ALSO BY KATEE ROBERT

RADIANT SIN

KATEE ROBERT

sourcebooks
casablanca

Published by Sourcebooks Casablanca, an imprint of Sourcebooks
P.O. Box 4410, Naperville, Illinois 60567–4410
(630) 961-3900
sourcebooks.com

Cataloging-in-Publication Data is on file with the Library of Congress.

Printed and bound in the United States of America.
VP 15 14 13 12 11 10 9 8 7

To Tim. I love you forever and always.

THE RULING FAMILIES OF
Olympus

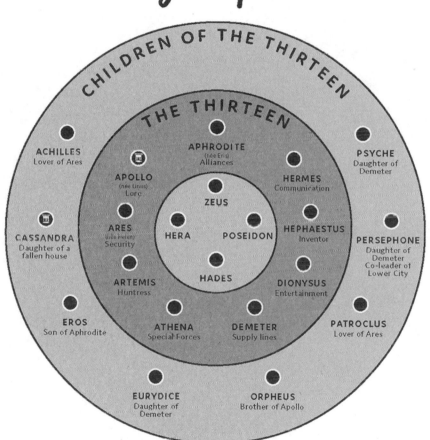

CHILDREN OF THE THIRTEEN

THE THIRTEEN

APHRODITE
(née Eris)
Alliances

ACHILLES
Lover of Ares

PSYCHE
Daughter of
Demeter

APOLLO
(née Linus)
Lore

HERMES
Communication

ZEUS

CASSANDRA
Daughter of a
fallen house

ARES
(née Helen)
Security

HERA   **POSEIDON**

HEPHAESTUS
Inventor

PERSEPHONE
Daughter of
Demeter
Co-leader of
Lower City

ARTEMIS
Huntress

HADES

DIONYSUS
Entertainment

EROS
Son of Aphrodite

ATHENA
Special Forces

DEMETER
Supply lines

PATROCLUS
Lover of Ares

EURYDICE
Daughter of
Demeter

ORPHEUS
Brother of Apollo

THE INNER CIRCLE
HADES: Leader of Lower City
HERA: (née Callisto) Spouse of ruling Zeus, protector of women
POSEIDON: Leader of Port to Outside World, Import/Export
ZEUS: (née Perseus) Leader of Upper City and the Thirteen

CASSANDRA

1

I HATE PARTIES, OLYMPUS, AND POLITICS...BUT NOT NECES-sarily in that order.

I can avoid two out of the three on good days, but today is promising to be anything but. It started this morning when I spilled my coffee all over Apollo's shirt. A rookie mistake, and one that might get me fired if my boss were anyone other than *Apollo*. He just gave a small smile, assured me it was his fault when it was clearly mine, and changed into the spare suit he kept in his office.

He should have yelled at me.

I've worked for the man for five years now, and even that isn't enough time to stop expecting the other shoe to drop. He's hardly perfect—he's one of the Thirteen who rule Olympus, after all, and there are no saints among them—but he's the best of the bunch. He's never abused his power over me, never turned his position as my boss into an excuse to be a petty tyrant, has never even raised his voice no matter how thoroughly I've fucked up from time to time.

It's maddening.

I shove my hair back, hating that I can feel sweat slicking down my back as I climb the last flight of stairs. Something is wrong with the elevator in Dodona Tower, and for reasons that seem suspect, it only goes halfway up. I glare down at the file in my hand. I *should* have just left well enough alone when I realized Apollo forgot it as he rushed out the door for his meeting with Zeus. He's an adult and is more than capable of dealing with the consequences.

But...he didn't yell at me.

No one who knows me would call me a bleeding heart—more like a coldhearted bitch—so I have absolutely no reason to have caught a cab to the center of the upper city, taken the elevator halfway up, and then proceeded to climb the rest of the thirty floors on foot.

In six-inch heels, no less.

There's something wrong with me. There must be. Maybe I have a fever.

I press the back of my hand to my forehead and then feel extra foolish because *of course* I feel overheated. I just did more exercise than I would ever intentionally participate in unless running for my life. And even then, I'd fight before I ran.

I curse myself for the millionth time as I push through the stairwell door and out into the hallway where Zeus's office is located. Then I get a look at my reflection in the massive mirror next to the elevator. "Oh no."

My red hair has gone flat, and there's a *sweat stain* darkening the line under my breasts—which means there's an answering one down my spine. I'm practically dripping. Without thinking,

I dab at my forehead and then immediately regret it when my blouse comes away with a smear of foundation. My makeup has to be melting off my face right now. I look like I got caught in a rainstorm, except it's not rain, it's sweat, and my face is the color of a tomato on top of everything else.

"Fuck this. He doesn't need the file that bad." I turn for the elevator...and then remember that to flee, I have to make the return trip down fifteen flights of stairs. My thighs shake at the thought. Or maybe they're shaking from the climb.

Does it count as a workplace accident if I fall down the stairs on an errand I technically wasn't asked to do? Apollo would probably find some way to blame himself and pay for my medical bills, but getting hurt like that means no paycheck, and no paycheck means my little sister might not have the money she needs to buy books or school supplies or all the other random shit being at university requires. I can't risk an injury, even if it means I'm humiliated in the process.

"Cassandra?"

I curse myself yet again and turn to face the gorgeous white woman walking down the hallway toward me. Ares is her name now, but it used to be Helen Kasios. I wouldn't call us friends exactly, but I've attended the parties she used to throw from time to time before she became one of the Thirteen. It always felt a bit like watching animals in a zoo as I posted up against a wall and witnessed the powerful people from Olympus's legacy families poke and snap at one another. I've learned a lot from playing the sidelines, nearly enough to protect me and my sister from the circling wolves.

But Helen isn't too bad, honestly. She's never cruel when kindness will further her goals, and she's perfected a glittery exterior that everyone seems to think means she's empty-headed but that I've always interpreted as a warning not to get too close. No one surfs the political currents as adeptly as she does if they're not smarter than most of the people in the room.

But that was before she became Ares. Now I can't take anything for granted when it comes to her. We aren't on the same level—two women from legacy families, even if mine is disgraced and hers rules Olympus.

She's one of them now, and I'm still me.

"Helen. Or, rather, Ares." I strive to keep my tone even, but her name still comes out too sharply. "What are you doing here?"

"Meeting with my lovely brother." She shrugs. She's built slim the way her mother was, though there's clear muscle definition in the arms left bare by her black sheath dress. She looks cool and professional and untouchable, her light-brown hair perfectly done.

I feel grimy standing next to her. I haven't wanted a thin body in over a decade—I love my curves out of sheer defiance of everyone who acts like they should be part of a *before* picture—but it's hard not to compare us when we stand like this.

I ruthlessly squash the urge to shift, to conceal. There's no fixing how messy I look, and trying to do it will just telegraph how uncomfortable I am right now. I raise my chin and focus on smoothing out my expression instead. "I see."

She gives me a long look. "Apollo's in with him now. I don't think he knew you were coming, or he would have waited for you."

There's no getting out of this. I'm here. I might as well see it through. I hold up the file between us like a shield. "He forgot this."

"Ah." She glances back down the hallway. "Well, I'll walk you down there."

"That's really not necessary."

"It really is." She spins on a heel and faces the same direction as me. "With things in a bit of upheaval right now, the security is ramped up. Honestly, I'm not sure how you got up here at all. My people are supposed to have the upper floors locked down."

That explains the elevator "malfunction" and why the guy downstairs was such an asshole. I shrug a single shoulder. "I'm persuasive."

"More like you're terrifying." She laughs, a sound so happy it makes my chest ping in envy. I don't want what Ares has—the title, the power, the responsibility—but it must be nice to be so comfortable in how she moves through the world, sure that it will bend to her impressive will.

I'm not naive enough to think that everything comes as easily to her as it appears, but I've had to fight and claw my way through the last decade of life. People look at me and don't automatically assume innocence. I'm painted with the same shame my parents were, even if I don't deserve it.

Not that it matters. I don't give a fuck what these peacocks think of me.

Not even Ares.

"Your people are specially trained," I snap. "If they can't take me, that sounds like a *you* problem."

"Absolutely." She agrees so damn easily. "By the way, is Orpheus still bothering you?"

Mention of Apollo's brother makes me frown. What does Orpheus have to do with anything? It takes several steps for understanding to settle over me. She's talking about that party where he was being an arrogant little prick, but that was months ago. I'm honestly surprised she remembered at all. "I can handle Orpheus." He might be bigger than me, but he's brittle. I could break him without lifting a finger.

"If you're sure... I know it's a touchy subject because he's Apollo's little brother."

I snort. I can't help it. "Apollo has more or less washed his hands of Orpheus." As much as Apollo can wash his hands of anyone in his family. What it really translates to is that he's stopped smoothing over Orpheus's messes and cut off his money. With how their mother babies the spoiled brat, it never would have worked if Apollo wasn't, well, Apollo. "When he shapes up, he can play prodigal son and get all the attention he's deprived of right now. He has bigger things to worry about than chasing some woman who doesn't want him."

"If that ever changes, don't hesitate to call me."

"Sure," I lie. I know better than to trust anyone in this godsforsaken city. When push comes to shove, Ares will look out for herself and her interests before helping someone else. Expecting anything else is like expecting a fish to sprout wings and fly. "I'll do that."

"No, you won't." Ares smiles. "But the offer still stands. Here we are." She stops in front of a large dark door with Zeus's golden nameplate on it. The current Zeus is Ares's brother. The last one was her father. I'd rather chew off my own arm than deal with either of the men who've held the title during my lifetime, but I'm here. It's too late to go back now.

I do my best not to hold my breath—not with Ares watching—and knock.

Apollo's the one who opens the door, and I instinctively brace myself for a whole new reason.

I hate looking at Apollo. He's too fucking perfect, a product of his Swedish father and his Korean model of a mother. Tall, broad shoulders, perfectly trimmed black hair, and kind dark eyes. It's the latter that always hit me like a blow to the chest.

I should have quit a long time ago.

As his executive assistant, I've got my fingers in an information network that spans all of Olympus and beyond. I'm the one who compiles the reports from the various sources, complete with my thoughts, before Apollo gets them. The work is challenging, and I actually enjoy it.

Not that I'll ever admit as much out loud.

But as much as I like what I do, this attraction is getting to be too much. Better to work in an office job I loathe than to have… feelings…about my boss. Even if the feelings in question are something as simple as lust. It complicates things.

I know what happens to people who get tangled up with the Thirteen.

They die.

I shove the file at him. "You forgot this." My voice is too sharp, too bitchy. He didn't ask me to do this, but I'm embarrassed and it's so much easier to snarl and snap than admit it. "I'm not your errand girl, and now I'm in overtime for the week."

Apollo raises a single dark brow. "You didn't have to come all this way, Cassandra. I would have done without."

Without a doubt. He's capable on a truly terrifying level and has nearly perfect recall of anything he's ever read. He would have been fine relaying the contents of the file without having it on hand. He probably only put it together for Zeus's benefit.

But he was nice to me this morning.

I am a *fool*.

"You're welcome." I turn on my heel. "See you tomorrow."

"Cassandra."

I ignore him and keep going. If security is the reason the elevators won't go above floor fifteen, then I bet they'll descend from here. They're keeping people out, not in. My exit won't be marred by having to take a breather on the stairwell and praying to the gods that no one stumbles on me. My pride won't be able to handle it.

"Cassandra." He's closer. Damn it, I should have known he wouldn't let this go.

I sigh and stop. It's beneath both our dignities to have him chase me down the hall in front of Ares.

Apollo stops next to me, his longer legs having covered the distance easily. He pauses. "Thank you for bringing this. If you'll hold on for a few minutes, I'm just wrapping up. I'll give you a ride home."

The temptation to say yes nearly makes my knees buckle. I've shared enough rides with him on the way from one meeting to another over the years. I know exactly how it will go. He'll slump back against the seat and loosen his perfect black tie. Not a lot.

Just enough to drive me to distraction. Then he'll pull out his phone and leave me to my thoughts.

Apollo never prattles on the way some people do. He's not one of those strong, silent types, but he doesn't feel the need to fill quiet moments with inane chatter. The car ride will be comfortable and lovely, and I absolutely cannot say yes to it. It's one thing to have those moments during the workday when I can tell myself there's no avoiding them. After hours?

No. Absolutely not.

"I'm fine."

He searches my face as if he can tell I'm being stubborn for the sake of being stubborn, but Apollo is a man who respects boundaries so he just nods. "Keep the cab-fare receipt and expense it."

I hate how weak I get at the simple thoughtfulness he continually demonstrates. Apollo is too savvy not to know how tight money is for me—his entire job is information, after all—and he also understands me well enough to guess I won't take charity. Not from him. Not from anyone. Not when it's never really charity and always comes with strings attached.

But a business expense?

My pride can handle that.

"Fine."

"See you tomorrow, Cassandra." The warmth in his tone almost brings me up short before I forcibly remind myself that this is just how he speaks to people. He can get tense from time to time, but Apollo really took that old saying about flies and honey to heart. Especially when it comes to me, as if he can smooth my sharp edges with pure charm.

It's nothing personal. It's certainly not *interest*.

My unfortunate attraction is one-sided and that's just fine with me.

It's only a matter of time before I get out of this cursed city once and for all. The last thing I need is to get entangled with one of the Thirteen—*another* one of the Thirteen—before I do.

APOLLO

I HAVE TO FIGHT NOT TO STARE AT CASSANDRA'S BIG, perfect ass as she stalks down the hall away from me. It doesn't help that she favors pencil skirts and heels, which only serve to showcase her generous curves further. I can't ask her to change her style simply because I want her. It's my problem, not hers. If I've taken more than my fair share of cold showers since hiring her five years ago? Well, that's a small enough price to pay for lusting after my employee.

That's the crux of the problem.

I hired her.

She works for me.

Letting her know I'm interested would be highly inappropriate. Even without the employer-employee power dynamic, I am one of the Thirteen and that skews things too far in my favor. If I asked her out and she felt she couldn't say no…

I shake my head and turn back down the hall. Which is right around the moment I realize I've been staring after Cassandra in front of the new Ares. She gives me a wide-eyed innocent look that I don't believe for a moment.

"She's got quite the mouth on her, doesn't she?"

Even though I *know* she's baiting me, I can't help defending Cassandra. "Wouldn't you after everything she's gone through? People in this city treat her like getting too close will poison them, too." The worst part is that they're not entirely wrong, if not for the reasons everyone believes.

Twelve years ago, Cassandra's family was one of the most powerful in the city...until, almost overnight, they weren't. As far as the greater population is concerned, her parents did something to anger the last Zeus and were set to be exiled. They died in a car crash before he could enact that punishment.

The truth is far more sinister. Her parents attempted to exploit an ancient, barbaric clause in Olympus's laws and were removed as a result.

The clause states that if someone manages to assassinate a member of the Thirteen—exempting the legacy titles of Zeus, Hades, and Poseidon—then that person will take the title. Our history is filled with black holes where information should be, but best I can tell, this immutable clause was added to protect the city if one of the Thirteen turned corrupt beyond all reason.

For obvious reasons, its existence is kept a closely guarded secret. It effectively paints a target on ten out of the Thirteen and would breed utter chaos if widely known. Yet if Cassandra's parents had succeeded, her role in Olympus would be very different. She'd be the daughter of one of the Thirteen rather than the daughter of a disgraced house.

Her parents would still be alive.

Ares shrugs. "Olympus is what it is."

A vague and unsatisfying statement. Our city might be home, but very few people would go so far as to claim it's fair and just. Not with power skewed so heavily in one direction. Maybe that will change with our new leadership...

I turn my attention back to Zeus's door as Ares nods goodbye and leaves me to my work. Zeus truly entered a trial by fire when coming unexpectedly into his title. Between how things hashed out with his sister claiming the title of Ares and the exile of the old Aphrodite, the transfer of power has been anything but easy. I glance down at the file in my hands. The information it contains is worrisome if not downright damning.

Olympus is in trouble.

But even with all the resources at my disposal, I can't say for certain *how much* trouble.

Up until this point, Olympus has mostly existed in its own little snow globe. The greater world wrote us off long ago as an unreachable prize. We all took for granted that it would always be that way, that the barrier keeping Olympus from the rest of the world would hold forever.

Now, it's failing. And no one can figure out why.

A problem for another day. We have enough to worry about right this second.

I step back into Zeus's office and close the door behind me. "Sorry about the interruption."

He sits behind the big desk in the middle of the room, a white man with blond hair and a perfectly tailored suit. He's the spitting image of his late father, though he wouldn't thank me for pointing it out. That's where the comparison ends, though. This Zeus doesn't have the same mercurial charisma that the last one could turn on at the drop of a hat, and that fact has made his taking of the title challenging.

Honestly, I prefer it. He might be difficult to work with at times, but I don't have to worry about any nasty surprises. It's a relief after dealing with his father.

He nods, and I resume my seat across the desk from him. Only then does he speak. "You were saying…"

I set the file aside. I don't need it, though I appreciate Cassandra taking the time to bring it all the way here. The woman is as foul-tempered as a wet cat, but she's remarkably kind when she forgets to snarl at everyone around her. "Despite exhausting my information network, I still don't know where Minos came from. He and his people are ghosts. For all intents and purposes, they appeared out of nowhere a few weeks ago to participate in the Ares tournament. We can't even pinpoint how they knew to come in the first place."

Zeus steeples his hands before his face. "They paid dearly to enter the city. That kind of money doesn't just appear when someone wishes upon a star."

"I'm aware, but maybe Poseidon should have asked more questions before he arranged transport."

"That's his prerogative." Zeus leans back. "If I start asking too many questions, he'll start growling about overreaching."

He's not wrong. Poseidon doesn't participate in most of the political squabbling, but he's no pushover. "This is important. Surely he realizes that."

"Possibly." Zeus shrugs. "But that's less important to him than protecting his territory and his power base. We know he brought in Minos and his people. That's enough. He was entitled to do so, thanks to the tournament. It's open to everyone."

I hardly agree that it's *enough*, but I let him move us along all the same. Ultimately, all that matters is that Minos and his people are still here despite the tournament being over. "It's no accident that Minos pushed his way into the city and is now brokering secret information about Olympus's enemies in order to stay."

"I know." Zeus sighs. "He was planning this from the beginning. If one of his people became Ares, we'd have less maneuvering power than we do now, but we're still not in a good position to ignore whatever information he claims to have."

If there *is* an enemy capable of taking the city, we need to know about it before we lose our main defensive measure—and so far, Minos has given us very little of what he supposedly knows. "I've spent the last few weeks searching, and there's nothing. Either Minos is bluffing or this group rallying against Olympus is good enough that they're essentially invisible."

"Fuck." Zeus presses his fingers to his temples. "We can't risk it if he's not bluffing. The information he's already let drop is enough to make me think there really is a threat."

"I agree." I, of all people, am aware that knowledge is power. There's no telling how much this shadowy enemy might know about us. Olympus might not broadcast all its secrets, but there are always exiles and I imagine most of them would be willing to talk for a price. Or out of sheer spite. "We have to assume worst-case scenario, that they know plenty about us."

"And we know nothing about them. Not without Minos."

Minos is well aware of the position he's put us in, and he's leveraging it for all he's worth. That's why we're having this meeting today. He's offering to tell us *all* he knows about this supposed enemy. In exchange, he wants money, a home, and Olympic citizenship for all the members of his family.

The first two are easy enough. The latter is complicated because Zeus granting citizenship is as good as elevating the family to the highest levels of Olympic society. It will change the balance within the upper crust of the city, and we might have a revolt on our hands as a result.

If there's anything Olympus hates, it's change, and we've had more than our fair share of it in the last year.

"We have to give him what he wants." Zeus curses. "This had better be worth it, because we can't take it back without an even bigger mess."

That's what I'm afraid of. No matter what steps we take today, the consequences are far-reaching. "If you give me more time—"

"I can't do that." Zeus pushes slowly to his feet. "Every day counts right now, and we've already spent too long trying to find a different solution. Another week or two won't make a difference."

Impossible not to feel the sting of his blunt statement. It's my job as Apollo to be plugged into information streams that aren't accessible to anyone else. I'm essentially Olympus's spymaster, and even with my team and all the resources at my disposal, I've failed. Between this and my inability to figure out *why* the boundary is failing, I can't help bristling. "There has to be another way."

"We've looked. There's not."

"You can't deny this feels like a trap. He has the whole world. Why settle here?"

Zeus sighs, suddenly looking a decade older—and even more like his father. Sometimes I wonder what it must have been like growing up knowing that someday the role would be his. Zeus has been a Kasios since the founding of the city. My distant relatives have been Artemis, Apollo, Hephaestus, and even Athena, but there are no guarantees among any but the three legacy titles. There were no members of the Thirteen in my parents' generation, so they were particularly pleased when I was named Apollo thirteen years ago.

Each position within the Thirteen is filled a little differently. Demeter is voted on citywide. Aphrodite names their successor upon stepping down. As Apollo, I was appointed by vote among the Thirteen.

I've been trying to live up to the expectations of that appointment ever since. In this way, I suppose, Zeus and I are the same.

"There has to be another way," I say.

"It's bad news no matter which way we look at it. We need the information he has, and we can't get that without bowing to his demands. He hasn't done anything to justify more...extreme measures."

"No, he hasn't." I've been coordinating with Athena to ensure we have a bead on Minos and his people at all times. Between covert operatives and my access to various information streams, we have as full a picture of these people as possible.

Which is the problem. They haven't given us anything at all. None of them have done anything noteworthy since the competition for Ares ended. It should be a relief, but it just makes me more suspicious. "It's a trap," I repeat.

"It's a trap we're going to walk into. We don't have another choice. We're just going to have to hope we can deal with the consequences when he springs it on us."

I intensely dislike being propelled to a course of action that's not of my choosing. Olympus isn't exactly a secret, but it's intentionally difficult to get information on the rites and rituals that keep the city running. Minos has more familiarity with our customs than is comfortable.

Almost as if someone is feeding him information.

But even if I can't track Minos's history, I *do* keep an eye on all people exiled from Olympus. Best I can tell, Minos hasn't had contact with any of them. Unfortunately, I can't trust that information. I can't trust anything. "If you'd just—"

"Apollo." He doesn't snap, but the harshness in his tone is enough to stop me in my tracks. Zeus holds my gaze. "We have to grant his request for citizenship. Whatever he's waiting for, he needs that first. I will get that process started so we can finally get to the bottom of this."

I stand and straighten my suit. "Fine. I'll keep looking in the meantime." I'll call in my people and see what we can come up with. The meetings so far have been fruitless, but the people who work for me are the best. We'll figure something out. We have to.

Thinking of my team has me thinking of one member in particular. I wish Cassandra had waited for me. She's more than capable of taking care of herself, but she lives on the edge of the upper warehouse district. It's not safe there, even if she cabs in. At least if I'd accompanied her, I could see her to her door...

The thought of her response to *that* almost makes me smile. She wouldn't be a fan. Ah well, boundaries exist for a reason and it's just as well. She wouldn't thank me for my interest. She might actually push me in front of a moving vehicle. Cassandra's made her opinion of the Thirteen and the people who aspire to be them clear—and honestly, who can blame her after what they did to her parents all those years ago?

The only reason she took a job with me was because I pay her nearly double what she can find anywhere else. I won't lie and say that charity didn't play into it. I saw her get turned away from job after job for weeks before she finally came knocking on my door. With her parents gone, she's been supporting her sister this entire time. I couldn't let them starve.

Ironic that she ended up being invaluable to my operations. She's smart and sees things I don't. Her reports have been priceless over the years. Truly, I should give her another raise.

"Apollo." From the edge to Zeus's tone, it's not the first time he's said my name.

Unfortunately, my fascination with Cassandra tends to have this side effect. Which is why I don't usually allow myself to think about her during work hours. "Yes?"

"Stay close to Minos. We need to know what he's up to."

Only a lifetime of practice keeps my distaste for the order from showing on my face. It's a logical thing for Zeus to command, but that doesn't mean I relish the idea of being in close proximity with Minos. The man is cunning and there's a glint in his eye I don't like. He's the kind of person who thinks he's smarter than everyone else in the room.

I mean to prove him wrong.

CASSANDRA

TWO WEEKS LATER

"YOU'RE LATE. IS EVERYTHING OKAY?"

I drop into the seat across from my sister and slump back against the chair. "Sorry, I got caught up in a report and lost track of time." Apollo has me wading through reports from the lower city. Hades rules there and doesn't take kindly to the rest of the Thirteen infringing on his territory, so information can be scarce, but ever since he married Persephone, there's been slightly more communication allowed. Which means more information.

Truly, the lower city doesn't sound half-bad. If I wasn't so determined to get the fuck out of Olympus the first chance I get, I'd consider crossing the River Styx and seeing if the lower city embraces toxic culture and ruthless power plays the same way the upper city does.

My sister, Alexandra, smiles sweetly. Everything about her is sweet. No one can look at us and mistake us for anything but relatives—we have red hair, skin that the sun seems to have a personal vendetta against, and bodies that people call *curvy* when they're trying to be oblique—but her lips naturally turn up at the corners instead of down. Our father used to joke that I came roaring into the world with a war cry and Alexandra arrived with a sunny giggle. She leans forward, dark eyes sparkling. "That seems to happen a lot since you started working for Apollo. I'm glad you like the job."

"'Like' might be overstating things a bit." My voice is too sharp, but I can feel a flush creeping across my skin. "It's interesting. Apollo has nothing to do with it."

"Sure he doesn't."

I open my mouth to snap, but I've worked hard to protect Alexandra from the worst Olympus has to offer. She's seven years younger than me and was still a minor when my parents attempted their ill-fated coup. I worried that she'd see the same derision and suspicion that I did once our parents' exile had been announced... so I made myself a target. It was easy enough to do. I'm already prone to spikes and snarls. It took very little effort to ensure they focused on *me* instead of Alexandra.

Mostly.

I take a quick sip of water. "Enough about me. How are classes going?"

"Cass, we never talk about you."

"Because there's nothing to talk about. I work and I go home. The most exciting thing about my week are these lunches with you." It's better that way. Most of the time, people forget I exist, which means they aren't staring and whispering behind their hands about the liar Cassandra, who once loudly proclaimed that the Thirteen had murdered her parents.

It's the truth.

Not that anyone believes me.

Alexandra smiles, oblivious to my dark thoughts. "Classes are going wonderfully. We're just wrapping up the summer quarter in a couple weeks and gearing up for fall."

With only a little prodding, she entertains me through lunch with tales of what her friend group is getting up to. I worried when she insisted on applying to the university instead of taking advantage of the free colleges Olympus offers. It put her directly in the paths of the scions of the legacy families, and I'm all too aware of what *that* can be like.

But Alexandra isn't like me. I've worked so fucking hard to ensure she doesn't have to fight her way through life. Our parents were selfish beyond belief when they put their own ambitions and desires above their children's safety.

I will never make the same mistake.

It's nothing less than a miracle that Alexandra has managed to maintain her sweetness through the years. I worry that it won't last past the reality of graduation. It doesn't matter that she's somehow managed to avoid the worst of the bullying and bullshit up to this point. As soon as she starts looking for her dream job, she's going to run face-first into the fact that everyone with a drop of power in the upper city hates our family and would love to see us both torn apart.

I have to find a way to get us out of here before that happens.

The waitress brings the check and I glance at my phone. "I

have to get going or I'm going to be late." Apollo doesn't usually care if I take slightly longer lunches with Alexandra once a week, but he's been in a strange mood since that meeting with Zeus.

"I can pay this time."

I smile even as I snag the check. "Save those pennies for school."

"*You* pay for my school."

I pull out my credit card and tuck it next to the bill. "Here's a wild thought. Why don't you do something fun?"

My sister's brows draw together. "I'm an adult now, Cass. You don't have to keep mothering me. We're equals."

"Of course we're equals." But that doesn't change the responsibility I feel for her. Twelve years ago, I was thrust into the role of her guardian, and I am still achingly aware that my sister needs protecting.

Whether she realizes it or not.

After the waiter returns with the bill, I sign the receipt and rise. "Same time next week?"

"You have a permanent spot in my calendar." She pulls me into a tight hug. "Do something nice for yourself, Cass. Promise me."

"I promise." It's even the truth, though I expect Alexandra wouldn't consider an early evening with a book, a bubble bath, and a jumbo glass of wine *something nice*. But then, my sister likes people. I don't.

"See you next week."

I walk her to the bus stop that will take her back to the university district and wait until the bus arrives. Only then do I check the time, curse, and hurry back to the office.

It takes me several minutes after arriving back at my desk to realize that something's wrong and another few seconds to locate the source of that wrongness.

Apollo's door is closed.

I stare at it. It's never closed. Ever. Honestly, I wish it were because he has the nasty habit of singing under his breath, but like everything else about him, his baritone voice is delightful. It's highly distracting. Sometimes I have to go over reports two or three times because I catch myself zoning out, trying to identify what song he's focused on.

A closed door should mean uninterrupted work. A closed door *should* make me happy.

I glare at it, arms crossed under my breasts. I can't very well go knock on it and investigate. Not only would that give him the wrong idea, but it's frankly none of my business.

Maybe he's not even in there. Maybe he left and locked up behind him. That makes more sense than him shutting himself up for privacy.

For a spymaster, he's really shitty at being secretive. If I were a romantic, I'd believe that means he trusts me, but it's really that he's strangely absentminded when he's not focused on something. And when he *is* focused on something, sometimes he mutters under his breath. At least when he isn't singing.

Gods, I'm a mess. Why am I obsessing over this man? I have work to do.

I start to turn for my desk—the only other piece of furniture in the small office that Apollo inhabits. He owns the whole building, of course, but he claims not to deal well with people— bullshit, people love him—so he prefers to have me run his communications with those outside the Thirteen. Technically, I guess that makes me some kind of manager, but my official title is executive assistant.

My job is challenging, and there's nothing quite like the thrill of putting together two seemingly unrelated pieces of information and having the full puzzle snap into place.

The door swings open hard enough to bounce off the wall. I jump and then fight to smooth my expression into cool disinterest. Not a moment too soon.

The man who limps out of Apollo's office is a beast. He's got to be six two and built like a tank with broad shoulders, broad chest, just *broad* body. Medium-brown skin, reddish hair cropped close to his skull, a nicely trimmed beard, and empty dark eyes. He catches sight of me and sweeps a look over my body that shouldn't feel threatening...but does.

I know who this is. I saw him compete—and fail—in the Ares tournament. Helen herself eliminated him, busting up his knee in the second trial before moving on to win the third and become Ares. The fight between them was brutal and I hadn't been sure she'd win. He'd looked like he wanted to murder her. If she hadn't prevailed, I think he might have attempted it.

Theseus.

"What are you doing here?" I don't mean to speak, but the words fly out all the same, sharp and brittle. Olympus is full of predators—I know that better than anyone—but they usually pretend they're just like the rest of us. Richer, more glamorous, more beautiful, maybe, but average and to be underestimated all the same.

There's no underestimating this man.

Theseus doesn't answer. He dismisses me nearly as quickly as he registers my appearance, brushing past me and out the door, violence in every uneven step.

I don't stop to think. I just rush into Apollo's office, half-sure I'm going to find his body instead of *him*.

Except...he's fine.

He sits at his desk, staring at something a thousand miles away, and appears entirely unharmed. I stop short, but it's too late. He focuses on me. "Cassandra. Come in and shut the door."

Annoyed with myself for having been worried—and worse, *betraying* that worry to him—I carefully shut the door behind me and move to sink into the chair across from his desk. Apollo's office is the very essence of rich-man chic with his oversize dark wood desk, a wall filled with floating shelves containing books and other knickknacks that are worth more than six months' rent on my shitty apartment, and a single large window that overlooks the street below. We're only on the third floor, which provides lots of people-watching opportunities; in the blocks around Dodona Tower, people purposefully walk the sidewalks looking to see and be seen.

He sits back with a tired sigh. "You're aware that Minos and his people now have Olympus citizenship."

"Kind of hard to miss it." The gossip sites have gone wild with the news. I'm sure it has to do with them covering the same players and same families since the city was founded. New blood is rare enough, let alone an entire new family to gawk and poke at. The last time that happened was when the Dimitriou family moved into the city proper when their matriarch became Demeter, but even then, they were still Olympians, if country ones.

Minos and his people are decidedly *not*.

"I've been invited to a house party he's hosting." Apollo's full mouth twists. "To celebrate."

"Sounds like you're going to have a ton of fun." The sarcasm flicks off my tongue without my thinking about it. What am I supposed to say, though? He's *Apollo*. Part of the job is hobnobbing with powerful assholes and getting close to people he hates because they have information he needs. Information *Zeus* needs.

He chose to take the title. No one forced it on him. I will not pity him, no matter how miserable he looks right now. He could always say no. He won't, but he *could*, which is more than most people in this city can manage if the Thirteen start meddling in their lives.

"I have a favor to ask."

"No."

He gives me a long look. "Will you hear me out before telling me no?"

"Let me think." I glance at the ceiling and then back at him. "No. You have that scheming look about you, and I don't want any part of it."

"Cassandra." There's a rare edge in his voice. Theseus must have really gotten under his skin. "Hear me out. Please."

I could walk out. Refuse to hear him out. I could…but I don't. My second mistake of the day, and one I'll no doubt come to regret.

He doesn't wait long to prove me right. "Minos has ulterior motives for being here, but I can't figure out what they are."

"I know that." Apollo has been muttering about it for weeks, ever since Minos's party showed up and two of them competed for Ares.

"He had bargained with Zeus to trade information for citizenship, but so far everything he's offered has been too vague to be of use. I'm sure that's intentional."

"Probably." If it's his only bargaining chip, he'll want to squeeze out every bit of its worth. It seems foolhardy to want the attention of the Thirteen on you, but what do I know?

"This house party is going to be my best opportunity to find those answers. It will last for a week, which would theoretically give me plenty of time to dig around for evidence. Someone bankrolled his trip here, and if I can find out who it was, we won't need Minos."

Apollo is something of a jack-of-all-trades when it comes to information. His title is technically Keeper of the Lore, and he does that by preserving records of Olympus's history. But he's also more than a little bit of a spymaster, sourcing information for the Thirteen and his own purposes constantly. Even after working for him for five years, I'm still not entirely sure how he comes by some of the info he finds. But it's always accurate.

A week in Minos's house should be more than enough time to get to the bottom of this mystery. I frown. "Why do I sense a *but* coming?"

"But..." He sighs again. "You've worked for me long enough to know my strengths. I am more comfortable with data and archives than I am scrying out people's motives."

It's true. If Apollo has one failing—and I'd hesitate to qualify it as such—it's that he's too honest. His brain doesn't work in the twisty, deceptive ways required to understand the layers beneath layers of plots that play out in this city. He's not naive; he knows the plots are there—he just can't divine the shape of them instinctively. "You've survived this long. I'm sure you'll be fine."

"Cassandra." He gives a rueful smile that makes my chest ping. "You know better. I'm only as strong as my team, and I won't be able to have you all there with me. If I can only bring one, I want you."

I want you.

Not going to think about how those words make me feel. Not even a little bit. "Well, you can't have me. Ask Hermes. She's good at this sort of thing."

"Hermes plays her own games and you know it." He shakes his head. "And I'm not on her level. I can't whisk in and out of rooms like magic."

What Hermes does isn't magic, though anyone who's walked into a locked room and found her rooting through their shit might believe otherwise. Most people don't pause long enough to realize breaking and entering is basically her love language and that she only does it to people she likes, but if I say *that*, then I have to explain how I would know such a thing, and I'm not about to get into my exes with anyone, let alone Apollo.

"You're very good at what you do, but *no one* is on Hermes's level," I finally say. "You'll have to find another way."

"Agreed. I *have* another way." He levels a look at me. "Come with me. Play the part of my date. You see things I don't, and I need that perspective to successfully navigate this."

Come with me.

Play my date.

At a house party that will last a week.

My brain skips and I shove to my feet. "No. Absolutely not." Bad enough that I spend so much time in close proximity with him while we work together. Attending a party like that... We'll be expected to share the same *room*. The same *bed*. He'll have to touch me. He's dated a few people in the years since he took his title. The soldier Hyakinthos. The model Coronis. Enough that everyone knows he's touchy-feely with his partners. Enough that if he *wasn't* that way with me, it would raise questions.

I can't do it.

I won't.

"You're out of your fucking mind, Apollo. I can't believe you'd ask me this." I'm still talking too sharply, my words filled with blades born of panic. "You know what that would mean for me and what everyone already thinks. You'd prove them right, and *I'd* have to deal with the consequences." No one in Olympus believes that I have no interest in power. They look at me and see the sins of my parents.

The bitter irony is that if my parents had just been content with their privilege and power, no one would look sideways at Apollo dating me. We were a legacy family, which meant I would be an acceptable marriage option for one of the Thirteen.

Everyone expects me to try to reclaim what we lost. They've been watching me like a bug under a magnifying glass for twelve years, and what Apollo's asking for means putting myself into the public eye in a way that invites attacks.

Even Hermes knew better than to ask *that*.

I had thought Apollo understood why I avoid anything resembling the spotlight, at least in theory. He's the one who offered me this job, who pays me far too much for the work and constantly seems concerned about my welfare. For him to ask me to play sacrificial lamb... It hurts. It has no right to hurt this badly.

"No," I repeat. "I won't do it."

"Okay." Apollo holds up his hands, looking guilty. "I'm sorry. It seemed the smartest route, and I trust you to be able to hold your own. I understand why you won't." His voice goes soft in a way that threatens to make me weak. "Cassandra, I'm sorry. I should have considered the implications."

I can't let him be soft to me. If he's soft, then I'll go soft, and then I'll end up agreeing to something against my best interests. It takes far too much effort to straighten my spine and offer him coldness when he's only given me warmth. "Yeah, you should have thought of it. If that's all?"

His sigh is nearly soundless. "Yes, that's all."

I flee from his office. If only it was so easy to flee from the guilt nipping at my heels.

APOLLO

I MESSED UP.

I was too rattled by Theseus showing up uninvited and issuing the command that I attend Minos's party. It *was* a command, too. Minos might not be one of the Thirteen, but he knows he holds power and he's throwing it around for all he's worth. It can't last, but it's inconvenient in the extreme while it does.

Still, that's no excuse. I shouldn't have made such an inappropriate offer to Cassandra. If she was anyone else, she might have felt compelled to say yes even though she didn't want to...

The thought makes me sick.

I have no illusions about what kind of place Olympus is. Power is the only law that matters, and as a member of the Thirteen, I have it in spades. I've seen the corruption that runs rampant, the way that some who hold titles abuse their influence to further their own goals and vices. I can't pretend I'm any different. I've used my influence to pull my family members out of the fire more times than I care to count. Especially my little brother.

If I pressured Cassandra, who's already suffered at Olympus's hands...

Fuck.

I drag my hands over my face. It was a good plan, at least from the outside, but I'll have to pivot to something else. I wasn't lying when I told her she's the only one who could accompany me. She's one of the smartest people I know. She might think I hired her out of pity, but the truth is she's become an irreplaceable asset. One I trust, though she'd never believe it if I told her.

There's Hector, of course, but he's so deliriously happy in his marriage that accompanying me to this kind of event would get tongues wagging. He won't say yes. His marriage might be able to weather any kind of media storm, but he wouldn't put his family through that. Not even for Olympus and the greater good.

The rest of my team is good, but they're not on Hector and Cassandra's level.

"Apollo."

I straighten so fast, I send my chair rolling away from my desk. "Yes?"

Cassandra's pretty face is locked down tight. Her lips naturally turn down at the corners, but they're molded into a frown currently. She flicks a glance off to the side. "Zeus is here to see you."

Fuck again.

I should have anticipated this. I'd texted him when Theseus arrived, but I expected a phone call requesting an update. I didn't think he'd show up here personally. I smooth out my expression. "Go ahead and send him in."

Zeus, of course, doesn't wait for her to relay the invitation.

Cassandra barely gets out of his way before he stalks into my office. "Tell me."

I bite back a sigh and bring him up to date. It doesn't even occur to me to keep the rejected offer to Cassandra to myself until his expression goes thoughtful. Zeus leans back in his chair. "Bringing her along is smart."

"It's a moot point. She said no, and I'm not comfortable compelling her into a situation like that."

His lips quirk in a bitter smile. "You don't have to play the bad guy, Apollo. That's my job." Before I can generate a response, he raises his voice. "Cassandra."

It takes several beats for her to appear in the doorway, looking justifiably suspicious. "Yes?"

Zeus moves his chair so he can see both of us. He studies her for a long moment. "You want to get out of Olympus and take your sister with you."

She crosses her arms under her breasts and narrows her eyes. "That's not news."

"You don't have the money to do it."

"Also not news," she snaps.

Later, it might awe me a little that she's one of the few people who doesn't seem to care that the de facto ruler of Olympus sits before her. Right now, I'm too busy fighting a wave of unease. I can tell where he's going with this, and I don't like it on a number of levels. "Zeus—"

He ignores me. "Do this one thing for us and I'll give you enough money to start over. Comfortably. Seven hundred grand."

Cassandra glances at me, and even though I know her well at

this point, I can't read her expression. She turns her attention back to Zeus. "You're serious."

"I am." He holds her gaze. "This party presents an opportunity we won't see again. You work for Apollo. You know the potential threat we're facing. We need that information. There's no lengths I won't go to protect Olympus." He doesn't move. "Name your price. As long as you deliver on your end of the deal, if it's within my ability to give it to you, I will."

She's silent for a long time, her gaze on something in the middle distance. We both wait silently, though I have to bite my tongue to keep from protesting. Zeus is correct in his arguments, but Cassandra just told me no. It's not right to put this kind of pressure on her. She's not one of the Thirteen. She didn't sign up for this kind of responsibility.

Finally she nods to herself and refocuses on Zeus. "Any price? Double your offer and provide me and Alexandra a safe way out of Olympus. If you agree to those terms, then I'll do it."

He doesn't hesitate. "Done."

I can't stop a choked sound. One point four million dollars. That's her price. I don't blame her for that, but *gods*, the audacity. She's amazing. Still, I can't ask this of her. I know she doesn't want it, and even throwing so much money at the situation doesn't change how uncomfortable she'll be acting the part of my girlfriend. "I'm sure we can find—"

"You will be paid upon completion." Zeus's blunt tone doesn't waver in the slightest. "While you won't be asked to do anything sexual with Apollo, you will have to sell the relationship, and that will mean acting appropriately enamored in public." He pauses. "I won't require you to be nice to people."

"I wouldn't even if you asked me." She doesn't look at me. "I'll be a good little girlfriend and spy, and that's all that you bargained for."

Zeus gives a grim smile. "So I did." He pushes to his feet and finally looks at me. "Update her on everything she needs to know. Start selling the story now so it's not a surprise when you show up with her next week." He pauses and sweeps a look over Cassandra that makes me bristle. Zeus frowns. "You have style, but that's obviously from the sales rack. Appearances matter, and we can't have you showing up looking like—"

"Like Apollo is fucking someone he picked up in an office," she says drily.

"Just so. My wife will be in touch to deal with your wardrobe." He glances at me. "Find me answers, Apollo. We can't afford another failure."

"I know," I finally manage. I'm still trying to process what just happened when he stalks out of my office and leaves me to deal with the mess he just created. One of the perks of being Zeus, I suppose. I clear my throat. "You don't have to do this."

"I know." Cassandra shuts the door and comes to sit across from me. She's got her expression shuttered, but there's new tension in her body language that wasn't there before. She holds my gaze. "I won't do it for the good of Olympus. The city can burn for all I care. It's nothing more than it deserves. But a true escape that doesn't mean losing everything?" She shrugs a single shoulder. "It's a price I'm willing to pay to get Alexandra out before this city smothers her innocence."

"If you needed money—"

"I'm going to stop you right there." She holds up a hand. "We both know you gave me this job as a charity case, and you pay me nearly double what others in similar positions make. You're already giving me money, Apollo. I'm not going to ask more of you." Her dark eyes go soft for a moment. "It might not seem like it, but I do appreciate what you've done for me."

"You'll take Zeus's money." It comes out like an accusation, but I can't help myself. I don't understand her logic. Sometimes I feel like I know Cassandra better than anyone else in this city, and sometimes it's like arguing with a stranger.

She laughs bitterly. "Fuck yes I will. That bastard has more than he could spend in a lifetime. If he's going to strong-arm me into doing this, he's going to pay through the nose."

"Cassandra..." So many things I can't say dance on the tip of my tongue. *Let me help you. Let me protect you. Let me take care of you.* I swallow them back down the same way I have every other time the temptation to press her arises.

I always knew she'd find a way out of the city eventually. I think the only things that have held her here are this high-paying job and her sister. Poseidon's people aren't above accepting bribes to get citizens out, but that costs money. She won't make that call until she has enough saved up to know she can land on her feet and keep her sister afloat. After next week, she'll have more than enough and have dodged the need to spend any of it in bribes.

So little time left. The thought leaves me ill at ease. I don't know what I'll do when she's gone.

She shakes her head slowly. "It's done, Apollo. I agreed. You can keep feeling guilty about it, but you'd be better spent updating me on what I need to know so I can prepare for the party."

She's right. I know she's right. I simply have a hard time pivoting in this direction with so little warning. I close my eyes and inhale slowly, stilling my thoughts. When I open them, I'm almost centered. "Minos has brought information of a threat against Olympus."

"Yes, you mentioned. I fail to see why we're dancing to his tune instead of just getting *all* the info out of him. You can't pretend worse hasn't been done in the name of the city's safety." She narrows her eyes. "Besides, there's the boundary to consider. What is this enemy going to do? Camp out a few feet from the city limits and yell at us?"

I glance at the closed door. There's little chance of someone overhearing this, but…I sigh. "The boundary is failing."

"*What?*"

"It's failing. It's not obvious yet, but there are weak spots. Poseidon brought it to our attention months ago." Months of fruitless searching for answers. I've never been so frustrated in my life. The entire history of Olympus is at my fingertips, and yet there's a giant blank spot when it comes to anything connected with the barrier. I tried to talk to the last Zeus about it when I first took over this title, but he wasn't interested in devoting further resources to finding answers—and forbade me from talking about it with anyone lest I cause a panic. Now he's dead and we're left to deal with the fallout without years' worth of lead time.

Cassandra stares at me. "You don't know how to fix it, do you?"

"No." Admitting as much feels like admitting my deepest, darkest sin. "I've looked, but someone scrubbed the records at some point." Some past Apollo, no doubt. My title is the only one with the authority to even access the records, let alone make a call to remove them. I don't understand *why*, though.

The boundary is the greatest mystery of Olympus. The average citizen just takes it as fact, whether chalking it up to magic or some advanced technology that might as well be magic. They assume that those in power, at least, know the details.

We don't.

If we did, we'd know how to fix it now that it's broken.

"Fuck," Cassandra breathes. "But how likely is a ground war or whatever? Most of the greater world has written us off. Why now?"

"I don't know." Another admission of guilt. I scrub my hands over my face. "This is why we can't toss Minos out, and even if someone was willing to resort to torture, it's not a surefire way to get accurate information. We're more vulnerable than we've ever been, and he has more information than he's telling us."

"I see." She taps her thigh with one black-painted fingernail. "Well, Zeus is paying me well enough. Guess I can help you save Olympus." She looks up and meets my gaze. "Let's do this."

CASSANDRA

I HOLD OFF TELLING ALEXANDRA ABOUT MY NEW "boyfriend" for as long as possible, but in the end I can't avoid it forever. The last thing I want is for my little sister to see news of us splashed across the gossip sites.

Still, I wait until the very end of our lunch to blurt out, "I have something I need to tell you, and I need you not to get your hopes up."

Alexandra laughs a little and folds up her cloth napkin. "With an intro like that, I'd almost expect you to tell me that I was right last week and you've fallen madly in love with your boss."

It would be so much easier if I could tell the truth, but if I share what's really going on, she'll worry. More, I am very careful to hide how much I go without to ensure Alexandra has everything she needs. She has enough hurdles after what our parents did. The last thing I want to do is add to her burden. She'd start making her own sacrifices to help *me*, and that I can't allow.

If she knows I agreed to Zeus's bargain to help her, she'll feel bad and tell me I don't need to do it. No, better to keep up the lie Apollo and I are about to spin to the whole of the city.

I'll come clean at the end, when I can explain why it was all worth it.

I take a deep breath. "Yeah, about that."

Her eyes go wide. "You're joking."

"I'm not joking." My skin heats. "I wanted to tell you first. You know how this city is. We're going to be photographed and they're going to say terrible things about me. Just, uh, heads up."

Her smile fades. "I wish it wasn't like that. You're not our parents. You'd think after twelve years, they'd have realized it."

"They don't care, Alex. Our parents dying wasn't enough. They need someone to punish and we're still here." Not that we have a choice. I don't know if our parents would have tried to leave the city after failing in their plan. They never got the chance. They died the same night they attempted to enact the assassination clause.

Leaving us to pick up the pieces. "They'll keep punishing us as long as we're here."

"I'm sorry." She reaches across the table and takes my hand. "You shouldn't have *them* putting a damper on a really great thing. I'm happy for you, Cass. He seems like a really good guy."

I swallow past the sudden lump in my throat. I hate lying to my sister, but it's for the best. "He is."

The entire walk back to the office, I wonder if I've done the right thing in not telling Alexandra the truth. I've been her guardian for nearly a third of my life; at this point, keeping the less savory details of my life from her is second nature.

I've done the right thing. I'm sure of it. She'll be happy when I explain the situation fully and have a solution to the problems that have plagued us for twelve years. A true escape.

In the end, pretending to date Apollo in order to investigate Minos is a small price to pay.

Being back at my desk feels particularly surreal. Nothing's changed and yet everything's changed. I don't know how to explain it. Apollo is still my boss, at least until Zeus's payment clears my account. That should be where it ends, but I can't help obsessing over how we're supposed to play pretend for all of Olympus. Not just in carefully constructed public dates. At a *house party*. The intimacy that will be required leaves me breathless and a little sick to my stomach.

I don't know what I'm doing.

I glance up to find Apollo standing in the doorway to his office, looking adorably ruffled and mildly uncomfortable. "Cassandra." He clears his throat. "We have less than a week until the party begins. We should, ah, make an appearance this weekend." He's still not quite meeting my gaze. "I've taken the liberty of booking us dinner at the Dryad."

Of course he has.

It's where he takes all his first dates, so I should have considered the possibility that this fake relationship would be expected to follow the same route. There's just one problem.

The Dryad is one of the most elite restaurants in the entire upper city. There's a wait list for the wait list. The fact that he's able to get a reservation so quickly is a minor miracle, but it doesn't change the fact that there's a firm dress code for the place and I don't have a single piece of clothing that fits it.

I've spent five years painstakingly building up a capsule

wardrobe that won't embarrass me while working for Apollo. My job puts me in contact with a number of the Thirteen and various families within power, and they might loathe me on principle, might make snide comments about my body just within hearing range, but they cannot fault my style. It's become a point of pride for me.

Shame heats my skin, and the fact that I feel shame for something so far beyond my control stokes my ever-present anger to the surface. "Yeah, that's not going to work for me."

Surprise lights his dark eyes. "It won't?"

If he was anyone else, I'd cut him off at the knees, but this is Apollo and not even I am heartless enough to go there. I look away, all too aware that my pale skin must be an unsightly crimson. "I don't have anything to match the dress code."

"Oh. That's all?"

I whip back around to face him. "Excuse me? What the fuck do you mean, that's all? If I show up in one of the dresses I already own, I'll get turned away and you'll be laughed out of the building. How does that help anyone? Maybe you have a humiliation kink, but I don't."

"Kink shaming, Cassandra? Really?"

My skin flushes hotter, and I can't tell if it's embarrassment or me dying a small death at the word *kink* on Apollo's tongue. "What? No. That's not what I meant."

"I know what you meant." He considers me. "You've agreed to this plan."

The abrupt change of course pulls me up short. "Uh, yes?"

"So you agree that my taking any measures to ensure the success of the plan is reasonable and not charity?"

I immediately see where he's headed and glare. "That's logical, but I don't like it."

"I know." His lips curve, his smile making my heart beat erratically. "You'll be paid for overtime, of course, but I have a call to make."

"But—" It's too late. He steps into his office and closes the door firmly behind him.

I glance at the clock. It's already three. I don't know what resources he's going to pull in to outfit me in a new wardrobe in twenty-four hours, but that's obviously his plan. I swallow past the pride threatening to choke me. He's right. This is to further the plan, not because it's charity. Come to think of it, Zeus made an offhand comment about my wardrobe during that last meeting, but I'd been too flustered to think much about it.

It doesn't matter. I know what Olympus will think when they see me at Apollo's side in clothing that's blatantly new. They'll call me a gold digger and whisper that I'm sleeping my way to the top to reclaim the power my parents lost.

It's not the truth, but Olympus never cared about the truth. Not when a juicy story is dangled in their faces. Not when a convenient lie covers up an ugly reality.

It's fine. I knew this was coming. It's why I warned Alexandra earlier.

I press my hands to my desk and focus on breathing through my anger. It doesn't matter what those piranhas of the upper city think. This relationship with Apollo isn't real and it's only temporary. I've dealt with the nasty comments and sidelong looks for twelve years. I can do a few weeks more.

At the end of this, Alexandra and I get out.

I can bear anything to reach that conclusion. As long as I don't try to follow in my parents' footsteps, the worst the Olympian assholes will launch at me are words. I'm not so thin-skinned to let that deter me from my end goal. Zeus's money will get us far, and I won't do anything to give him cause to say I didn't hold up my end of the bargain.

At five o'clock exactly, two dark-haired white women walk through the door. I instantly recognize Psyche Dimitriou and her oldest sister, Hera. Oh, Hera's name used to be Callisto, but since she married Zeus, she's secured a position within the Thirteen as the new Hera. The sisters couldn't be more different. Hera is tall and lean, a walking blade with an attitude to match. *She* can get away with cold eyes and snarling at anyone who comes close in a way I could never dream.

Psyche is a few inches shorter and my size, her abundant curves clothed in a really cute little sundress in a pin-up style with cherries printed on the fabric. I've met her a few times since she showed up at a party on Eros's arm, newly married and navigating the deep Olympus waters with apparent ease. She's sweet, but she must have teeth beneath that soft exterior, or the upper city would have eaten her alive already.

She focuses on me. "Cassandra. So wonderful to see you again. You look lovely as always."

"Psyche." I pause, flicking a glance at Zeus's wife. "Hera."

Hera surveys me. "Well, at least you have style. That's better than the last one."

"Callisto," Psyche hisses. "Be nice."

"Are you going to tell *her* to be nice?"

I raise my brows. "I can hear you."

"I know." Hera flicks her hair over her shoulder. "But you're a rare woman who appreciates honesty, so I'm sure you won't mind."

"*Callisto.*"

She ignores Psyche and stalks to Apollo's door to rap on it twice before walking in. Psyche gives a deep sigh that I recognize on a cellular level. It brings a reluctant smile to my lips. "Sisters, huh?"

"The best and the worst, both at the same time." She crosses to me. "This is all very hush-hush, but I'm to understand that you need a wardrobe."

I have to concentrate to keep my skin from heating. It works much better in Psyche's presence than in Apollo's. I thought I was prepared to be judged, but this is happening so quickly. "It's for work."

"No need to be defensive," she says mildly. "You know who I am. In my opinion, no one needs an excuse for new clothing." She casts a long look at my body. Unlike most people in this city, it's not judgmental in the least. More like she's assessing my size. "There is a designer who's recently branched out into more plus-sized fashion who I trust implicitly. She has a decent number of items in stock that will match the criteria Apollo relayed. Zeus is picking up the bill, so I suggest you take advantage of this because she's incredibly expensive."

Psyche Dimitriou is one of Demeter's daughters. She might have been raised outside the city proper, but even before her mother was Demeter, the family was richer than most people in Olympus. For *her* to say this designer is expensive?

I have to fight down a shudder at the idea of spending that much money on clothing. "Like you said, Zeus is footing the bill. Might as well charge up his credit card or whatever." Clever of Apollo to anticipate that I might dig in my heels if he was the one paying for things. He'll have known that I don't give a fuck if I max out Zeus's credit cards—if such a thing is even possible.

"Perfect."

Hera walks back into the room, looking smug. "Let's go."

Which is how I end up in the back seat of a town car with the two sisters, cruising onto one of the three bridges that connect the upper city with the lower. I've never been over the river before. There's some kind of barrier similar to the one that surrounds the greater city, albeit much weaker. It buzzes lightly across my skin about halfway across the bridge. Supposedly one needs Hades's permission to cross, but I think it must be more complicated than that. Both women must have standing invitations, seeing as how their sister is married to the man. That must have been enough to get me one as well.

At least this time.

I fight down a shiver as we turn south in the lower city and follow the street until the buildings grow into warehouses. The car parks in front of one with a stylized sign reading *Juliette's*. Recognition sparks. I've heard of this woman. She was run out of the upper city by the last Zeus because she got a bit too vocal about her suspicions that he killed his second wife, a suspicion most of Olympus shares, not that any case was ever opened. Since then, I've seen Juliette's pieces on everyone from Psyche to Helen—now Ares—to Hades's wife, Persephone.

Moving to the lower city hasn't hurt Juliette's career any. If anything, it's added to her notoriety and increased her perceived value. There's little the petty assholes in the upper city love more than novelty, and she's selective in her clientele, which only has them frothing at the mouth all the more. If I show up at events wearing her clothing, it will certainly send a message.

It doesn't matter. This is all temporary. I don't care what those assholes think of me, so I'm not going to let their perceptions change my mind about this.

Psyche leads the way through the front door. Inside, the warehouse has been converted, the ceiling lowered and a shining curtain blocking off the space toward the back. There are quite a few racks of clothing arranged by some system I can't quite identify at first glance. It's not color and it's not style. Maybe size? Though Juliette does custom pieces, and most designers who offer similar don't go into expansive sizing. Certainly nothing that would fit me.

Then again, Psyche is a client, so maybe I'm wrong there. I must be if they brought me here to shop. The Dimitriou sisters don't have a reputation for being needlessly cruel. More, Apollo signed off on this. He wouldn't allow them to set me up.

Really, Cassandra? Putting your faith in him? He might be kind, but he's still a member of the Thirteen. You, of all people, know what he's capable of.

Maybe to others. Not to *me*.

Or maybe I'm a fool and about to have pie on my face.

I straighten my spine and follow Psyche and Hera to a remarkably charming sitting area arranged around a platform with a half circle of mirrors. A door off to the side must be the changing room.

Psyche looks around. "Juliette?"

"Here." The rattling of a rack against the stained concrete floor precedes the tall Black woman who appears from between the racks. She used to be a model, and it shows in the way she carries herself, her simple but elegant black clothing, and the short, dark curls that leave her features on appealing display. I can't begin to guess at her age, but she must at least be in her forties if she was around when the second Hera was. Possibly even fifties, since most designers don't make names for themselves in their early twenties, especially when they were models first. Some models flicker and fade in the face of age, but time seems only to have polished this woman with something more than beauty. Strength.

She arranges the rack next to the changing room and motions long fingers at me. "Well, let me look at you."

I hold my chin high as I approach and do a slow spin. When I face her again, approval lights her features. "I like your style. I can work with this." She tilts her head to the side. "But first, what kind of vision do you have for this event?"

I hadn't really thought about it, but the words come unbidden. "They're going to talk about me regardless of what I do. I want to give them something to talk about."

Juliette's smile is knife-sharp. "Then you've come to the right place. Let's get started."

APOLLO

I ARRIVE AT THE DRYAD FIFTEEN MINUTES EARLY. WHETHER Cassandra admits it or not, she's got to be nervous about dinner for a number of reasons. She'll be thrust into the very pool of people she's spent twelve years avoiding. Not to mention this is where our fake relationship either launches...or crashes and burns.

We should have done a dry run somewhere private. Except that's not logical either, because despite working together for five years, we've never been properly alone. Even though no one works in our immediate area—the closest is Hector with his office down the hall—we're not really isolated. Cassandra has skipped every work party and after-hours event. Not that I blame her, but I can't help looking for her during the ones I'm obligated to attend.

Now we're supposed to be dating.

I can't believe I even suggested this plan, let alone allowed Zeus to bully his way into ensuring it happened after her initial refusal. My reputation is more pristine that some of my peers, but this will be a black mark for certain. Or, rather, it will be confirmation that I'm no better than the others. Dating my assistant? How cliché. The gossip magazines will be salivating at even the slightest hint of scandal.

It's still less a price than I'm asking Cassandra to pay.

"Apollo?"

I turn...and freeze.

Cassandra stands a few feet away. She wears her hair like normal, an undisturbed glossy fall of deep red. Her hair always catches my eye first. I'm still not sure if it's natural or not. I suppose it doesn't matter.

I try to keep my gaze on her face, on her artfully smoky eyes and dark-red lips. Truly, I do. But even as I tell myself to stop it, I can't help sweeping my gaze over her.

In all the time we've worked together, I've gotten used to Cassandra in a particular kind of clothing. Yes, she wears pencil skirts that hug her wide hips and big ass in a way that has inspired more fantasies than I care to admit. But she also trends toward high-necked frilly tops that might hint at her generous chest but never *more* than hint.

Her dress tonight is worlds different. It's a dark gray that's almost black, setting off her pale skin and highlighting her hair. It's also got a deep V in the front that shows off more than a hint of cleavage. *So much more than a hint.* I can't stop myself from following the line of the fabric to her waist, where it flares in folds that make her hips seem wider than normal before narrowing down to hug her calves. It's got a slight split in the front, probably to allow her to walk. Red heels complete the look. With those heels on, she might reach past my shoulder. The thought makes my chest thump painfully.

"Apollo." There's something in her voice. Not her normal snark or dry wit. No, it's almost panic.

Because I'm standing here, gawking at her like she's an animal in a cage. I'm her boss and I'm ogling her and making her uncomfortable. I'm acting like an unforgivable jerk. I give myself a shake. "You look adequate."

"Adequate." She blinks. "Be sure to pass your thoughts along to Zeus when he sees the bill."

Adequate. What am I saying? The dress is a masterpiece. I want to run my hands over it, following the folds. I want to kneel at her feet and start my way from the bottom. Or, better, start at the top. I want to peel the damn thing off her and...

I close my eyes, striving for focus. "You look lovely. I'm sorry. You caught me off guard."

"I'm not sure if that's a compliment but thanks."

I open my eyes to find her studying the restaurant behind me. She's not worrying her bottom lip the way she does when she's nervous, but it's a near thing. "So I guess we're doing this."

"It's not too late to change your mind."

She sends me an arch look. "I'm sure Zeus would have something to say about that."

Without a doubt, but I'd rather tangle with Zeus than put her in a position where she feels unsafe. "Let me handle Zeus."

Cassandra studies me for a long moment and shakes her head, her mouth pulling into a wry smile. "No, Apollo, I said yes and I plan to hold him to his end of the bargain. I won't give him reason to say I didn't do what I promised. Let's get these tongues wagging."

I want to keep arguing, but we're already drawing looks. It's too late. She won't change her mind, so the least I can do is make this as painless for her as possible. I turn smoothly and offer my arm. "Shall we?"

"By all means." She places her hand gingerly in the crook of my arm.

I should leave it at that, but she's right. If we're going to do this, we need to sell it. "Cassandra," I say softly. I wait for her to look up at me to continue. This close, her citrus scent threatens to derail my thoughts, but I power through. "You've seen me date other people."

She's smart. She connects the dots almost instantly. Her mouth goes tight and then relaxes into a surprisingly convincing smile. "Right. Sorry." She takes a deep breath and leans in to me, shifting one hand up to cup my bicep and wrapping her free one around my forearm. The new position has her breasts pressing against my arm and my hand is far too close to the juncture of her thighs and...

I almost break away. I actually tense to put some distance between us before I remember that this is the whole point. I might not touch my employee like this, but I certainly would touch someone I was dating. More, I'm known for it. Not effusive public displays of affection, but the casual intimacy that lets everyone in the room know who this person is to me.

"Apollo?"

The faint concern in her tone grounds me. I manage a smile, give myself one last mental shake, and force myself to make the switch to my public persona. I've been Apollo long enough that I don't have to bother playing games when I don't want to, but old habits die hard. Before I held the title, I had to play harder than anyone. I can do so again.

I give Cassandra a charming grin and can't help the slight vindication at the way she goes a little soft before she catches herself. If I tried to seduce this woman... Would she be just as sweet beneath the harsh exterior as I suspect? Would she go soft for me, let down her walls, and let me take care of her?

I'll never know.

This isn't real. It will *never* be real, because after Minos's party has wrapped up, Cassandra will take her sister and leave Olympus once and for all. I'll never see her again.

We walk through the doors of the Dryad, trading in the balmy August night for frigid air-conditioning. I've always liked this place. You get a sense of theater from the moment you arrive, the doors opening to a small landing space that leads to an arching bridge over a koi pond. There are rocks on either side with water trickling down them, the sound pleasing. It gives the impression of entering a grotto, and the rest of the restaurant only takes that flight of fantasy further.

It might be the spot to see and be seen after hours, but the owner keeps it from being absolutely unbearable with a particular brand of entertainment in the evening and the best food and drink Olympus has to offer.

Speak of the devil.

Pan himself is behind the host counter, talking to the hostess in low tones. He's what my grandmother would call *a character*. He is one of the few success stories that don't link back to a lineage stretching to the city's conception. Even I'm not sure where he came from—I suspect the lower city—but he showed up one day and bought the old restaurant that used to be in this space with cash. Within five years, he'd built a reputation that drew Olympus's elite families like magpies to glittering jewels. Now, he's nearly untouchable. No one wants to risk infuriating him and being blacklisted from this place, especially not after how things fell out with the last Aphrodite.

Pan is a short man with light-brown skin and a riot of short dark curls. He's got a wicked sense of humor and an infectious grin, which he's pointing our way right now. "Apollo." He excuses himself from the hostess and rounds the stand with arms outstretched. "It's been too long."

"Pan. You look well." I allow myself to be pulled into a quick hug. I don't know that Pan and I are what could be termed friends. I enjoy his company and we've shared more than a few top-shelf bottles of liquor after hours, but we don't see each other outside his place of business.

I turn him to face Cassandra. Here's our first test. "I'd like you to meet my girlfriend, Cassandra."

She doesn't flinch, but she does give Pan a dismissive once-over. "Nice place."

He bursts out laughing, the joyful sound filling the entrance-way. "You seem suitably impressed. I've never seen you in here before." He takes her hand and presses a kiss to her knuckles. It should be a ridiculous move, but a blush steals across Cassandra's cheeks, and I have the completely irrational urge to throw Pan into the koi pond. He glances at me, dark eyes alight with amusement. "She seems fun."

"*She* is standing right here."

"Indeed." His grin widens. "I have the best seat in the house set up for you. Have fun, kids." He clasps me on the shoulder and then he's gone, striding down a side hallway that leads to the offices and kitchen.

The hostess, a petite white woman with pale-blond hair, smiles warmly at us. "This way, please."

The Dryad is set up in a very interesting way, and I'm curious to see Cassandra's reaction. I watch her closely as the hostess leads us up the tall staircase and into the main restaurant. It leaves quite the impression from above, the room comprised of three descending rings with a circular stage in the very center. The lower the circle, the better the seat is considered.

Personally, I prefer the higher ring. I like people-watching, and spending time in the Dryad is a good way to see where alliances stand with the various power players in the city. Naturally, tonight we're led down to the very bottom ring. I press my hand to the small of Cassandra's back as we descend, a thrill going through me at the casual touch. She's so damn soft, I have to concentrate to keep my touch light and not let my hand stray.

Gods, I'm acting like an absolute cad.

I pull out the chair for Cassandra, moving too quickly and jerkily. She raises her brows but sinks into the seat. I can feel eyes on us as I move to sit next to her. An unconventional choice, maybe, but it will allow us to speak in softer voices. The walls have ears in this place.

Yes, that's all. It's certainly not because I want to be close to her, to have her thigh pressed to mine and her citrusy perfume teasing my senses, letting her presence distract me...

I realize my mistake the moment I sit down, but it's too late. If I move, our audience might take it as a slight or use it as an excuse to gossip in a direction I don't want them to go. I truly am acting like an unforgivable fool.

For once, Cassandra doesn't appear to notice. She's surveying the stage with a strange look on her face. "How can you stand this? Don't you feel like a bear in a cage?"

"I prefer the upper ring." I pick up the menu, mostly for something to do. "The tables up there are less sought out—comparably—but it's a more...relaxing...eating experience."

Her gaze tracks up. "Yeah, I get that." She sighs and picks up the menu. "I'm going to be frank. I'm starving and you're paying, so I'm going to order the most delicious thing I can find, and it's not going to be a salad. If you are one of those people who feels the need to critique my food choices because I'm fat, I'm going to dump wine on your head and leave."

I blink, trying to process the onslaught of information—and the implications. A slow anger flares to life in my stomach. "Do you make a habit of dating people who comment on your eating habits?"

"Not anymore." She doesn't look at me, but her hands shake a little where she holds the menu. "But I find it easier to state my intentions up front and avoid any bullshit. Or, more accurately, get the bullshit over with before it has a chance to ruin my meal."

"Cassandra." I cover her wrist with my hand, guiding the menu to the table. "Order what you want." I should leave it at that, but the strange anger steals my best intentions. "And to be perfectly frank, fuck anyone who acts like you need to change your body to fit some bullshit beauty standard. You're stunning."

She blinks those big, dark eyes at me. "Apollo."

I just overstepped, didn't I? I open my mouth to apologize, but her soft laugh stops me in my tracks. Cassandra doesn't laugh often, and never like this, with a strange sort of wonder on her face.

She presses her lips together and turns back to her menu. "I've never heard you swear before, and then you drop two in one sentence in my defense. I'm honored."

She's making fun of me, but I can't help a small smile in response. "I swear."

"No, you really don't. You're painfully proper and polite." She shakes her head. "But thanks for the compliment."

Compliment. As if calling her stunning isn't pure truth. Cassandra might not have the commonly sought-after body type in this city, but I don't see how that matters. Beauty is beauty in whatever shape it comes in.

Cassandra is so beautiful, it takes my breath away.

CASSANDRA

IT'S SO *EASY* TO BE WITH APOLLO. I DON'T KNOW WHY that surprises me, but I think I'd convinced myself that he was a different person outside the office. He *must* be. I've encountered his family from time to time over the years—first his parents before my parents were murdered, and more recently his shit show of a little brother, Orpheus. They are not good people. Oh, Orpheus might manage it one day if he pulls his head out of his ass long enough to look around and realize that in Olympus, beautiful tortured artists are a dime a dozen. The only reason he gets away with his bad behavior is because of who he's related to.

And Apollo recently stopped taking his calls.

But the man sitting next to me, his thigh a distracting weight against mine? He should be the worst of the worst. He's reached the pinnacle of power within the city. He should be abusing it left and right, at least according to the actions of the other members of the Thirteen. If he'd been one of the Thirteen when my parents attempted to assassinate Athena, he would have been part of their murder and subsequent cover-up.

Instead, he keeps sneaking glances at me throughout dinner as if *he* feels fortunate to share a meal with *me*.

It's fake. I know it's fake. One doesn't grow up within this city without developing a boatload of coping mechanisms, chief among them learning to craft a public persona. This is Apollo's. He doesn't bother with it in the office unless he has meetings with certain people, and I've never been in public with him before. That's all.

Still, it makes me feel strange.

Dinner is, of course, a masterpiece in culinary arts. My meal is nearly better than sex—or at least the sex I've been having for the last couple years. I can't help moaning a little bit with each bite. And the expensive wine he chose pairs so well...

This is how it could have been.

I shut the thought down. It's a little more difficult to do than normal, probably due to the amazing food. It's almost worth getting gawked at by everyone around us, most of whom are not even trying to be subtle. I even catch the lady above us snapping a picture with her phone. *Classy.* No food, no matter how mind-blowing, is worth living like this. Still, it's not a terrible evening.

And then the show starts.

The lights dim so slowly, I almost don't notice it. Not until it's dark enough that I'm left blinking at my plate. "This food is going to end up all over my dress."

Apollo's low chuckle makes my body go tight. It vividly reminds me of how he looked at me outside the restaurant, his dark eyes hot. It was...desire. I'm almost sure of it. Except even as I remember the expression on his face, my brain offers up half a dozen different alternatives that make more sense than Apollo wanting *me*.

I'm no slouch, but I'm hardly Ares or Aphrodite.

"Cassandra." He leans in, his voice low and intimate. "You're thinking so hard, you're going to miss the show."

My gaze tracks to the center stage, now being lit by a watery mix of blue and green and pale, pleasing light. The stage itself is maybe six inches taller than our table, but it's empty. I glance at Apollo, only to find his face *far* too close to mine. I don't jerk back, but it's a near thing. He smiles and tips his chin upward.

I follow the motion...and gasp.

Above us, a naiad swims through the air. Oh, my brain is already picking apart the magic of the moment, pinpointing the wires attached to a clever harness on her hips and tail that keeps her aloft. But it doesn't change the fact that with the light and her sinuous movement, she appears to be swimming as she slowly descends from the darkness of the ceiling toward the platform.

A second naiad joins her in the air. They spiral and seem to dance together, and I can't quite figure out how they don't end up entangled in each other's wires, but it's so beautiful, I don't care about the logistics. The show ends far too soon, and I press my hands to my thighs, forcing down an instinctive reaction to turn to Apollo and ask when we can do this again.

We won't have the chance to. This is our public fake date to convince people it's not strange for us to show up at a weeklong party together. There will be no second dates, no return trips to the Dryad.

I find it best not to want things that aren't meant for me, but it's still a strangely bitter pill to swallow. I take a slow breath, and then another. When I turn back to Apollo, he's watching *me* instead of the retreating naiads. "What?" I press my hand to my face. "Do I have something in my teeth?"

"No." He doesn't elaborate, though. He simply picks up a small menu that wasn't on our table at the start of the show. "Dessert?"

I hesitate and then curse myself for hesitating. I made a big show of putting him in his place at the beginning of this, and now I'm going to let insecurity deprive me of the chocolate cake I saw delivered to a nearby table before the show? No. Absolutely not.

I lift my chin. "Yes, please."

"Apollo!" The boisterous call comes from the stairs, where a large man with light-brown skin and a head full of striking gray hair is making his way down to us. Even without Apollo murmuring in my ear, I recognize Minos. He's been all over the gossip sites in the last two weeks. He's an attractive man in a brutal sort of way. I saw how the Minotaur wielded that giant sword in the competition for Ares. I bet he learned the skill from his foster father. Minos moves the same way Athena, Ares, and Zeus do: like he's got combat training.

He finally reaches our table and gives a charming smile. "Quite the show, wasn't it?"

"Pan offers premier entertainment," Apollo says neutrally. "Did you enjoy it?"

"Very much so." Minos glances up into the darkness of the ceiling. "I'd pay good money to know how they pulled it off without crashing into each other."

It's nothing more than I already thought, and he hadn't done anything wrong during this short interaction, but something about this man raises the small hairs on the back of my neck. As far as I know, we haven't confirmed him as an enemy of Olympus, so it might just be that he reminds me a bit of the last Zeus with his boisterous charm and steamrolling attitude. It might be...but I've survived this long by trusting my instincts and they're saying this man is dangerous.

Of course he is. Everyone in Olympus with a smidge of power is dangerous. Minos has gathered more than *a smidge* since he arrived and started making waves.

He turns back to us with an easy chuckle. "I hear you'll be bringing a guest to the party next week." He focuses on me for what appears to be the first time since he arrived at our table. It's not quite a lecherous look, but there's interest in his dark eyes that sets my teeth on edge. "Pretty thing, aren't you? I didn't know you were dating anyone, Apollo."

"Minos." Apollo's voice doesn't go tight, but he places his hand on my thigh. Just like that, I'm not thinking about Minos at all. My brain kind of...blips. Apollo keeps speaking as if he's not branding me right through the thin fabric of my dress. "This is my girlfriend, Cassandra. Our relationship is a recent development we kept under wraps for obvious reasons. You've tasted what the gossip sites are like in the city."

Minos grins. "Relentless."

"Exactly. Cassandra, this is our newest Olympian, Minos. He's...not from around here."

Minos booms out a laugh. "Not by a long shot." He holds out a broad hand. "Nice to meet you, Cassandra."

I gingerly place my hand in his, trying not to tense when he brushes a perfectly polite kiss to my knuckles. Pan did the same thing when we came into the restaurant, but it didn't give me the same reaction. His flirting felt harmless.

There's nothing harmless about Minos.

He releases my hand and turns that charming smile on Apollo. "Look forward to seeing you at the party."

"The feeling is entirely mutual."

Minos heads for the stairs and ascends to the third level, returning to an empty seat at a large table. I can see it from my position without craning my neck. I recognize Theseus and the Minotaur—what kind of name is that, anyway? There are another three people at the table, but they're sitting too far back in the shadows to get a good look. "Does Minos have a wife? Other children?" I don't think his foster sons have wives. If they do, they've kept the women out of the public eye since arriving because while both men have been photographed a number of times in the last few weeks, they've never been seen with anyone.

"No wife. A daughter and a son. They also have another woman in their party, but I'm not certain of her connection. She's not another daughter, though."

"I see." I drop my gaze to Apollo. He's still relaxed and smiling, but there's new tension around his dark eyes. "You really don't like him, do you?"

"I don't know nearly enough about him."

From Apollo, that's saying something. He knows everything about everyone. It's literally his job. It speaks volumes that there's nothing to find when it comes to Minos. I'm sure it feels like failure, and Apollo is not one to tolerate that. At least when it comes to himself.

He has a lot more grace when it's someone on his team who's come up short.

I open my mouth to attempt something reassuring, but then I register that he still has his hand on my thigh. It's...a nice hand. Everything about Apollo is nice. He's not massive by any means, but I've seen him haul around large boxes as if it's nothing, so he stays in shape. His hand is graceful, long fingered with perfectly maintained nails.

Even as I tell myself I'm being ridiculous, I know I'll feel the imprint of his fingers tattooed on my skin for hours afterward. It's all too easy for my imagination to take hold, to fill in the blanks of what it would feel like if he slid his hand higher, if he curved his fingers around to my inner thigh, if he—

"Cassandra."

I lift my gaze from his hand to his face. I don't know what my expression is doing, but he narrows his eyes and his tension bleeds away, replaced by...heat? His fingers pulse on my thigh. I feel that pulse all the way to my pussy, as if he skated his touch up to cup me there. I shiver. What did he say? My name? I lick my lips, achingly aware of the way his eyes follow the movement. "Yes?"

"Are they watching?"

I tuck my hair behind my ears, using the move to check. It seems like *everyone* is watching. "Yes."

He sighs. "Of course they are." Again, his fingers pulse on my thigh. "I'm going to kiss you now."

His resignation almost makes me laugh. Or it would if a pit hadn't just opened up in my stomach. Of course he's not kissing me because he wants to; it's all part of the roles we're playing. "Just like that."

"Just like that." But Apollo doesn't move. He's still searching my face for answers I'm not sure I have. This is all pretend. It will continue being pretend for the next week or so. I've kissed people I like less than Apollo. I don't know if I've kissed anyone that I like more.

I'm still processing *that* thought when he leans forward. "If you're not comfortable—"

My body overrides my still-spinning-out mind. I grab his tie and tug him down, lifting my face to meet his. To his credit, his surprise doesn't last long. He slips his free hand along my jaw to cup my head. At first, it's barely a kiss. His lips brush mine, perfectly polite and barely worth noting. Except it's *Apollo* and he's *kissing* me.

His grip tightens ever so slightly on my thigh and a shaky exhale ghosts against my lips. For a moment, I think that's it. He's kissed me. Everyone watching has seen it. We've accomplished what we set out to do.

But it doesn't stop there.

He only pulls away enough to adjust his angle and then his mouth reclaims mine. I don't intend to open for him...I don't think. Everything is a little hazy, my brain misfiring because *Apollo is kissing me*. And then his tongue slides against mine and I can't think of anything at all. He keeps it light, teasing kisses that make my head spin and my body pulse, but nothing so deep that I'm swept away.

I should have known. Apollo is focused and intentional about every single thing he does. Of course he'd bring both those traits to a kiss—to more. I try to keep my thoughts in order, but I'm swept away as he releases my thigh long enough to grip my chair and tug me an inch closer. It plasters us together from knee to hip and I shiver. We're fully clothed and sitting in the middle of a crowded restaurant, but I'm having trouble remembering why I can't climb onto his lap.

Just when I'm about to forget myself entirely, he finally lifts his head, breaking the kiss gently. I actually start to lean forward before reality slams into me.

This is pretend. We were putting on a show. Even if it wasn't, I would rather fling myself into oncoming traffic than give all these assholes even more to gossip about.

A deeply satisfied smile pulls at Apollo's lips. "Now. I think it's time for dessert."

APOLLO

THE DAY WE LEAVE FOR THE HOUSE PARTY, I PICK UP
Cassandra on the curb outside her apartment. As I step out of
the car, I can't help looking around with displeasure. We're a
few blocks from the upper warehouse district, and while crime
in Olympus isn't something of overt concern, it doesn't change
the fact that Cassandra lives alone and the door leading up to her
apartment doesn't seem very secure. I frown at it as she comes
through, battling two oversize suitcases. "I could kick that down
with one blow."

"If you do that, I'll lose my deposit, so maybe let's not." She
shoves one suitcase at me. "Here, take this."

"I'm not going to kick down your door." I reach past her and
pull it shut firmly enough to hear the lock engage. Then I rattle it.
"I wouldn't even have to kick it. Gods, Cassandra, you should let
me set you up somewhere safer."

"It's a moot point."

Because she's leaving. Right. I blink down at her. I didn't

realize how close we were standing, but I almost have her pinned between me and the door. The memory of our kiss washes over me. I can still taste her on my lips, even though it's been days. It wasn't nearly enough. I want her pressed against me. I want my hands all over her. I actually shift a little closer before I register the suitcase she keeps between us like a shield... I give myself a shake. "Sorry."

"The door is fine." She brushes past me and heads for the car idling at the curb. "I've managed to live here for years without someone kicking it down, so I don't expect they're going to do it in the next week." She flicks her hair off her shoulder. "Not everyone can afford to live in a gilded tower, Apollo."

"If you'd let me—"

"You don't pay for Hector's housing." She starts to wrestle the suitcase into the trunk, and I have to abandon the one I'm holding to nudge her aside and handle it. Cassandra huffs out a breath. "Honestly, Hector's been with you longer, and he barely makes more than me."

Something akin to embarrassment heats the back of my neck, but I keep my expression impassive. "How would you know what Hector makes?"

"I asked him."

It's not, strictly speaking, forbidden for employees to talk about wages among themselves, but I wish Hector had been a little less frank. "You're worth what I pay you." Truly, she's worth more. Her insight is priceless when it comes to divining people's intentions. She's much better at reading people and situations than I am.

"*I'm* not arguing that." The way she says it makes me think *someone* argued it at some point, but she continues before I have a chance to question her further. "But there are plenty of people who already think I'm sleeping with you so you'll pay my bills, so having you move me somewhere up-city would make that unbearable."

I understand what she's saying. I do. But I can't help arguing as I wrestle her second suitcase into the trunk. "You don't care what anyone in Olympus thinks of you. Why would you deprive yourself of a safe place to live just because people would talk? They already talk."

"I don't expect you to understand."

I slam the trunk closed and circle around to hold the door for her. She looks lovely today, wearing a sundress with a floral pattern on it. I've never been so attracted to flowers in my life.

Cassandra slips into the car and sighs. "Gotta love air-conditioning. It's hotter than Hades outside."

"Hades isn't that hot." I'm a liar. He's ridiculously sexy in a broodish sort of way, and he only seems to have gotten more so now that he's happily married. Every time he looks at his wife, he practically lights up the room, which only increases his overall attractiveness. Not that he's aware of it.

"Yes, he is, but that's not what I meant and you know it."

I do know it. I'm also not going to let her distract me from my earlier question. "Explain what you mean. What don't I understand?"

Cassandra leans back against the seat. "You're not an asshole."

I blink. "Thanks?"

"It's a compliment." She sounds mildly furious. "If you were anyone else, I'd happily take you for everything you had, but you're the reason I'm able to put Alexandra through school right now. Asking for more is just ridiculous."

I try to parse through all that. The logic is a strange sort of twisted, but she's right. It *is* a compliment. Still, there's something I can't leave alone. I stifle the urge to take her hand—there's no one here to watch us—and settle back against the seat. It will take just under two hours to reach Minos's country home. We have time. "Cassandra."

"Apollo." She mimics my tone. "You're about to say something unreasonably logical, and it's going to piss me off."

"Without a doubt." I spare a smile. "You're one of the smartest people I know. I value your input. I'm not bringing you to this party because you're a beautiful distraction. You see things I don't. It's why I pay you so much, and it's why I'd happily pay you more. If the only criteria for this task were a pretty face and gorgeous body, there are plenty of others to choose from. I need your keen mind at my side."

She looks at me like I've grown a second head. "I don't know how to deal with what you just said, so I'm going to ignore it."

"Cassandra—"

She holds up a hand. "We only have so much time before we're at Minos's place. I'm assuming we won't easily be able to have frank conversations on the property?"

"No." I shake my head slowly. She's right that we need to tie up any loose ends before we get there, but I can't shake the feeling that she just changed the subject because she isn't comfortable with the compliment. That doesn't make any sense, though.

Cassandra is one of the most confident people I know. Why would she be uncomfortable with my honest appreciation?

It takes more effort than it should to focus properly. "We have to assume he's bugged the place, both with audio and potentially video."

She narrows her eyes. "He'll expect you to sweep the room, at least, and remove anything you find."

"Yes." I am Olympus's spymaster. Minos is canny enough to know that, and he'll expect me to take precautions. That's the true rub. He knows I'm coming to this party to find information and yet he still invited me. It's a dare. "I have a solution to the cameras. It's blunt, and normally I'd just play along and pretend I didn't realize they were there, but I won't let anything that happens at this party harm you."

Cassandra waves that away. "My reputation has been in tatters since before you met me. Besides, this is a fake relationship, so it's not as if we're in danger of having him film and leak a sex tape. If it serves your purpose to keep the cameras in place, don't let me be the reason you don't."

Sex tape.

An image slams into my head, too quick to resist. Me on my back, holding my phone. Cassandra astride me and...

I abruptly stare out the window. The city has given way to rolling countryside. I focus on the trees, counting them until I have control of my body's response. When I finally turn back, she's looking at me strangely again.

"I won't let any harm come to you. The cameras go." The statement comes out too harsh, too bold.

"Okay. I trust you." Her easy belief in me is staggering, but she continues before I can fully process. "I don't suppose you have blueprints of the house?"

"No." The admission grates. "It used to belong to Hermes." Hermes is one of the few members of the Thirteen that I have next to no information on. She took the title about a year after me. The Hermes title is transferred by virtue of stealing an unstealable object or acquiring a piece of information about one of the Thirteen that no one else knows. This Hermes did both.

She appeared out of nowhere. No past, no active connections to any of the legacy families, no motive that I can see. She stood before the rest of us and recited things about the others that not even I knew while holding an heirloom vase from *my* family's vault. No one contested the truth of those facts, and she was instated as Hermes immediately.

Since then, she's been an agent of chaos, but she seems to genuinely want to protect Olympus. I wouldn't call her an ally, but she's not an enemy.

I think.

Either way, despite her apparent lack of boundaries and deep love of breaking and entering, Hermes is intensely private when it comes to her own home. Frankly, I'm shocked she sold this place to Minos. The country might not suit her, but she's owned the house since she took over the title.

"Well, shit." Cassandra sighs. "Then it's bound to be full of surprises. Hermes's sense of humor is too twisted not to have secret passageways and the like. It would appeal to her."

I can't argue that, though the familiar way she speaks of Hermes has my curiosity stirring. "Most likely."

She hesitates. "I'm still surprised you didn't manage to get the blueprints. The house didn't spring out of nothing. Someone built it. If you can't get to it through permits, applying pressure to one of the workers is the next best thing."

I love that she already made that logical jump. I shake my head. "I tried. She didn't use any of the known contractors in the upper city."

"She went to the lower city."

I smile reluctantly. "That's my theory. And they have no love for me as a member of the Thirteen, so it's a dead end." Not to mention Hades wouldn't have thanked me for trespassing in his domain. There are circumstances when it would behoove me to test him, but not over something as mundane as this. It aggravates my curiosity to no end that I don't know what Hermes did to the building after she acquired it, but ultimately it's a country house that I would never set foot in.

Or so I thought.

Cassandra examines her long red fingernails. "Will Hermes be at the party?"

"I don't know." The guest list is another thing that's been kept under wraps. Minos hasn't kept a convenient list to peruse, at least not digitally.

"Poor Apollo," she murmurs. Her eyes are alight with amusement. "It must be aggravating to have run into so many dead ends. So we need to map the house as quickly as possible, find out where Minos keeps the keys to the kingdom, and use them to unlock his mysteries."

"Nice metaphor."

"I try."

We share a grin that quickly becomes…something else. It's my fault. My gaze falls to her lips, and despite my best efforts, I can't help thinking about that kiss the other night again. She'd tasted of wine and had practically melted when I deepened the contact.

Not even cold showers were enough to combat that memory over the weekend. I haven't had my body take over so intensely since I was a teenager, but back then, I was jacking myself to whatever I could find on the internet that suited my tastes.

These days, my fantasies all revolve around one woman.

Cassandra frowns. "I don't understand why this is all necessary, though. If Minos bargained for information in exchange for his citizenship, why hasn't he given that information?"

"He has." I shrug. "Or so he says. He was recruited to a militant group fifteen years ago, but according to him, he was part of a cell that was only informed about the Ares tournament. Which we already knew, since he showed up here for that event. We don't know anything about their leader, their motivations, or their plans."

"You think he's still working for them?"

"That's what I am to find out. He says he defected. We're not naive enough to believe it. I need evidence of correspondence or a money trail or something to prove he's still answering to the enemy."

"Okay. That makes sense. We need to get you access to Minos's personal computer, since I doubt he's got paper files just hanging out with incriminating evidence." Cassandra licks her lips. "I, uh, suppose we'll be doing more kissing this week."

"Yes." The word is low. A command I'm practically daring her to challenge. If she did...

Well, it doesn't matter, because she just gives a jerky nod. "All for the cause, right? I've kissed worse people for shittier reasons."

I don't like to think about her kissing worse people for shittier reasons. I have very intentionally not looked into Cassandra's private life. Oh, everyone in the city is aware her parents were killed in a car crash after displeasing Zeus—and I know the truth behind that public lie—and that she and her sister were publicly shunned afterward.

That's one thing. Her personal life is something else.

I don't pry. I don't check up on her. I don't ask her who she's dating or why she's changed her perfume and started wearing redder lipstick about a year into working for me. I had thought she might be seeing someone, but she wouldn't have agreed to Zeus's bargain if she was. She wouldn't be leaving her partner behind when she walks out of Olympus for good.

Except all that's an excuse, isn't it?

I don't care if she *is* seeing someone. I will keep my priorities in order and find the answers Minos wants to keep hidden, but I won't lie; I am greedy for every minute with Cassandra. After this week, all I'll be left with are my memories of her. I only have seven days to shore up a lifetime's worth of them.

I don't know if it's going to be enough.

CASSANDRA

BY THE TIME WE REACH THE HOUSE, I'M ABOUT READY TO throw myself from the car. It's not that things got awkward with Apollo. He keeps looking at me with that strange expression on his face, but he's maintained a steady flow of easy conversation.

Still, I can tell it bothers him that he doesn't have all the information. Not on Minos. Not even on the house we're going to be spending seven days in. It makes me feel the irrational urge to comfort him. *What a laughable impulse.* Apollo doesn't need *my* comfort. No matter the setbacks, he'll get to the bottom of this and find answers. It's what he does. He might even end up enjoying the challenge.

The house is, of course, sprawling and beautiful. It creates an upside-down U shape that frames the circular drive. We're not the only car pulling up, and I catch sight of Hermes herself bouncing from the car in front of us, followed by an exhausted-looking Dionysus. They make quite the pair. She's a short Black woman with dark-brown skin and tight dark curls wearing bright-pink pants that sparkle in the sunlight and a teal graphic T-shirt that I can't read from here. Dionysus, on the other hand, is a white man with mussed dark hair, a truly outstanding mustache, and a penchant for dressing like he stepped out of another time. Today it's slacks, suspenders, and a dark printed button-down shirt beneath a vest.

I still like Hermes. First because she's one of the few people in the upper city who know what my parents did and didn't treat me like I'm carrying around a knife and just waiting to finish the job they started, and second because I truly enjoy being around her. Our relationship flared bright and hot, but we quickly realized it wasn't meant to be. I'll never willingly tie myself to a member of the Thirteen, and I highly suspect Hermes gave her heart to someone a long time ago and no one else can compare. These days, we're friends and that suits us both.

Apollo waits until Hermes loops an arm through Dionysus's and tows him into the house before he opens the door and steps out of the car. He catches my questioning look. "We have to deal with her eventually, but there's no reason to rush it."

I should probably tell Apollo that she's my ex, but the words keep sticking in my throat. Surely it doesn't matter? I accept his hand even though I'm more than capable of climbing out of the car without help. For the act, of course. Not because I like the way his fingers curl around mine. To distract myself, I say, "You really don't like Hermes, do you?"

"She's fine."

His clipped tone gives him away. I frown at him. "Is it you don't like her? Or that you're quietly furious that she's dodged any of your attempts to get more information on her?"

Apollo shoots me a sharp look. "I don't like mysteries."

I bet. "Has she broken into your house?"

His jaw goes tight. "Several times. I still can't figure out how she gets in."

That must irritate him to no end. He really does hate mysteries. Without thinking, I pat his chest. "Poor Apollo. That must bother you so much."

He glances down to where my fingers still rest lightly against his chest. When he speaks again, his voice has deepened. "I'll get over it."

"Welcome!"

I drop my hand guiltily and spin to face the woman approaching us. She's about my age, I think. About my size, too, and wearing a perfectly tailored blouse and shorts. She moves with an easy grace that reeks of some kind of expensive finishing school; no one moves like they're floating naturally.

The woman must be Minos's daughter, but she doesn't look like him at all aside from her coloring. Her light-brown skin is an identical tone, though her hair is a deep black and falls in a straight line past her shoulders.

She smiles at us, the expression lighting up her dark eyes. Being on the receiving end of that smile makes my spine straighten despite myself. I don't have a type. I'm not one to narrow my options, even if I don't date much as a general rule. But this woman is *pretty*. Very, very pretty.

I can't help glancing at Apollo to see his reaction. Apparently he had the same idea because our gazes meet fleetingly before we turn back to her. He steps forward and offers a hand. "I'm Apollo. This is my girlfriend, Cassandra."

"I know." Her smile widens. She looks so *happy*. Surely she's faking it, but I don't detect a hint of artifice in her. "I'm Ariadne. My brother, Icarus, and I are seeing to the sleeping arrangements. We have your room ready."

He has his children doing the initial entertaining. It's not shocking. After the encounter with Theseus in Apollo's office and watching the Minotaur during the competition for Ares, I don't expect either of them excel at playing nice. Not like Ariadne apparently does. I can't help wondering if Icarus takes after his sister or his foster brothers.

Apollo smiles down at her. "That sounds wonderful."

She turns and leads us through the front doors into an echoing entranceway. It looks like something out of a movie with two staircases circling the space opposite the front door to meet overhead. I knew Hermes had a sense of the theatrical, but this looks like a cross between a Gothic mansion and some hideously expensive southern manor.

Ariadne heads up the stairs, leaving us to trail behind. The archway at the top of the stairs flows into a wide hallway. She motions at the doors studding the walls all the way down. "These are converted rooms. They're essentially sitting rooms and will be open to whoever wants to use them throughout the day."

I raise my brows. "How many people are coming to this party that you need half a dozen sitting rooms?"

She tucks her hair behind her ears. "They were, ah, used for a different kind of entertaining purpose by the last owner, and my father decided sitting rooms were a more appropriate conversion."

A different kind of entertainment.

I look at the doors with new interest. Hermes's sexual tastes are just as eclectic as her fashion. She's kinky as fuck and a regular in the lower city where it's rumored that Hades has an honest-to-gods sex club, though she never took me there when we were dating, understandable considering Hades was supposed to be a myth at that point. Another of the secrets she kept close to her chest.

Still... *Six rooms?*

"I see," Apollo says faintly. I can't tell if he's actually surprised or scandalized or if this is information he already had filed away in that impressive brain of his.

"Dinner will be at seven tonight. Papa has a party game planned afterward." Ariadne shoots us a sweet smile. "There's an agenda in your room with details for the week. Dinner and lunch have scheduled times, but please feel free to have breakfast sent to your room. If you prefer to dine downstairs, there will be a small buffet available."

I make a show of looking around as we reach a T in the hallway and take a right. "I don't suppose there's a map with that agenda."

"No need." Another sweet smile. Is this woman for real? "Just follow this hallway back to the entranceway, go downstairs, and everything is a straight shot to the main area downstairs."

A straight shot doesn't sound very *Hermes*. This house holds some tricks up its sleeve. I'm sure of it. The only question is whether Minos and his people know it or if Hermes kept those secrets to herself. I'd bet good money on the latter.

Ariadne opens a door halfway down the hall. "This is your room. Please make yourself comfortable and feel free to explore before dinner if you're so inclined. The gardens are particularly lovely."

I step inside first. I'm vaguely aware of Apollo following me into the room and shutting the door behind him, but the only thing I can focus on is the oversize bed. I had foolishly thought this might be a full suite, but while there's a bathroom through the open door visible from my position, the only other furniture in the room is an antique-looking dresser and a pair of matching nightstands on either side of the bed.

Fuck.

I knew this was coming, of course. I just didn't expect to freeze up at the reality of it. "Um." Damn it, I can do better than that. I clear my throat. "About tonight, when we go to bed—"

"Hold that thought." He narrows his eyes and motions toward the bed. "Sit and be silent. Please."

I jerk back, a sharp reply on my lips, before my brain kicks into gear and makes the jump to what's going on. He's not telling me to be quiet. He wants to sweep the room for surveillance. I sit primly on the edge of the bed and watch him dig through his duffel bag for a piece of electronics I don't recognize. It's strangely difficult to stay silent as he goes over every inch of the room. The device dings three times. Once in the mirror over the dresser. One in the lampshade on the nightstand, and one tucked cleverly into the doorjamb. A fourth additional one dings from the bathroom.

I make a face. "Ugh."

"Not done. Checking for cameras."

I shudder a little. Obviously being watched and listened to was something we'd talked about before this. I'm not surprised when he pulls a tiny camera from the molding at the top of the mirror, but I feel vaguely violated all the same. "*Gross.*"

"Yes." He deposits it in the small pile on the dresser and brushes his hands together. "That's everything. About what we expected. I have a device that Hector can use to hack the system, but I need to be closer to the control room, which means we need to prioritize finding it."

"Consider it prioritized."

"Agreed." He nods. "About the sleeping arrangements...I'll sleep on the floor." Apollo hauls my suitcases to a spot near the dresser and sets his on the other side.

"But—"

"Don't argue." He doesn't look at me. "I know you're not going to insult me by suggesting I'd allow *you* to sleep on the floor while I take the bed. And no, we're not going to switch off. I don't care about being fair, so that agreement won't work."

A little forbidden thrill goes through me at his firm tone. Apollo almost never gets abrupt with me, and certainly never commanding. I can count on one hand how many times it's happened in the past five years and still have fingers left over. Including just now.

He finally faces me, brows drawn in a forbidding line. The thrill inside me only gets stronger in response. He eyes me. "Do you concede?"

"I was going to suggest the bathtub. It's got to be massive in a house like this."

"Absolutely not. You are *not* sleeping anywhere but on that bed, Cassandra. Do I make myself clear?"

Yes, sir.

I clamp my mouth shut so fast, I bite my tongue, but I manage to keep the snarky reply internal. Under *no* circumstances will I be calling Apollo anything other than his name, and certainly not something in a tone so sexually suggestive.

No matter how melty it makes me feel. In fact, that melty sensation in my core is a very good reason to never admit how he affects me. Ever.

I belatedly realize he's waiting for a response and clear my throat. "You're being ridiculous." I smooth my hands over my dress. "We're both adults. It's a big bed. There's no reason we can't share."

His jaw goes slack. "Cassandra—"

"If you're worried about me wandering in my sleep, I don't. But there are more than enough pillows to put up a barrier between us to protect your virtue." The words are a little sharper than I intend, but I don't like the idea of him sleeping on the floor. I can control the meltiness. I'm not going to throw myself at my boss, no matter how good his fake kisses made me feel.

Apollo runs a hand through his short black hair. "I don't want to put you in a position where you feel uncomfortable." He grimaces. "Though I guess I can't say that any longer because you're here and I know you'd rather not be."

There's not much to say to that, but I can't just not respond. "For what it's worth, I know I'm safe with you. That was never the issue." It's just everything else that threatens to make this so messy. None of that is Apollo's fault, though, and I can't stand the thought of him blaming himself for my shitty attitude. He should know by now that it's my default.

He gives a wan smile. "Well, with that out of the way, let's get ready for dinner and see about finding that control room to deal with the cameras."

"Sounds like a plan," I say faintly.

APOLLO

I UNDERESTIMATED WHAT IT WOULD BE LIKE TO BE IN SUCH close proximity with Cassandra outside the office. The sheer intimacy of sitting on the bed and going through my emails while she stands in the bathroom with wet hair as she puts on her makeup is...strange. Very strange.

I've dated several people seriously as an adult, and none of those relationships reached a point when moving in together made sense, but there were intimate moments. Relationships are built of intimate moments. I don't know why it feels so different with her. I'd be a fool to chase that feeling.

My phone rings as Cassandra finishes doing something to her eyes to give them a sexy, faintly smoky look. I bite back a sigh at the sight of my little brother's name on the screen. It's been several weeks since I cut him off, and I don't trust him not to revert right back to his spoiled self the moment he senses me wavering. Cutting him off wasn't easy, but it was the right thing to do.

It's *still* the right thing to do, but I'm not heartless enough to ignore his calls entirely, no matter how frustrating I find them. "Orpheus."

"Apollo." He sounds tired, his charm worn thin.

Guilt pricks me. Our mother's worried about him. She wants him to move back home, to let her look out for him. Since that translates to her meddling with his life, I don't blame him for digging in his heels. He's made changes, too. Downsized his apartment and moved away from the city center to somewhere more affordable. He doesn't have a job yet, but apparently he wasn't as careless with his money as I'd assumed. He has plenty of it to work through before he's anything resembling truly desperate.

"I need a favor."

"No."

He sighs. "I'm not asking for money or anything like that."

Cassandra realizes I'm on the phone and shuts the bathroom door. A few seconds later, the hair dryer starts, the sound muffled by the thick wood. I'm suddenly irritated that my brother caused me to miss being able to watch her dry her hair. "But you are asking for something, and that's not part of the agreement."

"I didn't agree to anything. You made that decision for me."

"Yes, I did. Someone had to." Our parents certainly weren't going to rein him in. He inherited our father's charm and our mother's audacity and boldness. Our parents have spoiled him from the moment he was born, and they never would have stopped if I didn't draw the line in the sand.

My brother is a selfish prick, but he's not a monster. Not yet. If he continues down the road he was on, though? I can't make any promises. He's an adult. I can't save him from himself. I can only remove some of the more tempting vices that poisoned him.

Orpheus curses. "Look, the last few weeks have brought some...clarity."

Clarity. Right. We'll see. I settle back against the headboard. "And the favor?"

"Eurydice is spending all her time in the lower city, and I can't get to her. I was hoping you'd pass along a message for me."

I pinch the bridge of my nose and strive for patience. "Orpheus, that woman wants nothing to do with you. If she's not taking your calls or agreeing to see you, the appropriate response is to leave her alone. It's not to find a roundabout way of contacting her."

"I know." For the first time in longer than I care to remember, he sounds absolutely hopeless. Maybe he's never sounded like that. "I know I fucked up, Apollo. I didn't realize how much at the time, but now that some stuff's come out about what happened that night... I thought it was Zeus pulling some shit. I didn't think she'd get hurt. I never wanted her hurt."

I'd be curious to know how that information *came out* because it's not common knowledge that the last Zeus used my brother as a pawn in a convoluted plan to endanger Eurydice, get Hades to cross the River Styx, and break a decades' old treaty. I shake my head. What am I thinking? I know exactly how that information got to Orpheus. All the Dimitriou women hate my brother—and with good reason, if I'm going to be honest. One of them no doubt informed him of just what they think of him and why.

"Intentions don't matter, Orpheus. Actions do," I finally say.

"I know. That's why I'm trying to make it right."

Orpheus is ten years younger than me and sometimes I feel more like a parent to him than our actual parents. If he takes this to them, they'll tell him exactly what he wants to hear. Unfortunately, it falls to me to give him the harsh truth.

Still, I speak it gently because even admitting that he was wrong is progress. "Sometimes the best way to make it right is to let that person move on without you. You're not entitled to her time, even if you want to apologize."

I expect him to argue. A few months ago, he would have.

He just sighs. "I know. Fuck, I know. You're right." He's silent for a few beats. "I hear what you're saying, Apollo. I promise I do. But the fact remains that I *do* need to apologize. If it doesn't go past that, then it doesn't. I'll have to live with that."

It's remarkably mature of him, though I'm still not convinced he should be anywhere near her. I've only met the woman in passing, and she's got a fragile air to her that makes me worry my brother crushed her carelessly. Apologizing won't help that.

It's still the right thing to do. "Promise me that apologizing is all you intend to do and that you'll leave her alone after that."

Silence for a beat. I've surprised him. "It's all I want to do. I promise."

Strangely enough, I believe him. I drag in a breath. "I'm not going to set up some meeting for her to be ambushed, but I'll reach out to Hades with an inquiry. If she agrees to see you, then you can apologize. If she doesn't, this ends now."

He hesitates but finally says, "Okay. Agreed."

I've had limited interactions with Hades since he officially reentered society, but he seems a fair man. He'll at least pass on the request and let Eurydice make her own decision. His wife, on the other hand, will not thank me for bringing this to her sister's door. I fight down a shudder. Persephone might have been a sunshine princess when she was only Demeter's daughter, but now she's a force to be reckoned with akin to her husband. It doesn't matter that she's not one of the Thirteen. Underestimating her would be a mistake.

Honestly, *all* the Dimitriou daughters are dangerous in their own way. Eurydice seems to be the exception, which has me wondering if maybe there's something about her that I'm missing. "I'll pass on the request."

"Thanks."

The bathroom door opens and Cassandra steps out. She's wearing a wrap dress in a deep red that somehow makes her hair appear brighter. It clings to her hips and stomach and breasts almost lovingly, offering a tantalizing glimpse of thigh and cleavage. I clear my throat. "I've got to go, Orpheus." I hang up while he's still saying goodbye. "You look lovely."

"Considering what this dress cost, I had better."

I frown. "Why do you do that?"

"Do what?"

"Every time I compliment you, you divert it. The dress is nice, but *you* look lovely."

She blushes, her pale skin going a delightful pink. "I don't know how to answer that."

I want to press her on it, but we're not here for that. It's frustrating that I have to keep reminding myself of that fact. I climb off the bed and put on my shoes as she does the same with some truly torturous-looking heels. "Will you be able to walk by the end of the week after wearing shoes like that?"

"Yes." She straightens and smooths down her dress. "They're only a little higher than what I wear normally. It'll be fine."

"It's not—"

"Apollo," she says firmly. "I know you are not about to lecture me on how wearing heels is not good for my health. Just because I agreed not to argue about sleeping on the floor does not give you the green light to start policing my choices. I'm more than capable of dressing myself, right down to six-inch heels if that's what I feel like wearing. Stop it."

"Sorry," I mutter. I don't know what's wrong with me. I move to the door. "Shall we do some exploring before dinner?"

"Exploring sounds great."

The hallway is empty, but there are faint sounds of conversation echoing from somewhere close by.

Cassandra looks around with raised eyebrows. "Interesting acoustics."

Something we'll need to keep in mind going forward. If even a low conversation carries through the area, the only place safe to have a frank conversation is within the bedroom. But we knew that already, even without the acoustics.

I offer my arm. "Let's see who else is on the guest list."

"Can't wait." She sounds less than enthused, but she takes my arm, sliding up against me. Her proximity threatens to make my brain skip the same way my heart is attempting to right now.

It takes far more concentration than it should to turn and start down the hall in the direction of the main entrance. We find a trio standing there. I recognize all of them as we descend the stairs to stand before them. I'm surprised to see Pan present; I hadn't thought he left his restaurant often. He's dressed in a pair of perfectly tailored slacks and a white dress shirt. Next to him is Aphrodite, a tall white woman with long, dark hair and a propensity to cause mischief. Until a few months ago, she was Eris Kasios, daughter to the last Zeus and sister to the current one. She's tucked under the arm of a handsome Black man with a shaved head and a bright smile.

Adonis. He's an up-and-coming socialite with a family legacy that stretches back through the history of Olympus. Off the top of my head, I can name three of his distant family members who have been one of the Thirteen, though the last was his maternal grandmother, who was Artemis for a number of years. A short reign as such things go, but she made an impact.

Aphrodite catches sight of us and waves a languid hand. "Do come down, Cassandra. Bring your little boyfriend."

At my side, Cassandra tenses and her smile goes knife-sharp. "Aphrodite, I know you did not just call *Apollo* my 'little boyfriend.' If you're trying to insult him, you can do better than that."

"You're right." Aphrodite's grin widens. "I'm delighted to see that your relationship hasn't softened you at all. I was worried."

Cassandra laughs, and I find myself staring down at her. I've never heard her laugh like that. She certainly doesn't in the office. She releases me and leans against the railing. "You know better."

"I guess I do."

I'm not certain whether I've just been insulted. It hardly matters. I clear my throat. "Nice to see you again, Adonis." I reclaim Cassandra's hand.

Adonis's easy smile never wavers. He's not a foolish man, but he seems to ride the political waves of Olympus without overmuch worry. It baffles me. "Apollo." He reaches out the hand not wrapped around Aphrodite and shakes mine. "Nice to see a friendly face here."

"And what am I?" Pan raises his brows.

"Cranky." Adonis laughs.

His charm comes off him in a pulse that I can almost feel. Not even Pan is immune, a slow smile pulling at his lips. "I have reason to be cranky."

"I don't doubt it for a moment. You're here as Dionysus's plus-one and he made you take your own car. Poor thing." He steers Aphrodite toward the stairs. "Now, let's go check out the bedroom."

She gives Cassandra a long look that seems to be a promise to speak later but allows her date to guide her to the stairs and away. I don't quite breathe a sigh of relief when they're gone, not when this thorny interaction will be the first of many. "I didn't realize you and Aphrodite are friends."

"Oh, we're not." Cassandra finally looks back at me. "But we get along just fine. I like watching her leave chaos in her wake. She enjoys the way I snap and how my presence at her sister's parties stirs the pot with the other guests."

I don't understand that. Parties in general are hardly my favorite thing, though they're rife with information so I can't afford to skip them often. But Cassandra can, and what she just described almost sounds like they set her up like a carnival attraction. I don't like it. "If you say so."

"I do." She turns to Pan. This time, her smile is much warmer. "It's nice seeing you again."

"The feeling is entirely mutual." He hefts his bag over his shoulder. "I'll see you at dinner."

As we turn and head for the back of the house, it strikes me that I don't know as much about Cassandra as I thought. It seems like every time I turn around, she's revealing a new angle, a new piece of information. It's disconcerting...and addicting.

I can't wait to see what she shows me next.

CASSANDRA

MINOS HAS INVITED QUITE THE ECLECTIC MIX OF PEOPLE. I sip my wine and study them situated around the long banquet table. Minos sits at the head of it, his foster sons Theseus and the Minotaur on either side. It's interesting that he's blocked himself off from his guests, but he obviously has a plan. His two children, Ariadne and Icarus, are here of course, practiced smiles in place. The last member of his people, though not of his family, is a plus-sized woman with light-brown skin and luxurious wavy black hair who sits next to Theseus and has a delightfully loud laugh that carries all the way down the table. I don't know what she's laughing at, because it's certainly not something *Theseus* is saying.

There are *six* members of the Thirteen here, most with plus-ones. Apollo, of course, sitting on my right. We saw Hermes, Dionysus, and Aphrodite earlier. But he's also invited Hephaestus and Artemis. They're cousins, both from legacy families, and both very much not on board with some of the waves the new Zeus has been making. If I were going to try to drive a wedge into the Thirteen, they're where I'd start. The foundation is already there.

But then why invite the others? Hermes plays her own games, and she always has. Aphrodite might like starting shit, but she's never going to side against her brother. I still don't quite understand Apollo and Zeus's relationship, but he wants what's best for Olympus and right now he feels that Zeus is the way to that.

Then there are the true surprises.

I glance to the group clustered at the end of the table around Minos's son. Pan and Adonis chat easily with a third person I recognize from school. Atalanta is an athletic Black woman with a scarred face and locs spilling down around her shoulders. Plus-ones for Dionysus, Aphrodite, and Artemis, respectively. If everyone is bringing dates or friends, I suppose that's not outside the realm of expectation.

But the gorgeous woman with light-brown skin and long, dark hair and the handsome white man with their heads close together across the table from him? *Them* I did not anticipate. Eurydice Dimitriou and Charon Ariti. Best guess, they're here representing Demeter's and Hades's interests, respectively, but I can't believe either Persephone or Demeter agreed to allow Eurydice into what could potentially be a dangerous event. They've worked hard to keep her as sheltered as someone can be in Olympus.

I ignore the flicker of jealousy the thought brings. Demeter might be a political monster, but no one with the tiniest bit of intelligence doubts that she loves her daughters. It's a different kind of love than most people experience, perhaps, but it's there all the same.

Apollo shifts closer and my foolish heart picks up as he leans down and speaks directly into my ear. "Eurydice is a surprise."

"I was just thinking the same thing."

"I need to speak with her."

That strange flicker of jealousy threatens to ignite, but I do my best to dowse it. If Apollo is interested in Eurydice, it's not my business. In another week, I won't even be in the city.

I nod. "She's a wild card." The others, I can hazard guesses as to why they'd be present, though I'll need a little time to fine-tune those suppositions. There are *several* powerful people heavily invested in keeping Eurydice tucked away from the rest of Olympus. Her being here doesn't make sense.

The problem with having a table full of this many people is that Minos and his foster sons might as well be in a different room. I can't hear anything they're saying. Ariadne on my other side is entirely wrapped up in some story Hermes and Dionysus weave across the table from us. I catch something about a scooter chase, but I'm not sure I need to hear more. Hermes and Dionysus might play jesters in public, but they're too smart to give away any kind of information without intending to.

Still… Can't hurt to try. We didn't manage to find the security room in our predinner explorations, though we did map out a portion of the downstairs floor plan.

Dionysus laughs uproariously as Hermes wraps up the story. I wait a beat and then lean forward, all interest and intent. "Is it true this used to be your house, Hermes?"

"Guilty as charged." Her smile warms several degrees when she looks at me. It was that warmth that first attracted me to her. So much about her is farce, but when she enjoys a person's company, she doesn't pretend otherwise. "But I'm a city creature right down to my soul. It's a shame to let such a lovely place waste away beneath dust and sheets, so when our friend Minos mentioned he was interested in purchasing a home, I offered mine up."

Our friend Minos.

I have to fight not to narrow my eyes. There's a bit of an ironic lilt to those words. There's absolutely no way that Hermes considers Minos a friend; he's far too similar to the last Zeus, and I'm intimately acquainted on her thoughts about *him.*

My voice comes out too sharp. "I would have thought a house owned by the vaunted Hermes would be less mundane."

Dionysus coughs into his cloth napkin, almost managing to cover up his laugh. "She called you *mundane*, love. Fighting words if I ever heard them."

"Cassandra does love a fight." The warmth on Hermes's face doesn't fade, though her expression goes crafty in a way that used to thrill me. It usually meant a whole lot of fun or pleasure in the future—often both. Now it just makes me wonder what she's hiding.

"Hermes—"

"You know me." She doesn't quite sink insinuation into the words, but it's a near thing. "What would make you think I'm the type of person to just hand away my secrets for free? If you suspect there's more to this house...go find it."

I don't have a chance to come up with a suitable response, which is just as well. In all the time I've known Hermes, I've never managed to outwit her, and I highly doubt I'm going to start tonight. She as much as admitted there's something to find, but it would also be just like her to pretend this house held great secrets, only for me to discover it's just as mundane as it appears to be. With Hermes, you can really go either way.

The table falls silent as Minos stands. He smiles at us, his gaze seeming to meet each person's in turn. Neat trick. He's had some public-speaking training because he manages to project his voice to the whole room without seeming to lift it at all. "Thank you for honoring me by attending this event. I hope you'll indulge me further tonight with a little game." His smile warms.

Gods, he's good at this. We saw it a bit at dinner the other night, but I hadn't realized *how* good. He's holding the entire room enraptured. Even Dionysus has stopped nudging Hermes with his elbow and is focused entirely on Minos.

He spreads his hands. "Through the back door, you'll find a hedge maze. I've left a little something in the center for whoever gets there first."

A hedge maze.

I can't help glancing at Theseus and the Minotaur. The second Ares trial was a maze, and it was the trial that eliminated Theseus—and was responsible for his current limp. Surely it's left bad memories? Especially with Atalanta here, another competitor in that tournament. I can't tell from his expression. He seems to permanently glower at everyone except the woman with the boisterous laugh at this side, and even she only gets a small curve of his lips in response.

Another look around the table shows that we're missing

Ariadne and Icarus, who must have slipped out at some point. I frown. It makes sense that Minos's children wouldn't participate, but he seems the type to care about appearances and so he'll want to keep his family and people close.

Everyone starts standing, and Apollo is quick to pull out my chair. He presses his hand to the small of my back and guides me along with the stream of people out of the room and down the hall to the French doors leading to the backyard.

Dionysus huffs out a laugh as we follow a winding path through carefully curated trees to the entrance of a tall hedge maze. "Really, Hermes?"

Hermes shrugs. "It seemed romantic at the time. Turns out it's just creepy."

"Imagine that," he says drily. "You came out here at night, didn't you?"

"Of course I did. What's the point of a hedge maze if you can't explore it at night and look for ghosts?"

Aphrodite laughs. "Don't tell me you believe in ghosts."

"Everyone should believe in ghosts."

I lean harder against Apollo. "We're playing?" With everyone occupied, it might be a good idea to use this opportunity to continue exploring without worrying about running into someone who's going to ask questions.

He nods. "Minos isn't really giving us an option." He smiles suddenly, making me rock back on my high heels. "Besides, I think we have a solid shot at winning."

I eye the tall hedges. "I hope you're not expecting me to pull a Helen and climb these." It was how she passed the second trial, in a feat of athleticism that had even me cheering at my television. Not that I'll admit as much to anyone. Ever.

"No." Amusement warms his voice. "I'll keep you by my side."

Minos finally reaches the backyard, a basket in his hands. Where did he pick up *that*? "There are several entrances around the edge of the maze, all with equal chance to reach the center. You will pick your partners from this." He shakes the basket. "The first pair to reach the center gets the prize contained there. My household will, of course, not be playing. Hermes has also agreed to sit out, seeing as how she'd have an unfair advantage."

This whole thing is so *weird*. Maybe weeklong parties and group games were the norm a few centuries ago, but they hardly are now. Even in Olympus. It's also strange that he said *household* instead of *children*. Not that it matters, but this entire situation is like a puzzle I don't have a map for. I can't even see the edges properly. It bothers me.

It's not until we start stepping forward to pick names that I realize the new pitfall. I won't be paired with Apollo. It's so statistically unlikely as to be laughable.

Apollo dips his hand into the basket and comes out with a piece of card stock. "Eurydice."

That horrible jealous feeling surges. I can feel eyes on me as I fight to keep any evidence from my face. Why would I be bothered that my fake boyfriend is pairing with the lovely youngest Dimitriou daughter?

I bet Demeter would fall all over herself to approve a marriage between them.

I shake my head, trying to focus. *It doesn't matter.* I will keep repeating that to myself as many times as I have to in order to make it stick. Apollo being paired with Eurydice is honestly a great move for him because it will give him a chance to figure out what she's doing here. It stands to reason that Hades wouldn't trust the rest of the Thirteen to sniff out Minos's plans, but that only explains Charon's presence. Not Eurydice. No matter what I considered earlier, I don't believe for a second that Demeter actually sent *this* daughter as her representative.

"Cassandra."

I jolt at the sound of my name in a familiar voice.

Dionysus smiles at me faintly. "You're my partner, love."

Of all the options, he's probably the least offensive. Only a fool would underestimate him, but it's not a bad way to pass the time.

Everyone else picks their partners up quickly. I get a dark sliver of amusement when Aphrodite steps forward, forcing Minos to look up at her. She pairs with Pan. Artemis is with Adonis. Atalanta is with Charon. And Hephaestus is left as the odd man out, given the choice to compete on his own or sit this one out.

He surveys the group and shakes his head. "I'll pass."

"Very well." Minos turns to the rest of us. "Let's begin."

It takes about fifteen minutes to actually begin. As Minos said, there are several entrances—I'd bet six—around the perimeter of the maze. Dionysus and I end up near the rear, far away from the lights of the house. There are cleverly lit lanterns periodically placed, but the shadows reign supreme in this area.

He twirls his mustache contemplatively as he looks around. He's wearing a remarkably simple suit for once, a plaid that's so low-contrast it looks black in the darkness. "Maybe Hermes wasn't far off with the talk of ghosts."

I fight down a shiver. I don't believe in ghosts, but there's something truly eerie about this place. Like we've somehow stepped out of time. Or maybe we'll reach the center of the maze to discover the body of one of the guests. "Ghosts aren't real."

"That's what ghosts want you to believe." With that confounding statement, a bell chimes in the distance. Our signal to start. He offers his arm with a flourish. "Can't be easy walking in the grass and gravel with those." Dionysus peers down at my feet. "You look absolutely devastating, by the way. A stone-cold fox."

If he were anyone else, I'd bristle at the compliment and start looking for the barbs hiding beneath. But Dionysus is as free with compliments as he is with affection—at least to those he enjoys. If he doesn't like a person, that charming wit turns downright lethal.

I try for a smile. "Thanks." I will absolutely not admit that my feet are killing me. I'm truly not used to spike heels, no matter what I told Apollo.

The hedge walls close in on us as soon as we step through. I can hear low voices in the distance, but the maze distorts them, giving them an alien quality. I shiver. "Hermes *would* have a damned hedge maze in her backyard."

"She's fond of the dramatic, yes." We take a turn and then another, coming up against a dead end.

I should be asking about what he knows of Minos, but that isn't the first question that springs from my lips. "Everyone has a plus-one except Hermes and Hephaestus."

"Oh, he does. He's sharing Atalanta with Artemis. Kinky."

I give him the look that comment deserves. "Now you're just being preposterous. Everyone knows Atalanta is too smart to get caught up in some family drama with those two."

"Not everyone, love. Just you." He squeezes my arm. "You have a knack for seeing what's really there instead of what the peacocks want you to see."

"Dionysus, *you're* one of the peacocks."

He chuckles. "And a splendid one at that."

If I don't rein this in, the conversation will spiral. I take a deep breath. "And Hermes's plus-one?"

"Surely you're not jealous when you have Apollo chasing you around with hearts in his eyes?"

I snort. "Don't be dramatic."

"Now you're just trying to hurt my feelings." We move deeper into the maze, hitting another few dead ends. Gods, this is going to take forever. Dionysus hums a little. "Hermes had someone coming to the party. I think?" He shakes his head. "No, I'm certain of it. They were supposed to be here for dinner. I wonder what happened with that? She was all secret smiles about the surprise."

A shiver cascades down my spine. It could be nothing. Hermes isn't exactly fickle, but she pivots easily and often. "Are you sure she didn't change her mind?"

"As sure as I am of anything." He peers at the high hedge walls. "Maybe they were murdered and we're going to find them at the center of the maze. This is beginning to feel like one of those kinds of parties."

I don't like how his words mirror my earlier thoughts. "Surely

Minos wouldn't start a murder spree. What could he possibly gain out of it?"

"That's for smart people like you to figure out. I'm just here for the free booze." Dionysus gives a mournful sigh. "On that note, I wish Minos had parlor games among the plans tonight. There's top-shelf liquor in the parlor."

As if Dionysus doesn't have the best alcohol and drugs Olympus has to offer in his warehouses. Like all the Thirteen, he's disgustingly rich. Calling him out on his lie won't earn me any favors, though. "Maybe tomorrow."

We walk around a few more turns before he answers. "I doubt I'll be so lucky. I imagine most of the events are like this. He'll likely force us to double up for them, too."

To what aim? Most of the people invited already know each other. There won't be any new alliances coming between Hephaestus and Artemis and the others. Minos isn't using tonight to network, not when his household isn't participating…

I stop short and Dionysus nearly drags me before he stops, too. I look up at him. "Is he trying to marry off his children?" It would make sense. All of the Thirteen present are unmarried. If he couldn't secure one of his sons as Ares, a marriage to a member of the Thirteen wouldn't be a bad consolation prize.

It's what most of the legacy families already do, after all.

"Maybe." He shrugs. "Good luck with that. I'm not in the market for a spouse."

"Not now or not ever?" It's not my business. I know Dionysus is asexual, but I can't remember him ever dating anyone, either. Maybe he's also aromantic. Which, again, none of my business.

Still, he brought it up so I can't help saying, "You brought Pan to the party."

"He's a friend and potential business partner. Nothing more." He shrugs. "I'm not overly interested at this juncture. I don't see that changing."

"Well, I guess Minos should let that ship sail, then."

"Yep." We start walking again. I can't tell if we're headed toward the center of the maze or just getting hopelessly lost. I'm so busy trying to figure it out, I almost miss Dionysus's next words. "But let's not talk about *my* romantic life when yours is right there and oh so juicy." He tugs me into a dead end and puts his hands on my shoulders. "Spill, dear Cassandra. Tell me every little sordid detail."

This is it. The first real test of this experience. Dionysus knows me well enough to know my reasons for never wanting to publicly date a member of the Thirteen. I can't say I've changed my mind without a good reason. No one will believe that, let alone *him*.

I take a deep breath and prepare to lie.

APOLLO

"THE WEATHER IS REALLY NICE TONIGHT."

Eurydice gives me a polite smile that doesn't reach her eyes. "Yes, very."

Gods, this is ridiculous. I move through the most powerful circles in this city, where one wrong word can create a cascade of political ripples. I'm *good* at it most of the time. And the best I can come up with in this situation is a comment about the weather?

After several minutes of awkward silence, I try again. "I'll admit, I was surprised to see you at the dinner table."

Eurydice doesn't look at me. "I was a last-minute invite." It's clear she has no intention of elaborating, which is interesting.

There's something different about her. This woman has spent plenty of time in my presence at family functions during the time she dated my brother, but in those interactions, she always seemed nervous and almost fragile. That feeling is gone now. She's still quiet and composed, but something's changed. "How have you been?"

"Good." Her answer seems to surprise her. She finally shoots me a sheepish smile. "I wasn't for a while, but I'm doing much better now."

I don't inquire about her obvious camaraderie with Charon, don't ask whether it's more than friendship. That's none of my business. I glance up at the stars overhead. I had intended to reach out via Hades about the possibility of Orpheus apologizing. It seems silly to wait when she's walking next to me, but I don't want her to feel like I'm cornering her out in the dark maze, either.

"Apollo?" She pauses as voices drift from somewhere close, but they move away quickly. This maze truly is a monster.

When she doesn't immediately continue, I say, "Yes?"

"How is he?" She rushes on before I can answer, some of her previous nervousness showing through. "I wouldn't ask because I most certainly don't care, but I saw him a couple weeks ago. It was just for a moment and across a bar, but..." She takes a deep breath. "He looked like shit. Not at all like the man I knew."

It's on the tip of my tongue to tell her everything, but it's no more my place to share Orpheus's struggles than it is to browbeat Eurydice into seeing him. I can't even promise he's changed, for all that I believe he has, at least based on our recent conversations. I clear my throat. "He would like to apologize." I hold up both hands. "You absolutely do not have to agree, though. You don't owe him anything."

"I know." Her lips curve in a faint, sad smile.

"Oh. Okay." I drop my hands. "You don't need to answer tonight, but if you end up deciding that you'd like to hear his apology, I can arrange it."

"If I decide to hear him out, I'll arrange it myself." She starts to move forward and glances over her shoulder at me. "Thanks, though. Regardless of how I feel about my ex, you've been nothing but kind to me."

A dozen comments rise and die before they ever leave my lips. That Eurydice is a gift and I hope she finds someone who appreciates that in full. That I would have liked to have her for a sister-in-law. That I think Orpheus wants her in his life again. That I hope she moves on from my brother and never looks back.

I don't say any of it.

A *whoop* goes up somewhere to our right. I turn that way instinctively, even though I can't see anything but hedge. A few moments later, Minos's voice booms from the opposite direction. "We have our winners! Charon and Atalanta."

Eurydice smiles. "Charon really is the best, isn't he?" She tilts her head to the side. "I wonder what the prize is."

We find out a little while later. I'm able to get us back to our entrance without too much trouble, having memorized the route, and I'm no small amount of relieved to see Cassandra and Dionysus chatting as they come around from the opposite side. Pairs trickle in slowly, but the last one isn't a pair at all.

It's a trio.

"You must be joking me," Eurydice murmurs.

Ariadne walks between Atalanta and Charon, an arm slung around both of them. "You've won me, friends. Whatever shall you do with me?" She's grinning and seems like she's actually having fun. I can't blame her. Both Atalanta and Charon are attractive and charming and have proximity to power that's almost as alluring as the power itself. It takes skill to do what they do and everyone knows it.

I'm pretty sure I hear Eurydice growl a little, which is confirmation enough that her interest in Charon goes beyond friendship. Impossible to say if it's returned, but he laughs and artfully slips from beneath Ariadne's arm. "I think it's time for a drink."

"A man after my own heart."

I search for Cassandra again in the group, finally landing on where she's still speaking with Dionysus. I start to pick my way toward them, but Minos appears before me as if by magic. The big man smiles. "Apollo, I'd love a word."

I fight down the instinctive desire to go to Cassandra instead of being diverted; this is what she's here for. Either I trust her to be able to handle herself, or I don't, and if I don't, I had no business asking this of her in the first place. I manage a smile for Minos. "Of course."

We follow the group inside, but he leads me down a different hallway. I make a mental note as he unlocks a door with an honest-to-gods skeleton key and pushes it open to reveal a traditionally decorated study. We're right in the heart of the house, which is a part of the downstairs Cassandra and I didn't manage to map before dinner.

What are the odds that he keeps the security room close to his office? Or, rather, that Hermes did when she built this place?

It's what I would do.

I slide my hand into my pocket and send out the prearranged signal for Hector to get to work. I won't know if he's successful until I can check in after this, but he needs a good ten to fifteen minutes to hack into the security system using the device in my other pocket as a booster. It's cutting-edge tech, the kind of thing I would have spent time inventing if I'd secured a spot as Hephaestus instead of Apollo.

Now, instead of inventing the tech, I have to use it.

To give myself time, I look around the room. There's nothing of Minos's personality here. He might as well have picked the big mahogany desk, the tasteful chairs, and the generic bookshelf out of a catalog. I wander over to the bookshelf, more out of curiosity than anything else, and have my suspicions confirmed. All the books are hardcovers with the wraps removed to show foiled edges. They're too uniform not to have been bought together, and they're so new, they're practically shining.

If Minos is a reader, his collection isn't in this room.

"Drink?"

I'm not overly interested in drinking with this man, but we're doing a dance as old as time. "Please." I move to take one of the chairs as he pulls a crystal decanter off a nearby cart. Truly, this room reminds me of a set off the soap operas my mother used to watch when I was young. I'm reasonably sure the glass he passes me is the exact style from the show, which just confirms that it's all new.

By all appearances, Minos didn't bring much in the way of personal effects when he came to Olympus. That seems to support his story that he's fleeing an enemy who intends to take the city, but it could very well be that he wants us to think that. He's smart enough to take that into consideration.

And someone is funding him. He got some resources from

Zeus as part of the bargain he struck, but he bought this house before that deal went through.

I wait for him to take a sip of his drink before I do the same with mine. It's whiskey, and expensive, but it's not my drink of choice so I don't know it well enough to identify the year and maker. It's tempting to break the silence, but he asked me here for a reason so I intend to make him execute the opening bid.

He doesn't make me wait long. Minos sinks into the chair behind his desk with an exaggerated sigh. "Have you spent much time out in the greater world?"

I raise my brows. "No. My responsibilities lie with Olympus." I've had cause to leave the city a few times for one reason or another, but most of my work is here, which means my time is spent here.

Best I can tell, the rest of the world isn't that different from our city. The people with the most money and power sit at the top, and the rest are left to figure things out for themselves. The true benefit of Olympus, the reason we are such a tempting fruit to Minos's former employer, is that we're essentially a sovereign nation.

When the rest of the world realized the barrier kept them away, they were forced to be satisfied with trading agreements some distant-past Poseidon set up. I don't know if those agreements will hold even if the barrier falls. It's a different world out there than it was a few decades ago, let alone a few hundred years. Instead of razing our city to the ground, there's more likely to be an attempt to take over our positions of leadership in a bloodless coup. They can't get around Poseidon, Zeus, and Hades, but if the rest of the Thirteen are united, not even those three can do much about it.

It's what I would do if I wanted to take the city.

"It feels different out there." He contemplates his drink. "I realize you have no reason to trust me, but I want what you have. Stability for me and my family. Surely you can't fault me for that."

Bold of him to come right out and say it. "If you really want that, then I don't see why you're holding back information that might keep you and yours safe." I set my drink aside. "Don't bother to lie. We both know you didn't tell Zeus everything. You're too smart to put in so much work without knowing what the endgame is."

Minos smiles slowly. "I like you. You're not the same as the rest of them. You actually care."

The pivot has my mind whirling. We're being remarkably frank with each other, so I risk a blunt question. "What's that supposed to mean?"

"I took the liberty of looking into Cassandra. She's lovely, but you must know your parents will never welcome her. Not after her parents brought so much shame on the family. Olympus doesn't like to forgive and forget. I've been here a short time, and even I know that."

"Do you have a point?"

"By all accounts, her parents reached beyond their means, and look what happened to them. It'd be a shame if something similar happened to her for the very same reasons."

The small hairs on the back of my neck raise. Is he threatening Cassandra? I can't tell. He's got his genial mask in place, all concerned kindness. The desire to shove to my feet and rush out of the room to ensure she's safe is nearly overwhelming. "I'm Apollo.

No matter what my parents think of my partners, they won't risk alienating me." I don't like that he looked into her. I don't like it at all.

"Perhaps." Minos nods easily. "But what about Zeus and the rest of the Thirteen? They aren't bound the same way the rest of us are."

Zeus knows what this really is, but if one of the others thought Cassandra was trying to follow in her parents' footprints? "That won't happen."

"So you say. That girl has worked hard to avoid the limelight, and there have been more articles written about her since your date a few days ago than in the last five years combined. People are talking, Apollo. If you care so much about her, you never should have brought her here."

No reason for guilt to prick me. We knew what going public would do. Cassandra is getting paid well and she has no plans to stick around after this task is finished. I can't quite unclench my jaw. "I'm honored, Minos. I had no idea you were so interested in my love life and the welfare of my girlfriend." I honestly can't tell if he's threatening her or not. It *feels* like he is, but he hasn't said anything overt that I can call him on.

"As I said, I like you." He swirls the whiskey in his glass, expression contemplative. "You're an asset and you're wasted on this place. I'd like to have you in the family."

I blink. "Excuse me?"

"Take your pick of my children." He waves a casual hand toward the door. "Icarus might be a bit flighty for your tastes, but Ariadne is a good girl. She'd make a lovely wife to you."

His boldness leaves me at a loss for words. Arranged marriages are hardly uncommon in Olympus, but people tend to go about it in a subtler way. I look away. "I'm not in the market for a marriage at this point." Under no circumstances will I allow myself to think of *Cassandra*, dressed in white and walking down the aisle to me.

"Pity." He shrugs easily. "I had thought you too smart to be swayed by your emotions, but it's clear that as long as Cassandra is by your side, you won't see things my way."

I send him a sharp look. "If something happens to her, I won't see things your way, either."

He holds up his hands. "Whoa, whoa, no one is making threats, Apollo. You wanted me to speak plainly, so I'm just doing what you requested."

For him to speak plainly about his motivations. Surely there's more to this party than a marriage mart? I barely resist the urge to look at my watch. How long has it been? How much longer do I need to keep him talking? Maybe someone else could sit here while he threatened someone they cared about, but that's not me. It never has been. "Why are you here, Minos?"

"I already told you." He laughs. "Do you think asking a few dozen more times will result in a different answer?"

This whole thing feels like he just threw a handful of sand into an already murky pool. I can't tell if he's being honest about wanting to match me with one of his children, but surely it's not that simple. He must be holding something back. "If you'd be transparent, we wouldn't have to do this song and dance."

"There you go, talking frankly again." He hefts himself to his feet. It's rather dramatic, considering I watched him bound down the steps at the Dryad less than a week ago. Minos obviously wants to be underestimated. It's a familiar ploy—a lot of people in Olympus use it, including myself—but it irks me all the same. "Truly, you stand out among the others. It's a wonder someone hasn't taken issue with your honesty."

Another threat that isn't quite a threat. I follow him to my feet. "Thanks for the drink." Hopefully Hector had enough time to hack the cameras.

"Anytime, Apollo. And I do mean that."

I follow him back down the hall and into yet another large room, this one designed for entertaining. It's divided into smaller spaces by the way the furniture is arranged. The group has fractured as a result. I catch Aphrodite and Adonis sharing a love seat, though all her attention is focused on Theseus sprawled across from them, smirking at her. If looks could kill, he'd be broken and bloodied on the floor. It's an unwise move to antagonize that woman. Aphrodite might not be cutting down people in battle, but she's more than a formidable opponent to those she considers enemies.

Eurydice, Charon, Hermes, and Dionysus have joined Ariadne on a trio of couches and are having what appears to be an animated conversation. Pan and Icarus are perched on chairs on either side of a small round table holding a chessboard while Atalanta watches with interest, a glass dangling from her fingertips. At first glance, Icarus appears to be winning.

I don't see Cassandra.

I also don't see the Minotaur.

Minos seems to come to the same conclusion as he surveys the room. "How will you keep her safe when she's obviously so prone to wandering?" He chuckles. "Best of luck with that."

Surely he's too savvy to hurt Cassandra in order to get to me?

That's the problem, though. I don't know what Minos will or won't do. I didn't expect the direction of our conversation, and I can't speak to what lengths he'll go to achieve his goals. He's obviously targeting her, and that's enough to have my instincts screaming at me to act, to do whatever it takes to keep her safe.

I turn for the door. "I'll just go see what's keeping them."

His chuckle follows me out of the room.

CASSANDRA

I DON'T MEAN TO GET SEPARATED FROM THE GROUP. I was walking next to Dionysus and realized my shoe strap was coming undone. In the fifteen seconds it took me to fix it, the rest of the group cleared out, leaving only the hulking Minotaur behind. I don't know why it surprises me that he keeps his deep-red hair long enough to brush his shoulders, but it does. It's startlingly beautiful, glossy and thick, and only contrasts with his harsh features and the scars that cover his face. There's a new one healing from where Helen—Ares—cut him in the last trial.

I tense, waiting for him to say something biting, but he just looks up and eyes the clear night sky. "Walk with me."

Under any other circumstances, I would decline. He's a strange man and obviously dangerous, and I have no intention of getting murdered before Zeus can pay me. If I do, he's likely to say my side of the bargain isn't fulfilled and then Alexandra gets nothing.

But he can make the same argument if he finds out I turned down a prime opportunity to get close to one of Minos's family members.

Really, I only have one option. "Sure." I can't make myself sound happy about it, but I turn and head back toward the maze. The Minotaur is huge—he's got to be nearly a foot taller than me, if not more—but he matches his stride to mine without any apparent effort.

I have absolutely no interest in entering the confined quarters of the maze, so I veer when the path branches, walking farther away from the house. I keep waiting for him to say something, since he's the reason we're out here, but he doesn't speak.

I catch sight of a body of water in the distance. A pond, judging by its size. I stop short. "If you're planning on trying to murder me, you'll probably succeed, but I am an excellent screamer and you won't get away with it."

The Minotaur stops and looks at me. I can't see his eyes clearly. The lights that made the maze navigable don't stretch out to here. I only have moonlight to judge, but it sure seems like he's amused. "I'm not going to murder you."

Did he put an emphasis on *you* or is the adrenaline surging through my body making me hear things? "That's what a murderer would say." I don't know why I'm arguing. There's something akin to panic fluttering at the back of my throat. I am not equipped to deal with this. The backbiting and politics, maybe, but this man went after Achilles Kallis, one of the best warriors Olympus has to offer, like he wanted to kill him. Like he'd killed before. "Why did you bring me out here?"

"Cassandra?"

I spin around as Apollo strides down the path. He looks calm and collected, but he's moving fast enough to almost be running. He doesn't slow down when he sees us, either. He narrows his eyes. "It's time to go in now."

"Until next time, Cassandra." The Minotaur turns in the opposite direction and stalks into the darkness.

I stare after him. *What the fuck was that?* I open my mouth, but Apollo shakes his head sharply. "Let's go back to the room." He practically hauls me off my feet, moving too quickly for my shorter legs to keep up.

I finally have to dig in my heels and force him to stop entirely. He *growls* at me. "Move, Cassandra."

"No." I pull back, fighting down a shiver that's certainly not desire when he doesn't release my wrist. "Either slow down or let go, because I'm tired of you dragging me along."

For a moment, it looks like he intends to argue with me, but he finally huffs out a breath. "I'll slow down." He maintains his hold on my wrist as he turns back toward the house, but this time, he checks his pace so I can keep up without struggling. We still make it back to the room in record time. Apollo hustles me through the door and slams it behind him. "What the fuck is wrong with you?"

Of all the things I expected him to say, this wasn't on the list. "Excuse me?"

"The Minotaur is dangerous. *Everyone* at this party is dangerous. You can't simply waltz off into the dark with them without telling someone where you went."

I know this is fear. Apollo would never yell at me without

good reason, but my own residual fear gets ahold of my tongue. I don't even try to stop it. "I don't need a babysitter, Apollo. You brought me here to do a job, and I'm going to do it."

"Not at the expense of your safety."

A bitter laugh erupts from me. "Right. As if I've ever been safe in Olympus."

He focuses in on me, narrowing his dark eyes. "This isn't harsh words and gossip, Cassandra. This is dangerous."

Oh good gods, he's like a dog with a bone. I throw up my hands. "You don't think *I* know that? The Thirteen murdered my parents and then covered it up to look like an accident." I'd been young and naive and too shell-shocked to think clearly in the aftermath. It's the only excuse I have for going to the police. Not that it helped. They all but laughed me out of the station.

Apollo narrows his eyes. "Then you have no excuse for wandering off with the Minotaur. He could have killed you and shoved your body somewhere on the grounds, and I wouldn't have known any differently."

Like Hermes's plus-one?

I shut that thought down fast. We don't even have confirmation that there was a plus-one to begin with, let alone that they're missing. Dionysus might have misunderstood or not been informed when the plan changed.

Either way, it has nothing to do with this conversation. "I knew the risks when I agreed to come here. So did you." I'm done with this conversation. As grateful as I am that he hunted me down to ensure I was okay, I don't need to be lectured on the dangers of Olympus by a man born with a silver spoon in his mouth. A man almost universally beloved by both the public and those who hold power.

"Don't walk away from me, Cassandra." He doesn't move from his position, but his firm voice stops me cold. "If you want to be done with this conversation, then say so. But don't storm out in the middle of it."

The rebuke stings. I spin to face him. If he wants a report, I'll give it to him. Honestly, this should be a relief. For a little while there, I almost forgot that Apollo is nothing but my boss. I should thank him for reminding me.

I straighten my spine and stare at a point just off his right ear. "I don't need you to protect me, Apollo. I'm here to do a job. Dionysus shared no useful information during the maze, aside from the fact that Hermes may or may not have invited a guest and they haven't shown. I'm still considering information about why everyone is here, but based on the party guests and the prize, I would wager Minos plans to set up at least one of his children with single members of the Thirteen. I did not gain any information from the Minotaur, which seems to indicate that whole performance was for *your* benefit and you walked right into it." My voice trembles, and I concentrate on firming it up. "That's all I have to report. I'm going to wash my face and change." When he doesn't speak, I snap, "That means I am, in fact, done with this conversation."

He doesn't call after me again.

I close the bathroom door and slump against it. My adrenaline is already draining out of me, leaving a stark kind of clarity. Apollo was worried about me. He thought the same thing I had—that the Minotaur meant me ill.

I push off the door and, after the barest hesitation, start the shower. I need to wash the maze and the fear off me. As it heats up, I consider my theory. Minos strikes me as a smart man. No one is leaving this party engaged, and if he wanted to play matchmaker, why allow plus-ones in the first place? Something isn't adding up. Drowning me in the duck pond might remove me, but he has to know Apollo is too smart to consider it an accident. It would eliminate any chance of pairing Apollo with one of his children.

But that logic only holds if the matchmaker theory holds. If something else is going on, I can't assume I'm safe.

I sigh and strip out of my clothing. I'm going to have to apologize. Storming out in the middle of an argument *was* childish. I'm better than that. Especially since I know he's not just snarling to be a dick. He's genuinely worried about me. There's a good chance he is right to be, too.

It doesn't take long to shower and go through my nightly ritual. It's only when I'm done that I realize I didn't bring my suitcase into the bathroom. Which means the pajamas I bought solely for this trip are out in the bedroom.

I eye the dress I was wearing before, but it's silly to put it back on. The towels are all oversize and ridiculously fluffy. One of them will cover me well enough for the thirty seconds it will take to grab the pajamas.

It feels like a much bigger deal than it is. Before I can talk myself out of it, I open the door and step into the bedroom. Apollo sits on the edge of the bed, his elbows propped on his knees, his head hanging. "I just talked with Hector. He was able to hack the system and shut down both the cameras and the microphones planted throughout the house. When they figure out what happened, they'll likely try to lock him out, but he's got a good handle on the system for now. He'll keep us updated."

"Oh." I should have asked about that before I stormed off.

"I already searched the room again for bugs. It's clean. The rest of the household should be settled down soon and then we can see about mapping out the second floor. Once we finish that, we can either see about the third floor or finish up the main level."

The reason we're here. Right. "Okay," I say meekly.

"Cassandra, I—" He lifts his head and, though his mouth keeps working, his words dry up.

I've been able to convince myself that Apollo wasn't looking at me like *that* up to this point, but there's no denying it now. Not when we're the only two people in this room. There's no reason to pretend, no one to perform for. He stares at the point where I've tucked the towel in over my breasts like he can will it to untuck through sheer force of concentration. As if he wants to see me without anything at all.

As if he...wants me. A lot.

I have the most absurd urge to drop the towel. To see what he'll do, if he'll cross the distance between us and fulfill the promise alighting his dark eyes. Will he be gentle? Even better, will he use that deliciously firm voice with me as he instructs me on what he wants me to do? I shiver.

That seems to snap him out of it. He shakes his head roughly. "If you're done with the bathroom, I'll take a shower."

The sinking feeling in my stomach most certainly isn't disappointment. I step aside. "I'm done."

Apollo doesn't move until I make my way around the edge of

the bed to where our luggage is. I've hung up most of my dresses, but there are still a few things in the suitcase itself. I hear the bathroom door shut and turn around to find him gone.

We haven't talked about the details of how we'll do our after-hours snooping, and it belatedly occurs to me that we have a problem. Once Minos realizes the cameras aren't doing their job, surely he'll set up some kind of security patrol. I haven't seen any on the grounds but...

I stop short.

I haven't seen any security on the grounds. That doesn't make any sense. We have *six* of the Thirteen here, and they never travel without teams, even if those teams excel at subtlety. Why in the gods' names would they agree to come to the country without their security in place? I know why Apollo did, but the rest of them?

There's no way they're that arrogant, right?

I shake my head. Yes, they definitely are that arrogant. They all believe they're untouchable. Even Apollo, though he's less obscene about it. I dig through my suitcase. Normally, I sleep in the nude, but obviously that's not an option for this trip. I shouldn't have let Psyche convince me to add pajamas to the list of things we bought from Juliette, but after she bullied me into trying them on, I couldn't resist.

Not to mention Hera insisted on my purchasing one of every-thing. Not even I was willing to argue with her when she had that glint in her dark eyes.

There are several shorts-and-tank-top combos that seem innocent until I put them on. The way they hug my curvy body makes me feel so sexy, they should be illegal. And then there are the other ones. They're a short shift-dress style that, again, looks chaste enough until I put it on. I don't know what clever magic Juliette pulled with the sewing, but they fit as if made for a body like mine. Not clinging where they shouldn't and gaping elsewhere. The damn things were created for seduction.

I should have said no. I *should* have stopped on the way home and picked up some fleece pajamas that cover me from neck to ankles. Or at least leggings and a T-shirt. I even packed some of the latter in case I chickened out.

I run my hands over the pajamas. I'm not quite brave enough to go that route, no matter how hot Apollo's gaze felt on me. But maybe it wouldn't hurt to make him squirm a little? He did yell at me, after all.

The excuse feels flimsy at best, but I quickly pull on one of the sets, a matching black one with red lace at the top of the tank and the bottom of the shorts that is almost the same color as my hair. I braid my hair back from my face and am just wondering what I should do next when Apollo steps out of the bathroom. He's wearing a pair of lounge pants...and nothing else.

I try to look at his face, but I don't try that hard. How can I when he's shirtless for the first time since I've known him and he's been hiding *that* body beneath his perfectly tailored suits? Oh, I knew he had muscles; I felt them every time I pressed against him in the name of our fake relationship.

But seeing them is another experience entirely.

He's not absurdly carved or anything. But his chest is defined and I kind of want to take a bite out of his biceps. I give myself a shake and drag my eyes to his face. He's not smirking at the fact that I'm practically drooling on the floor, though.

No, he's staring at my thighs.

I tense, fighting the urge to cover myself. Not out of shame or discomfort. More like in instinctive need to retreat, to see if he'll stalk across the distance between us and rip my hand away so he can look his fill.

I lick my lips. *Focus.* We have to focus. "Apollo." His name comes out too low, too intimate. I can do better than this. I know I can. I reach for something logical and reasonable to say that isn't *"Take off your pants right now."* I clear my throat. "We can't just wander around in the dark, obviously casing the place. Do you have a plan?"

"I did have a plan. It was a very good plan, but then you put on those pajamas." He clears his throat and subtly adjusts his pants. Holy shit, Apollo is hard. For *me.* "Now I'm having a hard time remembering what it is."

Lust clogs my brain, threatening to wash away what's left of my good intentions. A surge of desire rushes through my body and my nipples pebble. "I can't think when you look at me like that."

A flush creeps over his chest and up his neck. "We have a job to do."

He's right. I know he's right. I lick my lips. "What if... We're dating, right? Or that's what they believe. If we're caught, we can just say we're, uh, exploring the kinky rooms for kinky purposes. Exhibition. That sort of thing." I can't believe how normal my voice sounds. As if my heart isn't trying to beat its way out of my chest and closer to Apollo. As if I'm not about to go to my knees before him and beg for him to touch me.

"We were explicitly told they're not kinky anymore."

"Maybe we forgot." I don't know what I'm saying. This isn't

furthering the plan to explore the second floor. It's pure, selfish desire. I stare at the line of his shoulders. I want to trace it with my tongue. "I'm feeling very forgetful right now."

"Me too." The words come out lower. Deeper. He holds my gaze. The Apollo I know is there, of course—even when he was yelling at me earlier, he was so purely *Apollo*—but I've never seen this side of him before. He feels almost...dangerous. He seems to force himself to look away, his jaw tight. "Cassandra."

Oh no. He's about to do something honorable. "Apollo, I—"

"You don't have to do this. By inviting me, Minos all but dared me to find out what he's really about. Once he realizes the cameras are down, he'll know who's to blame. If you want to keep things...simple...we can say we're going to get you a glass of water or something of that nature."

I should go with that option. It's a flimsy excuse, but a much safer one for me. My emotions are already compromised, have been compromised since before I agreed to Zeus's bargain. I'm leaving the city as soon as I possibly can. Giving in to the lust saturating the air between us all but guarantees I'll be leaving Olympus with a broken heart. I might be able to separate sex and emotions well enough in normal life, but this is *Apollo*.

Fool that I am, I don't care what pain I'm guaranteeing myself. I want this too badly to say no. It's supposed to be the kissing and stuff that is designed to excuse the snooping, but right now it feels like the snooping is giving us the excuse we need to do a whole lot more than kiss. I take a step backward, toward the door. "Come on, Apollo. Let's go see the kinky rooms."

APOLLO

I AM NOT ONE TO LET MY BASER DESIRES GET THE BEST OF me. My brain rarely shuts off, and as a result, I overthink things to a clinical degree. It's been the reason behind the end of several of my relationships over the years.

Standing here, staring at Cassandra, I'm not thinking of anything at all.

She's always been beautiful. But in this moment, dressed in that little tease of pajamas that have her breasts straining precariously against their thin straps and have pulled tight across her generous hips? She's *devastating*.

I want to kiss that down-turned mouth. I want to run my hands over her lush body and pull her tight against me. Gods, I want to wrap that braid around my fist and force her to meet my gaze and admit she wants me, too.

I shake my head, trying to think. "Are you sure?"

"For fuck's sake, Apollo." She starts for the door.

Oh gods. Oh *fuck*.

If the sight of her from the front was enough to short out my thoughts, I can barely stay on my feet at the view she presents me with as she opens the door. I have seen her ass in tight skirts and hidden behind flared dresses and—on the very lucky days—on display with tailored pants. I've never seen her show so much skin.

Of course not. She's not in office wear. She's in her pajamas and you're panting after her like a creep.

"Apollo."

I'm moving before I decide to take the first step. I have the disconcerting thought that I'd follow her anywhere as long as she let me look my fill. "Wait."

She stops in the doorway but doesn't look back. "What?"

"I told you that no video or photo would get out that would…"

"Apollo, please. You said that Hector took care of it. If we find out otherwise?" Cassandra looks over her shoulder at me. "Either hack Minos's systems and delete it—I know you're capable of it—or I'll ask Hermes to do it."

I blink. "Why would Hermes do that for you?"

"We used to date a long time ago." It's hard to tell, but I think she's blushing. "We're…friends now. I guess I should have mentioned it before."

I had no idea, because I very intentionally did not look into her past. With Hermes in the mix, I'm not sure there'd be anything to find about this relationship, but I didn't even look out of respect for Cassandra. The fact that she's offering up the information now, freely, is a gift. I need to see it as such.

I'm only human.

I can't help the spike of jealousy that rises in response to realizing that Hermes has dated the woman I... I'm not even sure how to term it. Cassandra is not for me. She can't be for me. Asking her to stay would be so selfish it makes me feel vaguely ill, and yet the impulse is there all the same. I swallow hard. "I see."

She steps back into the room and closes the door. "I didn't say anything before because I wasn't sure if it was a strange thing to just bring up randomly." Cassandra tucks a strand of hair behind her ear.

The move brings my attention back to her body. Gods, those pajamas should be illegal. I have no excuse for the words that erupt. "Hermes is kinky."

"Extremely." Cassandra doesn't move, doesn't seem to breathe. "What are you asking me?"

You dated her.

You're kinky, too.

"You should have told me you dated her. Her tastes run a certain way, and if yours do as well, that's something I need to know." I almost sound normal as I say it.

"You're right." She gives one of those delicious little shivers that makes her breasts shake. Her nipples are hard points against the silky black fabric of her top. "I don't like pain. We played bondage and some light dominance and submission. Occasionally she got more creative with the games, but it was only ever the two of us. No sharing." She looks away. "And yeah, there was some nearly public stuff. I was young and foolish enough to think it wouldn't matter if we were caught—and Hermes ensured we never were."

My cock goes so painfully hard. Bondage. All too easily, I can picture Cassandra's body crisscrossed with Shibari. Art. The sexiest art in existence. And once she was well and truly tied...

"When was this?"

"Six years ago, give or take. We weren't public about it by my request." She gives a half smile. "Even as angry and impulsive as I was, I knew better than to be linked to one of the Thirteen officially."

I have to step back, have to turn away to avoid kissing her right now. This isn't real, no matter how visceral the attraction. We have a job to do. "I see. We'll..." I clear my throat again. "Let's get moving."

She arches a brow. "Do you have bondage gear hiding in that bag of yours?"

No, but if I'd known to ask these questions, I would have packed some. "I'm sure Hermes has some stashed somewhere."

"What an excellent way to mark your territory just like a real boyfriend." She licks her lips. "Let's go."

She's right. At this point, I'm stalling. Inexcusable. "After you."

We step into the empty hall and look around. My arm brushes Cassandra's bare shoulder and it's everything I can do not to press her to the wall and ravish her mouth. With so little clothes on our bodies, I'll be able to feel her skin against mine, will be able to slide my hands under the hem of her top and...

She starts moving down the hall toward the main stairs. Her ass is truly out of this world. I normally try to resist ogling her, but there's no resisting this. Especially not when she puts a bit of extra sway in her step. "You're doing that on purpose."

"Doing what on purpose?" She doesn't look over her shoulder at me, but the teasing in her tone confirms my suspicion.

I manage to keep it together as we check the first three rooms.

They're exactly as Ariadne described—sitting rooms. Truly, they're just as soulless as Minos's office.

Cassandra's soft laugh makes me look over. "What?"

"He missed this." She points up to where a hook is cleverly tucked into the ceiling. It's a sturdy thing, obviously meant to hold enough weight to suspend a person.

Again, the image of Cassandra's body patterned with rope hits me with the force of a freight train. Her arms bound above her head, giving me full access to her body...

"Apollo?"

I shake my head sharply. "Let's move on to the next room." I don't expect to find anything during this search, but I've been doing this long enough to know better than to make assumptions. We have to check every room we can get access to, if only to eliminate them as possibilities.

We slip back into the hall and start for the fourth door. It takes me several seconds to realize the sound I'm hearing isn't *our* footsteps. Someone is coming up the stairs. They're moving fast enough that we won't have a chance to make it back to our room.

I don't think. I wrap an arm around Cassandra's waist and drag her through the fourth sitting-room door. To her credit, she doesn't make a sound. A quick glance around the room doesn't show much to hide behind. There's only the couch, facing away from the door.

I haul her around the couch and press her down onto it. All someone has to do is walk fully into the room and look around the edge of the couch to see us, but hopefully that won't happen. Still, I press my hand to Cassandra's mouth and lean down. "Someone's coming."

Her only response is to shiver.

Which is right around the time I realize that I'm cradled between her thighs. It's like my mind shorts out and my body takes over. I have absolutely no intention of moving, but I thrust against her, just a little. Her breath catches against my palm and she whimpers.

That whimper stops me short.

I stare down at her in the darkness. The faint light from the window doesn't reach us here on the couch. The shadows are too deep to reach her expression, but I've just manhandled her in the darkness and now I've pinned her to the couch.

What am I *doing*?

I don't have a chance to figure it out because the footsteps stop outside the door. I strain to hear them over my racing heart. Did the person see us duck in here? Or are they going to check all the rooms?

The door opens softly. I hold my breath. Beneath me, I can feel Cassandra doing the same. The seconds tick past, but the person doesn't step into the room. Finally, a small eternity later, the door closes softly and the footsteps retreat. They pause at each door, though.

Looking for us?

Or just doing a nightly round since the cameras are down?

I don't shift my hand from Cassandra's mouth until I can no longer hear the footsteps. "We should be good."

Except my adrenaline doesn't fade. Not when she shifts against me, her breasts pressed to my chest and her thighs so soft around my hips. My brain glitches again and I thrust against her. Again.

She makes that delicious little whimpering sound. Gods, I want to bottle that sound up. I want to do whatever it takes to make her do it again.

"Apollo," she breathes.

Now is the time to move, to reclaim some distance between us. It's the honorable thing to do, and I pride myself on being an honorable man.

Instead, I settle down more firmly on top of her. "Cassandra."

She shivers and shifts a little, her thighs tensing on either side of my hips. "You are very, very hard."

"Considering the fact that I have you beneath me, I'm surprised that's all I am." I shift closer when I should be moving away, until my lips brush her ear. Until I can whisper, "Please ignore it. I'm sorry."

"Are you really sorry?" She shifts again.

This time, there's no mistaking her movement. She's rolling her hips a little, rubbing herself against my cock. I drop my head to the curve of her shoulder. "If you don't stop doing that, I'm going to embarrass myself by coming in my pants."

She doesn't stop. If anything, my attempt at control emboldens her further. "You want me."

"Of course I want you." I'm speaking too sharply for all that I match her low tone, but she's rubbing her pussy on me, and it takes everything I have to hold perfectly still and not grind against her. "But you're my employee and it won't be appropriate to make you feel like you had to do something you didn't want to because of an imbalance of power." It's hard to keep my voice down, to whisper to keep this conversation just between us.

To not potentially draw the attention of whoever is roaming the halls tonight.

She goes still for a moment. I both curse and praise myself in equal measure for causing that delicious torment to cease. But then Cassandra surprises me by laughing softly. I lift my head and glare down at her, not that she can see my expression. "What's so funny?"

"In what world would I give a fuck about our so-called power imbalance? I'm quitting in six days. You don't hold any power over me, Apollo." She arches up a little, pressing her breasts more firmly against my chest. Her lips brush my jaw. "Unless you want to. Only in the bedroom, of course."

"*Cassandra.*" I don't know if I'm telling her to stop it or commanding her to continue.

Her laugh is low and downright sinful. But she doesn't start rocking against me again. Instead, she seems to consider something. I find myself holding my breath while I wait for her to speak. Finally, she says, "Is the only thing holding you back that you don't want to take advantage of me?"

I should lie. It's the safe thing to do. I'm afraid to hope I'm correctly anticipating where she's going with this. Even as I tell myself not to, I answer honestly. "Yes."

"You want me," she repeats.

"Cassandra, I've wanted you for years." I don't exactly mean to say it. I've tread so carefully around her for a very long time, always painfully aware of her position within Olympus and her desire to keep as far away from the Thirteen and their political games—from us—as possible.

But I *like* Cassandra. It crept up on me slowly, but that's how it works with me. Emotions and caring come first, and desire follows. How could I not care for her? She's smart and savvy and prickly, and she might not think I've noticed all the sacrifices she's made for her sister, but how could I spend any amount of time around her with falling, at least a little bit?

Shock stills her, but not for long. "Gods, Apollo." She exhales in a shaky laugh. "You're serious."

It's too late to walk it back now. Besides, I don't want to lie to her. "Yes."

"You know what?" She eases back to the couch, opening up the tiniest bit of distance between us. My arms shake with the desire to close it, but I force them still. Cassandra rewards me a heartbeat later when she snakes her hands between our bodies and presses her palm to my stomach. "I'm only in Olympus for another week."

"I'm aware," I grit out.

She strokes me with her fingertips almost idly, as if she doesn't care about the very real danger of me losing it from this touch alone. "What if we...made it real? The sex, I mean. Not the dating for obvious reasons."

Disappointment I have no right to feel takes root in my chest. Of course she wouldn't want to date me for real. Asking something like that is absurd; as she said, she's leaving in a week. Inviting her to be my girlfriend in any real way during that time is unfair.

If this were a month ago—a week ago—I wouldn't say yes. I would tell her that I want all of her or nothing at all. That I don't operate like that; I don't have casual sex with people I don't care about. Sex means something to me. *Cassandra* means something to me. She has for some time.

Am I willing to compound the pain of her leaving for the pleasure of having more of her now?

I know the answer even before I finish thinking the question. Of course I am. If the pain is inevitable, then at least I'll have these moments to look back on, no matter how bittersweet. I swallow hard. "I don't want to pressure you."

"You couldn't if you tried." She moves her hand to my stomach and dips her fingertips beneath the band of my lounge pants. "Can I touch you, Apollo?"

I can't help feeling like I'm damning us both. I should be the one to put on the brakes here, but I want her too desperately to be logical. When I speak, my voice goes low and commanding. "Do it."

CASSANDRA

I START TO SLIDE MY HAND INTO APOLLO'S PANTS, BUT HE says, "Wait." I freeze, suddenly sure that this strange moment has passed and he's going to call a stop to the whole thing. Instead, he leans down, careful to maintain the distance and not crush my arm, and speaks directly into my ear. "Give me a safe word."

I want to argue out of habit, but there's nothing wrong with having a word just between us that means everything stops. I've used one before and I'll no doubt use one again. More, I like that he's setting that boundary very clearly to keep us both safe. I lick my lips. "Python."

He huffs out a laugh. "Very well." His lips brush my ear, my jaw, the corner of my mouth. "Touch me, Cassandra."

This time, he doesn't stop me as I slide my hands into his lounge pants and wrap them around his cock. I felt him earlier, of course, but there's something about his length filling my hand that makes my breath catch in my chest. I stroke him lightly, teasingly. "All this for me?"

"Just for you." His arms shake a little where they're pressed against my sides. "I'm going to kiss you now. Give me your mouth." It's not a request, but he gives me a bare moment to protest. I don't. Of course I don't. I've been thinking about our last kiss since it happened, replaying it in my mind more times than I'll ever admit aloud.

Apollo kisses me as if divining every facet of my taste. Short, drugging kisses that distract me so much, I forget to keep stroking him. Instead, I chase him every time he retreats, little whimpering protests slipping past my lips, only for him to take my mouth again, longer this time.

He reaches between us to clasp my wrist in a firm grip and lift my hand to press to the couch beside my head. Apollo doesn't break our kiss as he does the same with my other hand. I might complain about not being able to touch him, but he chooses that moment to lower himself onto me, pressing me into the couch. My brain shorts out. It's been so long since I allowed anyone close enough to be like this. I'm starved for more...for *him*.

He breaks the kiss slowly but doesn't move away. "Tell me how to make you feel good, Cassandra." Again, there's no question in his voice, no invitation to argue. He's commanding in that quiet, stern way of his.

"This feels good."

"Mmm." He thrusts against me slowly and lets out a tortured groan. "Too good." He hooks the back of my neck and pulls me up as he shifts back. I barely have a chance to process the fact that we're changing positions when he sits me up on the couch and kneels between my thighs. I reach for him, but he shakes his head and grabs my wrists in that same firm grip. He presses them to the couch on either side of my hips. "If you touch me, this will end too quickly."

Surely he doesn't mean he wants me so much, he's about to come sooner than he'd like to? I thought he was joking when he said it before. I almost laugh, but my entire body shakes like a leaf over the fact that we're here and we're doing this. If he wants me even half as badly as I want him, then maybe it's best I keep my hands to myself.

For now.

Apollo lifts his hands slowly, making a satisfied noise when I keep mine where he placed them. "Good girl." I can barely process *that* when he clasps my knees and gently presses them wider. The bottoms of my pajamas gape. He stares at the juncture of my thighs with an intensity that makes me squirm.

He coasts his hands slowly up my thighs, guiding them wider yet, until his thumbs brush the lace hem of the pajamas. "I'm going to touch you now."

I exhale shakily. "You don't have to narrate every move before you do it."

He gives me a sharp look I can *feel* despite the shadows. "You squirm so beautifully every time I do. I like it." He edges his thumbs into the gap between the silky fabric and my overheated skin. "No panties?"

"No," I gasp. "They...don't work with the pajamas."

"Best money ever spent," he murmurs. He brushes my pussy and applies the barest pressure, spreading my folds. "You're wet. Just for me?"

It takes several beats for me to realize it's not a rhetorical question. I try to hold still, but I can't help squirming just like he predicted. "Apollo—"

"Tell me, Cassandra." He strokes up and down either side of my pussy as if he has all the time in the world. As if I'm not going to come apart the moment he touches my clit. "Tell me what gets you off. Tell me what you like and what you don't. Tell me everything."

I will cut out my own tongue before I admit that I'm afraid everything works for me because it's *him*. I might have propositioned him for a fling, but that doesn't mean I'm going to bare my heart. I swallow hard. "I like knowing I affect you like this. It makes me squirm."

"Mmm." He rewards me by dipping his thumbs a little deeper into my folds. "Is that all?"

Damn him. I'm panting as if I've run a great distance. I can't think past where he touches me, his soft but commanding questions. I shake my head. "No, that's not all." This time, I don't make him prod me further. "I liked it when you hauled me in here and pinned me to the couch, even if you were doing it to keep us hidden instead of as foreplay. I—I like this."

"I like this, too." He leans down and presses his face to the fabric right over my pussy. He inhales deeply and I nearly come on the spot. Apollo kisses one thigh and then the other. "When we go back to the bedroom, you're going to let me look at you."

"Apollo..."

"You're so beautiful, Cassandra." He kisses a little higher on my thighs. "You wouldn't deny me after I've spent *years* picturing you naked, would you?"

I whimper as he presses a kiss to my pussy through the silk of my shorts. "Oh gods. That feels good." Between his mouth and my desire, the fabric has gone slippery and wet. He rubs the flat of his tongue against my clit. I want to touch him, to dig my fingers into his hair, to hold him in place until the orgasm rushing to the fore overwhelms me completely.

Instead, I press my hands harder to the couch, obeying the unspoken demand he gave when he placed them there. I can't stop myself from speaking, though. "More."

He doesn't respond with words, but he doesn't need to. He just keeps up that devastating stroke. I slump back against the couch, writhing even as I try to hold still. "I..." I moan. "I can't be quiet. It feels too good. We're going to get caught."

Without missing a beat, he reaches up and covers my mouth with his big hand. It's not a harsh touch. Even when Apollo caught me earlier, his grip was firm but not painful. It's so perfectly *him* that I lose it.

My orgasm draws a cry from my lips, and he presses his hand a little harder against my mouth as he keeps working me with his tongue. Pleasure rises and rises, cresting again and again. Too much. It's too much. How am I supposed to move on after this, knowing how good it can be with him? This was a mistake, but I don't care that my parachute is malfunctioning.

I'm in a free fall and loving every second of it.

Apollo moves his hand, only to replace it with his mouth. I taste myself on his tongue, and it drives me wild. More. I need more. If I'm setting myself up for pain, I will draw out every bit of pleasure in the time I have. I dig my hands into his hair and pull him close as he kisses me. This time, there's no teasing. He *devours* me.

Footsteps sound in the hallway again.

I tense, expecting him to stop, but he tugs me down to the floor. I'm still processing the fact that I *like* how he moves me around when he arranges me in front of him, kneeling on the floor facing the couch with him at my back. He slides one hand down the front of my pajama bottoms to cup my pussy and whispers in my ear, "Be silent, Cassandra. Otherwise, we're going to get caught."

Holy shit, he's really not going to stop.

My safe word is on the tip of my tongue. Not because I want to stop, but because we *should* stop...

I clamp my lips shut and spread my thighs. A clear invitation that he doesn't hesitate to take me up on. He wedges two fingers into me, catching my gasp with his hand over my mouth. Apollo fucks me slowly with his fingers, as if we can't both hear the footsteps coming closer and closer to the door.

I knew I had a bit of an exhibitionist streak, but this feels different. Heightened. We shouldn't be doing this, but I don't care. I don't want to stop. I roll my hips, rubbing myself against his cock, and am rewarded by his sharp inhale.

The door opens.

I can't see more than the top few inches of it from my position. Not enough to see whoever is standing there. I freeze.

Apollo doesn't.

He keeps up that slow slide of his fingers in and out of me, though his body is tense behind mine. This is out of control. *We* are out of control. I'm...going to come. I shiver against him, not sure if I want him to stop or keep going. Not sure if whoever's standing in the doorway walks up to the couch and looks down to see Apollo fingering me.

Can they hear us?

He's not being rough, but surely they can hear the faint sound of finger fucking? I lean back harder against Apollo, and he responds by wedging a third finger into me.

Oh fuck, I really am going to come.

The door closes slowly. The click of it shutting might as well be a gun going off. I reach down and cover Apollo's hand with mine, urging him to keep going, to finish this. I can't stop shaking, can't stop the little whimpers that his palm barely muffles.

He kisses my neck and nibbles on my ear. "Come for me, Cassandra. I want to feel it."

My body responds to his command, clenching around his fingers as my orgasm crests hard enough to make my head spin. He eases me down slowly. "That's my girl."

I'm not his girl. Not in any permanent way. I just can't quite make my mouth work to tell him so.

"That was a good start, but I'm nowhere near done with you yet." He presses one last kiss to the spot behind my ear. "Do you want to walk or shall I carry you?"

Habit has me saying, "I can walk."

He doesn't immediately move back. "Cassandra." There's quiet censor in his voice. "Do you want me to carry you?"

Very much, but my heart is already doing something funny and I need to wrestle it back under control and quickly. Allowing Apollo to carry me—to *care for* me—is a terrible idea. No matter how much I crave it. "I want to walk." I attempt to say it firmly, but the words emerge as a question.

Apollo finally nods. "Very well." He stands, easily pulling me to my feet with him, though he keeps his hands cupped under my elbows as if he knows exactly how shaky my balance is right now.

"Thanks."

It should feel silly to lace my fingers with his and allow him to lead me out of the room. Who walks around holding hands when they don't need to? Even with Hermes, this wasn't how I operated. She was into casual intimacy, but she wasn't *sweet*. And this is sweet enough to make my teeth ache.

The feeling lasts until we turn the corner and come face-to-face with the Minotaur.

Apollo moves before I fully register the man's presence. He uses his hold on my hand to tuck me neatly behind him and angles his body to stay between me and the larger man. Where before his body language was loose and easy, he's now so rigid, I press my hand to the middle of his back in support.

"Minotaur."

The Minotaur looks down at him with no expression at all. Apollo is tall, but the other man towers over him. His scarred face looks even scarier in the low lighting of the hallway. "You shouldn't wander."

That surprises me enough that I burst out laughing. "I'm sorry, but why not? Surely you aren't going to try and convince us that there are ghosts haunting these halls."

He shifts that eerie attention to me. "Your safety isn't guaranteed, Cassandra."

I blink. "What do you mean it's not guaranteed?" Is he talking generally? Or about me specifically?

"Your safety isn't guaranteed," he repeats. "No cameras now. Who knows what could happen to you in the dark?" Without another word, he turns and stalks down the hall in the opposite direction.

Apollo doesn't move until the other man is out of sight. Only then does he reclaim my hand and lead me back to the bedroom. He closes the door behind us and checks the lock. "Well, we have no cameras to worry about, but apparently they're going to use that as an excuse to wash their hands of anything that happens here."

A frisson of fear dampens my lust. "They really are planning something for this party, aren't they?"

"I don't know." His jaw goes tight. "And that worries me."

My body is still flush with two orgasms. It makes thinking hard, but I try anyway. "Do we ignore the warning and keep looking tonight?"

"I don't think there's anything to find on the second floor. The sitting rooms are all exactly what was promised, and the rest of the rooms have occupants. We'll have a better chance with the third floor and finishing out the main one. We also can't exclude the possibility that he's using the garage or some building on the grounds for storage." He drags his hand through his hair, making it stand on end. "We've done enough for tonight. Might as well call it and get some sleep."

"Or we could do exactly as promised earlier and finish what we started in the sitting room."

"*Cassandra.*"

I ignore the warning in his tone. In fact, it sends a delicious little shiver down my spine. We can't take back what we did in that sitting room, but I wouldn't even if I could. He wants me. I can barely believe it after so long of desiring him.

I'm leaving in a week. I'll be damned if I miss a single opportunity to fulfill the promise held in the heated way he looked at me, touched me. If we're not continuing the search tonight, then there's no reason not to give in to the inferno of lust that makes it hard to breathe when I look at him.

Even so, it takes more courage than I want to admit to hold his gaze and pull my top over my head. I barely register his sharp inhale as I shimmy out of my shorts. The way this man looks at me should be illegal. His gaze sweeps over me as if he can't take in my features fast enough, as if this is a gift I'll snatch back at the last moment and he wants to imprint the image of me in his brain. It washes away the last of my hesitance. This is happening. We both want this to happen.

Instead of crawling on the bed, I sink to my knees, taking up the traditional submissive position.

"Cassandra," Apollo murmurs. "We don't have to."

Gods, but I could fall in love with this man. I ignore that thought and shift my stance a little, arching my back and spreading my thighs. "We covered this. I don't do anything I don't want to do, and right now I want to do you."

"You want to do me." His lips quirk in a skeptical smile. "Is that so?"

"Yes." I eye the hard length pressed against the front of his lounge pants. "I think you want to do me, too."

He steps closer and sifts his fingers through my hair, tightening them abruptly at the back of my head. I jolt, but it doesn't hurt. He's just holding me immobile. He considers me. "You have your safe word. I will respect it, regardless of what we're doing when you use it."

I lick my lips. "I know."

That reassures him. Of course it does. Any dominant worth their salt cares about their submissive's needs. Not that I'm Apollo's... I swallow hard. Best not to think about that. Best not to think about a number of things.

He tightens his grip on my hair, bending me backward a little. Apollo's gaze coasts over my mouth, down my throat, to my breasts and belly. I start to tense, expecting self-consciousness to rise, but how can I feel self-conscious when he's staring at me like a man who's finally allowed to touch the one thing he's craved for years?

"Apollo."

"Don't rush me."

I smile and relax back against his hold. Instantly, he shifts from fisting my hair to cupping the back of my head. I let him take my weight a little and lift my chin. "You have me. What are you going to do with me?"

APOLLO

A SMALL VOICE IN THE BACK OF MY HEAD WHISPERS THAT I'm doing something unforgivable, but those warnings are washed away on a tide of desire so intense, it's a wonder my knees don't buckle.

Having Cassandra naked and kneeling at my feet is an experience I never thought to have for myself. I'm tempted to simply look at her for hours, but our time is limited.

Duty comes with the dawn.

I intend to have *her* coming plenty more times before that happens. I tug on her hair, careful to keep it tension rather than pain. "You can keep trying to provoke me, but I've told you what I like, Cassandra. Be a good girl and give it to me."

She shivers. "I hate it when you do that. Enough talking. Let's get to the foreplay."

"Talking *is* the foreplay." I prefer my kink with a softer touch, but anyone who's experienced knows you can cut a person right down to their vulnerable center with words as easily as you can with a flogger. There's nothing more satisfying than seeing my submissive fight between their pride demanding they stay silent and their knowledge that giving in will ensure I do exactly what they're craving.

What we're both craving.

She glares up at me, but it's nowhere near her usual cutting expression, not when her eyes are heavy-lidded and she's allowing herself to rest against my hold. Trusting me not to let her fall backward.

People tend to fill silences. It's an impulse I've never shared. Silences can serve all sorts of purposes, and they are valuable for a number of reasons. Like this one. I can see the argument she's having with herself. She wants to submit, but she's not the type to hand that over freely without a fight.

I have no interest in fighting.

Cassandra will give me her submission, and she'll do it gladly. She just needs a few moments to realize it.

She doesn't make me wait long before huffing out a breath. "Okay, fine." She stares up at me, a challenge in those big dark eyes. "I would very much like to suck your cock until you blow in my mouth."

It takes everything I have to hold perfectly still and give her no reaction. "And then?"

"And then..." Her lips curve. "Then when you've had sufficient time to recover, I would very much like you to fuck me."

Gods, this woman.

I tug her hair a little. Even if I can contain the majority of my reaction, the fact remains that she's affecting me deeply. I like that even her submission has thorns. My voice is more than a little hoarse when I finally reply. "Earn it."

"Excuse me?"

I jerk my chin down. "Suck my cock well and I'll consider fucking you."

Her jaw drops. "I don't know if I want to tell you to fuck right off with that nonsense or come on the spot."

"You want to do both, but you won't tell me to fuck off, because you want me to make you come again." There's reward in the submission freely given. I could nudge her easily into doing what I want—what we both want—but this is significantly more satisfying. "Remember how well I rewarded you in the sitting room."

She licks her lips, her eyes going hazy. "You barely asked anything of me there."

"I wanted your words. Now I want your mouth." I pull her hair a little. A reminder of what came before. A promise of what comes next. "And *you* want to please me, Cassandra."

She reaches up and hooks her fingers in the waistband of my pants. "Don't let it go to your head."

"Always with the smart comments." I allow her to tug me closer and ease my pants down my hips enough to free my cock. "Clever, spiteful Cassandra. Let's put that mouth to good use."

She wraps a fist around the base of my cock and licks her lips. I can hardly believe this is real. I've fantasized about this woman more times than I care to admit, but having her bend down and drag her tongue along the underside of my cock when I can still taste her on my lips?

I have to tilt my head back and stare at the ceiling while I fight for control. Cassandra, the little troublemaker, chuckles and then closes her mouth around my cock. She sucks me deep, not giving me a moment to adjust. Fuck, I'm not going to last long.

Even knowing it will fray my control further, I look down. She's staring up at me, and the sight of her sucking my cock... I don't mean to tighten my grip on her hair, but she moans in response and sucks me harder, faster.

"Gods," I breathe. "You really want to earn that fucking."

She eases off me and brushes my cock against her lips. "Fuck me, Apollo." She flicks her tongue against me. "But not yet. I'm enjoying this."

"I know." I hardly sound like myself.

Cassandra looks up at me, something wicked in her eyes. "Would you like to know what else I want?"

"You're going to tell me." The order lashes out of me.

"Come in my mouth." She doesn't give me a chance to respond. She simply sucks me down as if her very salvation lies on the other end of my orgasm.

I hold out as long as I can, making her work for it. Cassandra seems to be good at everything she does, and this is no exception. But I don't want it to end too soon.

It's going to end too soon no matter what happens tonight.

I ignore that thought. I don't have forever, but I have right now. It will have to be enough. She sucks me deep, until her lips meet my base. Even if I was determined to hold out longer, this is too much pleasure to deny. It washes away the last of my control and I cup her face and begin thrusting into her mouth. Cassandra relaxes instantly, submitting as I fuck her mouth.

I'm not rough, but I don't give her time to decide she wants to retake control.

"Take it," I grind out. "You've more than earned it."

She hums a little in response, her expression entirely blissed out. The trust she puts in me, her willingness to submit, tips me over the edge. I curse and come, pumping into her as she swallows me down. On and on it goes.

When I finally ease out of her mouth, she licks her lips and smiles up at me. Without thinking, I go to my knees in front of her and kiss her. She meets me halfway. Of course she does. Cassandra is my equal in every way that matters. A perfect partner...at least for now.

"Apollo." She leans back and bites her bottom lip. "Fuck me tonight. Please. I need your cock so much. *Please* don't make me wait any longer."

It's a struggle to rise to my feet—to leave her—and move to my suitcase and pull out a string of condoms. I toss them onto the bed. Cassandra is still kneeling, still looking a bit dazed. I circle back to her and lean down to cup her elbows so I can lift her to her feet. I intend to kiss her lightly. But those intentions vanish the moment she wraps her arms around my neck.

Suddenly, I can't get close enough. Can't touch her enough. Can't taste her enough. I grab her hips and jerk her against me, closing the last miniscule distance between us. Her breasts and stomach press to my chest, shorting out what little thought I had to go slow.

My recovery time is usually longer, but none of the usual rules apply when it's this woman in my arms. My cock goes hard as I back her toward the bed. She tastes of me and need and I'm drunk off the feeling of her tongue against mine, of the knowledge that I can kiss Cassandra as much as I want to.

At least for the next few days.

I break the kiss enough to say, "Lie down."

"Apollo, if you don't fuck me right now, I might actually die." She hooks the back of my neck and gives me another searing kiss. "I'm wet and I'm aching and I need your cock. Now."

I push her down onto the bed and the sight of her stops me in my tracks. She's soft and beautiful and, gods, I want her to be mine in truth.

Stop it. It's too much to ask.

Cassandra makes a whimpering sound. "Stop staring at me and come here. Don't make me beg."

Another time, I would. Another time...

I grab a condom and make quick work of rolling it down my cock. Cassandra spreads her legs as I climb onto the bed, giving me a devastating glimpse of the perfection that is her pussy.

I need to be inside her, but I can't stop myself from dipping down and dragging my tongue up her center. She gives a cry and digs her hands into my hair. "*Get up here.*"

Despite the fact that I'm having a hard time breathing through the sheer wave of desire bearing me along, I manage a laugh. "Always so impatient."

"Don't act like you're not." She wraps a fist around my cock and squeezes a little. "That recovery time was, what? A minute?" She smiles against my lips. "You want me so badly, you're shaking."

I kiss down her jaw and nip her earlobe. "Are you expecting

me to deny it?" I hold my breath as she guides my cock to her entrance. "Now, be a good girl and take this cock."

She shivers. "I hate that I love that so much."

"No, you don't." I have every intention of going slow. But like with the kiss, my wires get crossed somewhere between the intention and the doing. I thrust into her, sheathing myself to the hilt.

Cassandra cries out. I tense, reason warring with desire, but she makes the decision for me. She drags her fingers down my back and sets her nails against my ass. "Deeper. Harder."

I thrust deeper. Harder. All thought leaves my head. There is nothing but her soft body wrapped around me. Nothing but how good her pussy feels. Nothing but her words, urging me on. There is no slowing down. No teasing this out until we're both shaking and desperate for each other. There is only a rough fucking that fills the room with the sounds of our bodies coming together again and again.

I try to slow down, to regain control, but Cassandra arches against me, crying out as her pussy clamps around my cock. Sheer pleasure wrenches a curse from my lips and then I'm pounding into her, chasing my own release. I come so hard, I get light-headed. "*Cassandra.*"

We end up in a tangle on our sides. Distantly, I'm aware that I need to get up and deal with the condom, but I don't quite have control over my lower body at this point.

She presses a light kiss to my nose. "Damn, Apollo. Just…damn."

I want nothing more than to lose myself in this woman, to forget the rest of the outside world and make her mine for as long as she's here. To do whatever it takes to convince her to stay. It's the wrong call, the selfish one. Just like letting this escalate was selfish in the extreme. Maybe I'll regret it later, but I can't seem to right now.

I catch her chin and kiss her deeply. "You've pleased me greatly."

She grins against my mouth. "Well, with you I actually want to earn the good-girl title. Who knew?"

Me. I knew. I ease off her and take a few minutes to dispose of the condom. Walking back into the room is surreal in the way that dreams are.

Cassandra has crawled beneath the covers and she smiles sleepily at me. "Give me a few minutes and I'll be up for round two."

What she needs now isn't another round of sex. It's a soft easing down into sleep. This week is far from over, and we'll need all our wits about us for whatever is coming. I don't know what Minos is planning yet, but one thing is certain: I'll do whatever it takes to ensure Cassandra remains safe and that her trust in me isn't betrayed.

No matter the cost.

APOLLO

WHEN CASSANDRA AND I AGREED TO SHARE THE BED, I expected sleepless nights. That was before I knew her taste, knew how devastating she looks on her knees, knew the exact sound she makes when she orgasms.

I tuck us both into bed. Cassandra makes as if to move away from me, but I catch her wrist. "Come here." When she hesitates, I continue. "You don't have to stay all night, but you will allow me to hold you for a little while."

She huffs out a faintly amused breath. "You really are a dom, aren't you? We didn't even do anything particularly kinky—"

"Cassandra, you know better." Kink isn't defined so acutely and she's damn well aware of that. She's protesting for the sake of protesting.

Another huff, but she slides back toward me. "Fine, fine. You're right. Get your cuddles and aftercare." For all her snark, she drapes herself over my chest and buries her face in my neck. I run my hand down her spine, urging her a little closer, and she makes a sound perilously close to a purr. Immediately, she tenses. "You heard nothing."

I smile into the darkness. There will be plenty of time to worry about complicated things tomorrow. In this moment, I am so content, I'm in danger of purring myself. "I like this, too."

"Are you sure you're tired? We could..." Her hand starts to wander south.

I catch it and press a kiss to her palm before placing it back across my chest. "No more tonight. Sleep."

"Bossy."

I almost retort that I *am* her boss, but I'm not keen to be reminded of that right now. Instead, I keep up my gentle touch against her back. I want to touch so much more of her, but she's put her trust in me and I won't give her reason to regret it. Right now, Cassandra needs sleep more than she needs to have sex again.

I'm proven correct when, a few minutes later, her breathing slows and deepens and the last bit of tension leaves her body. Only then do I allow myself the shaky exhale I've been holding for what feels like hours.

I want to keep her.

I already wanted to keep her even before I knew we matched up so well. Cassandra is one of the most confounding and frustrating people I've ever met, and she will lash out first to prevent the people around her from sensing anything resembling weakness. She's downright mean at times.

She's also incredibly thoughtful and kind when she thinks no one is looking. She's sacrificed more than anyone could have asked for her sister, has ridden the waves created by her parents' assassination attempt. Not to mention she's probably the smartest person in Olympus. She notices things I miss, can make logical jumps that seem to defy the minuscule facts in front of her; she's very rarely wrong.

And after tonight, I know that she has a playful side in the bedroom. That she's bold and fearless and comfortable in her desires. That her kinks seem to be a perfect fit for mine.

I close my eyes and will my body to calm. It's a losing battle. Just like having fallen for Cassandra is. She's leaving. She was always leaving. She hates it here in Olympus, and I'd never use her trust in me to convince her to stay. More, being with me means inserting herself into the very things about this city that she hates the most. She'll be targeted. Not even I can protect her from that; I can guard her body, but what about the assaults on her reputation?

On her sister's reputation?

What would keep the two of them out of the political games that are this city's beating heart? Every day with me would be a reminder of the price her parents paid for their ambition. Every day would be a chance for my enemies to use Cassandra and her sister against me—to bruise them just to see me suffer.

I can't ask that of her. I can't be that selfish.

I refuse to be.

———————

I wake up achingly hard. We've shifted during the night, though not much. I'm on my side with Cassandra tucked back against me, her perfect ass pressed against my cock. She shifts again, and I wake fully. "You're doing that on purpose."

"Who, me?"

It would be so easy to let this spiral out of control. In fact...I check the clock and bite down an unkind statement when I see what time it is. "We can't."

"We can't what?" Cassandra lightly drags her nails down my arms and burrows back tighter against my body. "This feels nice."

Nice is the understatement of the century. But if we get going, I highly suspect we will miss our chance at breakfast and all the events Minos no doubt has planned today. We can't afford to allow that to happen, no matter how great the temptation or inevitable pleasure. "Cassandra."

She sighs dramatically. "You've being very responsible right now and I don't like it."

"I like *this*." I give her a squeeze and kiss her bare shoulder. "Be very good today and I'll reward you tonight." The Minotaur's appearance last night all but ensured midnight wanderings are off the table. We needed the cameras to go, but without any recordings to hold people accountable, there's no guarantee that someone wandering the halls at night won't suffer an unfortunate "accident." It's not worth the risk.

We'll have to find a different way. I try very hard not to be pleased with the fact that Cassandra and I will be essentially trapped in our room from nightcap to breakfast.

"I'm never good. You should reward me anyway." She gives one last wiggle against me and then disentangles herself from my arms. I almost tug her back, but I'm the one who put a stop to things and I can't very well walk back on it now.

Except, as she climbs out of bed and pads to the bathroom door, my mouth actually waters. Gods, this woman. I trace every curve, drinking in the sight of her. She's perfect. Utterly perfect. I want to map her skin with my hands and mouth, to learn exactly what she likes and what drives her wild. Last night was only the beginning.

As I watch, her skin blushes a charming pink. "You're staring."

"I said I wanted to look my fill." Gods help me, I actually lick my lips. "This is a good start."

Cassandra blushes harder. "Order me to go take a shower and get ready, or I'm going to come back to bed and—"

"Go take a shower and get ready." I inject a bit of snap into my voice and am rewarded when she blushes even more. "No playing with that greedy little clit, either. While we're here, your orgasms are mine and mine alone."

Her mouth works as if she wants to argue, but she gives a jerky nod instead. "Better keep me satisfied, then."

"Oh, Cassandra." I rake my gaze over her. "I plan on it."

She hesitates one moment more and then turns, giving me another spectacular view of her ass, and goes into the bathroom. I slump down onto the bed and curse myself for my timing. My responsibility to Olympus *has* to outweigh any personal pleasure or happiness I might try to seek. Especially considering that it will be short-lived with this woman.

I cannot allow myself to be derailed.

I need to get up and moving, but as the shower turns on, I can't stop myself from stroking my cock. I don't tease the way Cassandra did last night. No, I jack myself almost harshly, a slide-show of *her* flashing behind my eyes.

The way it felt to be cradled between her thighs, sinking into her wet heat.

Her sweet little moans that she didn't try to hide.

Her taste.

I yank my hand away from my cock before I can come. I'm not normally a masochist, but if I'm denying her orgasms, it's incredibly unfair to not hold myself to the same rule.

My phone rings and the moment I see the name flashing across my screen, the desire leaves my body. I still take a few seconds to compose myself before answering. "Apollo here."

"Can you talk freely?"

I eye the bathroom door. The shower is still running. Judging from yesterday's timetable, it will be a good hour before Cassandra emerges. "Yes."

"Update me." It's not surprising that Zeus wants to be kept in the loop, but he could have given me at least twenty-four hours before he started calling.

"I haven't had much time to gather information."

"Indulge me." His tone brooks no argument.

I bite down a sigh. "All I have are theories and the guest list. Minos and his people are here, of course. Six members of the Thirteen, including myself, Hephaestus, Artemis, Hermes, Dionysus, and Aphrodite. Then there's Pan, Adonis, Charon, Eurydice, and Atalanta. Information seems conflicting on if Hermes brought a plus-one or not, but if she did, I haven't seen them."

"Godsdamn it, Eris." He speaks so softly, I choose not to respond. That statement wasn't meant for me, after all, but for Zeus's sister—formerly Eris, before she took the title of Aphrodite. Zeus doesn't let Aphrodite's presence here distract him for long. "And your theories?"

"Cassandra thinks it might be a matchmaking attempt. Everyone invited is publicly single—or was until recently." I don't know what's going on with Aphrodite and Adonis. They seem to be in one of those on-again, off-again relationships, but they're never messy in public. Sometimes they're pictured together for weeks or months at a time and then they seem to be moving in different circles, only to gravitate back toward each other. Even before she took the title of Aphrodite, though, she had to know her brother would never agree to her marrying Adonis. He comes from a legacy family, but they're far enough down the food chain that they won't see a new member of the Thirteen in this generation at least, if ever again.

"I didn't ask what Cassandra thinks. I ask what you think."

I have to fight not to bristle at how dismissive of her theories he is. I might think there's another component to this party, but that doesn't mean Cassandra is wrong. Minos seems far too smart to only have one plan. He arrived in Olympus supposedly so his sons could compete to become Ares but didn't miss a beat when they failed to do so, pivoting to leverage his information about a supposed enemy to ensure his place in the city.

Something he didn't speak a word of until they lost.

"I suspect that the matchmaking might be a feint, the same way the Ares tournament was a feint." I hesitate, but ultimately there's no reason to keep it secret. "There's one other thing." I quickly recap my conversation with Minos in his office. "There's something else going on here. He's strangely focused on Cassandra and all but threatened her explicitly. And again last night, the Minotaur did the same. I don't see how that fits in with the information we already know."

"Find out what it is."

I clench my jaw for three beats in an attempt to stuff my frustration down deep. It's not Zeus's fault. He's difficult and abrupt to the point of rudeness, but he's doing the best he can with the given situation. Knowing that doesn't make dealing with him any easier, though. "That is what I'm here to do."

"I'm aware." He curses. "You know how important this is. We can't afford to misstep."

"I will call with any updates."

"Apollo..." He hesitates. "Be careful."

"I always am." I hang up and drag my hand over my face. As frustrating as I often find my conversations with Zeus, this one was timely to remind me of what I'm really here for.

Unfortunately, continuing my seduction of Cassandra will have to wait.

The shower is still going, so I pull on some clothes and head downstairs in search of breakfast. Eating in our room will give us a chance to come up with a game plan for the day beyond *make Cassandra come as many times as possible*.

I bet there is another entrance to Minos's office. This place used to belong to Hermes, after all. But that also means it will be cleverly hidden, and with the Minotaur roaming the halls, we're likely to get caught searching. No, our best bet is going through the door itself, though we don't have a good excuse to be in there, borderline exhibitionism or no.

We'll have to try for the office today during one of the downtimes.

There are few people about. I catch sight of Aphrodite and

Adonis through the window that looks out over the grounds. They walk down the path in the direction of the maze with their arms linked. She's laughing at something he said. They make quite the striking couple, but they aren't my problem right now.

As promised, there's a breakfast spread waiting in the same room we dined in last night. I consider my options and then grab two plates. Cassandra doesn't seem to eat heavy breakfasts, but I'm not entirely certain what she likes. I put a little bit of everything on her plate and then get to work on my own.

I'm just finishing up when Hephaestus and Artemis stride into the room. They give me nearly identical long looks and then veer around to the other side of the table, pointedly continuing their conversation and ignoring me.

I bite back a sigh. It's naive in the extreme to want all members of the Thirteen to get along and work toward a common goal. I think the titles themselves were designed to ensure that never happened—or at least that's what it feels like most days. Too many of them have specialties that overlap, which incites rivalries even in the most level-headed of people. Athena and Ares with their military forces. Me and Hermes with information. Demeter and Poseidon with their trade agreements and resource gathering.

Even without that factor in play, the fractures run deep in our current Thirteen. How can they not when most of us are members of legacy families who have long Olympian histories filled with alliances, feuds, and the kind of political backbiting that ensures there is no trust to be found?

"Oh, Apollo." Artemis turns to me with false cheer. "I forgot to congratulate you on that girlfriend of yours." She laughs, the sound edged. "Though, honestly, if I knew you were so hard up as to date the *help*, I would have set you up with one of my sisters."

Hephaestus doesn't give me a chance to respond. His laughter joins his cousin's. "It wouldn't be more than slightly scandalous if she was just an employee, but a member of the Gataki family?" He shakes his head. "You must really like living on the edge. You're liable to wake up with a knife between your ribs."

I grip the plates so tightly, I have the distant thought that I might shatter them. The desire to defend Cassandra wars with the need to continue my easygoing public persona. "Cassandra is not the same as her parents," I finally say.

"I guess we'll see, won't we?"

I refuse to continue this line of conversation. "Where's Atalanta this morning?"

They exchange a look I can't quite decipher. I frown, but Artemis speaks before I can question further. She waves an idle hand through the air. "Oh, I sent her on a task last night. She must be sleeping late, as I haven't seen her since."

"You sent her on a task…in the middle of the night…at a house party hosted by someone who's essentially an enemy to Olympus." The Minotaur's rough voice echoes through my mind. *Your safety isn't guaranteed.* Did he happen upon Atalanta in the halls?

I don't like to think about that. Like everyone else in Olympus, I watched their confrontation at the end of the second trial in the Ares competition. She fought hard and lost, and for a moment, I'd been certain he would kill her right then and there. "The Minotaur—"

"Thank you for your concern about one of *my* people, but I

can assure you, it's not needed." Artemis smirks and strides out of the room before I can come up with a suitable response.

Hephaestus, of course, lingers. He eyes the two plates in my hands. "You're playing this wrong. Throw your lot in with the loser and you'll go down with them."

I hold his gaze. "Is Atalanta okay, Hephaestus? Why isn't Artemis worried that she hasn't reported back?"

"She's not one of mine. It's not my business." He shrugs. "She knows the cost of loyalty and she's willing to pay it if it's asked of her. A lesson you should take to heart. Minos means fresh blood. A chance to disrupt some of the old way of doing things."

I hold his gaze. "Your family comes from the old way of doing things. Mine does, too."

"Yeah." He shrugs. "But we're the Thirteen. Nothing can touch us now."

"Hephaestus—"

"You may have this Zeus's ear, but we all know how quickly the winds can change. Who knows what kinds of opportunities and connections Minos can bring us from outside the city? If you miss out because you're too busy playing with a failed assassin's daughter, then I don't know what to say to you. Good luck, I guess." He follows his cousin out of the room.

Nothing can touch us now.

The words have the ring of a false prophecy. I truly hope I'm wrong about that.

CASSANDRA

I EXPECT THINGS TO BE AWKWARD. I SHOULD REALLY KNOW better by now. Apollo and I share a nice breakfast, and then he gets ready in a fraction of the time it took me. I chose my clothing with care today: one of the many deceptively simple sundresses from Juliette and a pair of flats. If the maze was any indication of how the games will play out during this week, I'm going to save heels for evening. I have no problem wearing them all day in the office, but I don't spend most of the day on my feet at work.

Apollo eyes my shoe choice but wisely says nothing. He just opens the door for me and motions for me to precede him through. "It will be lunch before too long. Let's see who else is about. Maybe Atalanta is back by now."

"I hope so." I don't like the fact that Artemis said she hadn't heard from her, though with the contentious relationship Artemis and Apollo have, it's entirely possible that she was just fucking with him. We won't know until we can confirm Atalanta is missing.

If she is... That might be two plus-ones. Or it's two if Hermes's actually showed up. We've never had confirmation of that, so we need to try to get it today.

If Minos is targeting the Thirteen's companions... *Why?*

It doesn't make any sense.

I slide my hand into the crook of Apollo's arm and walk with him down the hall to the stairs. We take a circular route to the dining room, exploring a part of the downstairs we didn't get to yesterday.

The house is utterly charming. Even with the changes Minos had made, it still feels very *Hermes*. Recognizing that is bittersweet in the extreme. She never brought me here. She never even offered. I don't blame her for it. We had very clear parameters on our relationship when we started dating. It was never going to be forever; it was never even going to be public. Very few people in Olympus even know it happened, which is how we both prefer it. Hermes might be one of the most ostentatious of the Thirteen, but she's fiercely private. Most people just never notice that because they're so busy being thrown off-center by her showing up where they least expect her.

We clock a massive library, three more sitting rooms that may or may not have been kinky playrooms previously, and a truly lovely sunroom that seems to beg people to spend lazy afternoons there.

Hermes is playing court in the living area just off the dining room when we finally make our way there. She lounges in a chair, one leg thrown over the arm and her lean body slouched. Today she's restrained herself a bit, wearing jeans and a graphic T-shirt that's large enough I suspect it belongs to Dionysus, and she has her curly hair styled in two buns on top of her head. Compared to everyone else in the room in their garden-party best, she stands out.

But then, Hermes always stands out.

She leaps out of the chair when she sees us, nearly toppling Dionysus off the artsy stool he's sitting on. He looks a little green, obviously nursing a hangover, and blinks blearily at her. "You're awfully spry right now."

"I have to use the little girls' room." She sweeps through the room, somehow managing to insert herself between me and Apollo on her way to the door. Even expecting it, I'm still mildly surprised to find myself holding *her* arm instead of *his*. She beams at Apollo. "I hope you don't mind if I steal your girl. House rules. Can't pee alone."

I don't even know what Apollo intends to say—he looks like he's about to argue—because she doesn't stop moving, towing me out of the room with her. "Hermes—"

"Hush." She doesn't quite drop her cheery public persona, but a thread I'm deeply familiar with creeps into her voice. She practically drags me past the bathroom and through a door into yet another sitting room. This one is understated, with a very neutral color scheme and dainty furniture that looks like it might break under a normal human's weight.

I look around. "Was this always a sitting room or is this another converted kinky one?"

"A lady never tells." She shakes her head. When she turns to look at me, she's uncharacteristically serious. "At least Apollo did something right and took care of the cameras so we can talk frankly." She grips my shoulders. "You have to leave, Cass."

"What?"

She holds my gaze. "You need to leave."

"I heard you the first time. I wasn't asking you to repeat yourself; I wanted clarification." I let her take my arm and guide me deeper into the room. I can't afford to be honest right now, not even with her. "My boyfriend isn't going to like you dragging me off like this."

"Your boyfriend. Right." Hermes rolls her eyes. "We both know you would never publicly consort with one of the Thirteen, even if Apollo is a sweet baby angel by comparison with the rest of us."

I should have suspected this would happen. The rest of Olympus might be willing to believe the worst of me, but Hermes knows me too well. I lift my chin. "I like him very much."

"Oh, *that* I don't doubt." She smiles a little, eyes going soft. "I see how you look at him. It's the same way you used to look at me."

Being called out like this makes me want to walk out of the room, keep walking, and never come back. I should leave this alone. I know all too well how circular conversations can get with Hermes, especially if she's got her mind set on something. I'm nearly as stubborn as she is, though. "If you see how I look at him, why is it so hard to believe we're dating? Jealousy doesn't look good on you."

"See last point: I know you." She waves that away. "And I'm not jealous, even though you're a catch and a half. You were never meant for me. That's not what this is about. You need to leave, Cass. It's not safe here."

"It's not safe anywhere in Olympus." That's why I *have* to be here. I need to get Alexandra out. I don't tell Hermes that. She already knows my goal to put this damned city in my rearview. She also likely has some idea of Zeus and Apollo's plan to suss out what Minos is up to.

In fact, this whole interaction is off. The Hermes I know never would have pulled me aside like this. I narrow my eyes. "What's going on? You've never warned me off anything before."

"You wouldn't listen to me if I'd tried to before, and you know it." She tries to maintain her cheery persona but abandons it halfway through. Hermes glances away and then back to me. The friendship that developed in the wake of our ill-fated relationship can be spiky at times and occasionally uncomfortable, but it doesn't feel like that's the problem right now. This isn't Hermes randomly acquiring a jealous streak. She's actually worried.

"Hermes—"

"If you trusted me at all before, I need you to trust me now. Get out of here."

I frown harder. "If it's so dangerous, why are *you* staying? Why is Dionysus? In fact, where is your plus-one?" Hermes can be cruel and ruthless, but she would never put the few people she actually cares about at risk.

Hence this conversation.

"Oh, Tyche went home sick barely after arriving. Food poisoning, you know." She says it like she doesn't care if I believe it or not. "And Dionysus can take care of himself."

And I can't.

I try to ignore the sting and focus on gathering what

information I can get. "Artemis said Atalanta disappeared, too. Do you have confirmation that Tyche made it back to the city?"

"I would like confirmation that *you* are heading back to the city."

A dodge, and not even a good one. I'm not leaving, but if Hermes is willing to share what she knows, that will put us ahead of whatever game Minos is playing. "If you're not willing to be honest with me, you can't expect me to leave."

She curses. "You're so damned *stubborn*."

"It takes one to know one." I hold her gaze. "If you know something about Minos's plans for Olympus, you should share with the group."

"Since when do you care about Olympus politics?" She rolls her eyes. "Really, Zeus could have picked half a dozen better people for this, but he let Apollo run around thinking with his cock and now they've endangered you. It shouldn't matter *why* you need to leave. If you trust me at all—if you ever trusted me—then go home, Cass."

I step back and tuck my hair behind my ears. If I were here for any other reason, Hermes asking me to leave would be reason enough to do exactly that. Frustration blooms inside me. "Why is Minos targeting the plus-ones?" It's a stab in the dark, but I fire it off without hesitation.

"Why won't you leave?" She shakes her head slowly. "Is it the money? Go home today and I'll pay whatever you lost in that devil's bargain with our fearless leader."

Gods, she really wants me out of this house. For a moment, I'm tempted to take her up on her offer. She's right that I hate being here, playing these games with people I mostly despise. But Apollo…

Apollo.

I try to focus, to parse out what she has and hasn't said. If there's danger, it's not only to me and the other plus-ones, or she wouldn't have said Dionysus could take care of himself. "Hermes." I start to reach for her but let my hand drop without making contact. "Is someone going to get hurt here? Has someone *already* been hurt?"

"A lady never tells." The words are right, rife with her usual trickster persona. Her tone is off, though, almost bittersweet. "With great power comes great risk. Everyone at this party knows that. Except you, apparently."

"That's not how that saying goes," I say faintly, my mind racing. "Minos wouldn't dare strike anyone here, not with the kind of connections they all have. Zeus would tear him into tiny pieces." Really, I'm the only one without a dozen strings tying me to powerful people in this city. Even Pan has strong alliances.

For a breath, it seems like she might give me some actually useful information, but Hermes shakes her head instead. "You know I care about you, Cassandra."

Damn it. This is going the way of so many of our conversations, though usually the stakes are so much lower. Gossiping and drinking and sneaking around to little hole-in-the-wall restaurants don't usually come with this kind of warning. But all that aside, I never doubted for a moment that she genuinely cares about me as much as I care about her. "I know."

She sighs. "This is not going at all how I wanted this conversation to go."

I give a choked little laugh. "Yeah, well, our conversations never quite go how I picture them either." It's a testament to our history and our friendship that she even tried to warn me. I try for a smile. "I appreciate the concern, but I have things under control." I hope.

For a second, it looks like she'll continue arguing. But she finally gives another of those world-weary sighs, her customary joy nowhere in evidence. "Just promise me you'll be careful."

It's an easy promise to make for all my bargain with Zeus. I have no intention of putting myself in danger. Money and a way out of Olympus are great in theory, but I can't get my sister to safety if I'm dead. I'm certainly not going to sacrifice my life for this city. The very thought is absurd. Hermes would know that if she were thinking clearly. The fact that she's apparently not worries me.

I nod slowly. "I promise that I won't put myself in any unnecessary danger." The promise is small and leaves much to be desired. If she's right, I'm already in danger simply by being here.

She shakes her head one last time. "If you get killed because of Apollo and Zeus's scheme, I'll murder them both myself." Again, her customary cheeriness is nowhere in evidence. This is the Hermes that I lost my heart to all those years ago. I loved her mischievousness and her ability to talk her way both into and out of trouble, but like calls to like.

Her inner core is just as dark and haunted as mine.

We've always had different aims, though. It's the reason why we were never going to work. I always wanted to leave Olympus behind, and Hermes wants... Well, she's never trusted me enough to tell me exactly what she wants.

Her motives might be akin to Apollo's aim to bring about what's best for Olympus, but I'm not so sure. Hermes has always played on a different level from anyone else in the city. Not one of the Thirteen is aware of how deep she goes. They all see the flighty, mischievous thief, the one who shows up where she's not invited and steals things for shits and giggles. They don't see this look in her eye that I see now.

This Hermes will kill to accomplish her goals.

I'm nearly certain she has, although we never spoke of it.

My glasses are not rose-tinted enough to think that she'll kill for me, ex or no, current friend or no. Or at least I didn't think so. Maybe I should let it go, but if there's even the tiniest chance she'll drop some useful information, I have to try. "Why are you here, Hermes? If it's so dangerous, and there's things going on that I'm not privy to. If people might get hurt. Why are you here at this party?" I cross my arms over my chest. "I know it's not because you plan to let Minos set you up with one of his children." Another stab in the dark. It's all I have at this point.

She bursts out laughing, that joyful tinge returning to her tone. "Marry one of his children?" She laughs again. "Have you seen them? Ariadne isn't so bad, but the sons? Absolutely not. I'd break those poor boys."

She's probably right about Icarus, but the others? Both Theseus and the Minotaur top her by a foot and a half and are more than willing to do violence in pursuit of their goals. Though I'm not entirely certain that she could take them. At least not in a fair fight. I'm not sure Hermes has been in a fair fight even once in her life. So actually, if I were those men, I'd be watching my back when she's around.

Still... "That wasn't an answer."

Her smile goes a little sad. "You know better than most that no matter what questions you ask, there are answers I can't give you."

I should have known better than to waste my breath asking. She keeps her secrets close. Even from those she cares about the most. I had to try, though.. "I've always tried to respect your privacy. Now I need you to respect mine."

Another of those joyful laughs. "Oh, Cass, you know I don't respect anyone's privacy." Her smile falls away. "But I'll try. Just this once."

Apollo might technically be the Keeper of Lore, but Hermes is the keeper of more secrets than I could begin to guess. And yet our history has words springing to my lips that I know better than to speak. She might already know that I've made a deal, but I can't help telling her why. "I'm getting out. Me and Alexandra. We're both leaving, for real this time, to start a new life somewhere no one knows our history."

Her smile falls away entirely. "I'm happy for you, Cassandra. Truly. I am." She reaches out and takes my hand. "I'm not going to pretend I won't miss you, though."

No matter my feelings on the greater city, no matter my feelings on the Thirteen as a whole, my relationship with Hermes has been a bright spot. Never a permanent fixture, but bright nonetheless. "I'll miss you, too."

There's nothing else to say after that.

We make our way back to the room where everyone has gathered. Apollo sends me a concerned look, a hint of suspicion in his dark gaze. Suspicion…or jealousy? I almost miss a step. Surely, he's not jealous of *Hermes*? It doesn't matter what our history is. There's a reason it's history. Not to mention that what I have with Apollo right now, real sex or no, is temporary. Our relationship is pretend. Fake.

I hate that I have to keep reminding myself of that, but it's necessary to avoid falling into him in a way I'll never recover from. As I just told Hermes thirty seconds ago, I'm leaving Olympus in less than a week. No one can change my mind about that.

If it was just me…

But it's not just me, is it? It's me and Alexandra. And if our parents were too selfish to consider their daughters when they attempted to assassinate Athena, I am not going to make the same mistake. I refuse to put my sister in harm's way and compromise her future.

Certainly not for something as mundane as good sex.

Even as I cross to Apollo and slip my hand into a crook of his arm, I feel like a liar. It's not just sex with Apollo. If it were, things would be so much easier. If we didn't have five years of working together, five years of knowing what a kind and thoughtful man he is, five years of having him take care of me as much as I would allow.

Now that I know that he would take care of me both in the bedroom and out… I shake my head. *It doesn't matter.* I will not let it matter. I will not be diverted from my path.

No matter how much it hurts in the end.

APOLLO

SOMETHING'S WRONG WITH CASSANDRA. I DON'T KNOW IF her conversation with Hermes made her doubt her presence here, or if the other woman tried to rekindle an old flame, or if the problem is something else altogether.

With Hermes, I can never be sure.

I have no right to be jealous. I know that. I'm very painfully aware of that. No matter what physical agreement we've come to, Cassandra's not mine. Even if she was, her history is her own. I have no right to this horrible roiling feel in my gut whenever I look at her and Hermes together. I've never been one for jealousy or worrying about my partners' exes. They choose to be with me, and that's enough. I have my own history, after all.

It feels different with Cassandra. The feelings are real. The attraction is more than real. But our relationship is as substantial as morning mist, and that has me off-balance.

I can't even ask her what they spoke about because we're standing in a room surrounded by Minos's guests. We must keep up the facade. It would be significantly easier if I could concentrate.

Despite myself, I can't help looking down at her, noting the furrow between her brows and the tension now high in her shoulders. She looks, as ever, absolutely gorgeous. Her dress today is black with a faintly chaotic print on it that my eye cannot quite make sense of. It gives a faint hint of cleavage that makes my mouth water and shows off her generous figure to perfection. The garment reminds me of the woman herself.

She holds as many secrets as Hermes does.

I realized early on in her employment that there were great swathes of this woman cut off from me. I tried very hard not to pry into her life and to respect her privacy, but I play my role within Olympus's power structure for a reason. The temptation to delve deep and find out everything there was to know about Cassandra was almost too much to bear. Instead, I settled for a cursory background check and comforted myself with the belief that I knew everything that could make her a potential threat or asset. I might not know her secret thoughts or innermost workings, but at least I knew enough.

"Everything okay?" I ask softly. A perfectly normal question from a perfectly normal boyfriend who isn't having a minor meltdown from finding out his fake girlfriend's ex—the one person who's constantly bested him at every turn—is near.

She shoots me a vaguely worried look and gives a half smile. "Of course, everything's perfect."

Lie.

She's not even trying to cover up the lie, which is a strange sort of compliment. Cassandra knows I'll see through her false reassurance. She expects it. I don't know if that comforts me or makes this worse. I don't have a chance to figure it out because Minos chooses that moment to enter the room, his boisterous energy flowing out ahead of him.

"Good afternoon," he booms. "I trust you had a good night's sleep." His gaze skitters over me and Cassandra, lingering a beat too long.

I don't like it, especially on the heels of his vague threat and the more explicit one the Minotaur leveled last night.

Minos spreads his arms and gives a winning smile to all his guests. He's just as much a showman as the last Zeus, and even the jaded people in this room can't help responding to him. I see it in the way Aphrodite sets down her cup and Dionysus manages to open his eyes to actually focus on our host.

"I have another game for us. I hope you'll forgive me my excitement at having such a captive audience." He laughs. "Call me a bit sentimental and indulge an old man."

Everyone laughs politely along with him, some more genuinely than others. Cassandra doesn't bother and neither do I. The games feel like Minos attempting to pull us into his orbit. Every time we agree to play along, it allows him more control over us. It allows him to slip that much deeper beneath our skin.

He circles the room and stops before the fireplace. "This afternoon..." He pauses, and every single person in the room leans forward a little in anticipation. "This afternoon, we're going to play hide-and-seek."

A chorus of faint, amused groans goes up among those

gathered. He wants us to play a child's game. When added to the maze last night, it truly does seem that Minos is seeking to recreate some strange sort of historical house party.

As a city, Olympus has a tendency to stand a bit out of time. We are more than capable of keeping up with the technology of the greater world, and Poseidon and his predecessors have done their job well when it comes to providing any resource we could possibly need. But our rules and laws are our own, and so are our customs.

Minos doesn't have that excuse, and even in this city, this kind of event is out of place. I shake my head. The temptation to write Minos off as exactly what he appears to be an indulgent old man with more money than sense—is strong, even though I know better.

He's good.

Aphrodite toys with a strand of dark hair. "What if we decide to pass on these little adventures you've planned? This game sounds tedious."

It's only because I'm watching Minos so closely that I notice how his jaw goes tight for a heartbeat before he turns in her direction. "I'm afraid participation is mandatory for all guests. Should you want to rescind your acceptance to the party, I'm more than happy to call a car for you."

Her brows wing up. "I see." She glances at Adonis, something passing between them too quickly to identify. "The game sounds lovely, Minos. When do we start?"

"Right about now." He motions to the door. "My foster son Theseus will do the finding this time. Be gentle with the boy. You know his knee is not what it used to be. Whoever evades him longest is the winner."

"And what do we win?" Hermes says, a deep amusement in her tone. "Another date with your child of choice?"

Minos's gaze doesn't waver, but a sharp look flares in his dark eyes. "Of course. Would you expect anything else?"

"Absolutely not," she says, merriment still painted across her pretty face. "You have a one-track mind, Minos. I can appreciate that."

His attention skates back to us, once again lingering on me and Cassandra. "The grounds and house are all fair game. We wouldn't want to make it too easy on dear Theseus, would we?" He strokes his beard. "Though he's a fine hunter. I do believe he'll give you a good run."

This is a game within a game, an invitation of sorts, a first parry. He knows what I'm here for. He's practically inviting me to search his house and see if I can manage to suss out what he's up to without getting caught.

"One more thing." He slides his hands into his pockets. "Do be careful. There are plenty of ways for a person to get hurt if they're wandering where they shouldn't be." His lips quirk. "We've already lost two of our house guests. I'd hate to lose more."

A warning...or a dare?

And what does he mean by *lost*?

There's only one way to find out. We only have so many days here, and I'm not likely to get another invitation to search openly. I squeeze Cassandra's hand. "Let's go, love."

Her smile wavers a little around the edges. "Right behind you."

"You'll have fifteen minutes to find your hiding space." Minos lifts his hand. "Then Theseus comes hunting."

People file out the door with remarkable speed, scattering the moment they hit the hallway. Hermes and Dionysus head to the back door, their heads close together and their laughter floating behind them. After a long speaking glance, Hephaestus and Artemis head in the same direction, breaking apart once they pass through the door and moving in opposite directions. Aphrodite and Adonis duck into a dining room, no doubt planning to exit on the other side and through the kitchen.

And the rest? Well, they follow the same route that Cassandra and I do, taking the hallway toward the front of the house. We reach the front entranceway and watch Pan duck out the front door. Eurydice and Charon start up the stairs. They aren't holding hands, but the way he moves at her back, one hand spread as if to catch her fall, further confirms there's more to their relationship than strictly friendship.

They aren't my business at the moment, though.

Most people have paired up, though the game doesn't specify the need for that. I pause, filing through the options of the best places to use this opportunity to search. Not Minos's office; it's far too obvious and it's the first place Theseus will look. It's tempting to split up with Cassandra to cover more ground, but I don't like the idea of letting her out of my sight. Not when we've *lost* two other people at this party. "Stay close to me."

"I'm not going to argue that."

I glance down at Cassandra. The faint line is back between her brows. She looks more worried than she has since we arrived.

What did Hermes say to her to put that look on her face? "Time to head to the third floor?"

"Yes, this will be our best chance to check out the family rooms."

"Right." I'm starting to wonder if there's anything here to find at all.

Or if we're actually playing right into Minos's hands.

APOLLO

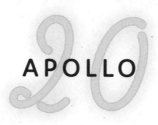

THE HALLWAY OF THE SECOND FLOOR IS EMPTY. THERE'S NO telling if Eurydice and Charon have split up or ducked into one of the sitting rooms to hide; there are enough of them that they might be a good option if the goal was truly to hide from Theseus. Better for us if that's their plan. I have no desire to have to explain why we're intentionally aiming for our host's private bedroom when there are plenty of good alternatives.

Cassandra waits till we turn the corner to pull her hand out of mine. "Let's hurry. Minos seems the type to cheat, so it's entirely possible that Theseus will head straight for us."

I don't argue, but I don't like the way she won't quite look at me. "What did Hermes say?"

"We'll talk about it later." She must catch the way I almost miss a step, because she exhales in a huff. "It's not new information, if that's what you're worried about. It's just...odd. This whole thing is *odd*."

There's no arguing that. It's not just the games or the

underlying threat that seems to become more blatant as time passes. Participate or be banished from the house. Watch out for danger on the grounds. Don't wander at night or something unfortunate might happen.

But to what end?

I slow, but Cassandra picks up the pace, tugging me along behind her. "If we're lucky, Theseus isn't cheating and will also cover the grounds first, but I would rather not bet on us being lucky. We don't have time to waste."

She's right. We hurry down the hallway past the guest bedrooms. This section of the second floor looks much the same as the rest, the grand hallway studded by doors at regular intervals. We'd have to check to be sure, but the number of rooms matches the number of guests, and everyone at the party seems to be staying on the second floor. "Hermes is one person. What could she possibly need with a home this large?" Best I can tell, she wasn't entertaining out here. Or if she was, the parties were so exclusive that no one spoke about them afterward. With how Olympus considers gossip an elite sport, I'm inclined to think the former is the truth.

"You'll have to ask her. I didn't even know this place existed." She's frowning harder. "I don't understand why no one is blinking at *two* missing people. Or at least one missing person. We can't verify that Tyche actually made it to the party, but Atalanta *was* here."

I squeeze her hand. "Everyone is here for their own reasons."

"And it's not the Thirteen in danger, so why bother to question it." Bitterness coats her words, and the worst part is that I can't argue with her. I'm not entirely sure of everyone's motivations, but there's a feeling of being untouchable that comes after you've held the title for a few years. Hephaestus said it himself.

That doesn't explain why Hermes and Artemis are okay with losing their plus-ones.

We finally find the staircase to the third floor tucked back into a relatively unassuming alcove. It gives the feeling of a haunted Victorian mansion with its narrow walls that almost feel like they lean in over a person. I can't tell if they're actually at an angle or if it's just a clever paint job, but I have to fight not to hunch my shoulders. The top landing is encased in darkness, a trick considering there's a stained-glass window there overlooking the backyard. It must be the fact that the walls are painted a deep green that seems to encourage an overactive imagination.

"Hermes certainly has a flare for the dramatic," I manage as we hurry up the stairs.

"Yeah," Cassandra says shortly. "She does."

On the third floor, the hallway looks very much the same as the second floor: broad space, thick carpet on the floors, the walls lined with more doors than are reasonable.

Cassandra once again pulls her hand from mine, and this time I allow it. We might be searching together, but it isn't a reasonable ask to maintain my hold on her the whole time, no matter how comforting I find it. "You take left, I take right?"

"That works for me."

The doors are locked. Of course they're locked. I glance across the hallway at Cassandra as she rattles another doorknob. "I don't suppose you're adept at lock picking."

"Why would I be adept at lock picking, Apollo? That's not a skill set that people have tucked up their sleeves outside fiction."

"You did date Hermes."

Cassandra eyes me, expression guarded. "I knew you were going to be weird about that."

"I'm not being weird about it."

"You are most assuredly being weird about it." She huffs out a breath. "*Lock picking?* Please. You have a propensity for kicking down doors. Go for it." She motions to the door behind her. "Besides, you're the spymaster. If one of us should be good at lock picking, it's you."

I make a face. "There's a reason I built the team I did. I'm good at managing and interpreting information, but I would have been much better suited to be Hephaestus. The spy-work part of the job doesn't come naturally to me. Hector tried to teach me to pick locks, but I'm terrible at it. I can get in...eventually, but time is of the essence right now." I clear my throat. "And I don't actually kick down doors."

"From how worried about it you were yesterday, I would have thought it was just as common an occurrence as lock picking."

Embarrassment heats my skin. "Your point is noted."

"Glad to hear it." She reaches the last door in the hallway and tries the doorknob. It twists in her hand and the door creaks open. Cassandra blinks. "Didn't see that coming."

"The odds weren't in our favor."

We share a glance. "This feels like a trap," she says.

"I can't argue that."

"Well, after you." She opens the door and steps back to allow me to precede her. Inside the room is bathed in shadows, thick curtains drawn over the windows. It's about the same size as our guest room downstairs, and I can make out the shape of a canopied bed, dresser, and two nightstands on either side of the bed. I feel around for a light and finally flick the switch. Disappointment sours my stomach.

Everywhere I look is evidence of Minos's daughter. The decor of the room leans toward frothy and dainty: the canopy made of lace, the comforter looking like some kind of antique bridal style, and even the rug beneath the bed seeming to be made of ruffles.

This is not Minos's room, and it certainly doesn't belong to the Minotaur or Theseus. I frown. "Well, this was a waste of time." It's likely that Minos's sons have some knowledge of his plan, but I'm not certain Ariadne does. I know better than to take things at face value, but Ariadne seems to be exactly what she presents: a lovely woman who has resigned herself to being a pawn for Minos on the marriage mart.

"You don't know that."

I look around again. "I suppose this could belong to the other woman in Minos's household. Her name is Pandora." She's not a foster like the two men, but she came with them to Olympus all the same. "It's unlikely either she or Ariadne have valuable information." It's even less likely when the unlocked door is taken into account. Minos hasn't misstepped yet. It's unlikely this is the exception to the rule.

"Don't be so rash." Cassandra slips past me. Her breasts brush my arm as she does, and I have to swallow past a physical response to her nearness. I *should* be focusing on the mission, on finding as much information as possible with the time allotted us, but suddenly all I can think about is whether she's as bare under that dress as she was last night. I actually clench my fists to keep from reaching for her instead of using this opportunity to search the room as she's begun to.

The hold this woman has on me. I swallow hard and follow her into the bedroom.

It takes three minutes of rifling through the dresser, feeling like the worst kind of creep, before I straighten. "There's nothing here." What did I expect, though? Minos is definitely keeping the information I need in his study. All the rest of this searching is only to ensure we're not missing something while we figure out a way into that locked room. Frustration surges and bubbles forth before I can call it back. "Fuck," I breathe.

"Language." She tuts. She doesn't look at me, flipping through a notebook left on the dresser. "Keep looking. If this is the only room we can get into this afternoon, then we need to ensure we search it fully." She carefully sets the notebook back down exactly where she found it.

"Minos doesn't seem to be the most forward-thinking feminist individual in existence," I finally say. "It's not entirely surprising that his daughter and her friend don't have useful information in their rooms."

"I suppose." She plants her hands on her hips and looks around the room. "We're missing something. I'm certain of it." Cassandra walks to the bookshelf tucked against the wall next to the closet and starts tugging on the books.

I recognize what she's up to immediately. "You really think that there are secret passageways in this house, don't you?"

"It's all but guaranteed, considering." She narrows her eyes at the full-length mirror, positioned against the opposite wall, and circles the bed to come and stand before it. "It would be really convenient to be able to find one of those right about now."

She's not wrong, but we haven't been lucky to date, and I don't expect that to start now. "There's little convenient about reality, Cassandra. You know that as well as anyone."

"Yeah, I suppose I do." She presses her hands around the ornate gilded frame that surrounds the mirror. I find myself holding my breath, even though I know better. As she said earlier, some things occur far more often in fiction than in reality. This is not the part of the story where the frame clicks and gives way. Yet I half expect it to happen. When it doesn't, we both let out a sound of disappointment.

I drag my hand through my hair. "Damn. I thought that might actually work."

"Me too." She sighs and tucks her hair behind her ears. "How embarrassing."

CASSANDRA

I HADN'T HONESTLY EXPECTED THE MIRROR TO CONTAIN secrets. It's too obvious. I bet Hermes put this mirror in here specifically to make people think that there *might* be something hidden behind it. It's exactly the kind of joke she'd find so amusing. I'm not entirely sure she's wrong, because we're the fools standing here, pawing at the mirror frame and hoping for a miracle.

I turn to Apollo, disappointment taking root. He's right. This was a dead end, a wasted opportunity. When I first agreed to Zeus's bargain, a week felt like an eternity. Now, I'm worried it won't be long enough. "Well, it was worth a shot."

For the first time, I wish I actually *had* learned to pick locks. Hermes offered to teach me once long ago, a fun little game while she distracted me, but she was far too good at distraction for me to get close to picking up the skill. I should have asked her to teach me properly. She would have said yes. It would have amused her greatly to do it. But I didn't. It honestly didn't even occur to me at the time. Lock picking is something out of thrillers and spy movies. It's fiction. When would I ever need that in real life?

Now is the answer.

I need it now.

I couldn't have anticipated that I'd be failing Apollo by not having this skill set. I'm pretty sure he doesn't consider me failing, but it stings nonetheless. "I'm sorry."

"You have nothing to be sorry for." He turns slowly, dark eyes narrowed. "This entire situation is less than ideal, and we're doing the best we can with the information we have." Apollo glances at me, expression going soft. "You're doing wonderfully, Cassandra."

His tone rings with sincerity and the praise warms me right down to my cold, shriveled heart. I drop my gaze, unable to look him directly in the face when I know I'm blushing furiously. "I haven't helped at all."

"On the contrary, you've done quite a bit. You just being here has shone the light on certain things, and I doubt Minos would have bothered to pull me aside without your presence pushing him to action." He huffs out a breath. "I can be rather dense about those sorts of things."

I snort. I can't help it. "Yeah, well, you didn't notice me making eyes at you for five years so I guess that statement checks out."

A choked sound has me glancing at him. His eyes have gone wide and his mouth is moving but no sound comes out. I jolt. "Apollo, are you okay?"

"What did you say?"

There's absolutely no reason to blush. I've had sex with this man. He's seen every bit of me. There is no reason that admitting I've had a thing for him should make me feel more vulnerable than that. Even if he's looking at me like I just hit him in the head with my purse.

I lick my lips. "Apollo, you have access to a mirror. You know that you're one of the most painfully attractive people in this damned city."

He surprises me—he always surprises me—with his response. "Don't do that." He shakes his head slowly. "Don't act like you would let something as simple as lust turn your head."

"There is nothing simple about lust." When he just waits, I relent. "Okay, fine. I like you. I've thought you were attractive since I took the job, but working with you so closely only added to that. You're a legitimately good guy. I...like you."

He drags his hand over his face. "Why didn't you say something?"

"I thought you didn't want me." I don't mean for the words to come out almost small. "I don't know if it would have mattered, but...I honestly thought you weren't attracted to me."

Heat and frustration flare in his dark eyes. "Cassandra, after five years of working with me, I would hope that you'd understand that I would never put you in a position where you felt uncomfortable. The more I got to know you, the more I was attracted to you, which just made me more determined to ensure you didn't feel obligated to..." He motions between us almost helplessly. "Anything."

"If you know me as well as you say, then you'd know I wouldn't feel obligated to do shit."

He shrugs. "I wasn't going to make your life harder just because I wanted you."

Last night, we definitely crossed a whole bunch of lines, and I won't pretend it's because we're fake dating. We were both pretty damn clear that we were on the same page about wanting each other. Still, it can't hurt to make things even more explicitly clear. "Apollo."

"Yes?"

I can't tell if he looks hopeful or if I'm just imagining things. It doesn't matter; I've come too far to back out now. I swallow hard. "I would like to have my filthy way with you again the first opportunity that presents itself, and also as often as can be managed before this thing between us ends."

The tips of his ears go a bit pink, but he sharpens in the same way he did last night. "Consider it a promise."

"Great. Good. Perfect." I'm stammering, but I kind of like that he flusters me because I know he won't use that flustered feeling against me. He seems to enjoy it, too, his attention snagging on my cheeks and lips before coasting down my body in a slow drag I can almost feel.

I start to turn toward the door but stop short. "Apollo, *look*." I point to the bed with its absurd number of pillows. Pillows that, until I stood at exactly this angle, hid what appears to be a laptop.

We exchange a glance and move quickly to the bed. He grabs the laptop and opens it. "Surely we're not about to get lucky now."

It boots up quickly, showing a desktop with a handful of icons on it. "Not password protected," I say softly.

He angles it toward himself and starts typing, agile fingers moving so fast through a series of commands that it makes my head spin. I'm decent when it comes to computers, but Apollo is on another level. Within seconds, he has Ariadne's search history, her password storage, and a whole lot of files of what appears to be fan fiction. "This is worthless."

"Give me a second." He narrows his eyes and leans forward. "There." A new browser window pops up for a different email account. "Minos logged into his email on this computer."

I lean back. "That seems very foolish of him." He's gone through all this trouble to keep things secure, and he logged into his email on a computer that isn't even password protected? It defies belief.

"Not looking the gift horse in the mouth." With a few keystrokes, he selects hundreds of emails and begins to forward them to Hector's email. "This will take a second, and Hector is going to have a lot to wade through, but this is the best lead we have right now."

All sorts of stuff is stored in email accounts. Log-in info. Bank notices. It will give a skilled hacker like Hector more than enough to work with. "This is big," I say. "But we also can't discard the fact that it might be a red herring. Doesn't it seem a little too convenient?"

"Yes. Absolutely." The emails finish sending, and he carefully exits out of everything and wipes the history. "But we can't afford to ignore it." He goes still. "Do you hear that?"

I hadn't noticed earlier, but there are footsteps coming down the hallway. "Apollo—"

It happens so quickly. One moment I'm frantically trying to

decide if we're supposed to hide or allow ourselves to be caught. The next, Apollo tosses the laptop back into the pile of pillows, sweeps an arm around my waist, and tows me backward into the closet.

He pushes the hangers out of the way and shuts the door, bathing us in darkness. I'm still blinking and wondering what the fuck just happened. I've never seen him move so fast...except last night when he dragged me down to the couch.

Despite the current circumstances, I can't help the forbidden thrill that goes through me. I'm not a small woman and I'm also a control freak, so the thought of someone hauling me around has never fully appealed, even in kinky play.

I get the appeal now.

I shake my head, trying to focus. Sex is not on the menu right now, and we have bigger issues at hand—like whoever is coming even with the bedroom door right now, their footsteps firm and thudding.

The only problem is I can't *see* who it is. Apollo's shut the door entirely, cutting off any chance at identifying our visitor. I reach for the door, intending to crack it a little bit so we can view who comes into the room, but he catches my wrist without hesitation.

I tug on his hold. Surely figuring out who's approaching is a better idea than just hiding and hoping for the best? It's not Theseus. The cadence of the steps is not uneven the way Theseus's is. This is someone else, and the knowledge of their identity might be a key piece of information.

But as I open my mouth to give a whispered demand for him to release me, Apollo places his hand firmly over my lips. The contact of his calloused palm shocks me to stillness. He takes that opportunity to lean down and speak softly in my ear. "Silence, Cassandra."

I realize within a few seconds that this is not someone looking for us. If they were, they wouldn't be pawing through things the same way we were several minutes ago. No, this is someone else looking for answers. I frown into the darkness of the closet. Who is it?

Not Hermes. She would never be so crass as to allow her footsteps to give her away. The woman moves like a cat, silent and always popping up where you least expect her. It's unlikely it's one of Minos's family members. There are still nearly half a dozen people it could be, not to mention the staff Minos has flitting about in the background.

Too many options.

If I had to place bets, I'd lay them on Charon or Aphrodite. Zeus is the type to hedge his bets, which means sending someone in addition to Apollo to search for information. He won't trust most of the other Thirteen with a task like that, but Aphrodite is his sister. And Charon is obviously here for Hades for the exact same reason—he doesn't trust the rest of the Thirteen to pass on the relevant information to ensure the lower city stays safe.

But I could be wrong. I won't know for sure unless I see them.

The temptation to crack the closet door is nearly overwhelming. My curiosity is a live beast inside me, all claws and teeth and irresistible urge to move. Only Apollo's presence, his strong body pressing me to the closet wall, keeps me still and silent. His words echo in my ear.

Silence, Cassandra.

I shiver.

He smells like expensive soap mixed with pure *Apollo*, and it's everything I can do not to bury my face in his throat and inhale deeply. I shift against him, not actively trying to... Except that's a lie, isn't it? I like the feeling of him holding me down, even in such a finite way, and I can't help pushing back against his strength. Just a little.

Apollo shifts, pressing a strong thigh between mine, and all thought flees my head. There are only this man and me in the close darkness. We might as well be the only two people left in the world right now, and that suits me just fine.

I go a little soft against him. There's something about this that I respond to on such a deep level. I've spent the last five years convincing myself that this is not what I wanted, and the first opportunity for things to change, it's as if a dam burst and all my needs and desires came flooding out, overwhelming everything.

I *want* Apollo. But I can't pretend it's just sex. I've cared about this blasted man for years, and if there was anyone in this city that would make staying here worthwhile...

I can't do it.

He hasn't offered me anything, for one. Even if he had, in that sweet, strong way of his, I can't accept. He's *Apollo*. He's a member of the very body of powerful people that I hate above all others. No matter what I feel for him, surely my bitterness would poison any chance of a long-term relationship. More than that, eventually he'd resent me. My parents ensured no one would ever trust me enough to allow me to play the games required of a partner of one of the Thirteen.

He needs a full partner, and I can never be that. Not with my history.

What am I thinking?

Apollo hasn't made any offers. He might want me, which means he cares about me enough to desire me, but he's hardly tried to convince me to stay in Olympus.

He intends to let me go, and I intend to walk away.

CASSANDRA

FOR HIS PART, APOLLO IS NOT UNAFFECTED. HIS HARD COCK against my hip is more than evidence of that. His fingers against my mouth move to grip my jaw lightly, and he shifts back just enough for his mouth to brush mine, a light kiss, both a warning and a tease. The things the man does with his kisses should be illegal. How am I supposed to keep my head on straight when he kisses me as if I'm his favorite dessert? It's just not fair.

He shifts over to speak directly in my ear. "Be silent. We're going to get caught."

I have never, ever considered getting caught in an intimate moment as anything other than something to be avoided. In the last twenty-four hours, Apollo has shown me the error of my ways. My breath hitches and I nod shakily.

"Good girl." He trails his fingers down my arm to my waist. Teasing me, the bastard. I might make a sound of protest, but he ordered me to be silent. I press my lips together hard, and he rewards me by cupping one breast and playing his thumb over my nipple. It's as if the thin fabric of my dress and bra don't exist. He's *scorching* me.

"You want more, don't you?" His voice is pitched lower than a whisper. It's barely an exhale against my ear. He touches me as if he'll never get another chance. As if I am a piece of artwork that he plans on appreciating at every level. As if we're not tucked into a closet together. The thought might make me laugh if I had the breath for it, but he's stolen it all. And how could he not?

This man is *everything*.

I nod shakily. Of course I want more. I want it all, no matter how ill advised. Apollo is a fire in my blood, and he might burn me alive, but I'll strike the match happily as long as he doesn't stop touching me.

He presses his leg higher until he actually lifts me a little. I roll my hips, the delicious friction making me catch my breath. Or, rather, he catches it for me, his mouth claiming mine. This time, the kisses are not teasing, not light, not conveying some hidden message. He's had his taste and now he wants it all.

I finally remember that I'm able to move and dig my hands into his hair, pulling him closer. In this moment, I don't care where we are. I don't care who might overhear or the implications if they do. All I need is Apollo as close to me as possible.

I need everything.

"Cassandra," he groans against my skin. On his tongue, my name feels like a curse and a promise at the same time. I've never felt more intoxicating in my life than I do in this moment. I've brought this man, one of the most powerful people in the city, to the breaking point with desire. "Show me where you need me."

I couldn't stop now if I wanted to, and I desperately don't want to. I ease back against the wall and grab the wrist of the hand gripping my chin. I tug his hand up to cover my mouth again. A silent demand for him to keep me quiet because gods know I won't be able to do it on my own.

Apollo goes perfectly still for a beat, two. On the third, he catches the back of my knee and urges my leg up to curl around his waist. The new position opens me, and he wastes no time taking advantage of it, pressing even closer and hitching me higher against his thigh.

I gasp against his palm, the sound morphing into a muffled moan as he skates his hand up the back of my thigh to grip my ass. "No panties, Cassandra?" He releases a shuddering breath. "You please me. I like knowing I can have you this way at a whim. That you're wet and ready for me."

His grip guides me to ride his thigh. The pressure and friction make my thoughts short out. It defies some kind of law that it's always so good with him. It doesn't make *sense*, except it's Apollo and somehow it was always going to be world-ending with him. I helplessly grind against him, seeking that rising tide inside me. It shouldn't be this easy, but something about Apollo takes *shouldn't* right out of the equation.

"Someone's going to hear you come all over my thigh." He drags his mouth down my throat and back up again. "I don't care. Let them hear. Don't stop."

His low words only drive me higher. My breath comes harshly, making me light-headed. I'm so close. I just need...

Apollo sets his teeth to the sensitive spot where my neck meets my shoulder. It's not quite a bite, more an intense pressure that doesn't veer across the boundary into pain. It's perfect.

I orgasm, my moan making it past even his hand covering my mouth.

"Are you fucking kidding me?"

Before I process that Apollo isn't the one to speak, the door's thrown open and light spills over us.

I try to jump back, but there's nowhere to go with the wall behind me, and I bump my head against it. "Ow," I say against his palm.

"Damn it." He releases me, only moving back enough to tug my dress down to ensure I'm covered. Apollo sifts his hand through my hair, feeling for a bump. "Are you okay?"

How can he sound so normal when seconds ago I was coming all over his thigh? I'm shaky and light-headed and still trying to process the fact that we were interrupted, but the only evidence in his tone is a slight gruffness that's not normally present.

That and the impressive hard-on I can still feel pressing against my hip.

"I'm fine," I manage. I take his wrist and tug it away from my head. "Seriously. I'm good."

"Okay."

We turn as one to look at the person standing on the other side of the doors. Ariadne. I frown. How long were we making out that we didn't notice the other intruder had left the room and someone else had entered?

The sheer level of distraction is worrisome, but there's no space to let that worry take hold. Not when we currently have some explaining to do. I give a pathetically nervous giggle. "Oh, you caught us. Whoops."

She plants her hands on her broad hips and gives us an exasperated look. "I understand that a game of adult hide-and-seek is exactly the kind of opportunity to sneak off and bone somewhere, but if you could *not* do that in my room, I would greatly appreciate it."

"Sorry." I actually sound more like myself this time. The desire is burning off, embarrassment waiting in the wings to make me wish the floor would open up and swallow me whole.

Apollo gives the back of my head one last caress, still testing for a bump, before he disengages and steps back. I catch him subtly adjusting the front of his pants and find myself grinning like a fool despite the blush that's no doubt turned me crimson. I can't deny that I love how thoroughly he reacts to me. It's a heady thing. Something to get drunk on later.

Right now, I need to focus.

Her laptop was a good find, but the woman herself might be more so. It still defies belief that she left her door unlocked and a computer sitting around by accident. It's enough to make me wonder...

I tuck my hair behind my ears and step out of the closet. "We didn't mean to get carried away." My voice is still not quite right, but I think I could be excused considering how she just found us. "Is the game already over?"

"Oh, that?" She waves her hand. "No, Theseus is still hunting down the rest of the party guests. I think he's out in the maze now." She glances out the door, her brows drawing together. "It wasn't this... I decided that... I'm not participating in the game right now."

"It must be a bit of a relief not to be the prize this time."

She turns to me too quickly. "Right. This time." Her gaze drops to the floor, which further confirms my suspicions that Minos's daughter likely didn't have much say in this whole circus.

It seemed a clumsy move when I first thought about it, but now that I have confirmation from Hermes that something else is going on, I think it's *designed* to be clumsy to make us underestimate Minos. I still don't quite understand what he could hope to accomplish by double-crossing the Thirteen. If Minos is facilitating an invasion or whatever else Zeus suspects, surely he realizes he won't survive the attempt?

But what if he does? What if he succeeds?

Apollo will still be here fighting to protect this city that does not deserve him while I'm off putting this all behind me. Who will watch his back without me here? Not that I'm the greatest protector, but no one else looks out for him. Hector is a great member of the team, but he will understandably put his family first. Same with the rest of the people who answer directly to Apollo. They all have families. More, he would never expect them to put the job before their loved ones.

Zeus uses Apollo as a blunt tool or scalpel by turn. The rest of the Thirteen are too busy engaging in backbiting and bullshit politics to ever care for one another beyond what power their allies can provide. Being an *ally* is as fraught as being an enemy.

Apollo alone stands apart. If I were Minos, a newcomer to this city who's obviously looking to make his own grab for power, Apollo is where I would strike. He's the cornerstone of the alliance that pledges to Zeus. Without him, Zeus would keep Ares and

Aphrodite at his side, by virtue of them being his sisters, but would he be able to keep the rest?

I doubt it.

"Are you okay, Cassandra?" Apollo clasps my shoulder gently with a firm hand.

"I'm fine." I don't sound convincing, but what can I say? Even if Ariadne wasn't here, nothing is going to divert Apollo from his mission. He is one of the Thirteen; more than anyone else, he knew the risk when he took the title.

The thought brings a bitter smile to my lips. Even if I lost my mind and begged him to come with me, he's far too honorable to leave Olympus, let alone when it needs him most.

Ironic that the thing that drew me to him in the first place is the very reason we'll never be together.

APOLLO

I CAN'T DENY THE SURGE OF SATISFACTION THAT GOES through me to realize that my kisses and my touch turn Cassandra into this blushing, stammering person. It's a heady thing to know that I affect her just as deeply as she affects me, but now's not the time to let myself get distracted. My cock hasn't quite gotten the memo, not with the memory of her softness imprinted on my body. I clear my throat. What had she just said? She's fine. Of course she's fine. She's never anything but *fine*.

I press my hand to the small of Cassandra's back and paint a charming smile on my face as I turn to Ariadne. "You're not a fan of hide-and-seek?"

She grimaces, the shadow of some remembered pain flashing over her face, gone almost too fast to catch. "No, I don't like the dark." Her tone is not quite right for the apparent lightness that she's striving for, but her fears are not my business. The information she possesses about her father is.

I step out of the closet after Cassandra and start inching

toward the door, taking my time. If she thinks we're attempting to extract information from her, she'll kick us out. Better to make all the right appearances of leaving and see what I can glean in the precious few seconds available to me. "How are you liking it in Olympus, Ariadne?"

"It's a lovely city." There's a reservation in her that wasn't present the last time we spoke. I can't tell if that's because she's unhappy that we've intruded on her private space or if she knows more than she's saying. I pulse my fingers against Cassandra's back and she, smart, savvy woman that she is, fakes a stumble and catches herself on the dresser.

"Oh, sorry," she says. "I'm just feeling a little dizzy."

Ariadne, true to my suspicions, is far too nice to ignore someone blatantly in need. "Here, sit down." She rushes forward and guides Cassandra to perch on the edge of her bed. She doesn't look particularly pleased about it, but her feelings are less import-ant than the opportunity Cassandra has provided us.

"Olympus is somewhat of an acquired taste," I offer.

Cassandra snorts. "Acquired, if you have the power for it." She shakes her head, pressing her fingers to her temples. Even knowing her as well as I do, I would be fooled by the misery on her face if I didn't know this was all an act. "Some people find Olympus to be exactly what it is, all glitz and glamour covering a rotted core."

Ariadne gives a faint smile, though her eyes remain serious. "Seems like you don't have a high opinion of your city."

"It's the truth, even if most people pretend otherwise." Cassandra shrugs one shoulder. "But it's all I know. Was it like this where you come from?"

"No," Ariadne says slowly. "Aeaea is nothing like Olympus. It was lovely when I was a child but...things changed."

I exchange a look with Cassandra. I've never heard of Aeaea. Is it a city? A town? A named property the way some people favor? "What changed?"

Ariadne shakes her head slowly. "You seem like a nice man, Apollo."

I don't get a chance to respond before Cassandra laughs. "Unlike everything else in Olympus, Apollo is exactly what he seems. You can't say the same for most of the guests here, let alone the members of the Thirteen, but Apollo somehow managed to be raised in a legacy family and take over one of the thirteen most powerful titles in the city, and yet he's a genuinely nice guy. He's practically a mythical creature." She lifts her gaze, her faux dizziness washing away and only seriousness remaining. "There are plenty of people in power in Olympus who deserve any trouble your father could bring and more, but not Apollo."

"Yes, well, my father does what he wants." She says it with the air of someone who's given up all hope, a stark contrast from the personality she's shown us to date. She seems to realize it, too, because she forces a bright smile. "You know how it is. Parents, right?"

It's not my business, I remind myself. *This woman is not my business. Olympus is.*

I cannot take every injured dove under my wing, no matter what Cassandra accuses me of from time to time. Even hiring her five years ago had my family blisteringly unhappy with me for months before they finally gave in and admitted that I'm more than capable of making my own decisions. They still think she manipulated me, seduced her way into my life to take advantage of my position. They especially believe that now that we're publicly dating.

That's neither here nor there, though.

"Ariadne, if you ever need a safe space," I find myself saying, "I know a few places that offer sanctuary." There aren't many in Olympus, but they are notable. The lower city offers a special sort of refuge for those Hades—and now Persephone—deems worthy, and the strength of that refuge has only increased since he forced the entire city to acknowledge that he's more than a myth.

The other lies within Hera's domain, a temple of sorts that now houses orphans but used to extend to anyone who claimed sanctuary. It has become mostly toothless over the last few Heras, courtesy of the late Zeus, but our current Hera is making moves behind the scenes to reclaim what power belonged to her title before it was gutted by a dangerous and greedy man.

I am very curious to see what our new Hera will do, given enough time.

Ariadne raises her brows. "That's quite the offer. You don't know me. I could say yes and then turn around and work against you."

I shrug again. I'm not normally one to let instincts guide me, but there's something about this woman that makes me feel like she's in trouble. Minos might play the part of the doting father in public, but he's already proven himself to be a superior liar. After the last Zeus...

I didn't have the power to fight that man and what he did to his own household. I was too green when I took over as Apollo, and even when I had enough experience to undermine him where possible, it was like trying to use a colander to bail out a sinking ship. Zeus was simply too powerful.

Ariadne is not Helen or Eris or Perseus or Hercules or even the last few Heras who died far too young from mysterious *accidents*...

But I wouldn't be able to live with myself if I didn't at least try.

"The offer is a standing one," I finally say. I hold out a hand to Cassandra. "We should get going and leave Ariadne to her peace."

Ariadne lets us get to the doorway before she speaks. "I, uh, appreciate the offer. I'm not going to take you up on it, but I do appreciate it." She hesitates. "I'm glad I was right about you."

Right about me? "Like I said, the offer stands." I give her half a smile and turn through the doorway, tugging Cassandra behind me.

I'm not sure what the plan is now. The game continues, but until Hector has a chance to go through those emails and chase down any leads he finds, we won't know if this mission was a success. Still, it's our best lead, and with how things have played out so far, it's likely the only one we'll have. Best to go back down to the second floor and make the appearance of continuing to participate.

I glance down at Cassandra, realize she's trying not to pant as I all but drag her behind me, and force myself to slow down. "Sorry."

"Penny for your thoughts."

"We should leave."

Cassandra misses a step. "*What?*"

"We should leave." I slow down further and look around. Hiding in our room is foolish. Better to aim for one of the many sitting rooms. Going back downstairs is a waste of time. Theseus will be headed up once he clears the grounds and the first floor. I readjust my grip on Cassandra's hand and tow her around the corner. The hallway is empty, but in the distance, I hear someone cackling with delight. It sounds like Dionysus.

"I heard you." Cassandra digs in her heels. "This one." She opens the door on her right and pulls me through. It's set up similarly to the one we were in last night, though the color scheme is a variety of purples that make my eyes ache. It's *almost* seamless, but there's something off, and so the many tones clash despite essentially being monochromatic.

I shut the door behind us automatically. "There's no good place to hide here."

"I don't care." She takes a step back and props her hands on her hips. "Why are you suddenly saying we should leave?"

"We're not getting anywhere, aside from that lucky find with the laptop. At this point, I'd be better spent back in the city center, working with Hector to go through all that information. I'm useless here. I don't know what game Minos is playing at, and he's laughing himself silly because he has us playing parlor games." Saying it aloud feels like almost too much. I'm so frustrated, I could throw something. "More, we've been warned twice now about your presence here. At least one person might be missing and that's enough for me to get you out of here now that we have something to show for all this."

"That wasn't an accident." Her gaze is focused on somewhere

in the middle distance. "The laptop and the emails. Did you catch what she said? That she was right about you."

I shrug. "I have a reputation. It doesn't mean much."

"Apollo, you are too innocent sometimes." She shakes her head. "I bet we're going to find exactly what we're looking for in those emails, and I would bet Alexandra's college fund that Ariadne knows that."

That stops me short. "You think she's working against her father?"

"It's possible." Cassandra frowns. "Or it's a double bluff and he put her up to this, but Minos doesn't give the vibe of someone who puts a lot of value on people he considers soft, and Ariadne is soft right down to her sunny center."

It always amazes me how she can make these jumps. I can usually reach the same conclusion, but it takes me a lot longer—and a lot more second-guessing myself—to get there. "If that's true..."

Excitement lights up her dark eyes. "We could have someone on the inside, or at the very least, if we could flip her to our side, we'd have an inside track to more information."

"Which means we can't leave." Up until this party, Minos kept Ariadne away from the public eye, and I don't expect that to change going forward. We won't have access to her again, not if we leave now. "We'll have to—"

In the distance, someone screams.

I freeze. "Did I just—"

"Yes." Cassandra starts for the door. "That was a scream. It sounded like Eurydice."

I snag her wrist. "Stay here." If there's danger, I want her as far from it as possible. "Or, better yet, go to our room and lock yourself in."

"You're out of your mind if you think I'm not coming with you." She jerks her wrist from my grip. "Are you going to keep wasting time arguing, or are you coming?"

She's right. We don't have time to waste. "Stay close." I lead the way through the door into the hall. Already, voices are raised somewhere in the distance. Downstairs. "Come on."

We find Eurydice and Charon in the library. At first, I don't see what the problem is, but then Charon wraps an arm around her shoulder and steps back, revealing the body of Pan. He lies on his stomach, blood pooling the carpet beneath him. "Oh no."

Tears pour from Eurydice's eyes and she allows Charon to pull her into his arms and tuck her face against his chest. "How did this happen?"

"I don't know." He looks at me over her head. "We were waiting in the parlor after we were found by Theseus and came in here when we heard a crash."

"Did you see anything?"

"No."

Cassandra pushes past me and moves to kneel next to Pan, careful to avoid the blood. Before I can say a word, she presses her fingers to his throat. A few seconds tick by. She looks up sharply. "He's still alive."

Just like that, this situation becomes vastly different. "Charon, call an ambulance. Now!"

He pauses long enough to guide Eurydice to a chair just out of the way—and out of sight lines to Pan—and then rushes out of the room. I join Cassandra at Pan's side. "Do we move him onto his back?"

"No." She shakes her head. "There could be a spinal injury. We can't move him until the paramedics arrive. They'll know what to do."

I stare down at the man. "What was he doing in here? I thought he went out the front door."

"He must have circled back."

It doesn't matter why he's here, only that he is. I sit back on my heels and look around. We explored the library briefly this morning, but it's just like every other personal library I've visited. It's relatively subdued compared to the rest of the house, a reasonably sized room with dark bookshelves and several cozy overstuffed couches arranged around a large bay window. It's probably a lovely place to spend an afternoon.

There's also nothing sharp to accidentally stumble and fall against. Not to mention Pan's wound is on the *back* of his head, as if someone clubbed him when he wasn't looking. But what...

"Apollo?"

I look up to see Eurydice standing on the other side of the chair, a marble tortoise held in her hands, blood spattered across its carved back. "I found this under my chair. Tucked away as if someone tried to hide it fast."

It's all the proof we need.

Someone tried to kill Pan.

CASSANDRA

THINGS HAPPEN QUICKLY AFTER THAT. MOST OF THE REST of the guests appear in a group, and under different circumstances, I might be amused by the sheer chaos of half a dozen members of the Thirteen trying to take charge of the situation.

Hard to be amused about anything when I'm watching Pan's back to ensure he hasn't stopped breathing.

I liked the cheerful man. I desperately want him to be okay.

Minos sweeps in five minutes later with two men in nondescript uniforms who *might* be paramedics, but they're not dressed like any I've ever seen. He stops short and looks down at Pan.

My adrenaline is surging. I can't stop shaking. It's almost enough for me to miss the pure fury on his face. He masks it quickly. I'm sure I'm the only one who witnessed it, kneeling at Pan's side as I am.

Minos snaps his fingers. "Stop bickering. We need to help this man." He motions to the two men who accompanied him.

"Get a stretcher and prepare him for the ambulance. It should be here shortly."

The impulse to throw myself over Pan's body so they won't take him is nearly overwhelming. Someone attacked this man, and the only reason he was here in the first place is because Minos invited him. No one else at this party wants Pan dead...

Do they?

I look helplessly at Apollo. He's got his expression locked down tight. He circles around and cups my elbow, guiding me to my feet. "Let the medics help, Cassandra."

"If they hurt him—"

"They won't." He says it loud enough that everyone stops arguing and looks at him. "Pan is a friend. A number of people in this room—and beyond—would take it amiss if anything happened to him."

It's on the tip of my tongue to snarl that something already happened to him, but if Apollo can assure no one finishes the job, that's the only thing that matters.

"Of course." Minos smiles, all charming host once more. "He's under my hospitality."

"Not that that helped him," I mutter. "He was attacked while under your hospitality."

The medics make quick work of getting Pan onto a stretcher and whisking him out of the room. Once he's gone, we're left staring at each other with an increasing amount of distrust. Pan didn't slip and fall on the stone sculpture. Someone hit him with it.

Someone likely in this room.

Eurydice opens her mouth, expression still distraught, but

before she can say anything, Aphrodite storms through the door. She takes in the scene with a single sweep. "Why does everyone look like their favorite dog got kicked?"

"Pan—"

The door opens again behind Aphrodite, cutting Eurydice off a second time, and in walks Theseus with his arm slung around Adonis's shoulders. Adonis has his smile firmly in place, and not even I can tell if it's fake or not. Ah. That explains the fury in Aphrodite's eyes.

Theseus doesn't immediately release him. "Adonis won."

"Wonderful. Let's take a quick break to, ah, deal with a few things." Minos looks around the room. "We'll rejoin for dinner."

"Rejoin for dinner," Eurydice repeats. She takes a step forward, ignoring the light touch Charon places on her arm. "You can't honestly expect us to ignore what happened to Pan. I thought he was *dead*."

"He's not dead," Minos says mildly. "He was drinking with Dionysus during lunch. He obviously tripped over the rug and injured himself."

I blink. Surely they're not going to buy that? It doesn't make the slightest bit of sense.

Dionysus chooses that moment to hiccup. "He was putting it away. Chap can drink me under the table."

I glare at Hermes, but she's got a small smile on her face and, for once, apparently has nothing to say. Aphrodite props her hands on her hips. "Someone explain what happened."

"I just did, my dear." Minos moves to the door, stepping easily over the bloodstain. "Shall we?" He walks out without another word.

Theseus tightens his grip on Adonis's shoulders and steers him after his foster father. It's at that moment that I realize no one else in Minos's household is in the room.

One of them was responsible.

Except we have no way to prove it. It can't be Ariadne. There's no way she got downstairs in time to attack Pan...but she's the only one I can safely mark off the list of suspects. I step back and take Apollo's hand. "We should call Ares. That wasn't an accident; it was attempted murder."

Charon shakes his head slowly. "No way to prove it."

I blink. "Excuse me?"

"There's no way to prove it," he repeats patiently. "They will come in and the first thing they'll do is sweep for prints. Do you know whose prints are on that tortoise?"

Eurydice's.

Apollo sighs. "There might be others."

"It will muddy the water." He turns to Eurydice. "We can leave if you want. I don't think we're going to find the answers we're looking for here."

Her lower lip quivers, but she makes an obvious effort to still it. "I'm fine. There's no reason to leave. Not until you've accomplished what you set out to."

That all but confirms my suspicions that Charon is here on a fact-finding mission for Hades, the same way we are for Zeus. It's a small blessing that Hades, at least, isn't looking to ally himself with Minos. I can't say the same for the others, except Aphrodite.

"Eurydice—"

"Would you leave if I wasn't here?" His silence is answer enough. She turns to the rest of us. "Are *you* leaving?"

"Nope." Hermes laughs. "This is just getting interesting."

Dionysus shrugs. "He's got good wine." His normal good cheer is nowhere in evidence, though. If anything, he looks far sicker than alcohol can explain.

I cannot believe what I'm hearing. They should all be heading for the front door. Instead, they're...staying. "You're serious. Someone just tried to kill Pan and you're just going to stick around and wait to give them another shot? And what about Atalanta and Tyche? That's *three* people."

"Pan will be transported to the hospital in the city." Dionysus hiccups. "I'm sure he'll be okay."

"Atalanta texted me. She's fine." Artemis examines her fingernails. "Sometimes parties get wild, Cassandra. You'd know that if you were invited to more of them." Behind her, Hephaestus makes a choked laughing sound.

"As if someone couldn't take her phone and use it to text you." I'm sorely tempted to pick up that fucking tortoise and fling it at *her*, but aside from that thing looking heavy, assault never solved any problems. If they won't see reason, trying to beat some sense into them isn't going to work. "You're fools. One of you will be next."

Hephaestus snorts. "Please. We're the Thirteen. We'll be fine."

"Of all the—"

"Collar your girlfriend, Apollo. Before one of us has to." Artemis turns away.

Her exit starts a cascade. One by one they follow her, even Eurydice and Charon. Hermes is the last one standing and she shakes her head slowly. "I told you to leave, Cass. It's not too late to go, but no one is going to believe your warnings." She leaves before I can come up with a response.

What is there to say? She's right.

I turn to Apollo. He looks troubled, but even knowing him as well as I do, I can't say if it's what just happened that's bothering him or thoughts of the future. He finally meets my gaze and squeezes my hand. "I hate to say it, but she's right. You should leave."

I don't miss the emphasis on *you*. "What about you? What about Ariadne?"

He ignores the question. "I don't know why someone would target Pan, but it's getting more and more obvious that you're not safe."

"Apollo—"

"If you're concerned about Zeus declaring the deal null and void, I can make the argument that you've more than done your duty and you never agreed to being in physical danger. He may attempt to dock the pay, but I'll make up the difference."

Exasperation takes hold. He's nothing if not stubborn. "You can't just write me a check for over a million dollars. Your family would chase me out of town with pitchforks and torches."

"You already intend to leave. What do you care what my family thinks?"

He's right. Of course he's right. That doesn't change the fact that the thought of leaving Apollo here alone makes my entire body clench in denial. "That's not the point."

He steps close and cups my face. "Let me worry about the money. Go home where it's safe."

I cover his hands with my own. "I'll leave if you come with me."

"I can't." He sighs. "Not if there really is potential for Ariadne to flip to our side."

"Then we'll call Ares." I'm reaching, and I know it, but I can't shake the feeling of impending doom.

"Ares can't interfere without a direct invitation or an order from Zeus, which he won't give for fear of alienating those members of the Thirteen who are guests." Apollo shakes his head. "I can't leave. Not yet. But you can, Cassandra. Please."

"No. Not without you." I wrap my hands around his wrists and squeeze. "If I'm not here, you have no one to watch your back. I'm not Ares or Athena or even Artemis, but I can't leave you alone. Don't ask me to."

"I'm not the one in danger, Cassandra." I refuse to budge. He looks like he wants to keep arguing but finally sighs again. "Short of stuffing you in a trunk and driving back to the city myself, I'm not going to convince you, am I?"

Despite everything, I laugh a little. "No. Short of kidnapping, it's not going to happen."

He presses a quick kiss to my forehead and drops his hands. "All right. If you're not leaving, let's go see what's next." He pauses. "No going anywhere alone, Cassandra. I won't risk you."

"Okay. I won't. I promise."

Apollo takes my hand. "Come on."

We find the rest of the guests gathered back in the living room. Aphrodite sits on the couch next to Dionysus, her arms crossed and dark eyes furious. He blinks at her but for once doesn't seem to have a witty comment ready. In fact, he looks to be in danger of losing his lunch, pale skin waxy and sweat dotting his forehead.

Theseus sits next to Adonis on one of the other couches. They aren't quite cuddled up, but Theseus has sprawled his big body out so that he's pressed against the other man...and Adonis doesn't appear to be complaining for reasons I can't fathom.

They do look quite the pair, though.

Adonis, for his part, has his charming smile in place. I've never been able to figure out if he's truly so easygoing that nothing ruffles his feathers or if he's got the best mask I've ever seen. I can't honestly say for certain, which would bother me if I gave a shit about Olympus politics beyond determining who to actively avoid.

Theseus, though? He's got a terrible poker face. Satisfaction comes off him in waves, there in the possessive way he touches Adonis and the smirk he sends in Aphrodite's direction. Considering I haven't seen him look twice at the other man since they arrived, this must be for her benefit.

Aphrodite has managed to piss off one of Minos's foster sons—maybe just by virtue of being related to Helen, who caused him so much damage and stole his chance to become the next Ares—and it certainly looks like he's going to make her choke on his "date" with Adonis.

If Minos intends to match his children with powerful people, Adonis shouldn't be on the list. He's arguably the least powerful person in this room, excepting me.

It makes about as much sense as attacking Pan.

I'm missing something. Something important. If I just had some time and space to reason it through...

"Cassandra?"

I startle and glance at Apollo. It's only then that I realize I was staring at Theseus and Adonis too intensely. I try for a smile. "Just thinking too hard."

He doesn't look like he believes me, but then I'm a normal human being who just went through a shock. Little tremors keep shifting my limbs without my permission. I don't understand how everyone is chatting easily as if one of Minos's people isn't in the library, cleaning bloodstains out of the rug. Only Charon and Eurydice seem bothered, and they make some vague excuses and leave the room quickly.

Even Apollo seems mostly fine as he guides me over to sit near Dionysus and Aphrodite. He drops into their conversation easily, charming Aphrodite enough that she stops sending murderous looks at her boyfriend and Theseus. Mostly.

This is what it means to be one of the Thirteen.

I knew they functioned differently than the rest of us, but spending so much time with Hermes and then Apollo lulled me into a false sense of thinking I truly understood what that meant.

I didn't then.

I sure as fuck do now as the afternoon stretches toward evening...and dinnertime.

I would like to say that I focus heavily on all the conversations around me during dinner. Minos is there playing his charming king routine. The others are speaking about...something. But all I can think of is that Pan was nearly killed and not a single person has inquired about an update from the hospital. Not even Dionysus, who is the reason Pan was at this party to begin with.

Everyone is very carefully not looking at me. They all think I'm paranoid and weak. Even Charon and Eurydice, who are handling this a thousand times better than I am. And why not? Neither of them have seen exactly what the elite in Olympus are capable of.

Is this how the Thirteen acted after they ordered my parents to be murdered?

Did they sit around and drink and laugh while Athena's assassins chased my parents through the streets of downtown, ending in their fiery death?

It was a different Apollo who held the title during that time, but I can't pretend that *my* Apollo would have made a different call. Not when his priorities are vividly clear. He will do anything to protect Olympus. Even if it compromises his personal morals. He knows what would happen to this city if information about the assassination clause got out. He wouldn't relish sentencing my parents to death, but he'd do it to serve the greater good.

If it had been me in the library, bashed over the head and left to die on the floor? I can't guarantee he'd do anything other than what he's doing right now—chatting easily with Aphrodite. He might enjoy me, might care about me on some level, but he won't put me before the city.

Expecting him to will only end in heartbreak.

I can't breathe. Oh gods, I can't do this.

Time moves strangely. On one hand, it feels like we just sat down for dinner when the staff is clearing away dessert and it's over. I don't eat anything. It's taking every bit of willpower I have to sit still and not flee the room. Apollo shoots me a few looks, but Ariadne is seated next to us and he's focusing on charming her.

It's only as dinner ends that I realize we still have another of Minos's godsdamned games to suffer through before we can escape.

Minos surprises me, though. He clears his throat. "I think, given the events of this afternoon, that it would be best if we postponed tonight's entertainment. There will be an after-dinner drink served in the lounge, but it's hardly mandatory."

I grab Apollo's arm as he starts to shift his chair back. "I can't—" My voice comes out ragged, and I have to clear my throat and try again, quiet enough only he can hear. "Apollo, I can't do more small talk. I'm going to start screaming and never stop."

His dark brows draw together in concern and he gives a jerky nod. "Of course. I had no idea you were that distressed."

I have no idea how you aren't.

I don't say it. It's not fair. It's not even his fault that we're built so differently when it comes to this. If my parents had been successful, maybe I'd be just as blasé. Maybe.

Whatever he sees on my face has him frowning harder. "Let's go back to the room."

"Okay," I whisper. I'm unraveling at the seams. I'm not built for this kind of thing. I thought Hermes was being dramatic when she said I was in danger.

I should have known better. She never gambles with those she cares about, even if she won't step in to save them from themselves. I chose to stay.

I never expected to be dragged down memory lane, triggered by one of the most traumatic experiences of my life. My parents didn't believe me that the Thirteen would never stand for them to trigger the assassination clause. The police didn't believe me that the Thirteen murdered my parents. Now no one is believing me about the danger this party represents.

Am I doomed to repeat the same warnings, only to have to stand by and watch the people I care about be hurt?

APOLLO

I'VE MADE A MISTAKE. I DIDN'T REALIZE CASSANDRA WAS SO upset until the moment she said something. Instead of taking care of her, I was focused on the mystery of who attacked Pan. On speculating what motivations could possibly keep the others here after the attack. No matter how they acted, the Thirteen are not usually so foolhardy. And to the best of my knowledge, Charon never is. It speaks to their determination to get close to Minos that they are letting his plans override their normal levels of caution.

It's enough to make me wonder if some of them know more about Minos and his connections to this enemy of Olympus than they're saying.

I lead Cassandra back to our room and shut the door softly behind us. Guilt swarms me as I take her in. She's *shaking*. "I'm sorry."

"I…" She exhales. "I forget sometimes that you're a completely different species from most people. You in the plural term. Not you specifically."

I catch her hands. "Cassandra." She's paler than normal, drawn. "Let me—"

"You should go have a drink or two." She gently extracts her hands from mine. "Ariadne is still down there, and if you can get her away from the group, you can give her a proper offer to get her to change sides."

She's not wrong. All through dinner, Ariadne was laughing a bit too hard and talking a bit too fast. She's obviously scared, and I might be a monster for using her fear to Olympus's gain, but it's a lever I can pull to convince her to do what I want.

But it means leaving Cassandra alone, upset and vulnerable.

"I'm not leaving you."

"Apollo." She gives a sad smile. "You don't have to play the hero for me. I know Olympus is your great love and responsibility. Do your duty. I'll lock the door."

She's right. I know she's right, but now that we're here and alone, the events of the afternoon come crashing back over me. I don't know why someone would target Pan, but the attack could have just as easily been against Cassandra. She's been threatened several times since arriving at this party.

If someone snuck up behind her, hit her before she could run...

The thought has me reaching for her. "Come here."

"Apollo—"

"I'm not fucking leaving you, Cassandra. You can keep arguing or you can come here and let me hold you until we both feel better."

It's a testament to how rattled she is that she places her hand in mine and allows me to pull her close and wrap my arms around her. With her body pressed to mine, I can feel the little tremors working through her. Part of me still wants to insist she leave, but she's made her choice and I'll respect it.

I'll also do my best to ensure she doesn't pay a price staying.

But it's neither here nor there tonight. I'll do whatever I can to make her feel better. With anyone else, that would include wrapping her up and tucking her in until she falls asleep, but I've learned not to make assumptions with this woman. "What do you need from me?"

She gives a hoarse little laugh against my chest. "You'll think the worst of me."

"Cassandra, I could never think the worst of you."

A long pause. I stroke her back as I wait her out. Finally, she fists her hands in the fabric of my shirt and mutters. "I need you to fuck me until I can't think anymore."

I freeze. "I—"

"If you don't want to, that's fine. I realize it's an unconventional choice." She's still speaking softly, still pressing her head to my chest so she doesn't have to look at me. "But if you're about to remind me that I don't have to feel obligated to have sex with you, I will point out, once again, that the only power you have over me is what I choose to give you."

My heart gives a painful lurch. "Cassandra, look at me."

She reluctantly lifts her head. Some of her shakiness has disappeared. "Please, Apollo."

I can deny her nothing. There's a kind of care in kink and sex, and it's not a route I would have suggested, but if she needs this, I'm only too happy to give it to her. At least *this* I can fix. I brush my thumb over her cheek. "Tell me your safe word."

Cassandra gives a faint smile, relief evident on her gorgeous face. "Python."

It's so easy to slip into the role with her. I press a soft kiss to her forehead and step back. "Take off your dress." My voice is softer than I've used with her in the past during these moments, but she needs a soft place to land after the events of today.

I can offer her that. I *want* to offer her that.

Cassandra is not one for unquestioning obedience in life, and I appreciate that deeply. I honestly expected her to be more of a brat in these kinds of interactions, but she submits so sweetly. She doesn't hesitate to pull her hair over her shoulder and turn around. "Will you unzip me?"

I step forward and catch the absurdly tiny zipper at the top of the dress. It would be so easy to rip, but while I can enjoy that kind of game, it's not what either of us needs right now. This might be working its way to sex, but it's about care, not pure lust.

I drag the zipper down the length of the dress and then run my knuckles up the center of her spine. She's so *soft*, it drives me to distraction. Even though I told her to remove the dress, I'm the one that eases the straps off her shoulders and down her arms. Then I coast my hands down her sides and over her hips, pushing the fabric before me.

As I discovered earlier, she's not wearing panties, but she *is* wearing a bra. I do away with it quickly, flicking the clasp open and repeating the motion of easing the straps down her arms. I press a kiss to one shoulder before I step back.

Then I allow myself to look my fill.

It doesn't take long for Cassandra to start squirming, each movement making her ass flex. I have to clench my fists to keep from reaching for her. Not yet. This is a careful dance between us, the tension strung tight. Too much anticipation will have her brain clicking on. Too little will dampen the escape she needs. More, I love looking at her.

She's perfect.

Thick waist, wide hips and ass, thick thighs that I really enjoyed having clasped around my head. I take a slow breath. Yes, that's enough. "Turn around."

She's slower to obey this time. As Cassandra turns to face me, she actually starts to raise her hands to cover herself before she lets them drop to her sides.

I clear my throat. She's just as perfect from the front as she is from the back. Oh, not in the glossed-over look that so many people seem to strive for; Cassandra is *real*. More importantly, for tonight at least, she's mine to care for.

I glance around the room and finally settle on the chair tucked into the corner by the dresser. I stride over and sink onto it. "Come here."

She obeys almost tentatively. I lean back in the chair and watch her make her way to me. She's standing on firmer ground, but she's not quite here with me yet. "Gods, Cassandra, the things you do to me. You're temptation personified."

She misses a step, her gaze snapping to mine. "Excuse me?"

"It's the pencil skirts. Every time you turn around, your perfect ass is right there and I'm fighting for my life to keep things proper and professional."

"Apollo." She raises her brows. "I am reasonably confident in how I look, but no one is going to look at my ass and label it perfect."

"Are you calling me a liar?"

She worries her bottom lip. "I guess not." She stops in front of me, a few inches short of my knees. "I've looked at you, too."

"Tell me."

The blush beneath her skin deepens. For someone who can be so cool and collected while facing down any number of powerful people, it's remarkably easy to make her blush. I like that. It feels like it's just for me. Cassandra tugs at a strand of her hair. "You know you're sexy as fuck. Don't try to pretend you don't. And you show up every day in these perfectly tailored suits. I'm human. Of course I've looked."

I check her expression. She's entirely focused on me now, not thinking about the scary things that happened earlier. Good. "Have you done more than look?"

She licks her lips. "It would be the height of unprofessionalism for me to finger myself the second I walk through the door of my apartment because I spent two hours in a meeting staring at the hollow of your throat after you loosened your tie."

I lean forward and catch her hips, urging her closer until she stands straddling me. Better. This time, I keep touching her as I lean back, running my hands lightly down the outsides of her thighs and back up again. Her skin is so *soft*. It makes me want to taste every inch of her.

All in good time.

"Did you do that, Cassandra?"

"Yes." She answers so simply. "More than once. It infuriated me every time. I didn't want to want you."

"And now?"

"I still don't want to want you." The words contain no edge, but they fall between us like stones. It's going to hurt her when this ends, too. Maybe that should be enough to make me change course, but the truth is that we've gone too far to escape unscathed.

We had even before we kissed the first time.

"Do you trust me, Cassandra?"

"Yes." No hesitation.

It makes my chest ache in the most glorious way to hold the trust of this prickly, capable woman. I love her. I've known it for some time, but I can admit it to myself right now, in this moment. It's going to break my heart when she leaves, and I'm not selfish or cruel enough to tell her how I feel with that deadline bearing down on both of us. She cares for me, but even if she felt exactly as I do, I won't put her in a position of choosing between me and her sister. She's suffered enough as the result of the powerful in Olympus.

"Go to the bed and lie down on your back."

She blinks down at me. I find myself holding my breath as Cassandra considers me. She doesn't make me wait long. "Okay."

I make myself stay seated as she obeys. I get a flash of her pussy as she crawls along the middle of the bed and eases onto her back, and the sight has me fighting down a groan. Patience. I can have patience. Tonight isn't about me and what I desire. It's about giving her what she needs.

"What did you think about the last time you touched yourself?"

"I—"

"I would like to hear it. In explicit detail." I push slowly to my feet and shrug out of my jacket. My fingers fumble a bit as I unbutton my cuffs and start on the ones down the center. I pause after two and raise my brows. "I'm waiting."

She smiles faintly. "You like hearing me talk, don't you?"

"It's one of my favorite things," I answer honestly. "You're the smartest person I've ever met, and I love your mind." I smile. "I also love hearing you go breathless when you talk about what you desire."

"What I *desire* is for you to take off your shirt."

I tug at the third button...and then stop.

She huffs out a breath. "Okay, fine. The last time was after that meeting about Aphrodite—the previous Aphrodite."

I remember exactly what she's talking about. The last Aphrodite was exiled from Olympus some months ago, but she's not the type to disappear quietly and leave everyone in peace. In the time she's been gone, she's attempted to launch no less than three smear campaigns against Psyche Dimitriou. At Zeus's instruction, I've managed to catch all of them early and dispel them; he doesn't want a whisper of scandal to touch his new wife's family.

That particular meeting had gone long while we sat in on a video call with the team tasked to take down all the posts she'd managed to publish, along with a particularly damning interview scheduled to go live the next morning. Afterward, I was furious enough to have gone through the same song and dance three times that I ordered my team to find a way to plant a virus in her computer and erase everything, with a threat that her finances would be next if she continued on this route. "What was it about that mess that got to you?"

"You were so mad." She shivers and my mouth starts watering. Cassandra watches closely as I unbutton my third button before she continues. "You never yell when you're mad. You just get sterner and it made me so hot to imagine you talking to me like that."

"I've never had to talk to you like that."

"You did last night." She laughs a little. "You're doing it right now."

I pause on the fourth button. "Keep going, Cassandra. You went home quickly after the meeting."

"Of course I did. My panties were soaked and I was halfway there before I even walked out the door." She clenches her thighs together. "I pictured you telling me to strip the moment I walked through the door, kind of like you just did earlier. And then I touched myself."

"Show me."

Her hand immediately shifts down to her pussy. She creates a V with her fingers and presses hard to either side of her clit. "I was so close, I knew I'd finish too quickly, so I teased myself." She pulses her fingers, parting her pussy a little. "I wanted your mouth on me." She sucked in a breath. "I want your mouth on me right now."

I fumble my way through unbuttoning the rest of my shirt and shrug it off. My hands are shaking. I need to touch her, taste her, make her feel good. I take one step before I catch myself and manage to exert some control. "When I fuck you in your fantasies, how do I do it?"

Her fingers pause and she blinks up at me. "You hold me down, but I feel so damn cared for even as you restrain me. You..." Her blush deepens. "You go slow and torment me until you lose control and then it's a little rough and hits exactly where I need."

"Like I did last night."

She gives a jerky nod. "Yes. Like that."

"It won't be hard tonight, Cassandra. It's not what you need."

Her brows draw together and she opens her mouth like she wants to argue with me. I wait. She finally gives a cute little growl. "Fine. You're right. It's not what I need tonight."

I consider her. "Spread your legs for me. Let me see all of you."

She eases her thighs farther apart. As she does, Cassandra become bolder with how she touches herself. She presses a single finger into her pussy and then brings her wetness up to circle her clit. My cock goes so hard, I get a little dizzy from the blood rushing south.

"Better hurry." Her voice has gone breathy and low. "Otherwise I'll finish before you ever reach the bed."

"No, Cassandra." When her hand pauses, I shake my head sharply. "Keep going." I circle the bed and hesitate when I catch a glimpse of something golden and shining in my suitcase that most certainly wasn't there when we left the room earlier. I bend down and pick it up, disbelief making me laugh. "Godsdamn it, Hermes."

"What is it?"

I turn to her with the golden bondage rope draped between my hands. "Your ex left us a little gift."

"She's real thoughtful like that." Cassandra hasn't stopped working herself. "Probably did it to fuck with you."

"Undoubtedly." But for the first time since I realized Cassandra and Hermes have a history, that prickly jagged feeling inside me has been washed away. It might be only for a short time, but Cassandra is naked and writhing in my bed. She's allowing *me* to take care of her, to see to her needs.

I test the length of rope. It's different from what I've used in the past, silky instead of sturdy. "Cassandra—"

"Yes, you can tie me up." She says the sentence so fast, the words are all mashed together. "I would like that very much, and yes I trust you, and yes I promise to use my safe word if something's wrong and communicate if anything feels like it's cutting off circulation. Please, Apollo."

I like that she's already anticipating the things that would make me pause, that she's communicating with me without hesitation. She's right here with me. "Sit up and put your hands in front of you in a prayer position."

Cassandra obeys immediately. She's breathing hard, but she manages to raise a brow at me. "Am I going to be worshipping tonight?"

"No, love. You're going to be the one worshipped."

CASSANDRA

MAYBE, GIVEN ENOUGH TIME, I'D EVENTUALLY BECOME used to the way Apollo's voice goes deep and stern when he's turned on and looking at me like I'm a buffet laid out for his personal enjoyment. Maybe.

No matter what else is true, I'm not thinking of anything but him and what he'll do next. It's a reprieve I desperately need, and he's giving me exactly what I asked for.

He circles back to the dresser and grabs a random hair tie I'd left there. It gives me the chance to take another moment to appreciate how fucking gorgeous he is. He has the kind of body that's seen on classical statues, muscled without being over the top about it. He obviously works out—something I was well aware of before, since he does it on his lunch breaks—but seeing his smooth skin on display makes me weak. I want to taste him and touch him and just press as much of myself against as much of him as possible.

He makes me feel safe, as if when he's in the room with me,

nothing else can touch me. If I'm honest, he's been making me feel safe for a very long time.

He turns and his cock is a painful-looking imprint on the front of his slacks. I swallow hard. "You should take your pants off."

"When I'm ready."

I shake my head. "I want you to have a good time, too, Apollo. This can't all be about me."

His eyes go wide and then narrow. "Cassandra." Gods, I love that firm tone he takes when I've done something to test him. "Tonight I'll have my hands on your naked body. No matter what else happens, I'm having the time of my life." He's smiling as he climbs onto the bed, and my brain does not have capacity to process Apollo crawling toward me with *that* look on his handsome face.

I expect him to stop a short distance away, but apparently we're past that now. He nudges my legs together and moves to kneel straddling them. His powerful thighs pressed against the outside of mine send a shiver through me.

Apollo reaches behind me and gathers my hair in careful hands. It takes a few moments to get it into what feels like a messy bun, and then he runs his hands over my neck and shoulders and upper back, obviously checking for stray hairs that might get tangled in the rope. I have to fight the urge to practically purr at the way he's taking care of me. Seeming to be satisfied, he sits back and begins running the rope through his hands.

I've seen dominants go through this ritual of checking rope before putting it on their submissives, but this feels different. Apollo lends a level of intent to the process that feels new and strange. It feels *good*.

The soft sound of the silken rope against his palms soothes me even as it makes the tension inside me coil tighter. I don't understand how these two things can exist at the same time, but none of my rules seem to apply with this man.

Apollo reaches the end of the rope and gives a low hum of approval. "Hermes takes good care of her toys."

I swallow hard. There's none of the tightness in his tone that was there earlier, but that doesn't change the fact that... "I don't want to talk about her anymore."

His lips curve. "Okay." He sifts back through the rope to the approximate middle and gently hooks it around the back of my neck. He eyes me and licks his lips. "If anything..." Apollo shakes his head. "This should feel firm but not pinching. If anything starts to tingle, tell me immediately."

"I will." When he still hesitates, I add, "I promise."

Finally, Apollo nods and begins.

It's slow, sensual work. That feeling of being taken care of amplifies and expands with each brush of his knuckles and tug of the rope as he carefully binds me. The rope crisscrosses in front of the hollow of my throat, angling down to catch my elbows in a very supportive position that allows me to rest them in the cradle of the silk. Then it crosses in a different pattern between my breasts to bind my hands together, palm to palm in the prayer position. The way he has my arms lifts my breasts and has them pressing tightly against my forearms.

He sits back and studies me. "Perfect." Apollo shifts around to my back and catches my chin in a firm hand, turning my face to the mirror over the dresser. "Look how beautiful you are, Cassandra."

As I look into the mirror, it's not my reflection I'm staring at. It's Apollo, and the way *he* is looking at *me*. He runs his hands lightly over my arms and brushes the undersides of my breasts with his thumbs. "Does anything feel too tight?"

There's not enough air in the room. He's teasing me right now and I might die if he doesn't touch me properly soon. "It feels good."

"Mmm." He lightly circles my nipples with his fingers. They're already pebbled, but his touch makes them tighten. I whimper and instinctively lean back, trying to get away from the pleasure so acute that it feels like pain.

Except there's nowhere to go. Apollo's hard body is behind me, and he's unyielding even as I squirm beneath his touch. "Apollo, please."

"I will give you everything you need, love." It almost sounds like a threat.

I can't process the fact that he called me *love*. My mind skips right over that word on his lips, spoken in that deep, firm tone. "But—"

He plucks at my nipples, drawing a whimper from my lips. "You can argue all you want, but I will have my way."

I press my thighs together, but it does nothing to assuage the need pulsing in my pussy. "I really hope your way includes orgasms and quickly."

His chuckle makes things low in my stomach clench. Part of me still can't believe this is happening, even as he resumes his position in front of me and eases me onto my back. Apollo's touch is just as gentle and firm as he is, his hands lingering on my stomach and hips in a way that feels downright worshipping.

As promised.

He nudges my thighs wide and exhales shakily. "Now I can finally see you properly."

"Apollo—"

"Hush."

I lift my head and give him an incredulous look. "Did you just *hush* me?" He doesn't respond with words. Instead, he drags his thumbs up the outside of my pussy, spreading me, and gives another of those deliciously shaky exhales. I bite my bottom lip. "I suppose I can be hushed if you keep doing that."

"I appreciate your obedience," he says in a distracted sort of way. He eases two fingers into me and a sound rumbles from his chest that's almost a growl. "Is all this for me?" He pumps slowly, exploring me. It's both similar to what he did last night and entirely different. "You're so wet, you're going to ruin the sheets."

I start to make a snarky response, but he presses his fingertips to my G-spot and my ability to think flees, leaving only stark truth in its wake. "It's for you," I cry out. "It's all for you."

"Good girl." His low words, his approval, send me over the edge. I orgasm with a cry that surely can be heard through the house. Apollo doesn't stop, though. He starts stroking my clit with his other hand, watching my face even as he keeps my orgasm going. "Give me another, love. You can do it."

As if I have a choice.

He leans down and presses a kiss to my knee even as he winds me up tighter, urges my pleasure higher. And, gods, the way Apollo looks at me. His heart is in his eyes, and it feels as if he's laying it at my feet even though he's most assuredly in the dominant role.

Every touch, every sweep of his gaze over my body... It's worship-ful, but it goes beyond that. He's not just happy to be fucking someone in general.

Apollo *sees* me.

The realization comes as he shifts down and presses a linger-ing kiss to my pussy. He keeps working me with his fingers, but his clever tongue drags leisurely over my clit, again and again. I reach for him without thinking, only to be brought up short by the bondage holding my hands together and my arms bent. "I want—" I fight against the bonds, which drives my need higher. "I need—"

He lifts his head long enough to say. "When I'm finished, you can make requests."

I blink down at him. "When you're finished."

"Yes. You asked me to take care of you. I'm doing it my way." He nips my thigh lightly. "If my nights with you are numbered, then I'll be damned before I cut any part of this short." A shadow flickers through his dark eyes, there and gone too quickly for my desire-addled brain to identify.

Something cracks and gives in my chest. To my horror, my lower lip quivers. "Apollo." So much in that single word. *I care for you. I might more than care for you, but I can't admit that because if I do, then I'll never leave. I* can't *stay.*

"Cassandra." His response contains just as many layers. I know him well enough to pick up on some of them, if not all. *I care, too. I won't ask you to stay.*

The moment stretches out between us, and all the things I can't say press against the inside of my lips. I didn't expect to feel this conflicted. I didn't expect…any of this. It doesn't change the circumstances, though, and we both know it.

Even if I wasn't planning to flee the city to save my sister, the events of this afternoon have been an unwelcome reminder of just how dangerous it is to be among the Thirteen. It wasn't Aphrodite or Hephaestus or Dionysus who was attacked. It was Pan. It could have just as easily been me. If I stayed, it might very well be me next time.

What happens to Alexandra if I get hurt?

If I die?

Apollo kisses me before I can ruin this with messy emotions and an impossible situation neither of us can solve without someone getting hurt. Better we be the ones to hurt than those who depend on us.

Again, I try to reach for him, and again, the rope pulls me up short.

This time, he doesn't leave me frustrated. He keeps kissing me as he starts to unwind the rope. The problem with the more elaborate forms of bondage is that it takes almost more time to get out of it than it does to get in, but with him, it doesn't feel like a chore. It's just a different form of foreplay.

The rope sags and he slips the last bit of it from me. I reach for him, but he catches my wrists in a light but firm grip. "No." He nips my bottom lip. "Tonight is about you."

"Well, *I* want to touch you."

He leans back enough to give me a rueful smile. "Later. I promise."

"Apollo…" Something resembling a whine works its way into my voice. "*Please.*"

His smile falls away. "At the beginning of this, you told me what you want. I'm going to give it to you." He picks up the rope again. "But I want better access to your breasts. Your hands."

It's not quite a command, but it's close enough. I slowly extend my arms and watch as he binds my wrists together. He's good. The rope loops several times down my forearms and around in those careful knots, ensuring that it doesn't put too much pressure on any one part of me.

He tests it. "Too tight?"

I want to be a brat about him removing the ability to touch him *again*, but I can't seem to summon the attitude. "No," I answer honestly.

"Good." He urges me onto my back and loops the tail of the rope behind the headboard and over the top. Then the bastard presses the loose end into my hands. "I trust you to obey me, love. Hold this."

Hold this.

What he means is to hold myself captive. I can't pretend he's tying me down and that I can't get free—safe word excepting, of course. No, he's ensuring I'm a willing participant in this because that's just who Apollo is.

It's a head fuck. Part of me wants to release it just to be perverse, to see what he'll do. The rest of me only wants to please him. That's the part that wins. I wrap the rope around my palm and tighten my fingers. "Okay."

"Good girl." He sits back on his heels and just looks at me. Again, I can't shake the truth that he sees me. Not just my body at the expense of my mind. Not my mind at the expense of my body. *Me.* All of me.

Apollo licks his lips. "Now, we can begin properly."

APOLLO

IN THE PAST, I'VE VIEWED SEX AS AN INTRICATE DANCE between myself and my partners. One of consent and power exchange and finding out exactly what makes them tick in order to bring them as much pleasure as possible. All those impulses are there with Cassandra. I am who I am, after all.

But they're superseded by sheer need.

My logical side has clicked off and there's only desire. It takes everything I have not to lose control now that she's naked and spread out, looking at me like I hold the keys to everything she needs. I want to be that for Cassandra. Desperately.

If I can't give her everything, at least I can give her pleasure. Escape. Comfort.

I smooth her hair back from her face and press a kiss to her forehead, the tip of her nose, her lips. She tries to arch and to deepen the kiss, but I keep moving before she can. I can't quite keep it light, though. I drag my mouth over the curve of her shoulder, the softness of her arm up to where the rope binds her, and then repeat the process on the other arm.

She shakes like a leaf, little whimpers slipping past her lips that I'm not certain she realizes she's making. It's a heady thing to affect this self-possessed woman so deeply. To have her trust me to guide this, to get her where she needs to be. I cherish the feeling, doing my best to memorize it as I move to her breasts.

I lavish attention on them, pressing them together so I can alternate between her nipples. I can't get enough. Gods, I can barely believe this is happening at all. It feels like a particularly vivid fantasy, as if at any moment I'll open my eyes and find myself alone in my bed, my fist wrapped around my cock.

I keep playing with her until her shaking has graduated to full tremors. Each breath is gasping and needy and her dark eyes have glazed over with desire. Only then do I move down, giving her stomach and hips the same thorough treatment. She's so lovely, it makes it hard to breathe.

As tempting as making her come again is, I promised to fulfill her fantasy and that's exactly what I intend to do. I deny us both and bypass her pussy, worshipping first one leg down to her ankle and then the other.

By the time I finally kneel between her thighs, we're both breathing hard and she's so wet, she's glistening. I drag my knuckle down her center. "Perfect."

"You keep saying that word." Her voice is ragged and hoarse.

"I mean it." I watch her face as I press two fingers into her. She's even wetter than she was earlier, her body more than ready for mine. "You're bold and smart and kind, Cassandra. It's a privilege to take care of you tonight, and I'm glad you trust me to be there for you."

She smiles, though her mouth trembles a little around the edges. "You're making it very difficult to protect my heart right now."

You don't have to protect your heart from me.

I don't say the words.

I run my hands up her thighs and press them wide. Her eyes slide half-shut as I grab a condom and rip open the package. It's quick work to get it on, but I make myself go slower than normal, ensuring it's properly done. This close to paradise, I'm determined to do nothing to taint the experience.

Now that the moment is here, it feels surreal. I prop myself up with a hand on the bed at her side to brace myself and press my cock into her. We both moan as I work into her in slow, shallow strokes. She wraps her thighs around my hips, urging me deeper. "More. Give me more."

"Impatient."

"For you? Always."

Kissing her is the most natural thing in the world. I can't believe I've spent the last five years *not* kissing Cassandra Gataki. She kisses me like she'll never get enough, like she wants to imprint this experience on her memory with the same intensity that I do.

It takes me a moment to gather my wits about me, to smother my instinct to drive into her as deeply as possible. She told me what she wants, and I'll be damned before I give her anything less than perfection.

I begin to move inside her slowly, but each stroke frays my ability to think, to plan. It feels too good to have her in my arms, her ankles locked at the small of my back. I lose myself a little more with each wave of pleasure that rises.

Time ceases to have meaning. There is only Cassandra. Her little helpless sounds. Her body moving against mine in a rhythm as old as time itself. Her eyes glazed with pleasure and yet focusing on me with an intensity that strikes right to my core.

Don't leave.

I love you.

Words I will never say.

I can only show her with my mouth, my hands, my cock. In this moment, everything I am is devoted to her pleasure. I change my angle so I can reach between our bodies to stroke her clit. Cassandra cries out. "More."

"Anything for you." The words have too much intensity, too much truth, but there's no recalling them now. I keep up the exact touch she seems to find the most pleasing and watch as she comes apart beneath me. I will never get enough of the moment of total surrender when she orgasms. The trust she places in me is staggering. I'll do everything I can to ensure she never regrets it.

I slow down, giving her time to come back to herself, giving myself time to wrestle back from the brink. She blinks up at me, dark eyes wide. "I want to touch you." I hesitate, but she presses harder. "Apollo, please."

Again, I can deny her nothing. The truth is that I want her hands on me and desperately. I nod jerkily. "Yes." I fumble for the rope binding her wrists, finally getting it loose with a curse that makes her laugh.

The first thing Cassandra does is cup my face in her hands

and tug me down for a devastating kiss. Everything falls away. This time, when I move inside her, it's with less control. It feels too good. *She* feels too good. She shifts one hand into my hair and coasts the other down my back to grab a fistful of my ass.

Just like that, my control snaps. I drive into her, needing to be deeper, needing to take her harder, simply *needing*. She cries out against my lips. Too soon. It's too soon, but neither of our bodies seem to care. Cassandra orgasms, her pussy clenching around me.

Words spill from me, drawn forth by sheer need. "You're perfect. Fucking *perfect*." I bury my face against her throat as I come. My body keeps moving even as my mind shorts out, grinding into her and making both of us moan.

Slowly, oh so slowly, the racing heartbeat in my ears starts to recede. I become aware of Cassandra tracing abstract patterns over my back. It feels good. Really good.

Still, there's the condom to consider.

I groan and start to shift away. She, naturally, responds by tightening her legs around my waist. "Just a little longer."

It's tempting to give in, but the longer we stay like this, the more likely for the condom to not work the way it was designed. I lean back enough to kiss her. "I'll be right back."

It's far more difficult than it has a right to be to leave her in bed and duck into the bathroom to dispose of the condom. I take a few seconds to clean up and hurry back into the bedroom, half-sure that the moment will have passed.

Cassandra is exactly where I left her, her body relaxed, her eyes closed. She opens them as I approach the bed. "Come here."

I'm all too happy to do exactly that. I climb onto the bed and settle next to her. It's the most natural thing in the world to pull her close. She fits perfectly against me and she does this achingly adorable little snuggling thing against me. She's not tense and upset like she was before. I've given her exactly what she needs, and that knowledge sits like a comfortable weight in my chest. I know I should hold her loosely in all things, but I can't help tightening my arms around her and drawing her closer yet.

If I only get this for a few more days, I will take everything she gives. Even these intimate little moments. Especially these intimate little moments.

"Apollo." She says my name slowly, dreamily. "You said fuck *three* times. That's got to be some kind of record."

That surprises a laugh out of me. "In that moment, I was... inspired."

"I'm taking it as the highest of compliments." She smiles against my skin. "I don't think I can walk. My legs are doing this little tremor thing that would be worrisome if I wasn't riding the high of like...multiple orgasms."

My chest can't decide whether it wants to expand or close. I settle for simply breathing. It's enough. Right here, right now, it's more than enough. "You come so beautifully, Cassandra. How could I not want to experience that as many times as possible?" I hesitate. Maybe now isn't the time to get into it, but I want her to know the truth. "I'm sorry that I brought you here and put you in a position where you were exposed to violence again, but I'm not sorry that this has happened between us."

"This afternoon..." She lifts her head, her expression going serious in a way that makes my stomach drop. "I know we don't move in the same world, for all that we both live in Olympus, but it's never been clearer." She swallows hard. "But I don't regret this time with you, either."

That's the crux of it. If it was a matter of money or power, I might be able to convince Cassandra to stay. But the reality that I cannot guarantee her safety if she didn't leave... It's too high a price to ask of her. No matter what my feelings are in the matter.

"Cassandra." I catch her chin in a light grip, enjoying the way her eyes flutter a bit at the contact. "Our time numbers in the days, the hours. I'm not going to do a single thing to shorten it."

"Me either." She lays her head down on my chest again and tightens her grip around my ribs.

The space between us is filled with things we've agreed not to speak about. I hold her close and smooth a hand over her hair. This moment is another to tattoo on my memory. Just as valuable as what preceded it. More, really.

Still, I am not going to waste a second of my time left with Cassandra.

I start to press her onto her back, but she wiggles out of my grip. When I raise my eyebrows, she smiles a little. "I feel a bit better now, and it seems a shame to waste all these hours alone with you." Her smile goes devious as she trails her nails lightly down my stomach. "May I, Apollo?"

I can deny her nothing. "Anything for you, love."

CASSANDRA

WE DON'T SLEEP MUCH THAT NIGHT. EVERY TIME WE START
to drift off, it's as if a frenzy overtakes us and then we're at it again,
burning through Apollo's condom stash. The way this man looks
at me... Even as pleasure washes away my thoughts again and
again, I can't quite shake the fear that this is the best it will ever be.

That I'll never be with someone who touches me the way
Apollo does.

That I'll never find someone who *sees* me the way Apollo does.

The temptation to stay in this bedroom and hide away from
the world is almost overwhelming. He feels it, too. It's there in the
almost desperate way he reaches for me upon waking, flipping
me onto my stomach and pleasuring me with his mouth until
I'm begging him to fuck me. This time, there's no slow teasing
or ramping up. He barely pauses long enough to roll on another
condom before he grabs my hips and fucks me like he can't get
close enough. I love every moment of it, even if I can't fully escape
the specter of what comes next.

Not even coming around his cock enough times to lose count can fully banish the threat of the future.

Or the memory of what happened in the library.

He finishes with a curse, grinding into me hard enough to shove me over the edge into yet another orgasm. I sob into the sheets. It's too much and yet at the same time I'm terrified that it will never be enough. Not enough pleasure, not enough memories to hold back the tide of time. Years passing have a way of dulling the edges, both good and bad. I know that better than most.

I will never forget Apollo, but will I always remember the feeling of his fingers imprinted on my hips? Will time eventually smudge the exact way he looks at me, as if the sun rises and sets at my pleasure?

I'm terrified of the answer.

He presses a kiss to the back of my neck and disappears just long enough to take care of the condom. He gathers me in his arms the moment he returns to bed. All I want to do is accept the comfort of his presence, his body, his control. The world seems so far away right now, and a selfish part of me wants to keep it that way.

We can't keep doing this, though. We have to talk about the party. About Pan. "Of everyone here, why attack Pan? Or make Atalanta go missing, if that's what has actually happened. Or threaten *me?* Why target the plus-ones? That's what I can't make sense of."

"I can't make sense of it, either. Pan is well-liked and there's no strategic reason to attack him. It's possible he has dangerous secrets, but I don't know why the attack would happen here, of all places."

That's the kicker. The probability of Pan's attacker *not* being a guest is so low as to be nonexistent. Looking at it from that angle is the wrong choice; I'm sure of it. "It has to be someone here. Maybe Minos wants the Dryad?"

"Everyone wants the Dryad." Apollo sounds so frustrated, I want to hug him. "It seems heavy-handed, but I suppose that could be part of it. Pan has no family, so if he dies without a will, the Dryad will go up for auction. But that's a lot of ifs, and even if it went to auction, there are people with much deeper pockets in this city. Dionysus, for one, would be the first in line and he can afford it."

I think about how sick he looked after the attack. Surely... I sit up. "Do you think Minos is offering to get his hands dirty so the party guests don't have to?" It seems a reach when the Thirteen are more than capable of murder on their own, but this Zeus is not the same as the last one. *This* Zeus wants stability, and you don't get stability in a time like this by murdering for profit.

I don't like thinking about Dionysus agreeing to that sort of bargain, but he's one of the Thirteen. I can't afford to assume anything.

"It's...possible. Gods, I hadn't even considered that it might be an option." Apollo frowns, obviously thinking hard. "But that doesn't explain the threats against you."

"Right, but you're not here to bargain with Minos. You're here to investigate him." The more I talk my way through it, the more sense it starts to make. "Maybe he thought if he threatened me, it would distract you from your task."

He glares at the ceiling. "He wasn't entirely wrong, if that's the case." He pinches the bridge of his nose. "But what about Atalanta? She's from a powerful family, but she doesn't have any holdings like the Dryad."

I sigh. "I don't know. Maybe she does have something Artemis wants, but we just don't know about it." That's the problem. Even with the progress we've made, we just don't know enough. "But that would at least explain why none of them are worried about being targeted—because they brought the targets with them." This theory doesn't apply to Charon and Eurydice, but they're here for the same reason we are. To find answers.

I wish I could say the same for Aphrodite and Adonis, but as much as I like her, the fact remains that she's a Kasios, and that family has more than proven that they will trample people to reach their aims. I'm not entirely certain what purpose removing Adonis would serve, but I can't ignore the possibility that she's more than ruthless enough to make that call.

I drag my fingers through my hair. "I need to try to talk to Hermes again. Out of everyone here, she seems to have some idea of what's actually going on. I don't know if she'll tell me the truth, but I have a better shot than anyone else." I'm nearly certain Tyche never actually arrived at this party. I don't know her well, but she's the mischievous youngest daughter of one of the legacy families. She's not in line to inherit and she's well-liked by most everyone.

Except Tyche's parents, who don't like that she spends time with Hermes.

Surely Hermes wouldn't hurt the woman to punish her parents?

No. I'm right. I know I am. Hermes can be just as ruthless as the rest of the Thirteen, and even cruel when it suits her, but she wouldn't hurt a friend just to punish an enemy.

Would she?

"You have a better chance at getting information out of her than I do." He makes a face. "Though after yesterday, I don't like the idea of letting you out of my sight."

I don't really relish the idea of wandering this house without him at my side, either. "It's the only way. She won't talk to me frankly if you're there." She might not even do it if we're alone, but...I have to try. And not only to fulfill my side of the bargain with Zeus. What happened with Pan yesterday more than proved that Hermes's warning has merit. Even if we don't fully understand why Pan was attacked, we don't know who did it or if they intend to strike again. That means *Apollo* is potentially in danger as well.

I have to keep reminding myself that he was moving through Olympus's shark-infested waters years before I ever came into his life, and no one stuck a literal knife in his ribs during that time. That they're unlikely to do it now, even if Minos is an unknown factor. Apollo doesn't actually *need* me to watch his back. The only real value I have is that I've spent so much time on the sidelines, studying the powerful in order to escape their wrath, that I have insight into people's motivations that he doesn't. If it comes down to a fight of any sort, I'm worse than useless.

Apollo does not need me.

The thought should reassure me, but it feels strangely like a lie. "Please be careful," I blurt out.

His dark brows draw together. "I won't be reckless, but I don't know that I can promise to be careful. If an opportunity comes to get the information we need, then I have to take it."

I know that. Of course I know that. But the panic bleating inside me won't listen. "Is Olympus really worth your life?"

He smooths my hair back. Anyone else would attempt to soothe me with meaningless reassurances. Not Apollo. He's oh so serious as he holds my gaze. "You don't think highly of the Thirteen, and with good reason. But the fact remains that we work for Olympus's benefit." He clears his throat at my look of disbelief. "*Some of us* work for Olympus's benefit. You might not like the method, but the people of this city are protected, both upper city and lower. No one goes hungry. Our crime rates are lower than any city of comparable size."

"Those things might be true, but it's not the full picture." I shake my head. "We both know that crimes committed by the powerful get swept under the rug."

He opens his mouth, seems to reconsider, and finally nods. "Fair point. It's not a perfect system, and I'd be lying if I said it was." He sighs. "I didn't take the title of Apollo to make a grab for power. That may have been what my family wanted, but I knew there might be sacrifices involved with being a member of the Thirteen. I will do whatever is required to keep this city and all the people in it safe."

The answer is so perfectly Apollo. Of all the people who currently hold titles for selfish reasons, he would be the one who saw the title as a custodianship instead of a throne elevating him over the heads of all those lesser.

I love you.

I clamp my lips together to keep the words from springing free. It's getting harder and harder not to tell him how I feel, no matter how selfish and unfair it would be to confess. There's nothing else to do but get ready and carry on with the mission. As tempting as it is to try to seduce him into staying in bed with me and pretending the rest of the party doesn't exist...it's impossible.

Everything about this situation is impossible.

"I'll take a shower, then."

He stops me with his hand on my shoulder. "I won't let anything happen to you."

I force a smile. "And what about you?" The risk to Minos's other party guests might be nonexistent if my theory is correct, but the same can't be said for Apollo. He's a threat and Minos knows it.

Apollo shrugs. "Like I said, risk goes with the territory."

We could go round and round like this for hours, but nothing will change. I'm leaving. He's staying, noble white knight that he is. It's why I love him, even if right now I wish he'd be selfish for once, look to his own interests instead of Olympus's.

But even if I was staying, this would never work in the long term. He's at home swimming in waters deep enough to drown me.

I head for the bathroom and take my time getting ready. Normally, my morning rituals and beauty regimen make me feel better and more centered by the end of the process. It's the kind of mindless repetition that usually allows my brain to work out problems the same way that driving is supposed to.

Instead, I seem to blink and I'm ready. There's no peace to be found. I glance at the bathroom door, worry gnawing in my stomach. When I agreed to come here, I honestly thought the only thing in danger would be my heart. I didn't expect actual assault.

I'm doing this for Alexandra.

On impulse, I grab my phone and dial my sister. The phone rings several times before clicking over to voicemail. Her happy voice says, "You've reached Alexandra Gataki. I'm probably in class or working right now, but if you leave a message, I'll get back to you as soon as possible. Have a great day!"

I sigh and hang up. She's working her ass off in order to pave the way to a better future. I can do no less than the same.

I open the door to find Apollo on the bed, working on his laptop. He looks so deliciously mussed with the sheets gathered around his waist and his black hair on end from me running my fingers through it. He looks up and smiles as if just the sight of me is enough to make his day.

It could be like this...

I ignore the little voice inside my head and move to get dressed. I feel a little shaky, as if the ground is shifting beneath my feet, so I choose the dress I'd saved for a time when I needed the emotional boost. My favorite. It's a deep silver that's almost black, and I immediately feel better when I have it on. I learned long ago that clothing can change a person's perspective, both the one I have of myself and that of others who look at me. It's a different kind of armor than Ares's soldiers wear but it serves much the same purpose, even if the weapons being sharpened by the upper crust in Olympus are words and ambition instead of guns and knives.

It won't protect me against either, though.

True to form, Apollo doesn't take long to shower and get

ready. He sweeps a glance over me as he steps out of the bathroom. "You look devastating."

"Thanks." I check my lipstick in the mirror and pull on my heels. I can't look at him directly because if I do, I'm going to touch him, and if I touch him, I can't account for what happens next. It's tempting to do it anyway, to prolong this relative peace when it's only the two of us, but I manage to restrain myself. "Is Hector still working through the emails?"

"Yes. He's managed to eliminate everything that definitely wasn't useful and now he's wading through the rest." He finishes buttoning his shirt. "It takes time to track down all the threads, but he should have an update later today."

"Good."

He offers his arm. "Shall we?"

Downstairs, most of the rest of the guests have beaten us to the table. The only two spots left are between Hermes and Pandora. I'm surprised when Apollo presses a hand to the small of my back and urges me to take the seat next to Hermes. Then again, is it really that surprising? From the start, he's aimed to protect me. Though from the beaming smile Pandora gives him as he takes his seat, maybe he'll be more successful at easing her into conversation than I would have been.

Then she turns it on me.

She reminds me a bit of Persephone Dimitriou, at least before she ran off and fell in love with Hades and shed the happy princess persona. Except...more. Having this woman smile at me is like getting a straight shot of the midsummer sun. I can only blink in response.

"I don't think we've been properly introduced." She reaches across Apollo with a charmingly apologetic wince. "I'm Pandora."

"Cassandra." Her palm is warm and smooth against mine. "Nice to meet you," I say. I don't stammer, but it's a near thing. She's *beautiful.*

"The feeling is entirely mutual."

On my other side, Hermes snickers. I remember myself enough to turn and shoot a glare at her. "Shut up."

"Always so cranky until you see a pretty face, and then you forget that you know how to talk." She nudges me with her shoulder. There's no edge to her voice, just a deep fondness that speaks of our long history.

Apollo, though, tenses. "Leave her alone, Hermes."

She holds up a finger, nails painted matte black. "One: you should know better, since I don't leave anyone alone." She lifts another finger. "Two: Cassandra is more than capable of defending herself if she feels the need to."

"Just because she can doesn't mean she should."

This feels strange. I can't decide if it's a good kind of strange or a bad kind of strange, but I'm not inclined to let them argue over me like two dogs with a bone. Even if they're both coming at the conversation with the intention of protecting *me.* "That's enough."

Apollo opens his mouth but seems to reconsider whatever he was about to say. He gives a short nod and turns to his plate. Hermes narrows her eyes like she wants to keep provoking him, but I catch her gaze and shake my head silently. She sighs. "*Fine.* I'll behave."

Lunch is a surreal experience. It's so...normal. Everyone chats easily as if a man wasn't almost murdered a few rooms away less than twenty-four hours ago. I knew the Thirteen and those close to them were different animals, but it's never been clearer than in the time since Pan was attacked.

Especially considering my new theory that they're here for Minos to do their dirty work in return for part of the profits.

Don't they realize that this will give him leverage over them? Or do they really think they're that untouchable?

Or maybe they're planning a double cross once they get what they want from him? All the gain and none of the possibility of sharing the rewards or future blackmail.

The possibilities make my head spin. I can't be the only one who sees the dangers. Surely I'm not. But they've ignored my warning so far. They truly think they're untouchable. Even Apollo, in his own way. He's willing to endanger himself for the greater good.

By the time they realize they might be wrong, it will be too late.

APOLLO

PANDORA IS A LOVELY CONVERSATIONALIST AND I DETECT some social training in the way she's so effortlessly able to keep the topics light but interesting. Safe. She also successfully dodges all my careful probes for information. She's cheerful in the extreme, but she's no fool.

Then again, no one in Minos's party appears to be a fool. Unfortunate, that.

Even Ariadne is making herself scarce after sitting next to me at dinner last night.

Minos clears his throat, and I can't help tensing up in response. Another party game is coming, another frustrating set of hoops to jump through for his amusement. They were irritating before. Now participating feels particularly ghoulish.

The facade of concern is gone from Minos today. He's smiling as brightly as I've become accustomed to, and his voice is boisterous as he comments on the quality of the meal we just consumed. But there's something… I can't quite put my finger on it. Something off.

Cassandra squeezes my knee and leans close. "You're glaring."

I make an effort to smooth my expression, but it's more difficult than normal. What is it about him that's making my instincts stir?

Minos gestures broadly. "This week has been more than I could have dreamed. I am incredibly grateful that you've all consented to come here and allow me to entertain you."

More like *he's* the one entertained by the whole process. It's not as if he's participating. He's sitting back and watching us—watching me—run around like a rat in a maze. I catch myself clenching my jaw and focus again on relaxing my expression.

"Did you know my dear departed wife, Pasiphae, was a great fan of historical romance books?" He continues without waiting for an answer. I catch sight of Ariadne across the table, looking like she wants to melt into the ground. "It's in her honor that we play these games."

I raise my brows. *And here I thought it was solely to humiliate some of the most powerful people in Olympus for your own amusement.* Or, if Cassandra is right, to commit violent acts to gain leverage on those same people.

As if sensing my thought, Cassandra squeezes my thigh. She doesn't look at me, but it's enough of a reminder to stop glaring. I've never had this much trouble controlling my expression, but I've never dealt with a frustration like Minos represents. Even with the progress we've made, he represents everything that is wrong with this city. Power and corruption, and too many of my peers are willing to wade into the muck if it means getting ahead.

Minos continues, ignoring the looks people are exchanging around the table. "With that in mind, this afternoon is her particular favorite for *her* favorite child. I'm not sure why. Since he was a little boy, he hasn't done a single damn thing right. Always the fuckup, aren't we, Icarus?" He laughs, but no one else at the table does.

This isn't the first time I've heard a parent be terrible to their child in what amounts to a public setting, but it's extremely uncomfortable. Icarus looks a little sick to his stomach, but he's been particularly quiet during the whole meal, his face drawn and dark circles beneath his eyes.

Minos continues, blatantly ignoring the strange currents that he caused. "Blindman's bluff."

"What the fuck is that?" Cassandra murmurs.

There's no way Minos could hear her, but he answers all the same. "One of the party is blindfolded and disoriented and must guess the identity of the person they touch."

It's a strange game, and an even stranger choice to pick a "winner" through. Aphrodite leans back, her dark eyes challenging. She's tucked under Adonis's arm, but there's a new tension in her since the events of yesterday. She keeps touching him almost possessively, and while she hasn't looked at Theseus once during the entire meal, there's no doubt it's for his benefit.

Now, she sarcastically raises her hand. "A question."

Minos's smile doesn't flicker. "Yes, Aphrodite?"

"The game ends when the blindfolded person guesses the identity of the person they touch. How can there be a group winner?"

"Ah, yes, that is traditionally how the game is played. For

our purposes, though, I propose an alternative way." He chuckles. "The one blindfolded will go around the circle and guess as many identities as possible. The person with the most correct guesses will take Icarus off my hands." His chuckle turns to a booming laugh. "Sorry, I misspoke. They win a *date* with Icarus. If only getting rid of this son was such an easy task!"

"I see," she says slowly.

"Shall we begin?" He turns and leads the way out of the dining room.

I exchange a look with Cassandra. "Wait until after." I don't dare say more with so many witnesses, not even speaking low in her ear. She'll understand. There's no point in trying to pull Hermes aside to talk now.

"Of course." She rolls her eyes, though the expression is half-hearted. "Let's do this."

Once again, we find ourselves back in the elaborate living room. If before I could not define why Minos made his choices with these games, today it's abundantly clear that he intends to humiliate Icarus for some unknown reason. Minos sits in the so-called place of honor in a high-backed chair that we form a reluctant ring around, with Icarus at the head. As at the table, he looks like he wants to be anywhere but here.

It makes me wonder if Icarus is just as unhappy with coming to Olympus as Ariadne seems to be. If one child is willing to work against their father, maybe the other is as well. I'll ask Cassandra after this. If my instincts are occasionally wrong, hers rarely are. She sees things that I miss all the time. Perhaps now is one of those times.

"For our first attempt..." Minos's smile goes sly. "Aphrodite, if you would be so kind."

She stands gracefully. Today she's wearing a pair of tailored black pants and a violet silk blouse that leaves her arms bare. Her dark hair hangs in a curtain down her back as she strides to Minos and turns around so he can slip a blindfold over her face.

"Now, of course, we won't want to make it too easy. Shift yourselves about the room, please."

Cassandra huffs out an exasperated breath as I follow her, moving to stand next to the fireplace, across from where we'd been. She doesn't say anything, though. We're too busy watching Minos carefully spin Aphrodite in place. Too many times, by my count, but I'm not the one running the game.

As it is, when he releases her, she stumbles. Not a single person makes a sound. It's strangely eerie to watch her move forward with her hands outstretched. She finds Adonis first. He holds perfectly still as her hands come to rest on his chest. From my angle, I can catch her smile in profile. She coasts her hands up to his shoulders and over his neck to his strong jawline. He smiles as she explores his face with her fingertips.

Aphrodite laughs lightly. "I would know that smile anywhere, Adonis." She leans up and presses a kiss to his lips.

Then she moves on. She's better at the game than I would have reckoned. She mixes up the Minotaur and Theseus, but that may be because she seems reluctant to touch both. She also mistakes Eurydice for Artemis, which has Artemis glaring holes in her back. The rest of us, she guesses correctly, working her way around the circle until she stands before Pandora, who's on my other side.

Though no one has confirmed or denied the guesses, she *must* know who it is she touches as she ghosts her fingers over the other woman's arms and cups her face in surprisingly gentle hands. Aphrodite gives a wicked smile. "Only one way to say for certain."

Then she kisses Pandora.

Without thinking, I look to Theseus. This is just another power play between him and Aphrodite, but I can't help a shudder at the sheer fury in his eyes as he watches them. I hadn't pegged his relationship with Pandora to be overly romantic, but they're obviously close, and he's undeniably enraged to see Aphrodite kissing her.

Aphrodite lifts her head, smiling. "Hello, Pandora."

"Hi." For her part, Pandora's a little breathless.

And so it goes.

Each turn, Minos spins the blindfolded person and the rest of the guests rearrange themselves. I give up trying to stay next to Cassandra after the second round. There's no reason to. She never leaves my sight.

The Minotaur does horridly, only guessing Theseus, Icarus, and Pandora correctly. Charon and Hephaestus only do slightly better. Dionysus seems to do poorly on purpose, though with him it's impossible to say if that's feigned or no. Adonis doesn't seem to care at all, rattling off names the moment he touches a person, usually guessing incorrectly. Artemis does nearly as well as Aphrodite. Cassandra gets everyone but the Minotaur correct.

Hermes, of course, has a perfect round. She tweaks Theseus's beard, plants a kiss on Dionysus's forehead, flirts shamelessly with everyone she touches, and kisses Cassandra with a little too much gusto for my peace of mind.

My jealousy has faded, though, nowhere near as pointed as it was yesterday. It helps that a blushing Cassandra sends me an apologetic look the moment Hermes moves on, that her gaze lingers on *me* even as we move on to Eurydice, who gets about half her guesses correct.

Then it's finally my turn.

While watching everyone else, I underestimated how disorienting it would be to be blindfolded. I try to listen for the movements of the others, but with Minos spinning me, it's an impossible task. When he finally releases me, I haven't the slightest clue where everyone has relocated to.

I hate this game.

I feel like an absolute fool as I stretch out my hands and move directly forward. I dislike having my senses distorted, and the sensation only gets worse when I gingerly touch a man. He's built lean, and the moment I reach his beard, I know. "Dionysus."

I move around the circle slowly. Most of these people, I would not consider friends, let alone someone I'd intentionally touch like this. I try to keep my hands up high enough that I don't accidentally brush against something I shouldn't, but it means that I end up bumping into Hermes's forehead instead of her shoulder when I reach her. "Sorry, Hermes."

I fumble my way through the rest of the guests. Though it's tempting to rush, my pride won't allow it. I guess as well as I can, finally ending on Cassandra. I know her the moment my hand closes on her soft shoulder. Still, I coast my touch up to cup her jaw and feel for her distinctive lips.

I smile. "Hello, Cassandra."

She's the one to remove the blindfold from my eyes, and she smiles up at me as I blink at the abrupt change. There's no time to say anything—I'm not even sure what I would say, since this is just a silly game—because Minos steps into the circle. "We have a clear winner! Hermes, congratulations."

Hermes grins and winks at Icarus. "We'll have some fun." In the face of her unrelenting cheerfulness, even Icarus manages a smile.

Minos laughs. "Without a doubt. Now, I do believe tea is ready to be served. I'll go check on the status of that. Please make yourselves comfortable." He strides out the door without looking back.

"Teatime. Of course. Why not?" Eurydice shakes her head and sinks down onto the love seat next to Charon. They're sitting slightly angled toward each other so their knees touch, and the careful way he holds himself at a respectful distance while maintaining that not-so-casual touch makes me both glad for Eurydice and sad for my foolish brother.

Charon gives a faint smile. "You like tea."

"Yes, I do. I'm also ready to go home. This wasn't fun before Pan got hurt, and now I'm jumping at every sound. I thought staying was the right thing to do, but that was obviously the wrong call. We're wasting our time here."

Charon takes her hand and lowers his head, speaking softly enough that I can't hear what he's saying. By my best guess, they'll be gone before dinnertime. Whatever Charon came here to find, if he hasn't found it by now, I doubt an extra day or two would change that.

Speaking of...

I turn to suggest Cassandra take the opportunity to speak with Hermes, but she's nowhere in sight. Both women are gone.

CASSANDRA

HERMES SLIPS THROUGH THE DOOR AS PEOPLE START settling in for the coming tea, and I don't pause to think. I go after her. I step into the hallway and find Hermes's dark hair and bright yellow sweater disappearing around the corner.

Where is she going?

She's already bypassed the bathroom conveniently located halfway down the hall, and she's not heading in the direction of the stairs to the second floor. I frown and start after her. I reach the corner in time to see her duck into what appears to be a random door. Strange.

I glance back toward the living room. The temptation to check in with Apollo before going farther is nearly overwhelming, but I already told him I planned to talk to Hermes. This might not be going like I expected, but everyone in the house is in that living room and I hardly think one of the staff is going to harm me. Probably.

I really hope that isn't the last thought Pan had, too.

Worry pricks me as I hurry down the hall to the door Hermes went through. I step inside and pause.

The room is empty.

"Hermes?" Her name comes out in a whisper, but I can't make myself raise my voice. I look around the room slowly. It's a mundane-looking bedroom, nowhere near as elegant as the guest rooms upstairs. The king-size bed is as simple as the dresser and nightstands. There's not even a door to a bathroom. There's also nowhere for Hermes to be hiding unless she's under the bed.

I shudder, but I make myself cross over and crouch down to check. Nothing. No matter what her reputation, Hermes is flesh and blood. If she's not in this room, there's another exit. A secret door. I'm sure of it.

I straighten and examine the walls more closely. There's no way she could have moved the dresser, so I bypass that and examine the mirror across from the bed. It's not as ornate as the one in Ariadne's room, but it's still on a hefty frame and stretches a good seven feet from floor nearly to the ceiling. The perfect size for a door. I feel a little silly, but I hold my breath as I touch the frame.

It moves beneath my fingers.

"What the fuck?" I whisper. Again, I glance at the door, but my gut says that this is a limited-time opportunity and if I go back to loop Apollo in, whatever it is will pass.

If I can find answers, we'll have no reason to stay here. We can leave, and that means he will be safe from whatever fate Minos might have planned for Zeus's spy.

That, more than anything, decides me. I slip off my heels and tug the mirror open all the way. It leads into a hallway that's dusty enough for me to see the faint prints of Converse shoes leading away from my position. I hardly need confirmation that Hermes came this way, and yet here it is all the same.

Following means leaving my own trail, but this is too good an opportunity to miss. I'll deal with Hermes knowing what I'm up to later. I step into the dark hallway and tug the mirror mostly shut behind me. The space is narrow enough to make me feel vaguely claustrophobic, but the walls don't actually brush my shoulders as I start forward.

Why would she bother with secret passageways right now? The house is all but empty and everyone who might be curious about what she's up to is in the living room. It's only as I take the narrow turn and blink into the darkness that I pause to wonder if Minos hired all new staff or if the people working here were inherited when he bought the house. He must have. Surely Minos is clever enough to realize that there would be people loyal to Hermes and only too happy to feed her whatever information they could acquire? So why did he allow this to happen? Unless… Suspicion takes hold.

Hermes wouldn't.

She *wouldn't*.

I pick up my pace as much as I dare and nearly run into the wall at the end of the passageway. I catch myself at the last moment, stopping just short of it. Now that I'm this close, I can see a faint outline of light around the doorway. It was all but invisible from even a foot away. I press my fingertips to it but hesitate.

Charging into whatever may or may not be going on in the

other room is a mistake. I might have followed Hermes with the intent to talk to her, but ultimately I'm here for information and this seems like exactly the situation that might relay the kind of information Apollo is looking for.

With that in mind, I carefully lean forward and press my ear to the cool wood of the door. I'm instantly glad I didn't open it. There are two people talking, both easily identifiable.

Apparently Minos made a pit stop on the way back from ordering tea.

I wish I could see, but I don't dare open the door. Instead, I close my eyes, blotting out even the faint light, and focus. Minos is pacing; I know Hermes's footsteps, at least when she allows herself to be heard, and they are not the heavy tread practically vibrating the floor beneath my bare feet.

"You're sure this will work."

Hermes's shrug is apparent in her tone. "It would work if you weren't wasting opportunities on innocent people. Pan wasn't part of the agreement. Neither was Atalanta."

"Take that up with my fuckup of a son. I told Icarus to deal with Aphrodite, but somehow he 'mistook' Pan for her." He curses. "Don't look at me like that, Hermes. It's the story he spun."

"It's not a very good one."

"It won't happen again. My other boys aren't half so inept." He laughs harshly. "And Atalanta is tied up in the basement. She's perfectly fine. I just can't risk her interfering with what comes next. You saw her in the Ares trials. She's formidable."

"Formidable enough to almost take down one of your prized foster sons."

"Your jokes leave something to be desired." A pause. "You're sure they won't run us out of town for this?"

"The laws are the laws, even if most people have no idea what little secrets from our founding the Thirteen have hidden all these years. If your boys follow my instructions to the letter, the clause will be triggered. But I never promised it would work."

"Hermes." Minos practically growls her name.

"What do you want me to say, Minos? There are no guarantees in this world. You asked me how to accomplish your goals and I provided the information." Her voice goes hard, harder than I've ever heard it. "Now, stop toying with me and give me the information that was promised."

Silence for several beats. I don't have to see his face to know that he's debating whether he can risk crossing Hermes. Finally, he curses. "Very well. The woman you seek is my benefactor."

"Excuse me?"

"She approached me a year ago with an offer that centered Olympus as the prize. She's not among those I brought, though."

"Minos." Something dark and dangerous flits into Hermes's tone. "You have strung me along for months with the promise of precise information on her. I have provided you a house, insider knowledge, and a vote to bring you into Olympus as a citizen. I sincerely hope you have more than 'she's my benefactor' as payment."

I can barely process what I'm hearing. In all the time I've known Hermes, she's been something of an enigma. Even when I shared her bed, there was always part of her held in reserve, and I respected that because I, too, held parts of myself back. But I never doubted for a moment that the protection of Olympus was her main goal.

I...

I close my eyes and try to keep my breathing under control. I don't know who she's talking about or what's going on, so all I can do is listen. I can have an emotional reaction to this later, when it's safe.

But...

What the fuck, *Hermes?*

Minos is silent for so long, I begin to think he might not respond to her threat. Finally, he sighs. "I agreed to those terms before I realized you know more about her than I do." A hesitation. "I have a way to contact her, though I can't guarantee anything will come of it."

"Is that all?"

I flinch, but Minos doesn't seem affected by the icy anger Hermes exudes. "She's not one to make herself available, which you should damn well know. This is all I have."

A tapping of a foot against hardwood floor. "I am very displeased, Minos. You can play the rest of the Thirteen all you want, but playing me?" She laughs sharply. "I highly suggest you come up with something more—and soon." The slide of a chair. "Do not tell her that I'm looking for her, or you won't live to see your little plan enacted."

"I understand," he grits out.

This is winding down. I didn't get nearly enough information to figure out what Hermes's game is, other than her wanting information on...someone...but I know enough. There's only one law they could be speaking of, and it's one I am entirely too familiar with thanks to my parents' ambition.

Minos means to kill a member of the Thirteen and take their place.

Possibly *multiple* members of the Thirteen.

The thought makes my entire body break out in goose bumps and I shudder. I hold little love for the Thirteen as a general whole, but Minos is an unknown in a number of ways. I saw his foster sons' brutality in the arena. If they bring that same violence to the ruling body of our city...

I won't be here to see it. Maybe that should mean I don't care, but I *do*.

There's no help for hiding my footprints and Hermes is too savvy to miss their existence, unless she's distracted by the new information, but I can't hope for that unlikely occurrence. Wiping away the proof is a waste of time, too.

In the split second it takes me to realize I have no way to conceal the fact that someone overheard, Hermes and Minos are wrapping up their conversation. I'm out of time.

I hurry back down the passageway as quickly as I dare, unable to resist casting looks over my shoulder. The door remains closed as I turn the corner and rush back through the mirror and into the bedroom where I left my shoes. I look down at my dirty feet, but there's no help for it. There's no time.

The temptation to confront Hermes is strong. Even now, when I'm questioning everything else, I don't question that she means *me* no harm. She wouldn't have warned me away from this place, this party, if she didn't care what happened to me.

Similarly, I can't believe for a second that she'd set Dionysus up on the chopping block. She must have negotiated his safety ahead of time with Minos.

But everyone else?

The thought leaves me cold. I slip on my heels and stride out the door, careful to close it softly behind me. I want to rush back into the living room and grab Apollo and get him as far from here as possible, but I make myself walk slowly to the bathroom and slip inside. I take the time to wash my hands. To attempt to steady myself, though it feels a fool's errand. My reflection stares back at me, too pale, eyes too wide. I'm shaking and I can't seem to stop.

We were wrong. So fucking wrong. Pan was a mistake. Atalanta disappeared because she's too formidable and would stand between Artemis and a threat. Hermes has been working with Minos to potentially assassinate one or more of our leaders at a moment when the city is most vulnerable to outside threat. An outside threat Minos seems to be playing vanguard for.

Treason.

They're talking about *treason*.

The murders have to happen at the party. Soon. It was a stroke of pure luck that the mistake with Pan didn't send everyone scattering. Once they return to their lives in the center city, there will be security and other things in play that will make it harder to target them. No one brought security to this party, which I didn't find strange until now. I know why Apollo didn't, but why not the others?

Unless... Maybe I wasn't as wrong as I thought. Maybe this really is the double bluff; it's just happening sooner than anyone could have dreamed. I saw Dionysus's face after Pan was attacked. He looked sick. With guilt?

If they thought they were making dark deals with Minos, they wouldn't bring security here to witness it. People talk, and if you start overtly betraying friends and your people, you won't have many friends or people standing around you in the future.

Only the Thirteen would be arrogant enough to think they had nothing to fear.

Charon, Adonis, and Eurydice should be safe, barring more *mistakes*. Their value lies in their connection to the various members of the Thirteen and the power they hold individually, but killing them brings Minos and his people no benefit.

Who will be the target?

I'm so wrapped up in worrying at the problem that I don't hear Hermes come in, don't even notice her until she appears at my shoulder. "Someone's been eavesdropping."

I jump and then curse myself for jumping. I hadn't planned on confronting her, but she's here and we have too much history to let this go. "What are you thinking? Minos? Murder? *Treason?*"

"Everyone who is in danger knows the law." For once, she doesn't have her easy smile in place. "Just like they understood that accepting the title of one of the Thirteen came with risks. If they choose to ignore that, it's their mistake."

"You're a member of the Thirteen," I grind out. "He could stick a knife in your ribs and then all your plotting and planning will be null and void."

"He could try." She nods slowly. "But I'm better than he is, and he knows it."

"Hermes…" I search her face for the woman I fell for all those years ago. "I never thought you would hurt this city for your own ambitions. Why are you doing this?"

"I have my reasons." An answer and yet no answer at all.

I shake my head slowly. "You won't get away with it. Not you and not him. I'll tell everyone. They'll leave and the opportunity will pass, and Zeus and Apollo will drive Minos and his people from the city. All this will be for naught."

"You can tell them, Cassandra." She smiles now, but it's bittersweet in the extreme. "But honey… No one other than Apollo will believe you. At least not until it's too late."

APOLLO

I KNOW SOMETHING'S WRONG THE MOMENT CASSANDRA walks back into the room. She's the kind of white that's leaning green and her eyes are too wide. In all the years I've known the woman, I've never seen her panic—not even when we found Pan—but I have a feeling that's what I'm witnessing now.

My body takes over even as my mind processes the little details. Her hands are damp, and her feet are dusty-looking in her heels. I reach her in two strides and take her hands. "What's wrong?"

"It's bad," she whispers.

It doesn't occur to me to make excuses. I simply slip my arm around her shoulders and guide her out the door. This close, I can feel little tremors working their way through her body, and I grit my teeth against the questions piling up.

She was gone less than fifteen minutes. I know, because I couldn't help watching the clock even as I chatted with Charon and Dionysus about a new batch of wine the latter had created over the winter. It isn't in distribution yet, and Charon wanted to negotiate something close to an exclusive deal for the lower city.

In that time, something happened to shake Cassandra up this terribly and I wasn't there to protect her. I hug her closer to me as we reach the stairs. "Are you hurt?"

"No."

That's enough to keep me quiet as we make the rest of the way back to our room. I shut the door and she staggers to sink onto the edge of the bed. Now that I can see her clearly, she looks even worse. It frightens me.

I cross to her and sink to my knees before her. "Tell me what happened."

"No one's going to believe me." The sorrow radiating off her makes my chest hurt. I would do anything to dispel it.

I cover her hands with mine. "I will. Tell me what happened," I repeat firmly.

She won't meet my gaze. Her eyes dart around the room and her lower lip quivers. "I don't know if I believe me and I actually heard them talking. It's too wild, too much."

I think back over the last little bit and make a few connections. "Hermes and Minos." It has to be. Surely the staff talking wouldn't shake Cassandra like this. From there, it's another leap in logic to guess what scared her so badly. "They were talking about the real reason he invited everyone here. It's worse than we guessed."

"Pan was a mistake." She closes her eyes and her shoulders slump. "Minos is going to kill one of the Thirteen and take their place."

Impossible. I barely keep the word inside, but she somehow knows. She opens her eyes and stares down at me. "I know it sounds unbelievable. Trust me, I've already gone through the denial phase, but the fact remains that Minos plans to use the same law that my parents attempted to exploit to set himself up as a member the Thirteen." She gives a bitter laugh. "He certainly has his pick of options at this party."

Again the denial nearly gets past my lips. I tighten my grip on her hands. "How could he possibly know about that law? Most of the city is unfamiliar with it. They kept your parents' attempt under wraps. It's in no one's best interest for every ambitious person in Olympus to start sharpening their knives." No one has successfully ousted a member of the Thirteen in this way in generations, well before we became the center of a culture of fandom and social media and gossip sites.

"He knows because Hermes told him," she says simply. "I don't know the details, but she's working with Minos in exchange for information on his benefactor—the person who's the real threat against Olympus. You were right in suspecting that he held back information, but Hermes is after it for her own reasons. She admitted it to me herself afterward."

I tense. "You spoke to her after? She knew you overhead?"

"Yes."

Hermes could have killed Cassandra. It would have been the wise move to ensure her and Minos's plan stayed secret. Or, at the very least, she could have locked Cassandra up somewhere and pretended she went back to the city. I might not have believed it, but I'd have no way to prove otherwise. Most of the rest of the party guests wouldn't care enough to be suspicious. "Why did she let you go?"

"I don't know." She looks so wretched, I want to hug her, but if what she's saying is true—and no matter how much I don't want to believe it, it must be true—then we need to move. Now.

"If he tries this, he'll be making it unsafe for everyone," I mutter. "I can't believe Hermes would hand him that kind of dangerous information. It has the potential to hurt her, too." We might—*might*—be able to keep it under wraps again, but the city has its attention on Minos.

Zeus ensured that when he made the man and his family citizens in a public ceremony. If Minos is successful, then it will destabilize Olympus more efficiently than literally anything else. Marriage or politicking or the normal ways of gaining power will forever be second to murder. I shudder. "We have to move now, before everyone scatters. We have to warn them."

"They won't believe you. Not when the information came from me."

"I'll make them believe." I rise to my feet and tug her up with me. "Change your shoes to something you can move easier in. Hurry."

"Apollo..."

Even with the urgency clamoring in my veins, I can't ignore the misery written across her face. I pull her into my arms and hug her tightly. "I believe you, love. The rest of them are too invested in their own safety to disregard a threat to their lives. I need you to trust me on that."

She nods against my chest. "Okay." Another pause. "Okay." Cassandra pushes away from me. "Let's move."

I wait for her to change her shoes, my mind already going to what comes next. No matter what I told Cassandra, there will be resistance from some of the party guests. It's the nature of the fractiousness of the Thirteen that if I say the sky is blue, several other members will shout that it's green. I hope that their self-preservation will override the instinctive desire to dig in their heels simply because I'm the one delivering the news, but I'll deal with whatever waves arise as soon as we get back down there.

Cassandra pulls on a pair of flats and rushes to the door. I'm right on her heels. She keeps up well enough as we start down the hall, but I still have to check my stride to accommodate her shorter legs. She huffs out a breath. "Just go."

Under no circumstances am I leaving her alone. Hermes might have spared her, but if Minos discovers that she knows his plan, he won't. "We go together."

Another huff, though this one sounds almost fond. She frowns as we hit the stairs. "What will happen to Hermes?"

"Likely nothing. She broke no laws." Even if inviting an enemy into our city is traitorous from where I'm standing, it's not technically illegal. The most unforgivable thing is that she endangered Cassandra in the process. I can't say as much aloud. Cassandra won't thank me for feeling so protective of her, and Hermes couldn't have known that I'd bring Cassandra here.

Which is enough to make me wonder... Did Hermes plan on *me* being one of the victims?

We race down the stairs and through the hallways to the living room. I barely manage to keep from bursting through the doors. The sight that greets me makes my stomach sink.

The room is half-empty. We're missing five people. Minos,

Theseus, the Minotaur...and Artemis and Hephaestus. "No."
I spin to pin Hermes with a glare. She's reclining on the couch,
her head propped on her hand, picking at a loose thread on the
cushion. "Where are they?"

"How would I know?" She shrugs a single shoulder. "I'm no
one's keeper."

"Hermes." Cassandra comes to stop next to me. "*Please.*"

Aphrodite rises, looking between us. Her sharp dark eyes
narrow. "What's going on?"

It's too late to play this hand close to my chest. "Minos intends
to utilize the assassination clause."

She flinches, her golden skin going pale. To her credit, she
doesn't flounder long. She spins to where Ariadne, Icarus, and
Pandora are huddled together on the couch across from Hermes.
"Is this true?"

Ariadne won't meet anyone's eyes, but Icarus lifts his chin.
"Ask our father. *He's* the one making plans."

"Oh, I intend to," Aphrodite says acidly. She turns for the
door, but Adonis is there. He moves quicker than I expect, catching her arm. She tries to shake him off. "Let go."

"We're getting out of here."

She blinks. "Excuse me?"

Adonis shoots me a look and then focuses on her. "It's not
safe, Eris. You can call for Minos's head later if you want, but
right now my priority is getting you to safety."

Her gaze goes flinty, and for a moment, I think she might
argue, but she finally nods. "Let's go." They hurry out of the room.

As much as I'm not keen on the group splitting further, Adonis was trained by Athena. He might not have stayed with her special forces, but he's more than capable of keeping Aphrodite safe. Just as well. If something happens to Zeus's sister, I can't guarantee what he'll do. His father wouldn't let a little familial murder get in the way of his ambitions, but Perseus—Zeus—is a different kind of man. Harsher, yes, but he cares very deeply for his siblings.

He might raze the city to the ground to get to the person responsible for harming his family.

I turn to find Charon ushering Eurydice to her feet. "You're safe enough."

"Safe enough is not *safe*." He starts guiding her to the door. "Besides, Hades and Persephone need a report on what's happened here, even if we don't know the final outcome. Good luck." Then they're gone.

There's only Dionysus and Hermes left. I eye them. "Where did Artemis and Hephaestus go?"

She tugs the string on the couch again, freeing another few inches. I clench my fists. If she won't tell us, we're at a severe disadvantage, but we can't afford to wait much longer. Finally, she looks up, though she isn't looking at me. "The Minotaur offered to show Artemis the duck pond. Hephaestus went with Theseus to the garage," she says to Cassandra.

"Thank you," Cassandra whispers.

No one moves, which means no one else will help us prevent what's about to happen. Maybe I'm being foolish. It's entirely possible Minos intends to wait and not strike in this specific moment.

But I can't be sure.

I rush out of the room, Cassandra on my heels. Where to go?

The locations are too far flung to reach them both in a timely manner. I have to pick. I drag my hand through my hair. "This is fucked."

"We split up."

I turn to look at her. Her eyes are too wide, but she's got a determined set to her chin. "It's the only way to warn them both. You take Hephaestus and I'll take Artemis."

She's right, and I know she's right. But even now, there are no guarantees that we'll get there in time. If I send Cassandra to warn one and she gets there too late, the Minotaur might decide she's a loose end in need of tying up. I can't forget how large and menacing he looked next to her that night by the duck pond. He could claim it an accident. Hadn't I thought as much then?

"No."

She grabs my arm. "Apollo, it's the only way."

"No," I repeat harshly.

"If one of them becomes a member of the Thirteen—"

"I don't care!" I stop short and lower my voice. "I do not give a *fuck*, Cassandra. I will not risk you." Not for Olympus. Not for anything. "I love you, and I will let this city burn before I intentionally put you in harm's way. We go for Artemis first. Together." She's the closest and while she's fierce and capable, against the Minotaur, I can't guarantee that she'll prevail.

Cassandra's jaw drops. "Apollo—" She shakes her head. "Right. Artemis. Okay."

We hurry out the back door and down the path toward the duck pond. I've stopped checking my pace, but Cassandra keeps up well enough as we sprint past the maze. It's only as we round the corner that I realize we have nothing resembling a weapon. Sheer numbers will have to do.

The path opens up and we get a view of the pond. Artemis is leaning over the water, looking at something the Minotaur points at. She doesn't see his big hand coming for her back. Once he gets those strong fingers around her throat... "Artemis, *run!*"

Too far. We're too damn far away.

The Minotaur surges forward, reaching for the back of her neck, but thank the gods Artemis is already moving. His fingers barely brush her long hair as she ducks. He's fast, though. The same speed that served him in the Ares competition serves him now.

She barely has time to take a step back when he strikes, plowing one of those massive fists into her stomach. Artemis crumples.

"No!" Cassandra shouts.

The Minotaur glances at us. It's the briefest hesitation, but Artemis isn't some helpless civilian. She claimed her title through the violence of a hunt, and she's obviously kept her skills sharp in the intervening years. She may not understand the full scope of what's happening yet, but she's ready to defend herself.

She lashes out with her feet. The blow appears aimed for the Minotaur's knee. He takes a step back, but she's ready for him, sweeping his legs out from beneath him. A bait and switch.

He hits the ground with an impact I'm certain I can feel even at this distance, and Artemis doesn't hesitate. She leaps to her feet and launches herself into the pond. She hits the water nearly six feet from the shore and is already swimming deeper. She's fast enough that the Minotaur will have no hope of catching her and smart enough that she'll disappear into the countryside the moment she hits the far shore.

Artemis is safe, for now.

I stop several yards away and hold out an arm to stop Cassandra from passing me. The Minotaur sits up and watches his prey escape him. "Lucky timing." For the life of me, I cannot decide if he's angry or disappointed to have been interrupted. His face and voice give nothing away.

"You won't get another chance. I'll make sure of that."

"Not today." He gives a slow, feral smile. "Will you be able to stop my brother though? I doubt it." He gives a dry, raspy chuckle. "We've already won."

That's what I'm afraid of.

CASSANDRA

I'M HOLDING APOLLO BACK.

I'm healthy enough but I am not, and never will be, a runner. Not like he is. Not like he needs me to be in this moment. We're halfway through the house on the way to the garage, and my lungs are on fire and the stitch in my side sears through me with every harsh breath. I'm slowing down, and I wasn't particularly fast to begin with.

Apollo is slowing down with me. I gasp out a curse. "Go. I'll be fine."

He shakes his head sharply. "No."

We've already taken too long. In order to trigger the clause, the would-be assassin has to kill their target with their own hands, in close combat. Considering how untouchable he felt, Hephaestus won't be on his guard...and Theseus has had more than enough time to corner his prey. If Hephaestus is alive, it'll be a sheer miracle.

"Apollo, please!"

"I am *not* leaving you." The vehemence in the sentence nearly makes me trip over my own feet. It's similar to how he sounded when he said we wouldn't split up earlier.

When he told me he'd let Olympus burn if it mean keeping me safe.

When he told me he loved me.

If he won't leave me, then there's no choice but to push through. I drag in a harsh breath and do my best to pick up my pace. We get through the house and burst out through the front door. I don't allow myself to stop; if I stop, I'm going to never start again.

I clocked the garage when we first arrived, and I head in that direction, Apollo at my side. The bastard is barely winded and I'll hate him for that later. He throws an arm out in front of me as we reach the garage. "Let me go first."

The temptation to argue for the sake of arguing is nearly overwhelming, but I press my lips together and nod tightly. He shoves the door open and heads through it. I follow closely. I'm not about to let him out of my sight.

The detached garage is huge enough that I spare a thought to what the fuck Hermes had in here before she sold the place. It certainly wasn't cars. She owns one, which is one more than I have or need, but she isn't the type to have a garage filled with vehicles she'll never drive. Minos doesn't seem to share the sentiment, because there are five vehicles in here. Aside from an expensive-looking red convertible, they're all nondescript SUVs and town cars in a uniform black similar to the ones every other rich family in Olympus drives.

Across from the neat line of vehicles is a set of shelving filled with various shit that seems to be in all garages. Apparently the rich also like to store their tires and miscellaneous tools just like normal people. *Rich people, they're just like us.* I bite down a hysterical giggle that is entirely spurred by exhaustion and stress.

Apollo slows and looks around. The lighting is relatively dim in here, thanks to the small windows overhead, but we can see clearly enough that it appears to be empty. He glances at me and jerks his chin in a clear command to stay close.

He has nothing to worry about there. I might have volunteered to split up to warn those who might be in danger, but I'm no hero. I have absolutely no desire to get myself killed for some member of the Thirteen who wouldn't piss on me if I was on fire.

A soft thud sounds somewhere nearby.

Apollo sprints in the direction of the sound, leaving me to do my best to keep up. When I round the corner of the farthest SUV, I wish I hadn't.

Theseus straddles Hephaestus's chest, his big fists descending in a steady rhythm as he beats the other man. I can't tell if Hephaestus is alive, but he's not fighting back. And there's...so much blood. I press my hand to my mouth and take a step back.

Apollo doesn't hesitate.

He throws himself at Theseus, taking him to the ground in a flying tackle. A normal person would respond to being attacked by surprise or freeze up. Not Theseus. I'm hardly trained in combat, but he looks like he simply switches the momentum of his punches from Hephaestus's limp form to Apollo. I can feel the impact of his fist striking Apollo's ribs from here.

I'm nearly certain I hear something crack. No, that has to be my imagination. It *has* to. I stand there helplessly as they whale on each other. For several seconds, it seems like Apollo will win. He's strong and he's trained and he's furious enough to have the upper hand.

But Theseus's punches have an impact.

Every time he lands a strike, Apollo crumples a little bit more. From here, I can see the precision in Theseus's attacks. He's aiming for Apollo's ribs and side. The next time he goes in with one of those nasty attacks, Apollo lowers his arm to block.

And then Theseus hammers his fist into Apollo's face. He takes advantage of Apollo appearing dazed by rolling them, coming up to straddle Apollo's chest the same way he straddled Hephaestus.

Hephaestus who still hasn't moved.

My heart stops as Theseus lifts one of those massive fists.

He's going to kill Apollo. Hephaestus might be a powerful title, but *Apollo* is arguably more powerful. If Theseus kills them both, he'll have his pick. From the bloody grin he gives Apollo, he knows it, too.

I don't make a decision to move. I blink and I find myself spinning to look for a weapon. My attention snags on the shelves with the tires, all perfectly stored in bags. Surely there must be something there.

I rush to the shelves and haul one of the tires down. It's heavier than I expect and I lose my grip on it immediately. "Fuck!" I risk a glance over my shoulder. Apollo still has his arms up, protecting his face from Theseus's attacks, but who knows how long that will last. He's bloodied and hurt.

I spin back to the shelves. "Come on, come on, come on!" There has to be something there that I can use. There *has* to be.

A gleam of metal catches my eye. A tire iron. I grab it and immediately have to shift my grip because my palms are so sweaty. I don't let myself hesitate. Apollo's life hangs in the balance. I simply act.

I sprint to where Theseus continues to beat him. No warning. I can't afford one. I plant my feet and swing the tire iron with all my strength. He must see me at the last moment because I don't hit his head like I was aiming for. He gets an arm up and grunts as the blow lands. It barely moves him.

If I don't stop him, he's going to kill the man I love.

Fear and panic give me the strength to hit him again. "Let him go!"

"Stop hitting me, or you're next."

"Run, Cassandra," Apollo rasps.

Fuck no. I'm not leaving him to die, not even if to save myself. I swing the tire iron a third time. I never make contact. Theseus grabs it and yanks it out of my hands. He gives me a bloody grin. "Checkmate."

"No!" Apollo surges up and knocks the tire iron out of Theseus's hands. The other man goes to punch him, but Apollo is already flipping them. This time, he comes out on top. He punches Theseus. Once. Twice. On the third time, Theseus's eyes roll back in his head, and he slumps to the ground.

I stare at the unconscious man, half-certain that this is a ploy and the moment I blink, he'll attack.

Apollo shoves him off and staggers to his feet. "Are you okay?"

"Me?" I have to look away from Theseus when Apollo tips sideways. I grab his arm to keep him on his feet. He winces and clutches his ribs. I follow the movement. "Are they broken?"

"No." He flinches again. "I don't think so."

As one, we turn to Hephaestus. He still hasn't moved. I don't know if it's adrenaline, but I plant my feet and can't make myself approach him. This is so much worse than the scene with Pan yesterday. There's blood everywhere, spattered all over the surrounding area. Too much violence. I never signed up for this.

Hephaestus never did me any kindness—in fact, he was cruel on the few occasions we had reason to interact—but cruelty is not a death sentence. No one deserves to die like this, alone and in pain.

Apollo gently extracts himself from my hold. "Stay there."

"Apollo—"

He reaches down to grab the fallen tire iron and presses it into my hand. "Guard Theseus."

It's a bullshit task and we both know it, but I can't help the gratitude that wells up inside me. This man continues to protect me as best he can. I nod, not quite able to clear the burning from my eyes. "Okay."

"Cassandra." He catches my chin for the briefest moment. "Thank you. If you hadn't intervened…"

A wet prickle at the corner of my eye betrays me. I can't make my bottom lip stop quivering. *You could have died.* I can barely think it, let alone say it. I can't comprehend a world without Apollo in it. "Check him," I finally manage.

He hesitates now when he didn't before. "Are you okay?"

"No. Not even a little bit." The tire iron slips against my

sweaty palms, forcing me to readjust my grip. "We have to know, Apollo. We have to end this."

He finally nods. I watch him closely as he walks to Hephaestus. Apollo is covered in blood and is holding his ribs in a way that scares me. Surely he'd know if they were broken? *Yes, but would he tell you the truth if they were?* The answer to that is a resounding no. I can't trust him to take care of himself if he thinks I'm in danger. "Apollo—"

"Fuck," he mutters. "He's dead."

My stomach tries to revolt, but I fight through the nausea that hits me in waves. We were too late and now a man is dead. "I'm sorry. If I hadn't—"

"It's not your fault." He pushes to his feet, swaying a little, and turns to face me. One of his eyes is swollen almost completely shut. "I have to call Zeus."

I nod, too quickly. I can't look at the man—the body—on the floor. "I'll just…"

"Cassandra, I need you to stay in the garage where I can see you." He walks to me and guides me to face away from the scene. "Don't look, love. But don't go anywhere. It's not safe."

Considering one of the culprits is groaning faintly a few feet away, I'm not certain it's safe *here* either, but at least I'm neither alone nor defenseless. I tighten my grip on the tire iron and give a shaky nod. "Okay."

"I won't be long. I saw a phone near the entrance. I'll stay within sight." He moves in that direction, leaving me with the body and the murderer. To stand guard? Or because he's between me and the entrance? Impossible to say, but it's easier to focus on that than the scene behind me. I still can't quite process that it happened at all. This...

I listen quietly as Apollo makes his calls. First to Zeus, explaining the situation. It goes about as well as can be expected. After he gives a quick report, there are a lot of low murmurs and apologies. It infuriates me. Apollo was sent here on a fact-finding mission. There's no way he could have known what would happen. *No one* knew what would happen.

Except Hermes.

I can't think about that too closely right now. I always knew what Hermes was capable of, but knowing in theory and seeing it play out are two very different things. She tried to protect me in her own way, but I'm not sure if that makes it better or worse.

They'll have one chance to keep this under wraps, and even then I don't know if it's possible. This isn't like my parents. They were the only two who planned the assassination, the only two who acted on it. *They* didn't have one of the Thirteen in their corner.

The Thirteen are still going to try to cover it up. It means more blood. More death. Maybe a fire this time instead of a car crash.

A broken laugh escapes my lips. I guess I have my answer on what Apollo would have done if he'd held the title when my parents attempted to assassinate Athena. Theseus got farther than my parents did, but he hasn't been successful. He hasn't completed the ritual required to trigger the clause.

Even as I think it, a faint groan has me turning despite myself. I don't think Theseus is going to be in any shape to do damage in the near future, but if he's already stirring, I'm not about to take anything for granted. "Stay down."

He's nowhere near as bloodied as Apollo. I stare at him, nauseous and my head swimming with adrenaline. He cracks open one dark eye and meets my gaze. I tense. "Don't say a word."

He rasps out a painful-sounding breath. "I claim Hephaestus's title by right of might and the laws written upon Olympus's founding."

"No," I whisper. I know what comes next. My parents rehearsed it often enough before their failed assassination attempt. "No," I repeat, louder this time.

He ignores me. "Cassandra…" Another harsh breath. "You stand as my witness."

The tire iron falls from my nerveless fingers.

APOLLO

THE NIGHTMARE ONLY GETS WORSE AS TIME GOES ON. ZEUS sends Ares. In the thirty minutes it takes her to arrive—she must have been waiting close by because there's no way to reach this location from the city center in such a short time—Minos and his family have already tried to bully their way into the garage. Holding that door while it takes everything I have to stay on my feet... Well, the less said about it, the better.

Three black SUVs of an identical make and model to the ones behind me in the garage careen up the driveway. They screech to a halt close enough to have the Minotaur taking several quick steps back to avoid making contact with the front bumper.

Ares steps out, her gorgeous face set in forbidding lines. She's wearing a perfectly tailored pantsuit, which would be at home in a boardroom if not for the shoulder holster clearly visible as she lifts her arm to motion the occupants of the other two vehicles forward.

I recognize one of her partners, Patroclus. He's one of the best strategists in the city, a tall white man with short dark hair and square frame glasses who prefers jeans and T-shirts to the suits the others under Ares's command favor. He'd been injured badly in the competition to become Ares but appears to have made a full recovery in the intervening weeks. There were rumors that Helen had a fling with Patroclus and Achilles during the tournament, but they turned the rumor mill on its head when they came out publicly as being in a polyamorous relationship a few weeks after Helen became Ares.

Zeus hadn't been thrilled with that, but there wasn't a single thing he could do. His sister had outplayed him. With all of Olympus salivating over her new relationship, he couldn't afford to meddle without worrying about *his* already precarious reputation.

Ares makes a beeline for Minos. "You. Get out of my way."

"With all due respect—"

She lifts her brows. She won't thank me for making the comparison, but she's never reminded me more of her father than in this moment while she faces down a blustering Minos and intimidates him into taking two large steps back without saying a single word. She gives him one last derisive look and turns to me. "Where is he?"

"This way." Cassandra hasn't move from my line of sight, and I haven't dared leave the door unmanned, but I'm eager to get back to her side and remove her from this whole nightmare. I never would have asked her to come here if I knew things would become actually dangerous.

"Patroclus," Ares snaps.

"I've got the door," he says, and he falls in behind her, blocking Minos and his family from approaching. Two of their people stay with him and the other two follow us as we head into the garage.

"This is fucked," Ares murmurs.

"Yes." There's nothing else to say. "Theseus was unconscious when I left, so hopefully he hasn't…" My voice trails off when I see Cassandra's face. Her lips are pressed together tightly and she's even paler than normal. I follow her gaze to where Theseus has dragged himself up to lean against the tire of the SUV.

He gives me a bloody smile. "Too late."

"He claimed the title by right of might," Cassandra whispers. "With me as witness."

"*Fuck.*" Ares closes her eyes for a long moment. "I don't suppose we can kill him and pretend we found them both like this?"

I'm not one to advocate murder, but I don't know how to explain Hephaestus getting replaced in a way that will continue to keep the assassination clause under wraps. If the rest of the city finds out how relatively easy it is to take on the title of one of the Thirteen…

"Ares." One of her people previously guarding the door hurries up, their pale features tight. "The press are here."

"That *motherfucker.*"

She turns toward the door, but I throw my arm out to stop her. "We have to clean this up. Now. It's too late to go back, but at least we can attempt to do damage control." I don't know how to manage it, but this will be our only chance to get ahead of things.

She presses her fingers to her temples. "Right. I'll face the press and send that little cockroach outside scurrying. Patroclus will help you with all this." She casts a furious look at Theseus. "Enjoy your time as Hephaestus. It won't last long."

He smirks. "This title suits me better than Ares anyways."

"Keep telling yourself that. At least *I* won my title honestly."

Theseus shrugs. "I didn't make the Olympian laws. Take it up with the founders."

"You son of a—"

"Ares," I cut in. "We don't have time for this."

She spins on her heel and stalks toward the door without another word. I take Cassandra's elbow, steering her deeper into the garage. "I'm sorry."

"You keep saying that." Her voice is wrong: strained and hollow. "We witnessed a murder, Pan almost died, and you were beaten badly enough that I thought he might kill you, too. Is this what your life is like, Apollo? You hardly seemed fazed."

I want nothing more than to whisk her away from this place, but Theseus has made sure that's impossible. By Cassandra being his witness, he's effectively chained her to Olympus until this is resolved. "Sometimes being one of the Thirteen means bumping up against violence and doing things I'm not proud of. I knew that when I accepted the title. I'm sorry you were drawn into this."

"Swimming in waters deep enough to drown me," Cassandra murmurs. She presses her fingertips to my jaw. "We really are different people."

I hate the reminder. I hate that she's shaking and there's nothing I can do to go back in time and spare her from this. "I brought you here. I know apologizing doesn't help, but I can't seem to stop doing it."

"I brought myself here." She shakes her head, her gaze clearing a little. "Stop trying to take responsibility for me, Apollo. I might be drowning a bit right now, but I jumped in knowing that was a possibility."

"I won't let you drown, love." I tug her closer and she comes willingly, slipping into my arms. It feels like I breathe a little easier as soon as I have my arms around her, even with my ribs screaming at me. "You shoulder too much. You never ask for help. I *want* to help you carry your burdens, Cassandra. Not because I feel an obligation but because it means I'm standing at your side and there's nowhere else in this world I'd rather be."

She buries her face against my chest and gives a broken laugh. "Only you could be romantic standing a few yards from a murder scene."

She's right. It's the wrong time, but it's always been the wrong time with us. Even if I'd never hired her, never brought her here, never known how good it could be between us...I move through a world she wants nothing to do with. I can't leave and she can't stay. Not if she doesn't want to drown. "If I don't say things now, I'll likely never get another chance."

Cassandra tightens her grip around my waist. When she speaks, her voice is muffled against my shirt. "It wasn't supposed to be like this."

"I know."

She lifts her head. "I love you." A broken laugh escapes. "Gods, I'm so pathetic. Now I have to apologize, too. I—"

I cover her lips with my fingers. "No. Don't take it back." I lean down and press my forehead to hers. "I love you, too. I have for a very long time."

"We're a mess."

"The messiest."

"I can't stay."

My chest goes hollow. "I know."

She takes a shuddering breath. "I... We can't do this right now. I'm stuck here until the tribunal of the Thirteen." She tenses. "Oh gods, I forgot about Atalanta."

"What about Atalanta?"

She looks up at me. "Minos has her tied up in the basement. He wanted her out of the way so he could..." She shudders. "Do what he did."

"Patroclus." I quickly relay the information she gave me.

Patroclus nods, but his gaze is on the scene before us. "Okay. I'll send people to retrieve her."

Cassandra starts to twist to look at the body, but I turn us away. "Don't. It won't help." It won't be long now. Patroclus instructs Ares's people to move the body into the back of one of the SUVs. They'll transport Hephaestus back into the city center where he'll undergo a quick examination, and then his body will be delivered to his family.

Somehow, I don't think Artemis will forgive me for failing to save her cousin.

I'm not sure I'll ever forgive myself either.

Things happen quickly after that. Patroclus sends two of his people to find Atalanta and another pair to ensure Pan actually reached the hospital. Another two are tasked with transporting Hephaestus's body back to the city. Patroclus approaches us. "It's time to leave. I'll be driving you personally." I start to protest, but he holds up a hand. "You can't go out in front of the press looking like that without giving rise to the kind of questions we're not ready to answer."

He's right. I hate that he's right. There's little I can do to fix this situation currently—or potentially at all—but there's plenty I can do to make it worse. If the press thinks I have something to do with the Hephaestus changeover, it'll be like throwing chum to a group of sharks. They'll go into a frenzy.

I glance at the doorway. Ares will have them well in hand, but... "They went after Artemis, too. No matter how capable she is, we shouldn't leave Ares alone with Minos and his people."

Patroclus's jaw goes tight. "Achilles will be here shortly, but Ares can take care of herself. The only reason they got the jump on Artemis is because she didn't see them coming." He casts one last look at the doorway and motions for me and Cassandra to get into the car.

If I were alone, I might argue, but Cassandra needs to get out of here and she won't leave if I don't. I can see it in the stubborn look in her eyes. "Fine." I open the back door for her and then follow her in.

Patroclus wastes no time getting behind the wheel. He presses the garage door and barely waits for it to rise completely before he backs out. The other SUV follows. I catch sight of several vans in the driveway and a cluster of people and cameras around Ares as we drive away at a perfectly reasonable speed. Our departure turns some heads, but Ares smiles and says something that makes everyone shift their attention back to her.

She's good at her job. The title of Ares has never been more beloved than it is now. And bringing in Achilles and Patroclus as her seconds-in-command has ensured that she has no weak points to speak of. It was truly well done.

Easier to think about that than what comes next. I squeeze Cassandra's hand. "I need you to know—"

"I have to stand in front of the tribunal and testify that Theseus successfully pulled off the assassination clause. Murder committed with his own hands, and the proper words spoken afterward in front of a witness." She's half-twisted away from me, staring out the window. "I'm aware of the steps."

I would spare her this if I could. It's not likely to be a comfortable experience for anyone. I clear my throat. "I'll ensure Zeus holds up his end of the bargain."

At that, she finally looks at me. There are tear tracks beneath her eyes and she looks more exhausted than I've ever seen her. "I know."

"Cassandra." I glance at Patroclus, who's doing his very best to pretend he can't hear us, and then back at her. "Please come home with me. At least until we get this figured out."

She looks like she wants to argue but finally gives a jerky nod. "Okay."

We don't speak again until Patroclus pulls the SUV to the curb outside my building. It's only then that I realize we're both a mess and Cassandra has nothing to change into. I clear my throat. "I'll send someone to your place to get your things."

"Thanks." It's a testament to how rattled she is that she doesn't argue. That she barely looks around as we head through the lobby and take the elevator up to the top.

All the members of the Thirteen who reside in the city center— Zeus and Hera, Ares, Athena, and myself—have what's come to be designated living spaces. The title of Apollo owns this entire building; I inherited that income as well as the penthouse itself when I took over the position. I'm so used to seeing it that I try to look around through Cassandra's point of view...but I'm too exhausted to make it work.

It's too much. That's about what it amounts to. Too much chrome. Too much marble. Too much money spent on things that hardly matter beyond aesthetics. But it's as safe as any place in Olympus, so it's home.

I lead us through my front door, not pausing in the open space that is my living room and kitchen, instead pressing my hand to her lower back and guiding her down the hallway to where my bedroom and home office are. She stands there silently as I turn on the shower but bats my hands away when I reach for her zipper. "I can do it."

"Cassandra, let me take care of you." I pause. "Please."

She hesitates and finally nods. "Only if you promise to let me bandage you up after we get clean."

Truth be told, I'm not certain there's anything to bandage. My eye is swollen and that side of my face throbs with each beat of my heart. Theseus got me several times in the ribs, and I have no doubt my skin is a rainbow of bruises, but I'm moving well enough now that I don't think anything's broken. But if it will make her feel better to see for herself, I'm hardly going to tell her no. "Okay."

I strip her slowly, letting her presence ease the fear still thrumming through me. She's safe. The situation might not be, but *she's* safe. I have never, not once, put my personal feelings or relationships above this city.

I did that today.

I have to live with the guilt of that. I don't know if it would have made a difference, but I don't know that it wouldn't.

Cassandra steps out of her panties and turns to me. "There's nothing you could have done."

"Are you a mind reader now?" I try for a smile but drop the attempt halfway through.

"No." She shakes her head, dark eyes serious. "But I know you. We were operating with the information we had at the time. If not for Hermes all but inviting me to eavesdrop, we wouldn't have saved Artemis, either. Even with the attack on Pan and our theories, we didn't have all the facts."

Rationally, I know she's right, but it's nearly impossible to look at things from any shade of positive light. "A man is dead because I failed."

"A man is dead because Minos orchestrated a plan to get multiple members of the Thirteen into one place and then his sons attempted a triple murder." She frowns up at me. "Lay the blame where it deserves to be, Apollo."

She unbuttons my shirt slowly and then carefully peels it away from my body. Cassandra hisses out a breath at the sight of the bruises already blossoming beneath my skin. "Promise me that you don't think it's worse than bruising, or I'm going to take you to the hospital right now."

I cover her hands with mine. "It's not worse than bruising. I'll be hurting tomorrow, but there's no sharp pain or difficulty breathing that would indicate something more serious."

She stares at me for several beats and then nods. "I want to get cleaned up and then…"

I wait, but she doesn't continue. Carefully, I take her chin and guide her back to look into my eyes. "And then?"

"Would it be okay if you held me for a while?" Her lower lip quivers a little and she makes a visible effort to still it. "I don't think I'm doing as okay as I'm acting."

My heart twists painfully in my chest. I would do anything to have saved her from this experience, from witnessing the very act that had such a horrific impact on her life twelve years ago. "Of course, love. Anything for you."

CASSANDRA

I CAN BARELY LOOK AT APOLLO'S BODY WITHOUT THE FEAR of what-if seeping in around the edges, the idea of a world without him so cold and dark that I can't stop shaking. He thinks I'm rattled because of witnessing a murder, and I won't pretend I'm remotely okay with that. Or the reminder that this isn't all that unusual for him. How can he live like this? How can any of the Thirteen?

Getting beaten barely registered as a blip for him; he immediately pivoted to worrying about the greater good of the city. I should care about the city. There are a lot of innocent people who live here.

But it's the potential loss of *him* that has me burrowing beneath his ridiculously expensive sheets and arranging my body carefully against his. I'm not certain I can touch him without causing him pain, but he tugs me close all the same and I don't argue.

I need this.

I think we both need this.

For a long time, we simply lie there. I allow his slow breathing and the steady thump of his heart against my ear to soothe me. He could have been hurt so much worse today...but he wasn't. That's the important thing. He's here. He's with me.

Only for a few more days.

The reminder hurts. It *always* hurts, but the bite feels particularly vicious and jagged now. We've been here for hours and not a single person has come to check on Apollo. Oh, his family won't know what happened unless he decides to tell them, but not even Zeus has checked in. He'll have already had a preliminary report from Ares about the situation and Apollo's injuries. Apparently that doesn't even warrant a call.

I want to beg him to come with me, to leave behind this city that doesn't care about him before it hurts him in a way he can't recover from. The loss of one Apollo might barely be a blip for Olympus, but it would be everything to me.

He won't leave, though. This is his world—it has been since birth—and he feels a responsibility for everyone in this city. His genuine care is part of the reason I love him, but I can't help the worry that wraps around me and squeezes tight.

I don't know who moves first. I shift against him, or he pulls me closer. Maybe both. But I tilt my head back and then Apollo's mouth is on mine.

This time, there's no finesse. No kinky games. No power dynamics. Just a deep heat that burns away everything but the need to get closer. He starts to push me onto my back and winces. That's all I need to shift away. "You're too hurt for this."

"Cassandra." He digs a hand into my hair and pulls me in for a searing kiss. "I need you." When I still hesitate, he curses. "I promise to tell you if anything hurts too badly."

It's a bullshit promise and we both know it, but my thoughts aren't orderly enough to navigate past the desire to reassure myself that we're both here, both alive, both safe. *For the time being.* I swallow hard. "Okay."

He tries to kiss me again, but I'm already moving down his body. He tightens his grip on my hair. "You don't have to."

"Apollo." I hold his gaze. "When have I ever given you any indication that I'm going to do something—sexual or otherwise—that I'm not fully on board with?" I don't give him a chance to answer, dipping down to kiss his chest. This part of him, at least, is bruise-free.

"Never." He says it almost hesitantly.

Gods, I love this man. I love him so much, part of me wants to dig that emotion out of my chest and set it on fire. To exorcise it because it's complicated and messy and the implications are more than I can bear to think about right now. I flick his nipple with my tongue. "I've been *dying* to suck your cock again. Please let me."

His chuckle is strained and raspy. "By all means, love. Don't let me hold you back."

I'm careful to bypass his ribs. In the fading light of the evening, his bruises look even worse than they did earlier in the shower. If he's able to move at all tomorrow, it will be a small miracle.

He widens his legs so I can kneel between them. I take a moment to memorize every detail of this. This man, who has exasperated me, confused me, and lifted me up for *years*. One of the very group of people I should hate beyond all others. The kindest person I've ever met.

The one who holds my heart in his gentle, battered hands.

"I love you." I said it earlier, but it feels different this time. It changes nothing. It *can't* change anything. But I need him to know it's true, that this isn't something as mundane as sex for me. "I think I've loved you for a very long time, even if I would have thrown myself from Dodona Tower before admitting it to anyone, let alone myself."

He gives a bittersweet smile. "I realized I loved you that day with the printer."

I instantly know exactly what he's talking about. It wasn't a good day. It was the anniversary of my parents' death, and my sister and I had a fight that afternoon when I'd taken her out to lunch. My emotions had been riding too close to the surface, boiling and ugly and awful. When the ancient printer went haywire, I'd lost control completely. But that means... "You're joking."

"I'm not."

"Apollo, that was *four years ago.*" I stare. "You can't have loved me that long."

"You were my employee, and you'd made your thoughts on the Thirteen and Olympus very clear from the start." He shrugs and winces a little. "I wasn't going to be just another selfish person in your life putting my needs and desires above yours."

Against everything, tears prickle at the edges of my eyes. "I took an office chair to the printer that day. Anyone else would have fired me."

"It was an old printer. I'd been meaning to replace it for a while, and you gave me the excuse to do so."

"Apollo..."

His smile falls away. "Up until that point, you'd been very careful with me. Walking on eggshells. After that day, you didn't bother. You gave me the real you." He trails his fingers down my cheek. "You're beautiful and complicated and the smartest person I've ever met. How could I not love you?"

If we keep talking like this, I'm going to start sobbing, and if I only have a short time left with him, I'm determined to fill it with as many good memories as possible. I turn my face and press a kiss to his palm. "Now lie back and be a good patient." I give a wobbling, wicked smile. "Nurse Cassandra will make you feel better."

I wrap my fist around his cock and lean down so I can take him into my mouth. His hissed exhale has me checking his expression, but there's no pain there. Only pleasure. *Good.* I give myself over to tasting and teasing him, taking him deeply and then licking my way to flick the crown of his cock with my tongue. Working him up. Making him forget himself.

Giving us both a reprieve from the horrific memories plaguing us. From the inevitable pain of the future.

At some point, he sifts his fingers through my hair, tugging it back from my face but doing nothing to try to guide me. Letting me have my way.

Letting me take care of him.

Every time I glance up, I find him watching me with a fevered, intense look that feels twin to the feelings pushing in my chest. The knowledge that we might love each other but we're destined to be temporary takes up too much space in the room with us. There's no escaping it.

"Come here."

I ease off his cock and give him a long look. "Your ribs."

"I'll hold perfectly still." He gives a surprisingly sweet smile. "I promise."

I hesitate, but the truth is that I want this, too. I narrow my eyes. "You'll tell me if it hurts."

"Yes." He motions to the nightstand. "Condoms."

I grab one from the nightstand and take my time ripping it open and rolling it down his length. I give him a slow stroke. "Apollo..."

"Come here," he repeats.

He's right. There's nothing left to say. There's only this. I carefully straddle his hips and lower myself onto his cock. Even with how turned on I am from sucking his cock, I have to fight to take him fully. I love it. I fucking *love* it. I take his hands and press them to my hips as I slide down another inch. "I feel so fucking owned by you when we're like this." I roll my hips. "Taking what's yours."

"No." He tightens his grip and drags me down to seal us together completely. "*You're* taking what's *yours*."

One of his hands drops to my upper thigh, his thumb stroking my clit as I ride him. The only sound in the room is our harsh breathing and the faint shift of our bodies against the sheets. I want this to last forever. For us to remain here for time unknown, to stay safe and isolated and happy.

Nothing lasts forever.

My orgasm takes me by surprise. One moment I'm luxuriating in the steadily building pleasure between us, and the next I'm coming. Apollo keeps me moving on him even as I lose control, crying out his name as I come. I manage not to slump onto his injured torso, but it wouldn't matter. He bends up and kisses me even as he keeps me moving on his cock. He grinds me down on him, sending another wave of pleasure through me. I cling to him as I come again, as he follows me over the edge with my name on his lips.

Too good. Too perfect.

I ease off him, and he carefully climbs off the bed and walks into the bathroom to dispose of the condom. His phone rings as he's heading back toward the bed. We exchange a look. Nothing lasts forever, but this was nowhere near long enough. I'm not ready for it to end. I'm not ready to leave him.

I don't know if I'll ever be ready to leave him.

He picks up his phone and sighs. "I'll take this in the living room."

I'm about to say that's not necessary when my purse starts ringing. It startles me so much, I stare at it, my brain shorting out. It's Apollo who walks over and digs out my phone, passing it over before slipping out the door to answer his call.

Guilt rises at the sight of my sister's name on my screen. I hadn't even thought to update her, but why would I? I try to keep the unsavory aspects of my life from touching her. Until this point, that included how gods-awful everyone with the tiniest bit of power is to me, how stressful the bills get, how much I resent our parents for painting us into this corner with their selfishness even as I grieved them.

This is different.

I take a deep breath and try to erase any fatigue from my voice. "Hey, Alexandra."

"What happened?"

I blink. "What do you mean, what happened?"

"Cassandra." Her exasperation practically pours through the line. "It's all over the gossip sites. Hephaestus is dead. And he was at the same party you were at this week with Apollo. What's going on?"

I open my mouth to tell her that she needs to worry about

college and not about me but stop short. I don't want to drag her into this, but dismissing her question is shitty. "Some stuff happened, but it's best if you stay out of it. I'm okay, but I don't want you to worry about stuff you can't control."

"Cassandra, I love you, but that's a load of horseshit."

"Excuse me?"

She doesn't sound angry. More like she's exhausted. That almost makes it worse. "I'm not a kid anymore. You don't have to shelter me from the bad stuff in this world. I know it's there." A weighted pause. "Be honest with me. For once."

She's...right. Alexandra is an adult. Wanting to shield her from all the bad stuff is as much about me as it is about her, and that's not fair. I sigh. "It's like it was with our parents. The new family in town? The Vitalises? Theseus killed Hephaestus and claimed right of might."

"*What?*"

"He..." I drag in a breath. Honesty only goes so far. I'm not going to expose my sister to the level of violence I witnessed at that party. "It doesn't matter. We're getting out of here. I have enough money to pay for us to start a new life outside Olympus. Poseidon has already agreed to get us out." A lie, but in the grand scheme of things, it's a small price to pay. I've shielded my sister from so much. I can't tell her the price I almost paid for this escape.

"What did you just say?"

I frown. There's something in her tone that I don't like. "I have a way out for us. A new life. It's what we wanted, Alexandra. This place is fucking poison, and you've been working so hard. You can finish out your degree at any college in the country. Gods, you could probably attend any college in the world."

"Cassandra." My sister's voice shakes. "What about Apollo?"

My heart cries out, and I can't keep the waver out of my own voice. "It was never going to work with him."

"Why not?"

"It doesn't matter."

Alexandra curses. "It does to me. You like him. You've liked him for a long time. Obviously he feels the same way. Why would you leave that behind?"

I start to tell her I'd do anything for her, but I've been dishonest about too much. I can't quite manage it now. "We're too different."

"Explain."

I frown. "You're kind of being an asshole right now."

"And *you're* kind of being a self-righteous martyr." Alexandra exhales slowly. "I don't fault you for wanting to get out of here. You don't exactly talk about it, but it couldn't have been easy to shoulder the burden of raising me while we lost everything. I don't blame you for hating this city and the upper circles, but... Cass, I don't. My friends are here. I love my graduate program and, well, I was going to tell you this at dinner next week, but I got accepted into an internship with Demeter's company. Cass, my *life* is here. But we're not talking about me right now. We're talking about you."

It feels like the world just flipped me around and dropped me on my head. I stare at the tangled sheets of Apollo's bed. "What are you saying?"

"I'm saying that even if I wanted to leave the city, it wouldn't make a difference. You've given up too much, Cass. Don't give up on him, too."

"It's not that easy." The truth bubbles up, all the fears I've been shoving down since I realized exactly how high the stakes were. "It's like our parents all over again. They were comfortable committing murder to accomplish their goals. They knew the risk and didn't care, and they were killed because of their ambition. That's the world they moved in. That's the world *Apollo* moves in. He's comfortable there. I never will be."

"Cass..." Alexandra hesitates. "If you need to leave Olympus, I won't hold it against you. But make sure you're leaving for the right reasons. You might say that you're not comfortable in the world Apollo moves in, but you've been his right hand for five years. You're *already* moving in that world."

"That's different."

"Is it? You interact with the other Thirteen and the legacy families all the time. What would be different if you and Apollo kept dating? If you got married?"

The thought of being married to Apollo nearly knocks me off my feet. I have to close my eyes and swallow hard. "I'll drown, Alex. The waters are too deep."

"So learn to swim. You're the smartest person I know. If anyone can do it, you can."

I don't know what to say to that. It feels too big, too easy, when nothing about this is easy at all. The violence we encountered at Minos's party shook me to the core...but even at its worst, Apollo was at my side. Refusing to leave me. Protecting me. Allowing me to do the same for him.

"I'm afraid."

Alexandra's voice warms. "When has that stopped you from doing something that mattered to you?"

She's...right. I've been scared for a very long time. Of failing her. Of letting the legacy of our parents drag us down. Of letting anyone close. My throat tries to close, but I swallow past the feeling. "When did you get so smart?"

"My brilliant older sister has set a really outstanding example for me to follow. If you want to credit someone, credit her."

Gods, now I'm going to cry. I blink rapidly. "If you change your mind about leaving—"

"Then that will be my choice," she says gently. "And I'll take care of it myself. Without you making any more sacrifices for me. It's time for me to stand on my own, Cass. You've shown me how. Trust me enough to do it."

"Okay." I wipe at my eyes. I barely know how to process this pivot, but I don't have time. Not yet. The crisis that started at the party isn't over. Not by a long shot. "What else are they saying on the gossip sites?"

Another pause, longer this time. "That Hephaestus was killed because of some legal loophole that no one's ever heard of. That there's a new Hephaestus being put in place, though no one knows it's Theseus Vitalis yet. The speculation is running wild, and they're focusing heavily on the clause itself. Someone somehow knew exactly where to look to dig up the specific law and it's all anyone is talking about."

They know.

The entire city knows about the secret the Thirteen have worked for generations to keep under wraps.

Ironic that Apollo was worried about Minos as a threat. He's only one man. The threat of the very city itself turning against the Thirteen? It's incomprehensible. They won't be able to walk down the street without worrying about every single person around them having a knife ready to sink into their ribs.

Some of them will take the threat more seriously than others. I'm sure Ares, Aphrodite, and Zeus will be fine. Hermes is too savvy to be caught flat-footed. Artemis won't be surprised again.

But Apollo?

Who will watch Apollo's back? His family is worthless when it comes to that sort of thing. He might be mostly allied with Ares and Athena, but they will have their hands full trying to ensure there isn't an uprising.

Not to mention there's nothing saying that Minos won't try again.

I swallow hard. "I'm sorry that I was high-handed."

"You have nothing to apologize for. I know you were doing what you thought was best. It's all you've ever done." Rustling in the background as she shifts the phone against her ear. "Please respect my wishes on this. And put yourself first for once, Cass. You deserve it."

"I will. Stay safe."

"You too, Cass."

I hang up and sink onto the edge of the bed. Too much information in too short of a time. I don't know how I didn't see that Alexandra was happy in Olympus. I chalked it up to her naturally sunny personality and projected my own issues onto her. I'm so used to taking care of her that it's strange to have the shoe on the other foot. Maybe she's right. Maybe it's time to take a leap of faith and learn to fly on the way down. To do it for those I care about.

Alexandra. Apollo.

I can pretend they're the only two people in Olympus who I would spirit away to safety if I could, but now, in this moment, I can admit it's not entirely the truth. No matter what she's done, I still care about Hermes. Not to mention Dionysus and Helen— Ares—have been nothing but kind to me. Even Eris—Aphrodite— mean viper that she is, has been a friend in her own way.

Am I really ready to leave the people I care about in a city gone murderous? Am I ready to let them face the potential threat coming from outside the failing boundary, too?

Chaos won't happen right away. The shock of the information will ensure that a large number of people disbelieve it. But eventually someone will try their luck. The gossip sites will report on it in a frenzy, which will only encourage others to try, too.

If I were an enemy waiting at the gates, I'd give the city enough time to fall into violence. Then I'd sweep through and ensure my win, staging a coup all but guaranteed to succeed with the Thirteen fractured and under attack.

I don't know what I can do to stop it. I'm not sure there *is* something to be done. But if I leave now, the city my sister loves will go up in flames.

If I leave now, the man I love will become a bastion alone without a single person to lean on.

I...have to stay.

I have to learn to swim in the depths.

APOLLO

I FIND CASSANDRA SITTING ON THE EDGE OF THE BED, looking lost. I hate that I'm about to add to her stress. I drop my phone on the dresser and sigh. "I would love nothing more than to give you a night of rest, but Zeus has called us in. The tribunal to officially deal with Theseus happens tonight."

She blinks at me. "Deal with Theseus."

"Yes." Zeus didn't yell when we spoke, but his fury practically iced over my phone. Up to this point, I could usually guess the direction of his thoughts, but I honestly don't know what he'll do. Murder—outside that damn outdated clause—might technically be a crime, but if he shoots Theseus in a room full of other members of the Thirteen, who will speak out against him? "I'm not entirely certain what he means to do."

She glances down at her phone. "It's too late. The gossip sites have ahold of this information and are running with it. Even if he tosses Theseus off a building, the secret the Thirteen have been fighting for so long to hide is out. None of you are safe."

I pick up my phone and pull up MuseWatch. They've been a boon and a curse in equal turns during my time as Apollo, and the flashy report on their landing page puts them firmly in *curse* territory this time.

Theseus Vitalis murders his way into the heart of the Thirteen!

"Fuck," I breathe.

"It's bad."

It took everything the last Apollo had to keep the information about what Cassandra's parents attempted to do locked down, but the timing of this news breaking is highly suspect. "Minos is behind this information leak."

"Without a doubt." She pushes to her feet and picks up her discarded dress. "Do we have time to stop by my house so I can change?"

I almost tell her yes, but then my mind catches up. "I can drop you off there if you'd like, but with this information public, the tribunal is all but unnecessary. There's no reason for you to go through the whole process if you don't have to. If Theseus disappears, Minos will ensure the public turns against Zeus. We have to instate him as Hephaestus. We no longer have a choice."

"Why not kill Theseus and the rest of his family? Name them traitors. Act like the assassination clause doesn't exist." She says it so hesitantly, I cross to hug her.

"Even if we're willing to do that—and I'm not—it's too late, love. The law exists, no matter how deep we tried to bury it. If people know to look for it, they'll find it. The information is out there and there's no taking it back."

"I figured as much. It was worth asking, at least." Her shoulders slump. "I'm not happy that this situation is so fucked. I'm not happy that you're in danger now because of what they've done." She lifts her head and meets my gaze. "But I don't think Ariadne had much to do with the whole scheme. And she tried to help us."

She did, but we could have avoided this whole nightmare if she'd just spoken frankly. She said nothing, which makes her guilty by association.

Or at least it will in the Thirteen's point of view.

I smooth back Cassandra's hair. "After the meeting, I'll ensure Zeus holds up his end of the bargain. The money will be in your account tomorrow. The passage out of the city will be ready whenever you are." It hurts to say it. Each word feels like I'm ripping out pieces of myself with my bare hands. "You'll get everything you wanted, Cassandra. I'll make sure of it."

She opens her mouth like she might argue, but my phone starts ringing again. I press a kiss to her forehead and release her. "Get dressed. We need to move." I scoop up my phone as I head for my closet. "What?"

"Artemis just reached Dodona Tower. She's calling for Theseus's head, and I'm inclined to give him to her."

I drag on my pants, holding the phone to my ear with my shoulder. "It's too late. Minos leaked the information to MuseWatch. The whole city is watching us now."

"Fuck." For the first time since this whole thing began, Zeus raises his voice. "*Fuck*. This is going to change everything."

"Yes." The only titles immune to this particular clause are Hades, Zeus, Poseidon, and Hera by virtue of being Zeus's spouse. But even that isn't a guarantee that they won't be targeted. "I'll be there shortly. I have to drop Cassandra at her apartment first."

A pause. "I'll hold to that bargain, but she's at the bottom of my list right now, so she needs to cool her heels while we deal with this."

I wrestle into a shirt and start buttoning it up. "You will transfer the money to her now, Zeus. It's not her fault this went poorly, and I won't have her punished for it."

"Fine." He curses. "It'll be in her account by the time you get here. Now, get moving."

By the time I finish dressing, my phone is lighting up. I scroll through the texts but stop when I see one from Hector.

> **Hector:** Saw the news. Sorry I didn't find the info in time. Are you and Cass okay?
>
> **Me:** Yes. Don't be sorry. It wouldn't have mattered. Things were already in motion.
>
> **Me:** Any progress on the emails?
>
> **Hector:** Some. I forwarded what I have so far to your email.
>
> **Me:** Thanks. Now get some sleep. Need to meet in the morning and bring everyone up to speed.

A quick check finds a trail between Minos and Hermes, confirming what Cassandra heard. They were in contact months before he came to Olympus. There's nothing in their communication that's actually new information, though. He reached out first, but she didn't turn him away.

No matter what Hector thinks, there wasn't enough here to make the leap to Minos's actual plans.

Cassandra has her clothing back in place. It's so tempting to try to coax her into staying here, but the longer she's with me, the harder it will be to release her. And I *will* release her. It's what she wants, and it's what I promised at the beginning of this. I won't go back on my word, no matter that the thought of a future without her is agony. "Are you ready?"

"Yes."

The drive to her apartment takes entirely too little time. She's lost in thought, only jarring back to the present when I stop next to the curb. I eye the empty sidewalk. "Do you want me to come up?"

"No, that's okay." She reaches over and takes my hand. "Be careful. Please."

Cassandra, of all people, understands the implications of what's coming. It's impossible to guess the scale of the public reaction. I don't expect it to happen overnight, but ambition is a river that runs deep in Olympus, and there will be those who look to this new information as a way to skip climbing the ladder entirely in their goal to end up at the top.

Not to mention Minos's benefactor. They've really set the stage to destabilize us and leave the city ripe for the picking the moment the boundary falls.

Athena and Ares will have their hands full.

We're *all* going to have our hands full.

"I'll be careful. I promise." I try for a smile. "I'll have your belongings retrieved from Minos's house and delivered here tomorrow."

She nods once and then she's gone, walking out of my life without looking back. I sit at the curb well after she disappears through that rickety door. She might not be staying in this place much longer, but I make a mental note to track down the owner and insist on the door being replaced so the next occupant doesn't have to deal with what Cassandra has.

I head to Dodona Tower. It's late enough that there's little traffic, and I make good time. It's only been a little over a week since I was here last, but it feels strange to step out of the elevator and into the doorway-studded hall that leads to the ballroom. That's not my destination tonight. Instead, I head to the previously mostly unused boardroom halfway down the hall. The last Zeus preferred to keep the Thirteen as separate as possible, but our current one has a different, more unified goal for the group.

I'm the last one to arrive. The rest of the Thirteen sit around the table. All except Hephaestus. Guilt surges through me. I didn't like the man; he was an active foil again and again to our current Zeus's attempts to bring the Thirteen into one balanced alliance. That doesn't mean he deserved to be murdered, though.

I sink into the chair between Ares and Poseidon, a giant white man with red hair and beard and a permanently furious expression on his brutal face. He hates these meetings the most out of anyone, preferring to stay in his shipping yard running the imports and exports out of Olympus.

Zeus sits at the head of the table, Aphrodite on his left and Athena on his right. The latter is a beautiful Black woman with black curls cut short on the sides and longer on top and a bearing that makes people take notice of her when she enters the room. She's as ruthless as she is brilliant. She flicks a quick look at me, taking in my bruised face. "I see you got your hands dirty, Apollo."

"Something like that."

Demeter sits on the other side of Poseidon. She has the look of her elder three daughters, a white woman in her fifties who projects the persona that she's all too ready to step in as a mother figure for anyone she comes across. Only a fool would underestimate her.

For once Dionysus looks entirely sober, and he's inched his chair away from Hermes. She doesn't appear concerned, though. She's got her chair balanced on the back two legs, her hands behind her head and her gaze on the ceiling. Personally, if Artemis was looking at me with *that* expression on her face, I wouldn't be so relaxed.

Hades and Hera occupy the end of the table opposite Zeus. They've become another pair that's a large pain in Zeus's ass, though they're usually subtle in how they dig in their heels and fight him. Hades is a brooding white man with dark hair and a neatly trimmed dark beard who favors black on black suits, like he's wearing today. Nothing shows on either of their faces.

Zeus clears his throat. "I had hoped to get ahead of this, but there's no help for it. Theseus has killed Hephaestus and claimed right of might. The title is his."

"The fuck it is." Artemis shoves to her feet. "Being a member of the Thirteen doesn't make him untouchable. I'll kill him myself for what he did to my cousin."

"You will do no such thing." Zeus doesn't raise his voice, but the bite in it cuts her legs out from beneath her and she drops back into her chair. "The press has picked up the story."

"How strange," Hermes mutters.

I had assumed Minos was responsible for the leak, but... "Do we have you to thank for that as well?"

"Who, me?" She rights her chair and gives me a long look. "Everything I do, I do for Olympus."

"I find that hard to believe," Artemis spits out. She's so furious, she's practically vibrating. "I know you told that bastard about the assassination clause. How does *that* help Olympus?"

Hermes looks around the table. "Minos didn't come here on his own. He's answering to someone more powerful."

Zeus looks like he wants to press his fingers to his temples but manages to resist the motion. "That information would have been helpful several weeks ago. Why not speak up before we instated him as an Olympian citizen? Why pass him information that allowed his son to infiltrate our highest body of power?" His voice is so cold, the temperature in the room seems to drop several degrees.

"Keep your friends close and your enemies closer."

"That's bullshit, Hermes." Ares twists to pin her with a look. "With one move, he's effectively destabilized the entire city."

"That remains to be seen." Hermes shrugs. "Maybe we need to crack a few eggs to make an omelet."

"Hermes." This from Hades. His voice is low with a faint rasp. He rarely speaks in these meetings, but I've seen how he runs his territory. He's a good leader. The lower city is arguably better off than the upper city when it comes to its citizens' individual lives. "You know I have no love lost for the rest of the Thirteen." He looks around the table. "But this is impulsive, even for you."

"If you say so."

Zeus sits back slowly, drawing the attention back to him. "No laws were broken, so there's no recourse to be had. We move forward with this because we have no choice, but we need to leash our new Hephaestus and do damage control. If the city has something else to talk about, we might be able to turn the tide away from speculation on how best to murder everyone in this room."

Artemis is still shaking. "And how, pray tell, do you plan to do that?"

"I am open to suggestions."

"A wedding." This from Aphrodite. "We've seen it before: nothing distracts the good people of Olympus more than a scandalous match."

Ares's spine snaps straight. "Oh, fuck no. Not this again. I already won in the arena; I am *not* marrying that murderous bastard."

"Not you." Aphrodite gives a thin smile, though her eyes are chips of ice. "Me."

CASSANDRA

I TAKE MY TIME PACKING A SUITCASE. THERE'S NO RUSH, though I don't intend to stay in my apartment overnight. It feels strange to be back here after the ridiculous luxury of the last few days, to pack my nice serviceable clothing instead of the high-end things I'd been wearing recently.

If I do this, my life is going to change dramatically.

It was *always* going to change dramatically, but this was never part of the plan. I'd been prepared to have to learn the way things worked outside Olympus and to be there to play support while Alexandra did the same.

Staying means learning to move through the very circles I've set myself apart from. It means learning to swim among them instead of watching from the outside. It means opening myself up to the potential of more pain.

It's worth it.

I finish packing and drag my suitcase to the door, cursing its broken wheel. I'll have to call a car before I go downstairs. Apollo would shit a brick if he knew I'd taken my things and waited on the curb. The neighborhood is safe enough, but he worries. I smile a little.

I'm so distracted, I almost miss the fact that I'm not alone. Almost.

I straighten and look at my ex. "What are you doing here?"

"Our meeting ended early with a bang." Hermes moves around my tiny kitchen, poking at things. "Apollo won't be home for ages, though, if you're worried about your timing. Zeus has him, Aphrodite, Athena, and Ares in a little war meeting. It's all very dramatic."

"Hermes."

She exhales slowly. "I'm sorry. I should have realized that Apollo would get over that moral high ground he clings to so sweetly and bring you along if he was invited to the party. I failed to anticipate that development and you got hurt because of it. I never wanted that, Cassandra."

"I didn't get hurt." Even as I say it, it feels like a lie.

She gives me a look that speaks volumes. "You witnessed a murder, honey. And two attempted murders. That's harm. I honestly thought if you heard me and Minos talking about the gory details, you'd leave. I didn't expect you to develop a white knight streak." She makes a face. "He's rubbing off on you."

I scrub my hands over my face. This has been the longest few days in existence and I'm not at my best right now. There was a time when I didn't bother to worry about that kind of thing with Hermes, but after the last twenty-four hours... "How could you? A man is *dead* because of the knowledge you passed on."

She leans back against the counter and crosses her arms over her chest. "If you had all the information, you'd see that this was the only course of action available to me."

"Then give me all the information." I know, even as I say it, that she won't.

She confirms my suspicions with a shake of her head. "If things go well, it won't matter because we'll have headed off the danger at the pass."

I don't understand her. How can this be the lesser of two evils? But I know better than to ask. She's more than proven she won't tell me. "They'll hate you for this."

"Maybe." She shrugs. "Or maybe they'll thank me in the end." She starts for the door and stops to squeeze my arm. "I'm happy for you, Cassandra. Apollo's the best of us, and he'll treat you the way you deserve to be treated. Like a queen."

I swallow hard. "I didn't say I was going to him."

"Didn't you?" She gives a bittersweet smile. "Try not to hate me too much. I'll be sad if I'm not invited to the wedding."

"I sure as fuck didn't say we were getting married."

"You will. Just like you'll live long, happy lives and have half a dozen children. Yes, by the way, I'd love to be a godmother." Hermes moves past me to the door. "Oh, and I called you a car. It should be here by now. Things won't be as safe as they used to be in the city, at least for a little while."

I barely wait for the door to close behind her to rush to open it, a thousand questions on my lips. Hermes, of course, is nowhere in sight. "I hate it when she does that."

Her words swirl through my head, threatening to distract me, but there's not much I can do about the greater Olympus problem right now. I can, however, set my path on the course that will bring me the happiness I've been too afraid to take for far too long.

True to her word, a car idles waiting for me at the curb. It's only when I climb into the back seat and direct them to Apollo's building that I wonder if this could be some kind of trap, but we make the trip without issue. It just confirms my ongoing belief that Hermes never meant *me* harm. It makes my feelings about everything that much more conflicted.

I walk through the fancy lobby, waiting for someone to tell me that I'm not allowed to be here, but no one stops me. They barely even look in my direction.

Upstairs, I use the key Apollo gave me years ago to let myself into his penthouse. After the slightest consideration, I change into an oversize T-shirt that's so faded, I'm not entirely sure what the graphic started out as, tuck my suitcase into the closet, and climb into bed. I fully intend to stay awake until he comes home, but my body has other ideas.

I jolt awake at the feeling of the mattress giving as someone sits down next to me. I open my eyes to find Apollo staring down at me like he just found his favorite gift beneath the Christmas tree, but he's afraid it's not truly meant for him.

He reaches out, pauses without touching me, and drops his hand back to his thigh. "What are you doing here, Cassandra?" The question isn't harsh, more...hopeful.

"You shouldn't give out your keys to people. It's going to be dangerous in the city for some time, and you might come home to find a stranger in your bed."

"You're no stranger." He can't seem to help himself. He strokes a hand over my hip. "You came back."

"I love you." It's not an answer, though, and we both know it. I sit up and shift back to lean against the headboard. "Apollo, I..." Gods, this is harder than it has any right to be. "When my parents died for their ambition, I promised myself I'd never be like them. I would never strive for power or prestige or anything except keeping my sister safe and getting the fuck out of this city. I closed myself off to everything. I, well, hated pretty much everyone. Except you, and that was despite my best efforts."

He watches me with serious eyes. "And now?"

"Now, with the stakes changing so dramatically, it's made things clearer for me. I..." I take a breath and push forward. "I have people who care about me, even if I haven't been the best of friends to them. My sister is happy here, though I had such strong tunnel vision, I didn't even realize it until today."

"Cassandra—"

"I'm not finished." I take another harsh breath. "Things are going to get dangerous in this city. We both know it's the truth. I am not going to let my pride dictate my choices, to leave just because it seemed like the only option. It's not. I can help, Apollo. You've said it yourself. I'm an asset, and you're going to need everyone in your corner that you can get."

He goes still. "That's why you're choosing to stay."

"It's part of it." I reach out and cover his hand with mine. "I've also been desperately in love with my boss for years now and he's really great to me, the best man I've ever met. I'd be a fool if I walked away from him." I squeeze his hand. "I want a life with you. I realize that I'm a cranky asshole and that I'll cause friction in the circles you move in even after I figure out how to move in them, too, but—"

He gently presses his fingertips to my lips. "I choose you, Cassandra. The opinions of those in the upper circles have never held much weight for me, and certainly never as much as *your* opinion does. I love you. If I thought for a second you'd say yes, I'd propose right now."

I smile against his fingers. "Ask me in a few months." I already know what I'll say, but even after knowing Apollo and working closely with him for five years, there will no doubt be kinks to be worked out while actually dating each other.

"I will." He lowers his hand. "I wanted more than anything to ask you to stay, but it wasn't fair to demand that of you. I'm having a difficult time believing you're actually here." He smiles. "You're choosing me."

"I'm choosing you," I confirm. I lean forward and press a careful kiss to his lips. "Come to bed, Apollo. Our happily-ever-after starts now."

APHRODITE

THE RECEPTION STRETCHES ON FOR AN ETERNITY. EVEN though I chose this, I can't stop the sinking in my stomach. I played right into my new husband's hands. A mistake, and one that will be costly. I can't afford to underestimate Hephaestus, and reacting to Adonis showing up unexpectedly before my wedding to the enemy? I might as well have waved a red flag in front of a bull or built a neon sign pointing to a vulnerable button. My new husband will be stomping on it in no time. I wish I could trust Adonis to avoid that pitfall, but emotions make everything messy and I hurt him badly by making this move.

He's not the only one.

All through the speeches and cake cutting and first dance, Hephaestus keeps that satisfied smirk in place. It makes me want to...

I manage to extract myself and part ways with my husband to grab a glass of champagne off a waiter's tray. Now's the time to follow him back to our seats at the center of the bridal party table, but I need a moment, so I drift over to the doorway leading back outside. The air has cooled with the sun setting, giving the first hint of the bite winter will bring.

I close my eyes and inhale deeply. The desire to strike back at Hephaestus after that little altercation is nearly overwhelming, but I haven't made it to where I am now by acting impulsively. Mostly.

Right now, the only thing that matters is getting through the rest of the reception and then managing to resist the impulse to make myself a widow on my wedding night.

Everything else can wait for tomorrow.

Even knowing that is the smartest course of action, I can't help searching the faces of the guests gathered in the ballroom. Adonis isn't here—I *know* he isn't— but that doesn't stop me from looking despite myself.

He won't have left Olympus; not without me. His life is here. His family and fortune and a whole city's worth of admirers. He has a way of drawing people to him wherever he goes, his charm and beauty making him the darling of MuseWatch and a good portion of the legacy families. Not enough to help him secure one of the titles of the Thirteen for himself, but Adonis lives a charmed life.

None of that really excuses what I've done.

Or the fact that I didn't talk to him about it first.

I smother the guilt trying to take root in my chest. Adonis knew what he was getting when we started this ill-fated on-again-off-again relationship several years ago. I was a Kasios before I became Aphrodite.

I drain my champagne glass and tuck all the messy emotions away. It doesn't matter what could have been, because this is my reality. I will not give my new husband and his family even an ounce of satisfaction thinking that I'm heartbroken.

Being heartbroken would require me to have a heart.

I make my way toward the table with the wedding party. It's slow going because everyone wants to stop the bride and wish me congratulations or use thirty seconds of their time to try to weasel closer to the power Aphrodite holds. My title's responsibilities include making marriage matches, and arranged marriages are one of Olympus's favorite way to consolidate power.

Again and again, my attention is drawn back to the bridal party. They've mixed up a bit. My people—Hermes, Eros, and my brother and sister—on one side and Hephaestus's—the Minotaur, Icarus, Ariadne, and Pandora—on the other. It's the latter who interests me.

In the brief time I've known their cursed household, she seems to be the only one whom my lovely husband more than tolerates. Even now, he's leaning over Icarus and there's an actual smile on his face. It's strange and soft and it makes me want to grab the nearest piece of silverware and gouge his eye out.

Instead, I focus on Pandora. She's a pretty little thing—short and soft with the kind of curves a person can sink their hands into. Smooth light-brown skin and a thick fall of wavy black hair complete the picture. But what really sets her apart is the way she lights up a room when she walks into it. Her laugh fills a space in a way I've never experienced before. I added her to my side of the wedding party out of spite, because I knew it would bother Hephaestus, but I actually found myself enjoying being around her.

If her attitude is a mask, it's the best I've ever seen.

Hephaestus sees me coming and sits back abruptly, his smile falling away and clouds gathering in his dark eyes. I dislike how attractive he is. Medium-brown skin and dark red hair that's actually trimmed properly for this event. His muscular frame marked him as a warrior before his injury, and I have no doubt that even with his injured knee, he can do plenty of damage.

He killed the last Hephaestus, after all.

I slip around the table and take my place at his side. I can do this. I chose this. The reception is all but over, and then all that's left is to consummate the marriage. After that, I can put the next stage of my plan into motion. For the next hour or two, I simply need to endure.

Even knowing it's coming, the rest of the reception passes in a blur of congratulations. And then it's time to see us off.

Hephaestus has only just moved into the penthouse he inherited with the title—likely because his predecessor's people made the transition difficult—and I have no intention of letting him into *my* home. As a result, we've booked a hotel room for the night.

It was the simplest solution, but I'm regretting the short trip now. The remaining wedding guests line the hall, tossing flowers before us, a perfect blend of red—roses and carnations and poppies. It creates a beautiful stage for us to walk down, holding hands as if we wanted this. Distantly, I note the photographer taking pictures furiously. Helen will go over which to release tonight, and the rest will be sent to me afterward.

What's the point in a wedding as a distraction if everyone isn't talking about it?

My sister appears at the end of the hall and pulls me into a quick hug. "Be safe," she whispers. Something cold presses into my hand.

I glance down and nearly laugh. It's a small knife, wickedly curved and designed to fit perfectly in the palm of my hand. "What am I supposed to do with this?"

"He's a murderer, Eris." She hugs me again, speaking directly into my ear. "Do what you have to."

I don't tell her not to worry. Truthfully, this wedding was a gamble. It could be as much a trap for me as I intend it to be for Hephaestus. If one of his family decides to kill me and trigger the assassination clause, they would be entitled to my title. Being alone with him is asking for an ambush.

But that danger goes both ways.

"I'll be safe."

"Don't make promises you can't keep." She steps back and then our brother is there. He doesn't hug me; he's not really the hugging type.

He just looks at me and nods. "Do what you have to do."

Helen makes an angry sound, but she's never really understood Perseus—now Zeus—the way I do. He's ruthless to a fault and clinically cold, both traits our bastard of a father encouraged, but he's never railed against his role in this city. Not like Helen. Not like Hercules. I wince a little at the thought of our youngest brother. He's not here. He was invited, of course, but he's made it clear he's not returning to Olympus, even if our father is gone.

I try not to hold that against him. He's happy and that's enough for the others. It has to be enough for me, too.

"I always do what I have to." I turn away from what remains of my family and walk with my new husband to the elevator that will take us up to the honeymoon suite. The doors close and I'm alone with Hephaestus for the first time.

I don't know what I expect. Threats or more taunting, perhaps. He says nothing. The silence unnerves me, but this is a weapon I'm familiar with. My father didn't utilize it often, but when he did, it was so bad I almost preferred his fists. He would ignore us when we made him a special shade of angry, would act as if he couldn't see or hear us for hours and sometimes days. Perseus always seemed to find that almost a relief, but it made me crazed. When I was fifteen, I destroyed an entire room while shrieking at my father, and he sat there staring mildly out the window and drinking his coffee the entire time.

I shudder. I'm not fifteen any longer. Control has been hard-won, but it exists. The doors open before I can make a liar out of myself, and I charge forward, leaving Hephaestus to follow behind.

The honeymoon suite is lovely. Everything about this historic hotel is lovely; it's why I picked it for the wedding. That and the fact that every member of my family going back generations has been married here.

In my father's case, multiple times.

I stare at the tasteful cream decor and my stomach twists. Best not to think about that. Or the fact that my brother and sister-in-law occupied this same room for *their* political marriage back in May. I shudder. Tradition is a trap, but I've gone too far to back out now.

Hephaestus steps around me and makes a beeline to the kitchenette. There's a bottle of whiskey there with a jaunty bow around it that seems to be made entirely of glitter. Even before he picks up the card and snorts, I know who it's from.

Hermes. Up until two weeks ago, I considered her one of my best friends in this world. Now, I don't know what to believe. My brother thinks she's a traitor, and she hasn't done much to disabuse him of the belief. Even though I *know* she's playing at deeper games than any of us first realized, I still can't quite believe that she means this city harm or that she's really allied with Hephaestus's family.

Maybe that makes me naive. I've been accused of worse.

I swallow past the complicated feelings her name brings and cross to join Hephaestus at the counter. "Give me that."

"I've got it." He rips at the bow almost violently.

I barely resist the urge to snatch it out of his hands and pick up the card instead. Hermes's sprawling handwriting greets me.

Enjoy the wedding night, you two love birds!

I sigh and toss it aside. "Always playing games."

"She's an Olympian. It's what your people do." He finally gets the bow off and drops it to the counter with a disgusted grunt. The bottle top soon joins it. Hephaestus takes a long pull directly from the bottle. Another time, I'd make a biting comment about his manners, but right now I need the same fortification he obviously does.

No. Damn it, *no.*

I am not some weak princess, married off against her will. This wedding is my design. If this were a story, I'd be the cunning queen, or even the evil witch. I am not helpless and I am not innocent.

If Hephaestus needs liquid courage, then that means *I'm* the one coming out on top of today, no matter his nasty little trick with Adonis earlier. I still take the bottle from his hand and lift it to my lips, holding his gaze all the while. One swallow, then two. I stop myself there and set it on the counter with a clink. "Shall we, dear husband?"

He shakes his head slowly. "You really are Olympus's wh—"

"I'm going to stop you there." It takes everything I have to resist clenching my fists...and perhaps driving one right into his face. "This marriage can be as awful or as pleasant as you choose." Lies. I have every intention of making each day a new torment for my *dear husband*. Anything to keep him distracted from the new power he stole with his title. It would be ideal to learn about the rest of his family's plans, but that's for others to discover.

My only aim is his suffering.

He looks at me as if he'd like to toss me out the nearest window. The feeling is entirely mutual.

I resign myself to a torturous experience and turn for the bedroom. "Let's get this over with."

ACKNOWLEDGMENTS

I will never ever get over my amazement and gratitude over the overwhelming support readers have given this series. We wouldn't have made it to book four without you, and I hope you enjoyed a slightly softer turn around Olympus. Suffice to say, we're ramping things up with the next book!

The biggest thank you to all the librarians and booksellers who've championed this series from the start!

This book wouldn't be what it is without Mary Altman's and Christa Désir's editorial comments. You helped me dial things in—and up!—and this book is way less a slow burn than it would have been without your help!

From cover to design to sales to production and everything in between, thank you to the team at Sourcebooks for all the support on this series, including (but definitely not limited to): Dominique Raccah and Todd Stocke; Rachel Gilmer, Jocelyn Travis, and Susie Benton; Pam Jaffee and Katie Stutz; Heather Hall; Stephanie Gafron and Dawn Adams; Brian Grogan, Sean Murray, and Elizabeth Otte.

I have the very best people in my corner and all my love and gratitude to Jenny Nordbak, Nisha Sharma, Andie J Christopher, Piper J Drake, Asa Maria Bradley, and RM Virtues!

Last but never ever least, my deep and abiding love to Tim. You're the wind beneath my wings and the rock that keeps me tethered. I wouldn't be able to do half the crazy shit I pull off without you by my side! And special thanks to my ever-patient children who are hauled along with my shenanigans!

ABOUT THE AUTHOR

Katee Robert is a *New York Times* and *USA Today* bestselling author of spicy romance. *Entertainment Weekly* calls her writing "unspeakably hot." Her books have sold over a million copies. She lives in the Pacific Northwest with her husband, children, a cat who thinks he's a dog, and two Great Danes who think they're lap dogs. You can visit her at kateerobert.com or on Twitter @katee_robert.